Wendi Jackson lives in the peaceful Wiltshire countryside and enjoys long walks in nearby Longleat Forest. As a single working mother of three, she forgot her long-held ambition to document the survival story of her family during World War II. During a visit to a psychic medium, she was told about the importance of a family book, but it wasn't until her grandmother, Thalia, passed away aged ninety-three, that her desire to write was rekindled. She joined a local Writing Circle and spent four years researching and crafting her debut novel in memory of her family.

This book is dedicated to my incredible grandmother, Thalia, who taught me that life isn't easy, painful things happen, but it is how you navigate through those times that matters. Throughout her life, she remained positive, modest, and never referred to herself as a victim, complained about life's misfortunes, or spoke with any malice for what she suffered. She glided through life with quiet strength and fortitude and for that, she has always been my hero. To my great-aunt, Terpie, without whose memoirs I couldn't have pieced together the gaps in the story.

To my family members, Thetie and Clio, who tragically lost their lives too soon in the conflict, and to my great-grandparents, Anthoula and Zacharia, who I wish I had the opportunity to know. Although since sharing this intimate journey with you, I feel our lives are now entwined and I carry you all in my heart.

It's been an honour to share your extraordinary story.

Wendi McAleese

THE LOST KEYS

AUSTIN MACAULEY PUBLISHERS™

LONDON * CAMBRIDGE * NEW YORK * SHARJAH

A CIP catalogue record for this title is available from the British Library.

ISBN 9781035859030 (Paperback)
ISBN 9781035859047 (ePub e-book)

www.austinmacauley.com

First Published 2024
Austin Macauley Publishers Ltd®
1 Canada Square
Canary Wharf
London
E14 5AA

The biggest thank you must go to my darling parents, who have supported me throughout this process and believed in me when I didn't believe in myself. Without their love and generosity this book would not have been possible. I'll be forever grateful to them for being my biggest champions, reading endless edits and offering advice to turn my dream into a reality. To my long-suffering family and friends, who allowed me the space to disappear to focus on this project and for their ongoing encouragement. To Becca, for her guiding hand with proofreading, and to the Warminster Writing Circle members for providing honest feedback and helping me gain confidence and overcome the fear being vulnerable to share my work with others.

Table of Contents

Prologue
The Shop
1911

A brand-new day peeks over the horizon on Singapore's High Street, and Zacharia has been impatient for this moment for as long as he can remember. Today marks the beginning of his ambitious dream. Standing on the pavement, he takes a moment to savour the emotions, the tingling excitement rippling through his veins, and it feels as good as he imagined. From across the dusty street, he admires the sign bearing his name, and his chest swells with pride. A heavy set of newly cut keys is clutched tightly in his hand, and the brass is cool against his skin. He beams at his young wife beside him, before bounding towards the door of his first and very own shop.

Fast-forward thirty years—the treasured shop is being ravaged by fire. Ugly flames devour the silk dresses and Panama hats for which Zacharia has become famous. All the years of love and passion he's devoted to creating his highly successful business fuels the flames. The front window explodes from the intense heat, littering the pavement with shards of glass, landing quietly on the thick carpet of fallen ash. His shop is just one of the millions of casualties of war.

In the early hours, whilst the city slept, Japanese fighter planes commanded the sky unchallenged, releasing a devastating air attack—the abandoned streets were filled with the sickening whine of air raid sirens and thundering explosions from enemy fire. No one was coming to their rescue.

Zacharia's world has shifted—he has no way back.

Chapter One
Zacharia, November 1941

Zacharia glanced at his watch; he was late again. It was almost seven. By his wife's standards, not being on time for dinner at six-thirty was deplorable. On the rare occasion, he missed it completely, he would receive her frosty furore until at least the following morning. The black Ford pulled onto the driveway and Lim turned off the ignition.

Tipping his Panama hat, he bid his driver goodnight and followed the melodic wind chimes tinkling on the veranda—a beacon guiding him to his haven. He staggered wearily over the crunchy stone driveway in the gloaming light, gravitating towards his home's warm, welcoming glow. After a busy day, he was always thankful to return to his family on the hill. He knew he was hopeless with the boundaries of time and had a propensity for hard work, often taking precedence over his family life. Throughout the last forty years, he'd struggled to balance the two. He also silently carried ever-present guilt for rarely being at home. His white linen trousers clung to his legs in the sultry Singaporean evening air as he wearily ascended the grand, white staircase. He loved the bones of this house.

Over the years, he and his wife Anthoula had extended it to accommodate their growing family. It was a simple structure, unlike the elaborate colonial bungalows in the city built for the wealthy English expatriates and Europeans. He had always desired an authentic, modest house in the suburbs, believing his home should exist in harmony with nature. Surrounded by palm trees and giant wax-leafed shrubs, his house was built in the Malay tradition with locally sourced wood from the Chengal tree. Perching high above the ground, it relied on sturdy white concrete pillars to protect it from the inclement monsoon floods.

Shortly after they had moved here, he planted a bougainvillaea, which had matured with the occupants of the house and became an unruly burst of crimson blooms. A tangle of twisted vines adorns the double staircase leading to the ornately carved veranda, where he would sit most evenings to unwind.

Briefly, pausing his climb, he replayed a flashback from years ago, when he would sprint up these stairs and back down the other side, making all five of his daughters giggle and shriek with delight. They watched like gnomes sitting on upturned plant pots on the driveway, legs dangling with long white socks and shiny black patent shoes, cheering him on, 'Again Pappa, again.' Just the thought of it exhausted him. With each step, he leaned on the stone balustrade for support which radiated warmth from basking in the sun all day. The scent of the rambling buds momentarily transported him back to his childhood many miles from here.

A cascade of excited voices and ribbons of laughter drifted on the breeze, smothering the sound of humming cicadas and evening birdsong. *All the girls must be home tonight.* An occurrence which was a rarity these days. A wave of guilt swept him up. *Have I missed an important event?* He thought back to breakfast that morning. Anthoula had made no special request for him to be home promptly, had she? No, he would have remembered. Anthoula had a way about her, meaning you dared not forget when she instructed you.

Before entering his home, he briefly marvelled at the picturesque city skyline. From this elevated view on the hill, he enjoyed Singapore city's splendour, radiantly lit in the amber glow of the distant houses and streetlights. The inky blackness of the ocean beyond was spattered with tiny pinholes of light from distant ships, flickering on the horizon. With the sun barely set, the louring sky promised rain before the night was out. The wooden boards creaked under his weight as he crossed the veranda, and like clockwork, he hung his hat and linen jacket on the stand, noting the satisfying jangle from the heavy bunch of shop keys inside his pocket. He removed his socks and shoes, preferring to be barefoot so the air could circulate between his toes, and he could feel the wood grain beneath his feet. He braced himself for his wife's admonishment for his late arrival. Catching him by surprise, Thalia sped towards him out of nowhere with outstretched arms; her tight embrace made him feel warm inside, and she planted a kiss on his cheek.

'Thalia, what a greeting! I've only been gone since this morning.'

'Pappa, you're late again. Come on, hurry. Terpie has wonderful news!'

Taking his hand, she led him to the large family room, with its high ceiling and rich, red-brown, polished meranti floor providing the illusion of grandeur and space. Delicate lace voile panels decorated the vast panoramic windows, bathing the room in golden sunlight during the day but preventing unwelcome flying insects at night. In the centre lay a fine Indian rug. Its colours, once vivid and bright, were now muted in dusky pinks and amber tones. From time to time, their loyal Amah, Shi Min, gave it a beating in the yard, the old-fashioned way. Various wicker chairs and a well-worn saggy couch faced the upright piano in the corner, where sheets of music were stored neatly in a wicker basket. Anthoula grew varieties of houseplants in jardinières, extending the garden into the home, which he appreciated. However, he tolerated the collection of china trinkets and ornaments on display for his wife's sake, but to him, they were unnecessary clutter. The walls were bare except for a large mirror and two dominating portraits.

The first framed photograph was of the family, and the second featured his younger brother Sotiri. Suited and slick; before he bankrupted the family business by making bad investment choices. Despite his brother's indiscretion, Zacharia still loved him. They hadn't seen each other since Sotiri had shamefully returned home to their father in Greece, leaving Zacharia to rebuild his reputation and start again from scratch.

Upon entering, he was met with shrill laughter and the sight of three of his daughters excitedly fussing around Terpie, his second youngest. Officially named on her birth certificate as Terpsichore, but no one ever dared to call her by her full name unless they were prepared for the repercussions. Named after one of the nine muses in Greek mythology, the muse of poetry and dance. When the girls were born, Anthoula insisted their names reflected their heritage, a decision that wasn't favoured by them all. Consequently, when they were younger, Zacharia referred to them as his "Greek goddesses". He smiled across the room at Anthoula, who was sewing in her high-backed chair. Neat rows of coloured threads lay on the table beside her; as he approached, he searched her features for signs of irritation at his late arrival. Peering over her glasses, she smiled and put her sewing down, and he knew he had been absolved.

'Good evening, family. What am I missing?' Zacharia leaned on the back of the chair and bent to kiss his wife. Her face was now aged with fine lines, and her thick black hair was peppered with striations of grey, but she was still a fine-looking woman. 'I'm sorry; am I late again? I had so much paperwork,' he whispered in her ear.

'I knew you would be. Don't worry. I delayed dinner, so you didn't miss it.'

'Pappa, I was going to wait until you got home to announce it to everyone, but I couldn't wait any longer and the others guessed, anyway. I'm hopeless with secrets.' Terpie paused for a second, biting her bottom lip. 'Benny asked me to marry him!' she shrieked proudly, displaying her new accessory, which sparkled as brightly as her beaming smile.

'Our daughter is engaged, Zac. Can you believe it? The first wedding in our family!'

'I'm so pleased for you, darling. Wonderful news.' Zacharia clapped his hands together.

'I can't believe she's engaged. It's so unfair. I should've been first.' Clio nudged her sister Ino out of the way to slump heavily onto the couch.

'Clio, that's enough. What a thing to say.' Anthoula scowled across the room. 'Don't ruin Terpie's good fortune with your jealousy.'

'I'm happy for her, but I should be married first, being the eldest.'

'Ahem, *I'm* the eldest.' Ino flicked her fringe out of her eyes. 'Only by two minutes, but still. So what if Terpie ties the knot first? It's not a competition.'

'You know what I mean. I thought I'd have a husband and a home of my own by now, that's all,' Clio sighed.

'Don't be such a spoiled sourpuss. This isn't about you. You'll get your turn one day,' said Thalia.

'Girls, come on now. Clio, you're still young; you'll have plenty of time to settle down. Be happy for your sister and her good news,' said Zacharia.

'Sorry, Terpie. Ignore me.' Clio hugged one of the cushions tightly, lowering her head sheepishly.

'I know you didn't mean it. Your time will come, Clio,' replied Terpie.

'All my friends are settling down and having babies, and I feel like it will never happen for me. Especially if we have a war, as people say, I'll never meet anyone.'

'Is that what you're worried about? Don't think like that. Anyway, life goes on even if we have a war,' Anthoula said matter-of-factly.

'Clio, we're only twenty-eight. We're not old maids yet. You talk like we're doomed to a life of spinsterhood. I want to get married and have a family too, and we will one day,' Ino shrugged.

'I'm glad that's not something I have to worry about. I'll never get married,' Thetie folded her arms.

'That's your choice. It's definitely not mine,' said Clio.

Changing the subject, Zacharia approached Terpie. 'Your mother and I are proud and happy for you both.' He hugged her tightly. 'Benny is a good man. He'll look after you and make a good husband.' In their close embrace, Zacharia spoke softly, 'Benny asked for my blessing, so I had an idea this was coming.' He took her hand to examine the classic solitaire diamond. It was a fine piece of jewellery and must have cost Benny much of his teacher's salary. Terpie awkwardly twisted the ring around her finger, not yet used to the feel of it or the attention it brought.

'We haven't chosen a specific date yet, but we don't want to wait too long.'

'It'll be the best wedding celebration. No doubt your mother already has ideas, and your sisters will be scheming and planning a big fancy event,' he kissed her on the forehead.

'Pappa, I'd prefer to keep it small. Next year in March, maybe, when it's warm but before the monsoon season starts.'

'That's only five months away! We'd better get planning then. Emily will be delighted.'

'We're going to pay her a visit later this week.' Terpie flounced across the rug, her long skirt swishing and sat beside Thetie. Zacharia had never seen his daughter look so radiant. 'I was saying before you came in, Pappa, that we've made plans for when the war in Europe is over.'

'Let's hear these big ideas, then.' His stomach contracted slightly in anticipation.

'Well … I know you won't like it. Benny's desperate to go home to introduce me to his family in Poland. I know the situation is terrible right now, but we'll go when the war is over. We're both saving every penny so we can travel around Europe.'

'The war is far from over, my darling, so you'll have quite a wait,' said Anthoula gently. 'Even then, I'm unsure how safe these countries will be for you.'

'I know. The world has gone insane. Benny's worried about his family since they hid after the Germans invaded.'

Zacharia bowed his head. 'Poor Benny. It must be awful for him and his family. Of course, he wants to go home. It's not safe for anyone there right now. I agree with your mother. Anywhere in Europe will be dangerous for quite some time. Let us help you with the wedding first, and if it's meant to be, it will happen when the time is right.' His words didn't convey his true feelings, and he silently berated himself for being selfish. The only positive thing he could glean from the current unrest in Europe was his daughter's delayed departure.

'Benny said the same!'

'He's a sensible man, like your old pappa,' he winked.

'Maybe a grandchild will put an end to your travel plans,' said Anthoula hopefully.

'I doubt that very much, Mamma. I don't want children. Well, certainly not until I've had the chance to travel. With the state of the world, I don't think it's right to bring a child into this chaos.'

'Anyway, let's not spoil the evening by talking about war. Will Benny be joining us tonight?' Zacharia approved of Benny and was glad to welcome him into the family. He liked his steady influence on his impulsive daughter. Whilst she hankered for foreign travel, Benny would only allow it once the troubles were over, which comforted him. Yes, he was very content with her choice.

'He should be here by now,' Terpie glanced anxiously at the clock.

'We can ask Shi Min to delay dinner if need be,' said Anthoula.

'Oh no; he'd be mortified to think he held up dinner. We'll start without him.'

'Thetie, why don't you play us the new piece you've been practising whilst we wait? I'm sure your father would love to hear it.' Anthoula slid her glasses back on and resumed her sewing.

Obediently, Thetie took her place at the piano and began playing; her lean fingers caressed the ebony and ivory keys with ease, and a Mozart masterpiece spiralled into the room, wafting through the air like vapour and seeping into the soft furnishings. Her audience fell silent and shared equilibrium.

Zacharia was already dreading the day when the piano would sit peacefully in the corner like a giant ornament, collecting dust. In only a few months, Thetie, his selfless and caring girl, would begin her new life as a Carmelite nun, a calling for which she was ideally suited. He knew the time would come when all his girls would leave the family home, which would hit him hard. For now, he cherished these nights when his daughters were together under his roof. These days, a dance, a charity ball, or a film at the cinema always seemed to lure them away. Thetie began another piece, and Thalia drifted out to the veranda. After a few minutes, Zacharia followed her to get some air.

Parents aren't supposed to have favourites, and without question, he adored each of his girls, but his bond was stronger with Thalia. She entertained him with her quirky sense of humour, and they could talk about almost anything; he relished their one-to-one time. Perhaps because she was the baby of the family, he felt more protective over her and called her his "little bird". She, like all the rest, would leave his nest one day.

Generally, his daughters had a closer relationship with their mother, except for Terpie, who distanced herself from the pack. Not only was Thalia different in personality, but also in appearance. Her four siblings were so similar that they could be mistaken for quadruplets; they reminded him of a set of Russian dolls. Clio was the tallest, and Thetie the shortest, barely reaching her sister's shoulders. The girls shared the same olive skin colouring, large circular eyes, and dense ebony curls. Thalia looked nothing like them with her fairer skin tone and light caramel hair; the difference was striking. It had been a long-standing joke among them that a stork must have delivered Thalia to this family.

Zacharia joined Thalia on the bench, and they sat in silence, allowing the music to wash over them as they gazed out across the familiar landscape. A last stubborn streak of pink on the horizon stood out from the grey clouds, marking the end of the day. Thalia leaned forward, clutching the edge of the seat and staring upward, her eyes vacant. He wondered where she had disappeared to and whether he should try to reach her.

'How was work today? Are you still enjoying it?'

Some strands on the arm of the cane seating had become loose, and she aggravated them further with her long fingernails. The scratching noise grated on him, but he chose to ignore it.

'Look, I understand if you don't want to. But you can talk to me about Charlie. I know you miss him.' He studied her unyielding features for a slither of emotion and patiently waited as she continued scratching and brushed the loose pickings onto the floor. She never talked openly about her relationship, preferring to keep the subject close to her chest. Thalia was fiercely independent. She believed she could take on the world single-handedly and rarely asked for help. Zacharia, however, was a good listener; he would wait all night if he had to. Eventually, she turned towards him.

'I didn't know it would be this hard. Sometimes, I can put him out of my mind, and other days I miss him terribly. It's driving me crazy, not knowing.' Her eyes glistened with the threat of tears, but he watched her fight them off.

'I know, my little bird.' Zacharia wrapped his arm around her shoulders and pulled her close, and she rested her head against his shoulder. 'When did you last hear from him?'

'It's been almost two months now. One letter is all I need. I think the worst all the time.'

He wished—as he had so many times—that he could control all his girls' fate and happiness. He wouldn't have chosen for his youngest daughter to fall in love with an Australian pilot, but no amount of fatherly concern could change her mind, as he well knew.

'I sincerely wish life was different for you, my darling. But I do know that you're stronger than you think, Thalia. Sadly, life isn't fair, and struggles will always arise for you to overcome. It's how we get through those times that matters.'

'I don't feel strong right now, Pappa.'

'It will pass, trust me.' If he could soak up her sorrow and take it on himself, he would do it gladly. It pained him to see the agony and worry on her face day after day. She thought she had fooled everyone, but he could see through her smiles. He knew her too well. 'I know it's easy for me to say but try not to think the worst. No news is good news, hey?' he gave her a reassuring squeeze.

'If he doesn't come back, I'll never marry anyone else.'

'Oh, Thalia. You have no idea where your life will take you and can't possibly make decisions like that yet. You can't imagine not loving him, but feelings change over time. Besides, he could be safe and well and return to you.' Zacharia kissed the top of her head, and after a moment, he added: 'Perhaps it would help to give yourself a timeline. You can't wait for him forever; you have your whole life ahead of you. Let him go if you haven't heard from him by your chosen date.'

'Hmmm, I'll think about it. He would still be here with me—if it wasn't for this blasted war. I know you don't like discussing war and politics at home, but do you think the troubles will get worse?'

He sighed. 'I have a feeling this war will test us in many ways before it's over, and yes, I think it's heading our way. But don't tell your mother I said so.'

'Come, everyone. Dinner is ready,' Shi Min's voice drifted out to them in the warm evening air.

'I'm not hungry,' said Thalia.

'Come on. You must eat. It's a celebration meal, and besides, Charlie won't want to cuddle a skeleton when he gets back, will he?' She smiled and allowed him to persuade her to take her seat in the dining room with the rest of the family.

Shi Min had dressed the table with candles, flowers and the best crockery. As Zacharia took his place at the table, he realised he hadn't eaten since breakfast. His stomach rumbled loudly at the mound of noodles and juicy prawns before him. The dish was Terpie's favourite, which was a thoughtful gesture. Shi Min coasted around the table, filling their glasses with chilled champagne.

'Why don't you both come and join us? It's a special evening,' Zacharia asked as Shi Min poured.

'Thank you. That's kind, but it's a family celebration, and besides, Lim and I have already eaten,' said Shi Min.

Zacharia laughed. 'You are part of our family. Well, come over for drinks later then. I insist.'

Shi Min agreed and scuttled back into the kitchen. Zacharia was incredibly fond of the elderly couple, who had worked for him for over twenty-five years and were like grandparents to the girls. With their home next door, they were as good as family.

Benny rushed in, apologising for his lateness. His face flushed red, his cotton shirt was damp with sweat, and his usually well-styled fringe stuck to his forehead.

'I'm so sorry! My extra classes overran. I got here as fast as I could,' he puffed.

Anthoula welcomed him in. 'You're here now; better late than never. Sit, sit!' she commanded. He took his place beside his fiancé to a chorus of congratulations and cheers from around the table.

Whilst they ate, lively discussion and laughter bounced across the table. With his hunger satisfied, Zacharia rubbed his full belly and was grateful for his forgiving, elasticated waistband. Shi Min looked after him too well. Enjoying the relaxed feeling, he sat back, and his shoulders loosened whilst he listened to their discussions about wedding plans, dances the girls were going to, and music he had never heard of. He silently hitched a ride on their adventures as they talked, gaining immense pleasure from observing them.

As a first-time parent, he remembered his shock and terror when he learned they were expecting twins. Anthoula had been desperate for a son, so they kept trying, but after five girls, they realised it wasn't to be. Back then, he was terrified of the responsibility of providing for the new lives which depended on him. Parenting was a job for life, and no matter his children's age, was the source of his constant worry.

'What is it, Pappa? You seem sad,' Clio quizzed. All eyes turned to him.

'Sorry, I was lost in my thoughts. I'm not sad. Quite the opposite.' He sat forward, placing his palms on the table. 'I was enjoying listening to you all making plans. I know your paths will take you further from your mother and me.' Anthoula placed her hand over his. 'Don't get me wrong. It's the natural order of things. You're adults now and will become independent of us. First, Thetie will leave us, and no doubt these two lovebirds will set up a home together after they're married.' He nodded towards the handsome couple. 'I don't think I'm ready for a quiet house, that's all.'

'Aw, Pappa, you old softy,' Terpie smiled.

Zachariah refilled the empty glasses around the table. 'Enough of listening to your soppy old father!' He raised his glass and beamed at the young faces staring back at him. 'Join me and raise your glasses in a toast. To Terpie and Benny!'

Chapter Two
Terpie, January 1942

The warm evening air was comfortable, with a gentle sea breeze on the rooftop terrace at The Adelphi Hotel. Terpie didn't need her pale lemon cardigan, but she wore it anyway to avoid her bare arms on show. Holding a full martini pitcher, she gazed at the stars, watching them sparkle against the black velvet sky. It was the perfect setting for a night of enchanted vaudeville, although Terpie would prefer to be a participant rather than a waitress. Up here, she enjoyed the uninterrupted view of the spire of St Andrews Cathedral piercing the sky. A chain of pale pink lights stretching across the courtyard swayed gently, and in each corner, large garden pots containing golden acers, lemon trees, and jasmine wafted their fresh scents of summer.

Only the city's wealthiest patrons were invited to this evenings' charity event, raising money for "The Malaya Patriotic Fund". On an easel near the entrance, a large poster displayed the face of a young soldier with the tagline underneath *He will thank you.* Recently, the same image printed on postage stamps had become a familiar sight drumming up support for the troops. All local businesses donated generously, including Zacharias's. In return for their goodwill, the affluent guests dined on mock turtle soup, pigeon fricassee, or a fillet of beef, followed by a selection of Swiss cheeses. Nevertheless, Zacharia politely declined his invitation as these social occasions filled him with dread and Anthoula more so.

In the previous month of December, the Imperial Japanese army launched a surprise attack on the American Pearl Harbour naval base near Honolulu. Shortly after, the Japanese declared war on the United States and the British Empire, intensifying the threat to the people of Singapore who lived under colonial rule. At the same time, in their conquest to gain control of the Pacific, the Japanese army invaded nearby Malaya. The province was already swarming with enemy soldiers heading south, and Singapore supported its neighbours as much as possible. As a safeguard, the military presence in Singapore increased, creating a sense of unease. Regardless of the growing threat, the authorities repeatedly reassured the public that the island was heavily defended and completely safe. Trusting what they were told, the people of Singapore went about their daily lives as normal.

Thalia sidled past Terpie with a tray of drinks raised high over her shoulder and winked.

'Not long to go now; cheer up.' She glided off to deliver her cargo to a table of rowdy, thirsty guests.

Their father suggested, or more accurately insisted, that both girls offered their services as hosts tonight claiming it would be an excellent experience. He allowed them each to choose a dress from his shop, which was a total bribe on his behalf, but a welcome outcome all the same. Terpie selected a simple wrap-around chiffon dress in canary yellow, and Thalia, bold as always, chose electric blue. Terpie assumed the other girls acting as hosts were not enthralled to be there either, judging by their sour faces and tedium expressed in yawns. Terpie empathised wholeheartedly. *Please let this be over soon*, her inner voice pleaded. Glancing around the terrace, she recognised the parents of girls she went to school with, colonial families who were all well connected.

The dolled-up women with sparkling gems wrapped around their necks, perfectly set hair, and overpowering perfume twittered effectually at the boorish men around the table. The men, loud and brash in smart dinner jackets, tossed their forthright opinions about the war to anyone who would listen, filling the air with pomposity and thick cigar smoke. By nine o'clock, the party was in full swing. Glass lanterns swayed, turning gently on the breeze, casting a kaleidoscope of colour, adding to the magical atmosphere. On the centre rostrum, the house band dressed in maroon velvet suits played jazz and swing numbers to entice revellers to the dance floor. Terpie watched in awe as couples danced and felt a sudden spike of jealousy as she had no rhythm at all. Her lack of coordination was proven when Clio tried to teach her, resulting in much hilarity to her family, as Terpie tripped, fumbled through the jitterbug and fell on the floor. She realised she would never impress Benny with fancy footwork, and dancing wasn't a skill she possessed, despite her namesake. Terpie circulated between the decorated tables serving guests graciously with a saccharine smile, making perfunctory conversation when needed. Drifting from table to table, she admired the striking glass trumpet vases overflowing with white orchids. The flower's sweet fragrance triggered memories of home as they were her mother's favourite and a typical arrangement in their house.

Between refilling glasses, she glanced at her watch. No matter how much she willed it, the hour hand hadn't moved. Terpie couldn't wait to meet Benny once her shift ended, and her tummy flipped with anticipation. During the last year, their relationship had blossomed since he abandoned his ambition of joining the priesthood. The couple became inseparable, and she was delighted when Benny confessed that his love for her was more significant than his calling—the day Benny proposed had been perfect. After sharing a picnic beneath the shade of an old woody Banyan tree, he knelt before her with an enormous grin and a small black box in his outstretched hand. Realising immediately what it meant, she flung her arms around his neck, not caring that passers-by were staring. With the threat of war on their doorstep, Terpie was impatient for the wedding, and it couldn't come soon enough. A silk dress embellished with pearls hung in her mother's armoire, waiting for the twelfth of March. She prayed the next few months passed quickly. Benny had found them a small apartment to rent after the wedding before fulfilling their desire to travel, and Terpie spent many hours daydreaming about their future.

The band stopped playing, and the sudden silence jolted Terpie from her trance. A stout lady wearing a lavender twinset tapped a spoon firmly against her glass to grab everyone's attention. It took a while for the boisterous crowd to settle enough for her to announce the prize winners of the raffle draw. *Great, another step closer to the evening ending.* Terpie was grateful these events didn't drag on too late, and typically the diehards and drinkers continued their evening elsewhere, usually at exclusive clubs reserved for British members only for late-night tipples and poker games. A roar of applause and cheering signalled the end of the raffle, and finally, the guests began leaving. Some were more unsteady on their feet than others and stifling the urge to giggle, Terpie and the hosts ushered them towards the doors until only the staff remained. With the terrace empty and the band packing up their instruments, Terpie collected empty glasses. The stench of stale alcohol turned her stomach. Thalia approached with her usual buoyancy.

'What are you still doing here? Go, I'll stay behind and do your share.' She flapped a cloth as if to shoo Terpie away.

'Are you sure you don't mind? I feel awful leaving you to clean up.' Terpie wondered if there was a catch to her sister's generosity.

'I wouldn't have offered if I minded. The other girls will help too.' Thalia turned and smiled at a pale, thin girl she had befriended earlier. 'Benny is probably pining for you like a lost puppy. Here,' she giggled, handing her sister her handbag. 'Besides, I know you would do the same for me.'

'Thanks. Tell Pappa not to worry. Benny will bring me home. Don't wait up,' Terpie replied over her shoulder as she headed out the door. She flew down the stairs with her handbag swinging and her heart racing. Stopping briefly on the bottom step to fix her hair, squirt perfume, and smooth down her dress before bursting through the heavy hotel doors. Straight away, she spotted Benny standing under one of the hotel's many ornate canopies with his back to her. Casually dressed in short-sleeved shirt and linen trousers, he stood stiffly bouncing from one foot to the other with his hands deep in his pockets. He hadn't noticed her yet, and Terpie's heart beat a little faster. Sometimes she couldn't believe her luck. Benny was a handsome man. Turning when he heard footsteps, he greeted her with a boyish grin. Benny embraced her, and she inhaled his musky aftershave, committing his smell to memory.

'I thought the evening would never end.' Terpie pulled away and saw his smile fade. Benny avoided her eye, and she knew something was wrong. 'What's the matter?' she asked.

With a stern frown, Benny grabbed her hand and started walking, still refusing to look at her.

'Let's walk. I've something to tell you.'

He was acting out of character, which unsettled her. Terpie didn't like this feeling at all, and her thoughts raced. *Was he breaking up with her? Had she done something to upset him?* The last time they were together, everything had been fine. Terpie couldn't think of a reason for his brittle demeanour. They walked the length of the hotel, which dominated the corner of Coleman Street with its intricately white stone-carved façade. Neither tried to engage in conversation, with only their footsteps on the concrete marking the silence. Eventually, unable to stand the void between them any longer, Terpie boldly made the first move.

'Benny. What's going on?'

Benny tightened his grip, rhythmically stroking the back of her hand with his thumb. His other hand remained in his pocket, jangling his keys.

'Let's walk for a bit. There's nothing wrong between us. That's not the issue.' Benny stared ahead, and Terpie squeezed his hand as a reassuring prompt for him to continue.

'What's the problem then?'

'I've been playing out this conversation for days. I've wanted to talk to you for a while, but the timing was never right. I've no choice now,' he mumbled clumsily.

Terpie registered his discomfort by the stiffening of his body and the way his hand felt rigid beneath her fingers. Could it be that he had to go back to Poland? She mentally prepared herself as there was no doubt in her mind that the news would be bad.

'Let's go down to the seafront first. Tell me about your night,' Benny said, stalling for time. Terpie talked about her evening with scant detail, but she was too preoccupied with the looming conversation they were about to have. The couple passed the cricket club and were headed towards the Fullerton Building, which overlooked the bay. Terpie bristled with nervous energy, trying to guess what was so troubling that he couldn't tell her about it. Trams and cars passed by, their occupants oblivious to her discomfort. They continued in strained silence until reaching the waterfront; the lapping of the waves against the harbour wall did nothing to calm the uncomfortable knots in her stomach. Facing each other, Terpie pulled her cardigan tighter and folded her arms across her body; the air was cooler here.

'This isn't easy. I feel so awful.' Benny pinched the bridge of his nose and inhaled deeply before continuing, 'I never told you something I did months ago, and I should have mentioned it long before now.' His face creased with turmoil.

'Have you met someone else?' Terpie asked, staring at the ground, afraid of his answer.

'God no, nothing like that. I'd never do that to you. I love you.' Benny grabbed her by the arms.

'Please, Benny, the suspense is killing me. Spit it out.'

'A few months back, I signed up to become a volunteer. I thought it was the right thing to do, and no one thought anything would come of it back then. I forgot all about it.'

A shiver ran down Terpie's spine, but there was still hope she could be wrong at this stage. She stepped back. 'Sorry, a volunteer, for what exactly?'

'I enlisted with the army, and I've been called up for service. I'm so sorry.'

The weight of the news crushed her like an avalanche. Suddenly her body felt heavy, and her legs gave way. Benny scooped her up and wrapped his arms around her, holding her upright. She leaned into him whilst her brain tried to process it and what this meant for them.

'Everyone is confident the fighting won't reach us. It's a precaution, that's all. I know I should've told you.'

'When do you leave?' Terpie asked.

'Monday. I don't want to go. I've stalled for as long as I could. Most of the volunteers were mobilised last week,' he rattled on. 'I love you. I'm sorry. Are you angry with me? Please don't be angry.' He cupped her face, his eyes searching hers for reassurance. Unable to speak, Terpie was helpless to prevent the hot stream of tears stinging her cheeks.

'I'm not angry with you. I'm angry at this stupid war and the Japanese. It's forcing us apart.' She pounded her fists against his chest in frustration. Benny didn't stop her. Once her sobs subsided, he held her close, and she nuzzled against him, tuning into his heartbeat whilst tears soaked his shirt.

'We'll get through this. With any luck, it won't be for long. Everyone says it will all blow over. Are you okay?' Benny asked.

'You should've told me. I could've prepared myself.' Terpie sniffed and wiped her stubborn tears on the back of her hand. She realised it wouldn't have mattered *when* Benny told her the news; it hurt regardless. 'What about the wedding? Do you think we'll have to cancel? It's only a few months away.'

Stray strands of ebony curls fell across her face, and he gently tucked them behind her ears.

'We'll have to see how things go. We will be married. It might just be postponed until this madness is over. It's all I want.'

'Look at the state of me. I don't want you going off to war and remember my blotchy swollen face.' Terpie laughed, playing down her despair whilst patting her cheeks on the sleeve of her cardigan. Within the space of an hour, her life had dramatically changed course. 'I can't believe you leave Monday. Will we have any time together?'

'I'm all yours tomorrow, and we can do whatever you want.'

Terpie bit her lip to ward off the tears which threatened again and turned around so Benny couldn't see her face. She placed her hands on the cool, sturdy concrete and leaned into the wall for support. Benny cuddled in behind her and slid his arms around her waist.

'How about a picnic tomorrow, at our favourite place?' Benny suggested, and Terpie nodded silently. 'I know this is awful, but the unit I'll be joining is just outside the city. I can write. It won't be so bad. We can ride this out, can't we?'

Benny nuzzled into her neck, and his warm breath tickled her skin. Knowing he wouldn't be far away eased her nerves slightly, and she considered it might not be so bad. The fighting could end before it reached the island, and he would return to her quickly. However, the threat was real and playing on her mind.

'I'm scared. What if the Japanese do make it here?'

'With any luck, they won't. But if they do, we've got more troops on the ground with the allied forces, so the numbers are on our side,' Benny replied convincingly.

'You'd better write to me every day!' Terpie playfully thumped him on the arm. 'I need contact and to know you're safe. I've seen how hard it's been for Thalia.'

'I'll try. Maybe *every day* will be a bit much.' Benny spun her around, scanning every contour of her face before kissing her. Terpie's legs weakened under the intensity of it, and her heart swelled. The pair remained wrapped in each other's arms, observing the shades of black and pinpricks of light far out to sea, trying to envisage what the immediate future looked like for them. To avoid the subject of their marred future and impending concerns, they kept conversation light with day-to-day triviality until, realising it was late, Terpie suggested they make their way home. As much as she wanted to spend every minute together, her pappa would be worried.

Nothing from now on would be the same. They travelled the journey in silence. Terpie glanced at Benny's profile in the darkness whilst he concentrated on the road ahead and she wished they could disappear together and run away. The reality of Benny becoming a soldier frightened her; an icy chill bore into her bones. What if they were incredibly naïve, the authorities got their predictions all wrong, and the Japanese invaded the island? Benny was a teacher, not a soldier, and she couldn't picture him fighting a war with his kind heart and gentle temperament. The thought of him not returning to her was unthinkable and too horrifying to contemplate. She told herself not to think too far ahead; dwelling on the worst scenario possible was not helpful. After all, the fighting was still hundreds of miles away in north Malaya. The car crunched over the stones of the driveway, and Terpie gripped the straps on her handbag, forcing herself not to cry again. With the car idling, Benny turned towards her, stroked her cheek, and reassured her he loved her for the hundredth time that evening. They agreed Benny would come to the house tomorrow morning so that they could tell her parents together. He kissed her tenderly and said goodnight as they had done many times before, but this parting felt so final. Reluctantly she slid out of the car and blew him a kiss as he drove away. Even though he couldn't see her in the darkness, she waved until the car lights disappeared. Upon reaching the steps, she removed her shoes, patted her puffy face and entered her home. All the lights were out, so the family must be in bed, for which she was grateful. She couldn't face anyone tonight. Once inside, she tiptoed across the wooden floor and snuck quietly into the room she shared with Thalia, who thankfully, was asleep. To avoid making unnecessary noise, she slid into bed, fully clothed. This was not the evening she had been expecting, and she wasn't ready to explain it to her family. She didn't think she would ever be.

Chapter Three
Zacharia, January 1942

Zacharia seized the opportunity to glimpse the world outside his shop on the High Street whilst he had no customers. Standing in the doorway, clasping his hands firmly behind his back, his paunch thrust forward; he glanced up and down the street. A coolie wearing a straw hat and flimsy canvas shoes ran by under the burning sun pulling his rickshaw laden with passengers, sweat pouring down his face. Locals came and went about their daily business as usual, but people were afraid since the surprise air attack by Japanese bombers a few weeks ago. The city shone brightly like a welcoming beacon as bombs fell without warning, and there was no time for blackouts. A shiver ran down his spine. Sixty-one locals lost their lives that night, and over a hundred more were injured, and the city was still grieving their loss. In the days since, he appreciated how fortunate he was that his family and livelihood had escaped untouched. For now, the people of Singapore waited in trepidation for what might happen next. Following a recent heavy downpour, the air smelled of earthy freshness. Zacharia squinted in the bold sunlight, noticing the sun's rays bouncing off the pristine dome of the Supreme Court, towering above the city, keeping watch. He sighed. Zacharia loved this city, but things were changing rapidly. He didn't recognise the sellers on his street anymore, and so much had changed since arriving as a young man in his twenties.

Only he and De Silva from the jewellery shop next door were the mainstays of old, and he worried himself to sleep at night on how his business would survive in this changing world. Independent shops like his were gradually disappearing from the High Street, pushed out and replaced with shiny contemporary department stores like Robinsons and Co. The smaller businesses struggled to compete with their lower prices and far-reaching suppliers bringing exotic goods from all corners of the globe. Zacharia remained sceptical. How could they possibly offer the personal service he could? Did they know their customers by name, for example? Perhaps he was old-fashioned, and customers didn't value such things these days. Zacharia knew he was a good businessman. To compete with the larger stores, he pioneered the first importation of Bata shoes and traded with some of the biggest fashion houses in Paris; he wouldn't go down without a fight. Zacharia was nostalgic for the old Singapore. Life seemed easier then. People were happier, the money went further, and there were no cliques or social groups; everyone knew each other or pretended they did.

He gently rocked on the balls of his feet, and the spicy aroma of caramelised onions from the hawker stall drifted down the street, stirring his hunger. A jamboree of trams, cars, bicycles, rickshaws and people on foot shared the road with good manners. He greeted a passer-by with a "good afternoon" and received no response reiterating his earlier sentiment. He was about to return to his shop when the sound of three large military vehicles stopped him. Their large tyres kicked up dust and stones in their wake, and cyclists and rickshaws hurried out of their path. The rumble of the engines shook his window, and the ground vibrated beneath his feet. Blank-faced soldiers stared at him from under the khaki canopy, cradling their weapons tightly to their chests. The youngsters appeared exhausted and terrified in equal amounts. He scanned their faces as they passed, searching for the one he may recognise as Benny's. Zacharia raised a hand in salute. He felt sorry for them and was relieved he was too old to fight. The presence of soldiers was becoming a familiar sight and a constant reminder of unrest with invasion brewing on the horizon. Once the trucks passed and the street was quiet once more, he returned inside to settle up for the day. The sound of footsteps and light chatter alerted him to customers entering, and he instantly recognised the smartly dressed British couple standing in the doorway. He smiled, greeted them by name and welcomed them.

'Good afternoon, Mr Pattara. I hope we're not too late?' Mr Henderson asked, shaking his wrist and giving Zacharia a glimpse of his expensive gold watch. His elegant wife beside him, her blonde hair perfectly set in tight waves, and her arm looped possessively through his. When she smiled at Zacharia, all he noticed was her ruby-red lips. In contrast to her shade of lipstick, her powdered skin appeared pale and pasty.

'Not at all. What can I do for you?' Zacharia ushered them in. His customers were a priority, even if the day was drawing to a close.

'The thing is old chap. My wife needs a new outfit. There's not one in the wardrobe that will do, apparently.' Mr Henderson glanced at his wife and winked.

'That's a little unfair, darling. I haven't bought anything new in weeks. You know I don't need an excuse to visit Mr Pattara.' Mrs Henderson placed her gloved hand on Zacharia's forearm and laughed in a singsong manner. 'I do adore your little shop. We've been invited to an event at The Raffles tomorrow, and one can't possibly be seen in the same old rags.' She cast a playful glare towards her husband.

'You have impeccable timing, Mrs Henderson. I've got a new line of summer dresses from Paris.'

Mrs Henderson's eyes lit up, squealing like an excited schoolgirl.

'I'll bring out a selection for you to try. The delivery has just arrived, so they're not on the rails yet. No fear of being seen in the same outfit, another bonus, I imagine.' Zacharia nodded knowingly.

'Perfect. That would be wonderful. You know my taste.' Mrs Henderson sauntered past and flicked through clothes on the hanging rails.

'Please, take a seat. I'll be right back.' Zacharia gestured them towards the blue velvet couch and disappeared to the storeroom at the back of the shop. He didn't need to check her size as he memorised these essential details about his regular customers. It was his business to know. He selected four dresses and seized the opportunity to pair the ensemble with matching shoes and a handbag. He worked on the assumption that the customer didn't always know they wanted something until it was suggested. More often than not, this technique worked in his favour. He had known the Henderson's for years. Not only were the couple long-standing customers, but their daughter Julia used to attend the same convent school as his girls. Zacharia wasn't sure what Mr Henderson did for a living, but knew he worked in the government buildings around the corner and some mornings saw him striding along the street with his leather briefcase. He returned to his customers with the dresses draped over his arm, pulled back the dark green velvet curtain of the changing room and placed them on the hooks.

'The dresses are ready for you. I've taken the liberty of matching some accessories I thought you might like,' he placed the shoes and handbag in the changing area. 'I have plenty more we can try if needed.'

Zacharia held open the curtain whilst Mrs Henderson removed her silk scarf and gloves and placed her handbag on the seat beside her husband.

'Thank you, Mr Pattara, you're a real gem.' Mrs Henderson ducked beneath his arm, and Zacharia closed the curtain with a firm swoosh. He stepped away to give her privacy and returned to her husband.

'Can I tempt you to a coffee whilst you wait?' Zacharia asked.

'Ahh yes. The famous Pattara Pure Mocha.' Mr Henderson picked up a tin of Zacharia's blend of coffee from the display on the counter and read the label aloud 'The Nectar of the Gods. This is the good stuff. I'd love a cup,' he said, pointing to the logo on the tin.

Zacharia removed a cup from the shelf, and within minutes, a roasted, nutty aroma of fresh coffee beans wafted through the shop, clinging to the fabrics. After his original business with his brother failed, Zacharia sold cigarettes. But industry giants pushed him out of the market, so he learned to diversify by importing coffee. A decision that had rewarded him enormously over the years. The process for his unique blend was jealously guarded and appreciated by connoisseurs throughout Singapore. He never wanted to go through the experience of bankruptcy again and expanded his business into couture, importing the finest silks from India and the latest fashions from Europe. With his collective endeavours, he had created the perfect fusion for a pleasurable customer experience. His coffee had gained notoriety, and the prominent and wealthy Sultan of Johore in Malaya regularly shipped orders over the causeway to his palace. About a year ago, Zacharia became concerned because he stopped placing orders. He realised why when he saw grainy images in the newspaper of the Sultan in England consorting with a glamour girl. They met whilst he was staying at the Grosvenor hotel in London, where Cissie Hill, a dancer half his age, was a performer. He reportedly showered her with expensive jewellery and brought her an art deco house in Herne Bay. Their love affair was heavily documented in the newspapers, causing quite a scandal as the Sultan was already married. The story ended tragically when Ms Hill was out shopping in Canterbury when bombs struck the building, killing her instantly. Her body was identified by the extravagant rings he had brought her. The Sultan returned, reportedly heartbroken. Zacharia couldn't be less interested in his extramarital affair, he was only concerned for his dwindling sales.

'How are your family?' Mr Henderson asked, removing his manila hat and placing it on the counter. Zacharia recognised it as one purchased from him a little while ago and was pleased to see it was still in excellent condition.

'They're well, thank you. Getting on with life as best they can under the circumstances. Terpie's fiancé signed up, so naturally, she's on edge with him gone. It's all such a worrying time. And Julia? She's well, I hope.'

'She completed her nursing training and is working at the Alexandra Hospital. Absolutely loves it.' Mr Henderson dug deep into his linen jacket pocket and removed his wallet to proudly reveal a black and white photograph of his only daughter posing in her starched white nurse's uniform.

'Excellent, I'm pleased for her. I'll tell my girls. They always ask after her.' Zacharia placed the hot cup on the counter, and Mr Henderson perched on the high stool, helping himself to the tray of milk and sugar and began reading the newspaper.

'This trouble will blow over, you mark my words,' said Mr Henderson, flicking his fingers against the two-page article on the Japanese advance. 'Tell Terpie not to worry. Her man will be back sooner rather than later.' His spoon clinked against the cup as he stirred. Zacharia was irked by his smugness.

'How can you be so sure? Only yesterday, I read that the Japanese soldiers are advancing through Malaya at quite a pace, riding through the jungle on bikes, of all things. And today were told Kuala Lumpur has been invaded, and Percival's troops are being pushed back again. I don't see how this will blow over.'

'That is true. But I'm confident our boys will stop them before they get anywhere close. Our island is a fortress! We have it covered. The Japs won't get their hands on it,' Mr Henderson said, slurping his coffee loudly.

'I hope you're right. I'm doubtful since the Pearl Harbour attack. You see, I think people are underestimating the Japanese. I wish I had your faith, but I can't see this ending quickly at all.' Zacharia leaned on the counter and shook his head. Mr Henderson sat upright and lowered his newspaper.

'Mr Pattara. Don't worry. The British outnumber their army. I know we lost our battleships and planes early, which put us on the back foot, but honestly? From what I've heard, their soldiers are fresh from the paddy fields with pitiful old weapons, and they're no threat to our soldiers.' His coffee cup hovered by his lips, he sipped his coffee noisily and continued. 'And did you know? Their soldiers can't see in the dark. That General Yamashita, or whatever his name is, will run for the hills and take his midget soldiers with him with a flea in his ear. You wait and see,' he prodded the counter with his index finger to hammer home his point. He acknowledged the uncertainty on Zacharia's face and added. 'If it reassures you any, my wife and I recently turned down the chance to evacuate to Australia. That's how sure I am this won't come to anything. We wouldn't stay if we thought we would be invaded, now would we? Relax. Singapore is perfectly safe,' said Mr Henderson smugly.

'How do you know all this, or is it your expert opinion?'

'I have it on good authority. I've got friends in the military old boy. The papers like to scare monger; upset the locals for no reason.' Mr Henderson picked up the newspaper and continued reading.

Zacharia found his customer's view incredulous, and the nerve in his forehead started to twitch. Zacharia was far from a military expert himself. Still, he'd been following the events in Europe and closer to home, and he believed the capabilities of the Japanese Imperial Army had been grossly misjudged. He knew that Mr Henderson wasn't alone in his opinion. For months, propaganda telling the public the island was heavily protected through posters, radio announcements, and newspaper articles had been drip-fed. The authorities had drummed the message that Singapore was an impregnable fortress into the population's psyche, and no one questioned it as anything but the truth. Zacharia excused himself to avoid saying something he regretted, allowing his customer to finish his coffee in peace, and busied himself rearranging folded shirts on display. A few moments later, the changing room curtain swished open, and Mrs Henderson appeared, modelling a pale blue spotted tea dress with a sweetheart neckline, holding the seams of the skirt out wide.

'What do you think, darling? It's just what I was looking for. Although they're all beautiful, it's difficult to choose.' She glanced over her shoulder, admiring herself in the mirror. Zacharia returned and was pleased to see the dress was a perfect fit, flattering her slender figure, and the shoes complimented the ensemble.

'If you like it, then get it. Well done, Mr Pattara, you've made my wife happy again.' Mr Henderson rose from his stool and slapped Zacharia's shoulder firmly.

'I like this one too… would it be awfully greedy of me to take the two with the shoes and handbag, as they do go so well together?' She appealed to her husband coyly, knowing full well he would never refuse her. Zacharia resisted his urge to smile triumphantly as his ruse with the accessories paid off. He didn't get to being "A doyen of the shop keeping fraternity" without learning a trick or two, which was how the newspaper article in the *Straits Times* described him

35

recently when they interviewed him for a piece to celebrate his thirtieth anniversary. The framed publication took pride of place in his office, and he read it to remind him of his worth, on the days when he felt like a failure.

'Yes, yes, if it makes you happy.' replied Mr Henderson, and his wife squealed in delight so loudly it irritated Zacharia's ears. Before returning to the changing room, she pecked her husband on the cheek and winked at Zacharia.

'I don't know. Sometimes it's hard to keep up. Dinner dances two or three times a week. Quite exhausting.' He lowered his voice to avoid the scorn of his wife. 'Does your wife always drag you out?' he mumbled, opening his wallet.

'No Sir. Luckily for me, my wife doesn't care for them much, and neither of us enjoys dancing. But my daughters love them. They'd be out every night of the week if they could.' he replied, reaching below the counter for some tissue paper.

'You're a lucky man. I can't say I care for them much myself, but I do as I'm told.' He raised his eyebrows towards where his wife was changing, and Zacharia responded with a knowing smirk. Mr Henderson paid in cash, and his wife joined them at the counter with a satisfied glow. Zacharia wrapped the goods neatly with lemon tissue paper, placed them in a white box, and slid them across the counter. The couple wished him well and said goodbye, promising to return soon. From the window, he watched Mr Henderson striding across the road and his wife scurrying behind to keep up with his pace. He silently congratulated himself for another satisfied customer. He yawned, suddenly feeling drained, turning over the sign to "closed" and retreated to his office to complete paperwork before going home.

Some hours later, Zacharia stopped writing in his ledger, rubbed his forehead with the back of his hand, and folded the black, leather-bound book for the day. Leaning backwards, he stretched before levering himself out of his office chair. Whilst tidying his desk, he knocked over a photograph in a silver frame. Covered in dust, he blew it off, wiping the glass on his shirt, before returning it to its rightful place. He studied the sepia scene where a younger version of himself with a head of jet-black hair leaned over the veranda of his home. Beside him, Anthoula, her swollen belly, carried Thalia. Standing on the ground directly below, equally spaced between garden pots, stood little Thetie, flanked by her sisters Clio and Ino. Their angelic smiles struck his heart, and to the left of the shot, Shi Min, with one-year-old Terpie, sitting in a pram.

Where did that time go? Zacharia had always thought it was a bit cliché when customers would talk about their children and say the time goes so fast. Now that

36

his family was grown, he could fully support that statement. Life seemed so carefree back then, and lately, he felt more at odds with the world than ever before. The photograph ignited a familiar niggle of concern he hadn't thought about for some time. None of his daughters showed any interest in the business, and the idea of having no successor to continue his work was troubling. A small clock chimed seven o'clock. This wouldn't do, Lim would be waiting, and he was late again. He shook himself from his nostalgic reverie and replaced the photograph, picked up his half-read newspaper tucking it under his arm. Walking through the stillness of the shop, he patted the piles of stacked shirts as he passed. With a flick of a switch, the shop descended into silence as the fans slowed to a stop above his head. Satisfied all was in order, he grabbed his cotton jacket and hat off the stand and locked up for the evening. Scanning the parked cars along the street, he spotted Lim, his chauffeur dutifully waiting for him. Zacharia strolled across the road and slid across the seat, tossing his jacket before winding down the window to replace the stale air.

'Good evening, sir. Good day?' Lim asked, glancing into the rear-view mirror before pulling away.

'I can't grumble, Lim. It's been busy. Are the girls home?' Zacharia flapped open his newspaper to continue where he had left off earlier in the day. It was depressing reading with page after page of war updates, and he wasn't sure he could face it this evening after his conversation with Mr Henderson and folded it up again.

'Yes, they've all been collected from work, and I believe Clio, Ino, and Terpie are all out this evening to a dance.'

'Terpie's going?' queried Zacharia.

'Yes, Sir. Shi Min said the girls are trying to cheer her up and take her mind off Benny.'

'Good, I'm glad. It'll do her good. No point brooding: she needs to have some fun whilst she can.' Zacharia relaxed his head back, watching the familiar buildings and landmarks pass by, and anticipated a quiet evening with his wife.

Chapter Four
Zacharia, February 1942

The lion city slept peacefully under a moonlit, cloudless sky. The sleeping occupants of Singapore were unaware of the faint humming barely audible over the chorus of birds and nocturnal insects buzzing with their courtship songs. The unusual droning steadily grew louder but was still unrecognisable. In the Pattara house, white muslin net curtains billowed into the bedroom on the gentle breeze. Zacharia was a light sleeper and didn't want to be awake, but his body defied him. Unsure why he had woken, he lay still and kept his eyes closed; perhaps he could drift off to sleep. The harder he tried, the more his mind seemed to chatter. It was no use, he was fully conscious, and no amount of stillness would work. Anthoula lay on her side beside him, facing away, but the familiar rise and fall of her breathing told him she was in a deep sleep. He listened. Something wasn't right, but until he had investigated the unusual noise, he knew settling back to sleep would be impossible.

Leaning on his elbows, he shook his head to ease the fogginess sleep left behind. Swiftly swinging his legs over the edge of the bed, he eased himself into a seated position with minimum movement without waking Anthoula. He rubbed the light stubble on his chin and yawned. It was still dark outside, and moonlight poured in, defining the edges and shapes in the room. He squinted at the clock beside the bed; just gone four a.m. Beyond the walls of his home, he heard the usual symphony of night-time sounds and something else... straining to identify the sound, he turned towards the window. As realisation dawned, a chill ran through his body. His heart pounded loudly inside his chest. If he was right, they were in trouble. Where was the warning? There had been no siren. His mind raced. What should he do? Feeling paralysed and stuck to the bed, he knew he must protect his family, but how? Leaping to the window, he searched the sky for answers, although a bank of palm trees hindered his view. There was no mistaking the droning sound, and pulling on a pair of baggy house trousers, he stumbled, waking his wife.

'Zac, what is it? Come back to bed,' Anthoula mumbled, full of sleep.

'Stay there. I'll be right back,' he told his wife firmly, staring at him in confusion.

He padded out of the bedroom barefoot as quickly as the poor light allowed, through the house to the veranda. Gripping the rail, he viewed the open sky beyond the trees. Despite the darkness, he could make out the black silhouette of planes against the cobalt night. Directly above, the patch of sky was saturated with fighter planes in a "V" formation headed for the city. His stomach lurched. He averted his gaze downwards in case somehow his scrutiny attracted their attention. A long shrill whistle followed by a thunderous explosion split the ground, sending out shockwaves from the impact. Zacharia steadied himself against the railing as the house trembled on its stilts, and the tremor rattled his insides. Open-mouthed, he watched in horror as planes approached their target, bomb doors open, ready to release their deadly cargo on his city.

'Good God, no, this can't be happening again,' he said out loud. He knew from the last raid that there were no shelters nearby, and the authorities had been so confident the attack was a one-off that they hadn't considered building more. Behind him, a jumble of frightened sleepy voices called out.

'Pappa, are you okay?'

'What's happening?'

'I'm scared!'

Rooted to the spot, he had no plan, no solution to offer them, and no idea what he would say. After one last glimpse at the fiery scene, he gathered his thoughts and hurried indoors. Assembled in the family room, his confused and frightened family gathered barefoot on the rug in long linen nightdresses. Their pale and terrified faces looked to him for answers.

'They're bombing the city again,' he blurted.

'We guessed that much, Pappa. What shall we do?' shrieked Terpie.

'Not again. They told us the island was safe,' said Ino, wrapping her arm around her mother's shoulder. Thetie and Clio clung to each other, visibly shaking, their faces white and ghostly. Before he could stop her, Thalia ran to the veranda to see for herself.

'Get back in here. It's not safe!' he called as another explosion shook the foundations, forcing them to the floor. Family memories in photo frames on tables fell like dominos, glass smashed, and the girls screamed. Boom after boom rang out, and the family huddled on the ground covering their heads in protection.

'The sky is full of planes,' Thalia yelled breathlessly, rushing back in. 'Bombs are falling like rain. It's worse than last time. Should we go to a shelter?'

Zacharia managed to stay upright, hovering over his crouching family with his arms outstretched protectively to shield them from the tirade above. Thalia grabbed his arm and tugged, prompting him to provide a solution. His mind stalled; it was blank. Before him on her knees, Thetie caressed the cross on the chain around her neck and quietly recited a prayer. The other girls held on to each other for comfort whilst bomb blasts shattered the dawn. Zacharia wasn't prepared for this. How could he protect them?

'The nearest shelter is in Tiong Bahru, and it'll be full by the time we get there, and I don't know of any others. It's not an option. We stay here,' he said.

'Are you sure Zac? We need to leave!' Anthoula insisted, tugging on the seam of his trousers. Kneeling to her level, he tried to ease her terror.

'From what I saw, they're targeting the city. Besides, the advice given for a raid was for families to stay put. It's too dangerous.' He scanned the room. *Come on, Zac. Think, think.*

'This house. It won't protect us,' replied Anthoula, pale with fear.

'Maybe not, but it's all we have. We're far enough out to be safe for the time being. Just until I have time to think of a better solution.'

He prayed the planes didn't change course or turn around. The fear on the faces of his girls made him feel inadequate. He hoped, for all their sakes, he was making the right call.

'Should we hide under the house, Pappa?' Terpie suggested, scrambling off the floor.

'No, if the house collapses, we'll be crushed,' replied Zacharia.

'And there's snakes and bugs under there,' said Thalia, screwing up her face in disgust.

'I have an idea. We need to stay together. Everyone, go to your rooms and grab pillows and blankets. We'll shelter under the dining table until the worst is over. Go quickly.'

'The table?' queried Ino.

'It's the best I can come up with. It's robust and solid as an ox. Does anyone have any better ideas?' Zacharia asked, and his daughters stared blankly, shaking their heads. 'Well, go then! Don't just stand there.'

The girls dispersed with a sense of urgency as instructed. Zacharia rubbed his temple. He didn't mean to shout but wasn't sure what to do and was just as terrified as they were. He reached out to help Anthoula to her feet, and she followed him like a lost lamb to the bedroom. Zacharia darted across the room to the chair in the corner, the dumping ground for clothes with at least one more wear in them before washing and flung items on the floor until he found a shirt.

'What are you doing?' asked Anthoula.

'I'll check on Lim and Shi Min and see if they need help. Stay with the girls and keep them calm if you can.'

'Please don't go out there. Stay with us for now,' Anthoula pleaded, hanging on to him.

Zacharia cupped her face in his hands and kissed her, tenderly stroking away the stray tear rolling down her cheek. 'Don't worry. The sooner I'm gone, the quicker I'll be back.'

Gently prising himself away, he buzzed with adrenalin pumping through his veins as he hastily threw on a shirt. Thetie hovered in the doorway.

'Pappa will be straight back. Come and help me with the pillows,' she said, catching her father's grateful nod before guiding her mother out of the room. Resounding booms continued in the distance, and the futile wailing of the air raid siren began. For peace of mind, he needed to see what was happening outside his four walls and check on his staff. Still fumbling with his shirt buttons, he raced to the veranda, where the sky glowed amber and fires raged in every direction. A surge of emotion stopped him in his tracks. There was no time to be sentimental. He descended the stone steps as fast as he could without tripping over his feet and hurried along the side path leading behind the house. Nothing appeared out of place, and he couldn't see any signs of fire, filling him with relief. As long as the bombers remained focussed on the city, they should be out of danger. He'd charged out of the house without thinking to put on his shoes, and shards of stone dug painfully into the soles of his feet. Flinching with each step, he tiptoed across the drive taking in the city's red aura glow and unfurling smoke clouds, further darkening the sky like a blanket. He prayed that his precious shop would be lucky for a second time and escape the bombs unscathed. That would have to wait, but he would head into town at the first safe moment to check. It struck him as odd that there was no air combat retaliation from British planes, so the Japanese enemy dominated the sky unchallenged. Then he remembered the news report he read some days back of an attack at the airfields, and it all made sense. This wasn't random; it was a well-planned assault. Singapore was a sitting duck. The enemy had gained superiority in the sky, and would progress to ground battle at some point. It was apparent the Japanese were smart, they had the upper hand, and Zacharia felt sick to his stomach.

Within the boundary of his grounds stood the wooden house where his employees lived, and he hammered urgently on the door and waited. With a creak, the door opened slowly, and Lim's pale face appeared. Seeing it was Zac, he opened the door and invited him in. Zacharia stooped to avoid banging his head on the low beam. A large window with a forest view allowed their home to bathe in the orange glow of dawn. The house smelled of spices and was immaculately tidy, with clean white walls and a bare wooden floor.

'Do you need me to drive you to a shelter? I'm ready to go,' asked Lim.

'No, Lim, that won't be necessary. I came to check you're both alright.' Zacharia placed his hand on Lim's shoulder.

'Yes, Sir. We're shaken, but we're fine. I can't believe this is happening again,' said Lim, and Shi Min appeared behind him in her nightdress. She appeared younger with her long grey hair draped over her shoulder, which Zacharia only saw styled into a neat bun.

'Are the girls okay?' she asked.

'Yes, like you, they're in shock and frightened. I can't believe there was no warning. All we can do is ride this out and sit tight.' Zacharia nodded towards the window. 'It looks like the city is taking the brunt of it. We're taking shelter in the house for now. I don't know what else to do.' He thought momentarily and asked, 'Are you and Shi Min okay here, or would you feel safer in the house with us?'

'We'll be fine here,' said Lim, glancing at his wife, who agreed with a nod.

'If anything changes, don't hesitate. Come over. You know you're always welcome, and there's plenty of room. I'd better get back.'

Zacharia brushed off the stones embedded in his feet before bolting up the stairs to the veranda. When he reached the top, he gasped for breath, a reminder that he wasn't a young man. It was impossible to ignore the view and he felt compelled to look, even though he knew he wouldn't like what he saw. This familiar scene he observed everyday which he took for granted, was altered forever. From left to right, he scanned the depressing view. Funnels of thick black smoke created a smog across the rooftops, fires raged, and familiar landmarks steeped in history vanished from the skyline. Surprisingly, the sixteen-storey tower of the recently constructed Cathay Building appeared for now to be untouched. The scene of destruction angered him, and he wondered how many innocent lives would be lost today. Families tucked up in their beds had no chance to save themselves or take cover. It saddened him to imagine the city full of chaos and heartbreak, and he grew concerned for people he knew and prayed none of them was among the casualties. Explosions continued, but the intensity had slowed at least. A nasty feeling in the pit of his stomach told him this was the beginning, and there would be far worse to come. When he reached the dining room, he found his family huddled on blankets and cushions under the sturdy table. The chairs stood abandoned at the side of the room, and the blinds were closed. Never in a million years could he have imagined the sight before him with the table pushed hard against the wall and his daughters propped up with cushions, knees under their chins, leaning on the wall for support. Thalia and Terpie sat cross-legged, heads bent, and Anthoula lay on her side propped on a cushion with her feet poking out from under the table. He leaned on the table and bent down.

'I know this situation isn't to be taken lightly, but it does look funny walking in and seeing you all under here.'

'Oh Zac, thank goodness you're back. Join us under here,' said Anthoula, patting a cushion beside her.

His bones gave an audible crack in protest as he crouched and squashed beside his wife.

'How long do you think we have to stay here?' Anthoula asked, pulling on the tassels on one of the cushions.

'As long as it takes. We have everything we need, besides the bombing won't go on forever.'

Cramped under the table, Ino and Clio played cards to pass the time. Terpie had bought her journal and was scribbling away furiously, and Thetie read a book whilst the rest sat in their thoughts in silence. The frequency of explosions seemed to be slowing, which relieved their shattered nerves. After some time had passed, Zacharia yawned and poked his head out from under the table to check the clock. They'd been under the table for almost two hours. His joints ached, and sitting around doing nothing didn't suit him. As the raid continued, all he could think of was his shop, the stock, and what he could do with it if the building were still standing and not burnt to the ground, but he didn't want to dwell on that possibility. Thinking of solutions was the only way to tame his restless mind. He had it all planned out. Lim could drive him, they could pack the car with as much stock as possible and bring it back to the house, and it would be safer here. He must be patient and pitch his idea to his wife at the right time, as she was already on edge. Whilst the girls and their mother chatted, he crawled out from under the table and stretched his stiff arms above his head, releasing a huge sigh. He noted the disgruntled look from his wife.

'It's only for a minute. I can't stay cramped under there.' He wandered to the solid wood credenza on the other side of the room. He scrabbled around until he found what he was searching for and pulled out a large wooden box. Blowing off the thin layer of dust, he opened his old chessboard. The delicate hand-carved pieces had not seen the light of day for many years, and he wondered why he'd stopped playing. When the girls were much younger, he tried to teach them, but only Thalia had the patience for the strategic game. They would sit for hours poring over the board, neither wanting to admit defeat. One game, he recalled, went on for days, but he couldn't remember who won. Zacharia crawled beneath the table once more and set up the board.

'We haven't played chess for years. I bet I can still beat you.'

'Let's see, little bird. Let's see.'

Chapter Five
Benny

Benny sat on the side of the road near the Kallang Airfield with his platoon; a menagerie of volunteers thrown together over recent months to defend the island. Across his lap lay a woefully old rifle he had inherited, with barely any preparation for how to use it. During their brief training, the men had laughed in response to the inadequate lessons in survival and defence, although Benny doubted they would find it funny when faced with the enemy—a prospect which was becoming more certain by the day. Lambs to the slaughter sprang to mind.

A wide yawn escaped, and Benny stretched to bring life to his limbs. Night after night with little or no sleep played havoc with his body clock, plus the lack of a decent meal made him weak. His anxiety levels had gone through the roof since the air raids started, and constant overthinking only added to his fatigue. Benny had no idea whether Terpie and her family were safe and had no opportunity to find out being stuck here in the middle of nowhere roasting like pork chops in the heat. He hoped he wouldn't be digging trenches and lugging heavy sandbags today. If he never saw another shovel again in his life, he would be elated. Even raising his flask to drink was a painful reminder of his efforts.

Teaching a class of hormonal fifteen-year-olds didn't require physical strength; his muscles had been screaming in protest daily. Adding to his discomfort, an itchy red rash recently appeared on his neck, made worse by his poorly fitting uniform, a size too big for his lean frame. The stiff collar chafed and irritated his skin. His boots rubbed blisters the size of golf balls, contributing to a myriad of reasons he strongly regretted his foolhardy decision to sign up in the first place. By mid-morning, it was impossible to get any relief from the sun's relentless rays, and he leaned back on the grubby tyre of his vehicle, trying to find a smidgen of shade. The metal carcass radiated more heat, so keeping cool was out of the question.

'Hey, where did you go? Earth calling Polak, is anybody there?' Jimmy nudged him out of his thoughts.

Jimmy assigned him a nickname the first day they met, others may take offence, but Benny didn't care. Jimmy was in his thirties and had scruffy, brown hair. Taller than Benny with a robust physique, he always seemed cheerful. 'You look like you've got the world on your shoulders. What's up?'

'Ah, nothing, just thinking about stuff.' Benny stared across the airfield watching the heatwaves shimmy in the distance blurring the landscape.

'You can do better than that. I haven't known you long, but I'm telling you. Whatever it is, it's better out than in. We have time on our hands, so we might as well fill it with something,' prompted Jimmy, and Benny sighed. He wasn't sure he had the energy to explain but got the impression Jimmy wasn't prepared to give up that easily.

'It's my fiancé, Terpie. She lives with her family outside the city, and I can't stop worrying something has happened to them.' He couldn't bring himself to say the words he meant. To avoid making eye contact with Jimmy, he picked up small stones and sifted them through his fingers, hoping he didn't sound soft.

'No wonder you've been quiet. I know how it feels to worry constantly.' Jimmy flashed his wedding band towards Benny. 'My wife Charlotte and my little one Daisy, she's three—a right little handful.' A wide smile lit up Jimmy's face at the mention of her name.

'I had no idea. You always seem so carefree, I guess. Where are they now?' Benny asked with concern.

'Most days, I feel like I've swallowed a grenade. I must hide it well. Charlotte's parents insisted they return to England, so they left in December after the first raid. I couldn't leave because of my job, so I'm stuck here with you.' Jimmy pulled a crumpled photograph from his shirt pocket and handed it to his friend. Benny studied the two smiling faces staring back at him. Charlotte, a petite woman with long dark hair, held her daughter on her knee with her arms wrapped around her. He noted Daisy shared her dad's wide-set eyes and dimpled smile. Messy blonde curls framed her chubby face, and in her arms, she hugged a rag doll tight under her chin. He returned the photograph, and his heart weighed a little heavier than before. Benny was thankful he and Terpie didn't have children. At least their situation spared them from that particular heartache.

'You have a lovely family. I don't know how you do it. Stay so cheerful, I mean. It must be tough knowing they're so far away.'

46

'It breaks me to be here and not with them. I get through the days by telling myself it won't last long. We'll be together soon.' He tucked the picture back in his breast pocket and patted it three times. Jimmy lit a cigarette and offered one to Benny, which he declined. He'd never smoked and didn't intend to, but he understood why many men did. If nothing else, it helped pass the time.

'We can only hope this war ends quickly. I feel bad now. At least I've been able to write to Terpie, but even her letters have stopped.'

'My last letter came at the beginning of January, and England isn't much safer.' Jimmy puffed on his cigarette.

Benny felt sympathy for his friend's suffering, and they shared the same anguish the enforced separation bestowed upon them with no idea of when it would end. Jimmy's story reminded him to be grateful for the letters he'd received from Terpie, albeit mundane information. In a few months, the rote of his everyday life had become a distant memory; now, his days were filled with digging trenches and playing at being a soldier.

Adding to his worry, the worsening situation in Europe meant he hadn't received word from Poland for months. His torment always crept in at night, niggling at his consciousness as he tried to sleep, wondering whether his parents and sisters were safe and well. He'd heard stories of the German concentration camps and had no way of knowing whether his family had been captured. At times, the loneliness and isolation of being stuck out here felt crushing, and Terpie's letters kept him going.

'We're in the same sinking boat, so we keep each other going. Deal?' said Jimmy, holding out his hand, and they shook on it. 'The postal service isn't going to be a priority in this crazy situation. I'm sure Terpie is fine. Don't overthink it.' Jimmy dragged on his cigarette and blew the smoke upwards. 'You'll go insane otherwise.'

Benny felt lighter somehow for confiding in his new friend, which helped him to know he wasn't alone. Jimmy was right, it was better to share, and now he'd gained a comrade in more ways than one. Their conversation was interrupted by the voice of their commander instructing them to move. New orders meant the troops were needed to help with the clean-up following the air strikes.

'You wanted a break from digging; well, now you've got it.' Jimmy tossed his cigarette to the ground and slapped Benny on the back.

Their commander waved the men towards a row of trucks waiting across the tarmac. Benny swigged the last of the water from his hip flask, sprang to his feet, and grabbed his rifle. The group sprinted to the idling trucks, and Benny waited patiently behind the others before climbing in. Squashed and uncomfortable against his comrades, the mixture of pungent body odours assaulted his senses. He wriggled uncomfortably, his back was drenched in sweat, and his shirt stuck to his skin. The truck lurched forward, and he grabbed the bar of the canopy, holding himself steady, swaying and bouncing along the rough terrain. The truck rumbled past the airfield filled with lifeless, buckled and burnt-out aircraft in the distance, damaged by enemy bombs. It was nothing but a metal graveyard. Benny watched funnels of black smoke rising on the skyline, chilling him to the bone. The bombing over the last four days had been constant and unforgiving, and Benny was afraid. His stomach churned with a life of its own, but he was stuck here with no choice but to face it head-on. Sir Arthurs Bridge carried them across the Kallang River, entering the smog through the city's industrial landscape. The tall towers of the gas works loomed ahead, and the sawmills were an untamed blaze of rage. The troops encountered widespread devastation the further they travelled towards the residential areas, where the full extent of the carnage was realised.

The two friends locked eyes; Benny could see from Jimmy's vacant expression that they shared the same disbelief. The colour drained from Jimmy's face, and Benny felt queasy himself. Everywhere he turned, destruction and decay bled out into the streets. Overhead stretching from one side to the other, washing lines full of smoke-blackened laundry flapped in surrender. Benny coughed, covering his mouth with his arm, and the fumes stung his eyes. Wooden framed houses engulfed by flames stubbornly stood tall whilst locals fought to save them.

The inadequate water supply would never be enough to suppress the fires since the city was now down to reserves. Streets he knew well were unfamiliar, and he viewed straight into homes ripped open. Suddenly the reality of the war punched him in the gut; he wasn't prepared for this. Whole neighbourhoods were demolished, leaving rubble and bricks blocking the road and limp bodies lying unclaimed. The truck weaved around the debris, giving Benny a slow-motion panoramic view. He tightened his grip on the rifle, pulling it close, his knuckles turned pure white, and he thought he might vomit, but he swallowed hard. Benny's body churned with a rage he never knew was possible. He closed his eyes to block out the horror of families clawing at fallen bricks and wailing in the street for lost loved ones. But the images were firmly imprinted on the inside of his eyelids. The injured victims aimlessly staggered along the road, their clothing ripped or covered in blood, not knowing where to go or what to do.

Further along, water flooded the street from burst pipes, wasting precious reserves. When the truck stopped, Benny was first to jump out, splashing in inches of water swirling around his feet. His comrades barged against him in their dismount, but Benny couldn't move. His attention was fixed upon a group of locals furiously shovelling bricks into a lorry, searching for survivors beneath a three-story building. Jimmy grabbed him by the arm.

'Are you all right, Polak?'

Benny couldn't summon any words to answer and nodded. On the opposite side of the road, rescuers lowered casualties strapped to a ladder from first-floor windows, transferring them to makeshift stretchers made from sheets and curtains. A few feet away, a Chinese woman sobbed hysterically, cradling an infant and rocking the bundle back to life. The woman's piercing cries sliced through him, but he couldn't take his eyes off her. The child's arms hung limply, and its skin's pallid sheen confirmed to Benny that the child was dead. His heart cracked. Calling them to attention, his commander's voice brought him back to the present.

'Right men. You four, help clear this debris. The rest of you split into twos to help the wounded. Do what you can.'

Only one pitiful Red Cross ambulance was available to treat the casualties and wounded. Feeling a tugging on his arm, Benny swayed shakily on his feet, unable to move as if set in concrete.

'Benny, come with me.' Jimmy pulled at his friend's sleeve.

'It's so awful, I don't know what I was expecting, but it wasn't this,' Benny stammered.

'All we can do is help the living.'

Jimmy was right; the dead were spared from this nightmare. Suddenly adrenaline kicked in, and Benny sprinted down the road searching for people needing help, sidestepping bodies beyond rescue. Ahead of them, an older man struggled to support a wooden beam to keep it from falling on his injured wife below. Benny spotted his frailty with the beam balanced precariously on his shoulder and his legs buckling beneath him. When the older man saw the soldiers running towards him, his features softened with relief. Benny came alongside him and wedged his shoulder under the beam taking the weight.

'It's okay, we've got this.'

The man ranted hurriedly in Chinese, collapsing onto his knees beside his wife, partially buried beneath bricks and rubble with only her head visible. Glancing down, Benny noticed a deep cut on her head and a trail of blood mixed with dirt and dust trickling down her neck. For a moment, he couldn't tell if she was alive, but after a few seconds, she blinked. They had to act quickly. The two soldiers, with youth on their side, effortlessly lowered the beam setting it down away from the injured woman. Benny leaned over her face, sensing her faint breath on his skin.

'She's breathing but only just. Help me get this rubble off her,' Benny said whilst her husband knelt on the ground, gently stroking her hair and expressing words of love as tears streamed down his face. Benny lowered onto his knees, feeling the dig of shrapnel from splintered bricks puncturing his bare skin. His shins screamed in agony, but he carried on. Leaning over the injured woman, he grabbed bricks, glass fragments, and lumps of wood, frantically throwing it clear. This woman would not survive under this weight for much longer. Opposite him, Jimmy worked hard and fast, tossing debris far and wide until her body was clear. Benny instructed the weeping man to step back, and on the count of three, he and Jimmy lifted her frail, bruised body and carried her to safety.

The welcome bell of another Red Cross ambulance arriving brought Benny relief and his shoulders relaxed. Having a lack of first aid skills, he felt panicked at the thought of dealing with blood and broken bones. Jimmy found an abandoned sheet, and they draped it over the woman to keep her warm and to spare her husband from seeing the extent of her injuries. The woman pointed weakly to her mouth and croaked for water, and Benny cradled her head and offered his flask to her dry lips. A little water dribbled down her chin, but she swallowed some. Spluttering and coughing, she lay in his arms whimpering like a child.

'You're safe now. Help is coming. You'll be fine; hold on,' Benny consoled, not knowing if that was true or whether she even understood him. 'Get the medics from the ambulance,' Benny shouted across to Jimmy. Whilst waiting for help, he prayed their rescue efforts weren't in vain and they had rescued at least one casualty from this catastrophe. Thankfully within a few minutes, two medics running with a stretcher arrived. Benny stumbled backwards, and the old man grabbed his hand, shaking it vigorously and repeating a phrase that Benny could only assume was "thank you" in Chinese.

Benny noticed a new stinging sensation in his legs as he watched the stretcher being loaded into the ambulance. Glancing down, he saw blood from scrapes and cuts dripping down his shins. His injuries were not a concern, so he ignored the discomfort and searched for others in need of help. For the rest of the day, Benny and Jimmy aided locals in clearing fallen rubble and glass, uncovering more buried bodies. Some weren't so fortunate and were beyond saving by the time they reached them. By evening, much of the debris had been stacked and swept into piles, and buildings had been made as safe as possible. With the light fading, it was too dangerous to carry on. The homeless survivors were directed to one of the many emergency shelters which had popped around the city, and the exhausted troops stood around the truck awaiting further instruction.

During the last few hours, Benny had been so preoccupied, he had no room to think of anything other than the immediate mayhem, but now a familiar terror rose in his chest. He prayed Terpie was safe. Every fibre in his body wanted to run, run to find her, to hold her tight and not let her out of his sight. His racing mind wasn't helping by conjuring visions of her crushed body like the poor souls he'd seen today. His throat tightened, tears stung his eyes, and he quickly blinked them away, hoping no one noticed.

Reaching inside his pocket, he grabbed the only photograph he carried of her, depositing a streak of his blood and dirt as he stroked her smiling face. Searching her image, he desperately wanted a feeling or sense that she was alive. In the dim light, he noticed his hands covered in blood mixed with grit and dust. Deep cuts across his palms stung and throbbed whilst the rest of his body felt numb. Benny staggered to the Red Cross ambulance and found an Australian nurse tending to a man with a head wound.

'Can you wait until I've finished here, and then I'll see to those hands?' she smiled kindly, nodding towards his bloodied hands. He hadn't even considered asking for medical help.

'I don't suppose you know if the St Michaels Road area was hit?' he asked.

'Sorry, no, I don't,' the nurse replied whilst deftly wrapping a bandage around her patient's head.

'I don't know whether my fiancée is safe. We're due to get married soon. Thanks anyway,' he replied, wondering why he told her that. The nurse seemed kind, and his emotions were all over the place.

'You could try the emergency hospitals or the refuge centres. Most schools, churches and convents are taking people in. I hope you find her ...' Benny had already turned away and sauntered towards the truck wiping the worst of the blood on his grubby shorts.

'Hey, where did you go? One minute you were behind me, and then you were gone. Thought you'd done a runner,' Jimmy said.

'I asked the nurse if she knew how bad the bombing was in Terpie's neighbourhood. I need to know she's safe; it's driving me crazy.' He rubbed the back of his hands over his eyes, feeling the emotion rising, and willed himself to keep it together.

'I'm sure she's fine,' said Jimmy, placing a reassuring arm on his shoulder. Benny nodded, but no amount of reassurance would be enough until he saw her face for himself. 'You should've got those hands seen to whilst you were there. Let me clean them up.' Jimmy busied himself, ripping cloth to make a bandage. Benny held his hands out and winced whilst Jimmy poured water from his flask to remove the dirt and blood. The water stung like mad but compared to the pain in his chest, it was nothing.

Chapter Six
Zacharia

Japanese planes continued releasing their barrage of bombs over Singapore, so Zacharia and his family spent much of their time sheltering under the dining table, cramped, exhausted, and terrified. Unlike the air attack a few months ago, it was apparent that this wasn't an isolated event, and Zacharia grew afraid of what else was to come. The attacks came relentlessly three or four times a day and throughout the night, keeping the family isolated in the only place they felt safe. The government advice they had received was to stay in their homes, but in the moments of stillness between the strikes when the skies fell silent, Zacharia encouraged his girls to stretch their legs and take a walk in the fresh air whilst they could. Clio and Thetie needed some convincing, comforting each other with arms entwined; they stared back at him with chalky white faces like marble. It required all his powers of persuasion to reassure them it was safe, and he eventually coaxed them out. Not for long, but enough time for them to eat a meal or take a walk with him around the garden. Zacharia's agitation was growing for the imposed restrictions placed upon him, along with his curiosity and concern for his business.

Life was normal for a few hours until the familiar wailing of the sirens would repeat the nightmare all over again, and the family would scuttle back under the table like scared rabbits. His wife had become subdued and overly anxious in recent days. She was clucking around her brood like a mother hen, unable to protect them from the raging storm above. Without a doubt, he felt it too, a sense of hopelessness and lack of control over anything. He knew the air assaults would end eventually and tried not to dwell on what would come after. The family read, played card games, listened to music, or wrote in their journals to pass the time. Sitting around doing nothing for hours and with only a racing mind to occupy him, Zacharia huffed and sighed, twitched and fidgeted. Shi Min kept them fed as best she could with rapidly dwindling food supplies, although no one felt much like eating. On the fourth day of attacks, the dispirited whine of the air raid sirens wound up again, and Zacharia experienced the familiar simmer of foreboding. On this round, the strikes were within range of their neighbourhood, making the house shake on its foundations. Dislodged shaves of plaster and fine particles vented from the ceiling. His girls screamed, and he attempted to calm them as best he could.

'Shh, girls, it will be all right. It'll be over soon,' Zacharia soothed, somehow managing to sound unfazed, despite being terrified too. The family trembled beneath the table, clinging tightly to each other or holding hands with sweaty palms and closed eyes in silent prayer. Zacharia had never prayed so hard in his life. When the floor beneath him tremored like an earthquake and his ears rang from the deafening blasts, he was convinced he wouldn't live to see another day. Keeping his eyes squeezed shut, he drew Anthoula in close and braced himself for the end. But to his astonishment, the danger passed, and the skies fell silent again. When Zacharia felt sure the raid was over, he exhaled with a slow breath and wiped his tremoring sweaty hands on his trousers.

'Is everyone okay? I think it's passed,' Zacharia asked his panic-stricken family.

'The bombs were so close this time,' said Ino.

'I don't think my heart can take it. Zac, we need to reconsider and move somewhere safer,' replied Anthoula.

'Let's just take a few breaths. I can't think about that now.'

'I'm worried about Benny. I hope he's safe,' Terpie said tearfully.

'I know, my love,' Anthoula replied, petting her daughter's hair.

'They can't keep up this level of bombing for much longer; there will be nothing left.' Zacharia crawled out from hiding and stretched out his buckled spine. 'We need to know what's going on. I know I said no more radio reports, but an update would help,' he guided his girls to assemble around the wireless. Up until two days ago, the family listened to news reports throughout the day, but Zacharia became concerned about their levels of distress, so he restricted their exposure to evening broadcasts only.

At the beginning of the week, British forces had failed to hold back the strong advance of the Japanese soldiers in Malaya, meaning the enemy had progressed to the south of the country and already reached the peninsular with only a three-mile stretch of the river separating them from Singapore's shores. On Tuesday, they learned that General Percival, the British commander, had tried to cover every eventuality by positioning troops around the seventy-mile perimeter of the island to defend the coastline. A day later, the Japanese leader Lt. General Yamashita, had established his headquarters in the tall towers of the Sultan of Johore's palace across the causeway to plan their attack. When Zacharia heard this, the stab of betrayal was as good as an attack on him personally. Not only was the Sultan a loyal customer, and up to now, a man he held in high regard. How dare he collaborate with the enemy. With a degree of churlishness, Zacharia vowed in future he would never sell his precious coffee to a traitor, regardless of being his wealthiest client. The following day the situation deteriorated as the British made a last-ditch attempt to prevent the Japanese army from crossing the causeway which failed. General Percival ordered his men to blow up the bridge, which only delayed the advancing enemy by a few hours as Japanese soldiers swiftly restored the crossing. Eight thousand Japanese soldiers had made their way across the stretch of water to arrive on the northern shores of Singapore island. A mere seventeen miles away. Zacharia convinced himself there was still a chance the British could turn this around, as the alternative was too unpalatable to digest. But if they failed, Zacharia calculated that the advancing army could reach the city within a few days, depending on the resistance they met on the way. He leaned forward in his seat, wringing his hands together eagerly, hoping for good news but silently fearing the worst.

Terpie and Clio clung to each other on the couch so closely that their bodies appeared to be joined. Anthoula, bolt upright in her favourite chair, rested a hand on the shoulders of Thetie and Ino huddled at her feet. Like a tableau painting, the expectant family focussed on Thalia tuning the radio. A grating hiss and crackle swallowed the silence, and Zacharia's stomach churned. The newsreader delivered his stolid report, and the family listened intently to every word.

The latest updates from the front line are as follows. After fierce fighting and hand-to-hand combat, the troops at Bukit Timah were defeated. The Japanese Imperial Guard gained control over valuable water reservoirs, food stores, ammunition, and vehicles on the island. Allied troops have been forced to retreat yet again and are preparing to defend the city. The Dalforce and Chinese soldiers have suffered heavy losses. The relentless air strikes continue, and all bomb shelters are full. The British government strongly advise British citizens to evacuate the island. Ships rallied from around the region are waiting at the docks at Keppel Harbour and will leave within the next 48 hours. To register for a place, families must report to the registration office with passports and there is a restriction of one bag or case per person. Spaces are limited, and tickets will be allocated on a first-come, first-served basis.

Leaping out of his chair Zacharia instructed Thalia to switch off the radio. She glanced furtively across to her father and did as she was told, and the click of the dial plunged the room into silence once again. No one uttered a word as the severity of the situation slowly filtered through. Bukit Timah was barely five miles away. Desperation and frustration fuelled Zacharia to want to do something. The futility of sitting around day after day gnawed away at his insides. Throughout his adult life, he had been a problem solver, a provider, and a protector, and he felt powerless to do any of those things. House arrest didn't suit him; days of being cooped up had rattled his nerves. The broadcast played over in his mind, and he paced around, biting his fingernails. The room was quiet except for his bare feet slapping on the wooden floor.

'What are we going to do, Zac?' Anthoula asked.

Zacharia barely heard her as he had become stuck on a train of thought. After days of worrying about the state of his shop and what might be left of it, he was desperate to see for himself.

'Zac, did you hear me?'

'Huh? What? Firstly, I'll need Lim to take me into town so I can check the shop and talk to the locals to get a feel for what is going on.' He paced in circles.

As soon as the sentence left his mouth, five incredulous faces, mouths open, stared back at him, and his wife had anger written all over hers.

'You'll do no such thing, Zacharia Pattara! Why on earth would you risk going to town?' Anthoula growled.

'Sitting here doing nothing is driving me mad. I don't know if I have a business anymore.' He waved his hands above his head in frustration.

Anthoula stood firmly in his path to stop him from wearing out the floorboards and entwined her hand in his.

'I understand, but what's the point? You can't do anything either way and if you go to the shop and find it's been destroyed, it'll only upset you. It's not worth the risk. Anyway, that isn't our priority. There are more important things we need to think about,' said Anthoula forcefully, searching his eyes for a glimmer of common sense.

He hated to admit it, but she was right. Unlike himself, whimsical and impetuous, his wife could always be relied upon to be pragmatic and sensible. Over the years, on many occasions, she had been the one to reign him in before his wild ideas took hold.

'I suppose you're right, and whatever state the shop is in, I won't be able to do anything. But I do want to visit the city.'

'What purpose would that serve? I'm more concerned about the army of soldiers heading our way. The report said they have ships for families to leave the island. *That's* what we should be talking about. We're not safe here, so I think we should evacuate.' Anthoula plopped heavily into her chair and resolutely folded her arms. The girls exchanged looks between them, waiting for their father's reaction.

'Leave? We can't just up and leave. Our home is here, Anthoula. My business is here!' yelled Zacharia, rubbing his forehead and struggling to make sense of the suggestion. Even with the advancing army, he never considered *leaving*. Striding around his territory like a defensive lion, he sensed all eyes burning into his back whilst rolling the unpalatable idea around. 'I've lived here over forty years. I'm not being chased out of my home by Japs or any other army for that matter,' he roared.

'Zac. It's not safe. You've heard the news reports. They'll stop at nothing to take our city, and I don't want to be here when that happens.' Anthoula stood her ground.

'I can't believe you're serious,' he challenged, shaking his head in disbelief at the impossible situation he found himself in, having to consider the genuine possibility of abandoning his home. Thrusting his clenched fists into his trouser pockets, he concentrated on breathing to calm the rising palpitations. The couple never argued in front of the girls, always showing a united front. How could Anthoula expect him to leave everything he'd worked so hard for, to give up and run away?

'I'm scared, Zac. Our best chance is to get away. I know how much your shop means to you, but your family's safety is more important,' Anthoula pleaded, her eyes glistened with tears and something inside Zacharia melted.

'I agree with Mamma. I think we should leave too,' stated Clio, towering above her mother and taking her hand in solidarity. One by one, the girls echoed their mother's sentiment. Saying they were terrified and wanted to evacuate. Only Terpie remained silent, alone on the couch, staring out of the window.

'Zac, we must go. I'm terrified of what I've heard, the brutality of the soldiers, and what they've done to innocent people in Malaya. I couldn't bear it if those things happened to our girls.'

His body softened, and the red mist of rage melted away. His wife had hit a chord about the girl's safety. It was true that the Japanese had bulldozed their way through Malaya, and he was aware of the reputation they had gained; stories of their cruelty towards women and the massacre of innocent families had reached the people of Singapore. He realised he was being selfish and allowing his silly pride to dictate. Anthoula was right; the girl's safety was a priority. If anything happened to them, he wouldn't forgive himself. He'd been so absorbed thinking about his business and his precious home that he hadn't considered they were in real danger by staying here.

'Your mother's right. We should leave. I'm sorry. It makes me so angry that we're forced to leave our home behind. What will become of us? Shipped off to goodness know where.'

'None of that matters Zac,' said Anthoula.

'Are we all in agreement then? We head to the docks tomorrow morning to leave?' Zacharia scanned his daughter's anxious faces.

Before anyone could answer, Terpie spoke up.

'I'm not going anywhere. Benny's here, and he needs me. I'm staying.' Terpie smoothed down her skirt, placing her hands in her lap, and fiddled with her engagement ring, avoiding eye contact with anyone.

'Are you mad? You can't stay by yourself,' Thalia screeched.

'We must stay together, Terpie, as a family. I'm not leaving any of you behind, you're coming, and that's final. It's far too dangerous.' The matriarch of the family had spoken, and she turned to her husband for support. 'Zac, you agree, don't you? Girls, go and pack. We're leaving.'

There was a desperation in his wife's voice he had never heard before. No one moved a muscle except for Terpie, who sprang from her seat in defiance.

'You can't make me go, Mamma. I'm an adult and can make my own choices. I'll be fine here. Benny has no one else.'

Zacharia alternated his gaze between the two women he loved; their eyes locked together in a mother-daughter stand-off, their chests silently heaving with emotion. He hated conflict and felt inadequate to referee this battle of wills. Anthoula broke her gaze first and glared at him, willing him to intervene, and for the first time, Zacharia was frightened for his family's future. Terpie pleaded her case honestly from the heart. He couldn't deny her reasoning. She had always been the most wilful of all his daughters. With a flicker of acceptance, he recognised the same trait within himself, remembering how he came to leave Greece all those years ago. With this knowledge, he found it difficult to deliver his words with any conviction. He knew from experience he'd be a fool to attempt to persuade her to change her mind, but feeling the pressure from his wife, he tried anyway.

'Please reconsider for your mother's sake. Benny wouldn't want you in danger, would he? It won't be safe. Those soldiers do terrible things,' he said, knowing full well his words sounded feeble against her pertinacious resistance.

'Pappa, stop. I don't care about any of that. I won't change my mind for you, for Mamma or anyone. I mean it.' Terpie mulishly cut through the air with her hand to draw a line under it. Zacharia saw the colour draining from his wife's face. Before he could speak again, a chorus of raised voices crisscrossed over one another in a heated debate which escalated quickly to a shouting match. He couldn't make sense of anything in this racket, and his head pounded from the tension. They weren't getting anywhere, and Zacharia needed to take control of the situation.

'All of you, stop! There's enough fighting in the world without us joining in. Nothing will be sorted by yelling at each other,' he pleaded, sitting heavily on the piano stool and resting his hands on his thighs. Six expectant faces stared back at him, and he breathed deeply before pleading with them to see reason.

'No one can deny we find ourselves in an exceptional situation and don't have the luxury of time to devise a better plan—your mother's right. We should evacuate, so we'll leave for the docks first thing in the morning. Please go and pack a case of essential items only and leave your mother, Terpie and I to sort this out.'

The girls reluctantly left their seats and drifted out of the room, murmuring to each other in speculation about what might happen next. A lump rose in his throat, and there wasn't a solution he could think of which would appease everyone. He knew Terpie couldn't be swayed, which frustrated him no end. He also loathed the anguish on his wife's face and despised going against her, but a resolution must be found.

'Anthoula, my love. Terpie's made it clear. She's twenty-two and can make her own choices. I can't command her to leave, and we must respect her decision.'

'What are you saying? She'll be in danger, a young woman on her own. She can't protect herself against those brutes! What if she's raped, attacked, or murdered?'

Terpie opened her mouth to interject, but he raised his hand to silence her and delivered his following words as calmly as possible.

'You're right… I'll stay behind. You and the girls will evacuate.' He allowed the statement to hang in the air, waiting for retaliation. When none came, he sighed heavily and continued. 'It's far from ideal, but at least you and the girls will be safe. It's not responsible to leave Terpie by herself.'

'You never wanted to leave anyway. You made that blatantly clear,' Anthoula said viciously. Her anger stung him.

'Now that's not entirely true. In the beginning, yes. But I was fully prepared to evacuate as a whole family. But that's not possible. I want to leave with you, but what other choice do I have? I can't leave Terpie alone,' he answered equably despite his churning insides and divided loyalty.

'You're the head of the family. Make her come with us!' Anthoula protested.

'We've been over this. She's not a child. I can't make her leave against her will!' he yelled in frustration; they were going around in circles. Terpie stood before them.

'I'm sorry I'm splitting up the family, but I'm all Benny has left. Surely you can understand that?'

'I understand, Terpie, I do,' Anthoula answered, turning towards her husband. 'Besides, how can you keep her safe here, Zac?'

'Don't worry. I'll think of something. We can't allow this to destroy us. I don't have a better solution. Do you?' Neither of the women answered. 'I'll arrange for Lim to take us to the harbour tomorrow, and Terpie and I'll return here. If it gets too dangerous, we'll head into the city. Okay? Terpie, go and help your sisters pack and let me speak to your mother alone.'

Terpie left the room, avoiding eye contact with her mother. Zacharia enveloped his wife in his arms, feeling her emotion dampen his shirt.

'It'll be all right,' he soothed, holding her close.

'I can't believe this is happening to us, Zac. What if I never see you again? I can't bear to imagine a world without you.' Anthoula wiped her tears. Her feelings were raw and painful, silently mirroring his own, but he couldn't afford to languish in fear. He found the idea of separation just as abhorrent, but he must remain positive to get through the difficult weeks, maybe months ahead for all of them. Since leaving Greece, Anthoula relied on him for everything. Did she have the resilience to cope without him? Only time would tell, but it eased his mind knowing she would have the girls supporting her.

'Come on now, don't think that way. It won't come to that. It'll be a period of separation, that's all.'

'I'm worried about Terpie too. Don't let her go looking for Benny.'

'Don't worry. I'll look after her.' He patted her hand. 'I'd better go and speak to Lim.'

On the veranda, he slipped his feet into his sandals, and sadness descended like a mist; this would be the last night his family spent together under the same roof indefinitely. It was such a difficult decision in the heat of the moment, but his fatherly instinct was to protect Terpie from harm. He fought off the niggle of doubt that he was making a mistake. The decision had been made, and there was no going back. As he descended the steps, for some reason, he thought of Emily. Her apartment was in the city's centre, and knowing how stubborn she could be, he doubted she would evacuate her home. He knew she would willingly take them in if the suburbs became too dangerous. By the time he returned, the girls were packed and sitting in the family room waiting for him with faces as long as a rainy monsoon.

'Come on, girls. I don't want our last night together to be miserable. Thetie, play us something so we can have a sing-along like the old days,' he rallied them to their feet around the piano.

Chapter Seven
Terpie

Terpie sat crossed-legged on her bed in the room she shared with Thalia, furiously writing a letter to Benny. Naively she still grasped the possibility that their wedding might go ahead next month as she wanted so desperately to be married. This deep longing contributed to her steadfast reasoning for staying on the island (not that she would ever tell her parents that, as they would only chastise her for being foolhardy). It had been an emotional evening and she shocked herself with her resolve to stand up to her parents so forcefully. Of course, she hadn't intended to hurt them or cause distress, but no reason or no one could convince her to leave the island now. Not even Winston Churchill himself. Being separated from Benny tore her apart and was adamant she'd remain nearby. Her pen glided across her crisp white writing paper. There was no guarantee her letter would reach him with the city in chaos, but she had to try. Since their final day on the beach a few months ago, correspondence had bounced back and forth, and she clung to his words like a life raft. When a letter arrived, her heart lifted, and she closed herself off in her room to savour every word in private. Often Benny's letters lacked any substance; he described his new comrades, how boring patrols were, and how fed up he was with digging trenches. Sometimes she craved more detail to understand what he was experiencing fully. Equally, her news back to him made dull reading with the schools closed and everyone at home, her banal routine reduced the content to mindless rambling. Since hearing the news earlier today, she was more worried than ever. The door slammed, jarring her out of her train of thought, followed by the heavy thud of footsteps across the wooden floor. She drew her eyes away from the paper to see Thalia in her nightdress looming above her bed with a face etched with fury. A red rash spread across her chest and neck, her eyes on fire under her heavy scorn. She wasted no time in launching her attack.

'You're always difficult. Because of you, we'll be apart. Pappa's trying to do the right thing, but do you honestly think he wants to be away from Mamma at a time like this? You're so stubborn and selfish, thinking only of yourself as usual.'

The rage tumbled out of her like hot lava, and Terpie felt she wasn't done yet.

'I didn't ask him to stay behind, did I! It was his choice,' Terpie retorted, finding the injustice of the attack hurtful. In her heart, she had been expecting at least *one* of her sisters to kick back at her, and it came as no surprise that it was Thalia.

'Choice! He had no choice! I know you want to stay close to Benny, but he's out there. God knows where. You won't get to see him. You don't care about anyone else. It's breaking Mamma's heart and it's your fault.'

Terpie slowly set her writing paper down and heaved herself to the edge of the bed knowing she must select her words carefully to avoid fuelling her sister's diatribe against her. She wasn't wholly cold-hearted, and of course, she felt guilty. It was hard for her to understand, let alone verbalise the strength of conviction compelling her to stay. Leaving was just not an option for her.

'Of course, I feel bad and never expected Pappa to stay behind. I never intended to cause trouble, and you have to believe that. I'm sorry it hurts all of you, especially Mamma.'

'You're not sorry at all, you've always been self-centred, and this proves it to everyone.'

'Listen, this isn't all about me. Benny has no one, his family are thousands of miles away, he is fighting a war, and he is scared,' Terpie said, hoping her explanation would be enough to appease her sister, and by way of a truce, she raised her hand aloft towards her, hoping she would take it. 'Please try to see it from his point of view if you can't see it from mine. Sit with me.'

Thalia accepted the invitation to sit but refused her hand. Thalia sat quietly, and Terpie hoped some of her words might invoke sympathy for Benny's situation.

'I do feel for him. I hate what this war is doing to everyone. I hate that I don't know where Charlie is and most of all I hate that we're being forced out of our home.' The anger in Thalia's face faded, replaced by sadness, and she continued. 'I don't understand why you won't come too. You can still write to Benny from where we are, and once the war is over, we can come back, and you and Benny can pick up from where you left off. It seems Mamma and Pappa are paying the price, which is unfair.'

Terpie sensed her sister searching for a flicker of hope that she might yield and change her mind. She reached across the void between them, taking Thalia's hand.

'I'm staying here Thalia, and that's all there is to say. I won't abandon him. Please don't let us part with hard feelings,' Terpie pleaded and waited for her sister to answer.

'Everything's falling apart. I'm so emotional lately.' Thalia paused and, sensing she had more to say, Terpie held her tongue. 'I miss Charlie so much. Not hearing from him is eating away at me. He could be dead for all I know. I doubt I'll ever see him again. If something happened to him, how would I even know? At least you get letters.' Her voice began to crack under strain, and she turned away.

'Oh Thalia, why didn't you speak to me about it? I would've understood. You keep everything to yourself.' Terpie identified with her sister's feelings. She now understood first-hand the need for reassurance and the pain of missing someone. Instinctively she put her arm around Thalia's shoulder and pulled her close. What could she say to make it better? Not much. They weren't very close, that was true, but she didn't enjoy seeing her sister so pained.

'It's hard, and you've been so brave. This thing is bigger than us, and we can't control what happens in our lives anymore. I wish I could promise you everything will be alright.' She gently rocked her sister as she used to when they were children. 'We're all scared.'

Thalia straightened, briskly wiping away her tears, drawing a line under her emotions.

'No one knows if everything will be all right anymore. I can't say I agree with you, but I respect your reasons. I still believe we should stay together. Pappa's not as strong as he makes out. But if you won't change your mind, then we'll have to agree, to disagree,' Thalia said bluntly.

Terpie found her sister's behaviour bizarre and wondered how she could turn her emotions off like a tap. Thalia made no further reference to Charlie as if it had never happened. It was a brief insight into her vulnerability, and Thalia pulled away. A short knock on the door interrupted them, it creaked open, and the trio of sisters appeared in their nightgowns.

'Can we come in? We couldn't sleep and heard voices,' said Ino and the three sisters filed in and sat in a row across from them on Thalia's bed.

'What's going on? Thalia, have you been crying? Are you okay?' asked Thetie.

'I'm fine. Don't worry about me. I was challenging Terpie on her decision, that's all,' replied Thalia coolly.

Thalia didn't divulge the part about missing Charlie. Terpie had witnessed her little sister's stiff upper lip before, like when she was bullied at school because she looked different to her siblings and had fair skin. It continued for months before Shi Min got to the bottom of her sultry mood swings. Thalia hated to appear weak in front of her sisters; the baby of the family was a tough role to fulfil. Once again, Thalia firmly welded on a brave face. Terpie and Thalia never really had the kind of sisterly relationship where they confided in each other about anything, so this brief baring of her emotions was a privilege. Thalia only held the door to her feelings open to one person and that was their pappa on their special walks or nights out on the veranda. If Terpie was honest, she was jealous of their relationship and often felt left out. Especially as she wasn't close to her mother or other siblings, but she had Benny now and clung to him instead.

'It's an impossible situation. Terpie's made her choice as much as we don't like it.' Ino glanced to her twin for confirmation, and Clio nodded in agreement.

'I don't want to leave without you, Terpie, but I understand. If I were engaged, I'd do the same. Mamma will have us so she will be fine, we'll take care of her,' added Clio.

'Thalia, try not to worry. With any luck, we won't be apart for long,' said Thetie. She rested her hand on her sister's knee before Thalia sprang off the bed.

'I don't agree with any of you. I think Terpie's being utterly selfish, but there we are, I'm obviously outnumbered,' Thalia said defensively, leaving the conversation to sit at her dressing table.

'Let's not fight anymore. It's been a long night. Thalia, whatever your opinion is, you need to accept the decision has been made and let it go,' said Ino.

'That's right, I'm the baby and know nothing,' Thalia huffed, turning her back on her sisters. Grateful for her older sister's support Terpie hoped that Thalia would calm down and forgive her in time. A strained silence followed whilst Thalia heavy-handedly lifted and replaced lids on the glass storage jars containing cotton wool and creams and set about cleaning her face.

Ino was about to go over to her, but Thetie whispered, 'leave her.' Terpie nodded her head, also signalling to Ino to leave it alone.

'How do you all feel about leaving tomorrow?' Terpie asked.

Picking at the embroidery on her nightdress, Thetie's eyes welled up. It didn't take much for them to become lachrymose lately with so much uncertainty and fear hanging over them.

'I'm scared of leaving. It wouldn't be so bad if we knew where we were going or for how long. The Japs terrify me, so the lesser of the two evils is to go. I had contemplated going to the convent to start my order early, but I can't leave Mamma now.'

'Very commendable of you, Thetie. It's nice to see that at least one of her daughters cares about her welfare,' Thalia jibed, dabbing moisturiser on her face. Terpie let the comment go, it wasn't the first time they quarrelled.

'That's unfair, Thalia. Terpie does care,' said Ino, speaking to Thalia's reflection in the mirror and seeing her shrug in response. 'I'm seeing at this as an adventure, and I can't wait to get out of here. This war can't go on forever.'

'There's a whole world out there we haven't seen. I might not want to come back,' said Clio.

Terpie admired her attitude, and she might have felt the same if her circumstances were different.

'Can we talk about something else, please?' Thalia snapped, raking the hairbrush through her hair. No one could think of anything to fill the empty silence until Clio found some common ground when life felt more normal.

'Isn't it crazy to think we were at the cinema two weeks ago? If you'd told me then we would be leaving home, I wouldn't have believed you. How things have changed so quickly.'

'It feels like a lifetime ago,' said Thetie wistfully, caressing her necklace.

'It'll be a while before we set foot in a cinema again.' Ino paused momentarily. 'Do you think the Cathay cinema even exists anymore?'

No matter how hard they tried, the war dominated everything; nothing in their lives was sacred or untouched by the horror of it.

'I don't want to think about what's been bombed. It's too sad. No doubt we'll see for ourselves tomorrow, and on that point, we should try and get some sleep,' suggested Clio.

'It does feel strange to think this will be the last night in our beds.'

'It's all a bit terrifying. From tomorrow, our lives will be totally different.' Ino stood up to leave. 'I'm not sure I'll be able to sleep.'

'Well, I need my beauty sleep… to look ravishing for a naval officer perhaps?' Clio smirked. The others groaned at her one-tracked mind, and Ino playfully nudged her off the bed.

'Come on. Thalia you too.' Thetie beckoned her sisters with outstretched arms to rally them for a group embrace. Reluctantly, Thalia joined the group, and the girls hugged each other and said goodnight. Clio, Thetie and Ino returned to their rooms, leaving Thalia and Terpie facing each other. Thalia climbed into bed without saying another word, pulled her mosquito net around her, and turned her back on her sister. Hurriedly Terpie resumed her writing, but events of the evening had needled her train of thought, so unable to think of anything else to say she signed off. With her swiftly crafted letter sealed in an envelope placed on her nightstand, she turned off the lamp and settled into bed under her mosquito net.

'Goodnight,' Terpie called out, which met with a wall of silence. It would be a while before Thalia would forgive her, if ever, but she hoped they could make it up before she left tomorrow. Lying in the semi-darkness from the light of the moon, Terpie was mesmerised by the shadows of palm leaves sweeping across the ceiling in the breeze and listened to the night-time nature sounds, but sleep wouldn't come. The cotton sheets tangled and stuck to her legs in the humid air, so she kicked them off. Ino was right, their lives were about to change irrevocably, and it was a daunting prospect. Terpie would miss her family, but nothing would deter her from what she felt she must do. Lying still, she became scared, not for herself but Benny. As she did every night, wondering if he was awake and thinking of her.

Chapter Eight
Zacharia

'Do you think the girls are okay with all of this?' Anthoula asked, returning from the bathroom in her nightdress.

'They're sensible, they understand. It makes me feel easier knowing you'll be together.'

'I wish Terpie weren't so stubborn, and if we had more time, maybe we could change her mind.'

'Honestly, it wouldn't make any difference. Her mind is set. As hard as the repercussions are for us, I understand her reasons. Remember when we were her age? I'd do anything to be with you,' he said, preparing for bed. Anthoula laughed.

'That's precisely what you did. Running away to get married to spite our parents.'

'And I'd do it again in a heartbeat. You know, I was thinking. We won't be the only family with tough decisions to make. I'm certain hundreds if not thousands will be leaving tomorrow. There'll be others divided by their choices. Strangely, that makes me feel slightly better about the whole thing.'

'I suppose you're right, but I can't say it makes me feel better,' said Anthoula glumly.

They were both acutely aware that their lives would be uncertain for the foreseeable future. Anthoula wasn't happy about the arrangements. That was obvious, but neither was he. After saying goodnight to the girls, they discussed their options again and could not find a more palatable solution. Begrudgingly they accepted that separation was their only option. Zacharia knew his wife was terrified and he felt frustrated that all he could offer were words to soothe her anxious mind. He was desperate to provide Anthoula with something tangible to help her through this challenging period. He sat on the edge of their bed and removed his watch. When they met her dream had been to travel the world and as a brash young man on the shores of Greece, he promised that he would be the one to take her. Now he felt nothing but contempt for his dogged ambition and for allowing her dream to fade into insignificance. In all these years, she never once reminded him or made any demands of her own. In a moment of clarity, it came to him. If the last few weeks had taught him anything, it was to seize the moment and be bold because in an instant, the path you're travelling along can crumble beneath your feet and the opportunity is lost.

'Anthoula, I know this might sound crazy. Whilst we're apart, I want you to visualise all those places you wanted to visit. Paris, Rome and London and anywhere else you fancy.'

'What are you talking about?' asked Anthoula, opening the covers and climbing into bed.

'You always wanted to travel, and I wanted the business. I got my dream, and you've patiently waited for yours.'

Anthoula laughed. 'Have you lost your mind? Where's this coming from?'

He wasn't crazy; it was the perfect thing to do. 'When the war is over, I'll sell the business.' He couldn't believe he'd said it, and it felt surprisingly good.

'Zac, you can't give up the business just like that!'

'But don't you see? This is the right thing to do. Yes, the business is a success, I'm proud of what I've achieved, and I couldn't have done it without you, but none of the girls wants to take on and it's time to let it go. I've been so blinkered. We must do something for ourselves. We'll go travelling like you always wanted.' The words he could never imagine saying tumbled out effortlessly in his excitement. He felt a sense of release. What was that? Burden?

'Well, you do have to retire at some point, and I worry you'll work yourself to the grave, so I'll support you if that's what you want. Perhaps the stress of the past few days is getting to you. You're not thinking straight.'

Zacharia leapt from the bed with a buoyancy he'd not felt in years and paced around the room with a mind full of ideas. However, he forgot the minor obstacle of a raging war on their doorstep, hammering at their door like an unwanted visitor about to take up residence. His hand was forced, and he had no choice but to wait it out. A fleeting thought crossed his mind that he may not even have a shop to sell once the dust settled, but he'd been shrewd with his investments which they could draw on. Either way, his life's work was complete. He needed a change of direction.

'I think it's called an epiphany, my darling,' he grinned, and Anthoula watched him in confusion.

'You're acting very strangely, Zac. What about the girls?'

'The girls don't need us as much as they did. If anything, cutting the apron strings will do them good. I realise I've been holding on to them, fearing change, when all the time change is exactly what we need!' His skin bristled with enthusiasm for their future.

'Zac, come to bed. It's late.' She patted the bed. 'I need some sleep, and your pacing makes me dizzy.' Bouncing back into bed, he snuggled against his wife and wrapped his arms around her.

'It'll all be all right, Anthoula. I know it.'

Zacharia hoped the night would be free from air raids and pondered on the decisions they had made. There was no way of knowing whether he'd made the right ones and it was too late to change his mind.

After a night of fitful sleep, Zacharia's eyes flickered open. He stretched and yawned, feeling stiffness in his joints. Obdurate gnawing above his left eye announced the onset of a headache he could do without; he massaged the area hoping to chase it away with a bit of pressure. The night had passed without any raids, although he didn't feel well-rested. A contented smile crept across his face as he recalled the last evening his family shared, singing some of his old favourites around the piano. However, his frown returned when he remembered their imminent evacuation tearing them apart which was tightening its noose around their necks. He needed something positive to hold on to as much as Anthoula. They had to get through this separation, and life would be better on the other side. Cuddling up to his sleeping wife, he wrapped his arms around her like twine and inhaled her sweet floral fragrance. He would miss this. Fragments of last night's conversation flitted across his mind; Anthoula stirred, her body stiffened against him as she stretched the sleepiness from her limbs; he hugged her tighter and bathed in her warmth.

'Good morning my love, did you sleep?'

'Eventually. I can't quite believe we're going today. It's all happening too fast. I don't want to leave you.'

'I feel the same. In a few months, this will be over, maybe weeks even and we can start planning our retirement,' he replied positively.

He pondered on the juxtaposition of his emotions. Feeling excited about his future travel plans with his wife, but the impending loss of his family left him feeling hollow. Anthoula rolled over and kissed him. Zacharia mentally framed a picture of this moment to recall on the mornings when he would be waking up alone. A tight ball clumped in his throat, threatening to topple his emotions over the edge. He swallowed hard. He was in no rush to get up to start the day and wished he could rewind time or at least pause it. Reluctantly the couple rose from their bed and prepared for their parting, packing bags and gathering valued keepsakes. The positive future he imagined last night slowly drained away as he watched his wife folding her clothes, and the reality of her departure was sinking in. The war was unpredictable so anything could happen, and that realisation scared him. Anthoula fastened the buckle on her case. It was unnerving to see her dressing table so empty, with no hairbrush or face creams, and a wave of sadness rolled over him once again. He had to hold it together.

'We won't be away for too long, will we? I don't think I can bear it.'

Standing beside the bed, Anthoula anxiously picked at the loose stitching on her case. He walked around to embrace her, feeling her cool hands on the back of his neck. She nuzzled into him, and they swayed slightly in each other's arms. He wished he could assure her that their time apart would be short, but it was not in his gift. These were unprecedented times, and no one could predict the future. War rides roughshod over everyone and everything without regard for feelings and sentimentality.

'I wish I knew. When it's over we'll pick up our lives, and things will be different, I promise. We'll spend more time together. I'll hate being apart from you every single minute.' He caressed her hair and kissed her head. They remained bound together until Anthoula pulled away, breaking their bond.

The family set about their morning routine, albeit more subdued than usual, and approached breakfast with a generous serving of apprehension. Zacharia greeted each of his girls with an embrace and a peck on the cheek as he always did. However, this morning, the ritual pulled at his heartstrings. Dressed casually in pale summer dresses, hair neatly styled with shiny pins and wearing sandals, they appeared so innocent, and he feared they were not prepared for the journey ahead. Shi Min had set the table with a large bowl of warm porridge, a steaming coffee pot and jugs of freshly squeezed orange juice. The cushions from their temporary shelter were stacked neatly against the wall and there was no sign of her. Usually, she could be found pottering around the kitchen, talking with the girls, and clearing up around them. Their Amah was noticeable by her absence. They assembled in their seats at the table, and silence floated in the air like a bubble waiting to burst, but the conversation didn't come easily to anyone this morning. Their only focus was forcing mouthfuls of porridge down purely because their next meal was unknown. Zacharia wasn't hungry. Abandoning his breakfast, he clasped his hands under his chin and studied his girls' faces around the table. The growing anxiety was palpable as the departure time neared, fingers tapped, spoons chinked against half-eaten bowls whilst restless legs jiggled uncontrollably under the table. Zacharia's emotions were all over the place. He found himself torn between a raging desire to leave right this minute to get this difficult parting over with and staying to savour every possible second with his family. He'd never experienced this feeling before. Such a rush of dread as if snakes writhed around in the pit of his stomach, and by the strained expressions around the table, he was sure he wasn't the only one feeling it. The silence was oppressive; he had to break it.

'I told Lim to be ready by nine, and we need to allow time to say goodbye to Shi Min. I expect the docks will be busy today.'

Around the table, a few apathetic murmurs bounced back to him. Anthoula stared at the contents in her bowl, her spoon hovering over her porridge and placed his hand over hers.

'All okay?' he asked.

'I know it's silly with everything we have to worry about, but I'm not looking forward to being on a boat after last time,' Anthoula replied.

'Why? What happened?' asked Thetie, pouring herself some orange juice.

Anthoula explained her dislike of boats, which she had never spoken of before. She wasn't much older than Thalia when they made the long voyage from Greece, and she suffered the most debilitating seasickness and hoped she didn't embarrass them by being ill this time. She laughed at the memory now but at the time, she was so sick, her legs turned to jelly, and she swayed on dry land for days after. Zacharia remembered it well. Their journey carried them through the Red Sea, the Gulf of Aden to the Indian Ocean and lasted almost forty days; his new bride spent most of the voyage with her head hanging over the side of the railings.

'I hardly saw your mother's face during the trip. I almost forgot what she looked like. Her skin was a peaky green colour for days.'

'I pray it won't be that bad,' Anthoula said, holding her stomach as if experiencing nausea all over again.

'With any luck, the journey will be short. I imagine many boats will head for Java or Australia,' said Zacharia.

'I hope it's Australia. I might meet my future husband there,' quipped Clio as she collected as many breakfast bowls as she could carry and flounced into the kitchen. Terpie nodded her head despairingly as she followed her out with the remaining breakfast bowls.

'We'd better warn him you are coming then so he can run a mile,' Ino jibed under her breath, but only Thalia caught what she said and snorted into her hand giving her sister a playful nudge. Clio lived in a perpetual state of longing for her future husband and Zacharia often wondered if she came across as desperate to potential suitors causing them to back off. Clio would have to work it out for herself as he wasn't brave enough to intervene and point out where she was going wrong.

'If it's Australia we might see koalas or maybe a kangaroo,' said Thetie.

Anthoula chuckled at her daughters childlike naivety and wiped the corners of her mouth on a napkin.

'I doubt it. It's not a holiday.' She shook her head in amusement as Ino and Thetie continued discussing landmarks and cities they could visit.

Hearing their ingenuous hopes and desires revealed to Zacharia how closeted their lives had been, so this experience would broaden their horizons if nothing else. It came as a relief that on the face of it, the girls were embracing the evacuation as a positive experience which would certainly help make the parting easier to bear. It suddenly occurred to him that he'd be excluded from their adventures making him miserable. None of them had travelled abroad before, and he wouldn't be there to protect them. He glanced at the clock again which ticked on regardless. Zacharia noticed Thalia seemed reserved and unusually quiet, and for once he couldn't read her mood. She hadn't shared in the excitement of travel like her sisters. After attempts to start a conversation, he gave up as all he received were monosyllabic answers. With breakfast over, the girls ran through their checklist of packed items ensuring nothing had been forgotten. Clio dragged her bulging case across the floor with two hands.

'It's essential items only remember. Have you packed everything you own?'

'But I need all these things, Pappa. Outfits for daytime and evening, plus my makeup, face creams, change of shoes, hair styling kit, a selection of hats…'

'Clio. You've packed too much. Don't forget there's no one to carry your case for you and you can barely lift it,' Zacharia responded with a sharpness to his tone.

'It's fine. I have room. Put some in mine,' Ino offered and helped her sister rearrange her case.

Zacharia glanced at the clock for the hundredth time that morning; it was time. He summoned all his strength to sound jovial and like his emotions were under control his, whilst in reality; he was feeling quite the opposite.

'It's time to go, my important ladies have a boat to catch.'

Leaving the room on mass, he felt his heart bruised by their absence already. All the positive energy being sucked out of the space left him breathless. Photograph frames around the house stood empty, their contents removed as keepsakes. They hadn't gone yet, and the cold empty void from their departure enveloped him like a thick fog. The house wouldn't feel like home without their laughter, music and company. Picking up Anthoula's case, he chivvied them out the door. The air outside was stale with fumes, and low black smog engulfed the city, reaffirming the need to evacuate. Clio led the solemn procession down the concrete staircase to Lim, who was waiting by the car. The chauffeur greeted the girls and hugged them farewell, then packed the cases into the boot and strapped the stragglers down on the roof with rope. Anthoula was the last to leave the house. She lingered on the veranda and observed the view once more before ambling down the steps, her fingers gliding over the magenta petals as she went. Shi Min hugged each girl, and their tears fell as they said their goodbyes.

'Stay safe all of you. I'll be here to welcome you back, don't worry about the house. I'll take care of it. Here, I have a little gift for each of you to remind you of us, it's nothing much.' She handed them individually wrapped parcels in red tissue paper. They thanked her and pecked her on the cheek. Zacharia stood awkwardly by and watched his wife say goodbye to Shi Min, and he could see Anthoula's strength wavering. Tears trickled down her cheeks as she embraced the tiny grey-haired lady his girls had come to love as a grandparent.

'Thank you for everything. I know my words are not enough to express my gratitude for all you have been to my family over the years.'

'Hush now, this isn't goodbye forever! You'll be coming back.'

'Zac and Terpie won't be travelling with us. They're returning once we've been dropped at the harbour.' A flicker of surprise crossed Shi Min's face, but she didn't pass judgement or ask questions. 'It's a long story, and I'm sure Zac can fill you in later.'

'I'll take care of them, don't worry; please take these. I made some food for the journey.' Shi Min passed her a cloth bag filled with individually wrapped cartons. 'It's not much but will keep hunger at bay for a while.'

'You're a treasure, Shi Min. Thank you. I feel awful leaving you behind, and you should be leaving too. It feels so cowardly,' said Anthoula.

'Don't talk like that. I won't hear of it. You've got a chance to save your family. You take it and get them far away from here. Those ships are not for the likes of us anyway. We'll be fine.'

Anthoula hugged her once more and joined the girls in the waiting vehicle. There had never been the requirement for the whole family to travel at once, so the back of the usually roomy Ford was a tight squash. Thalia, the slightest, sat on her case in the foot well, and Thetie, the shortest, perched on Ino's lap. Zacharia never considered staying behind because he wanted to be with them until the last possible moment. He sat up front with Lim and they slowly rolled down the hill, with the girls waving furiously out the rear window to Shi Min waving tearfully on the driveway. Zacharia had made this journey a million times, but the altered landscape looked unfamiliar. The immediate leafy neighbourhood was somewhat unchanged, but as they travelled further, the full extent of the bombing was evident, and recognisable streets were now foreign to him. Few buildings had escaped the attacks unscathed, almost all bore scars of damage or were entirely felled to the ground. At the roadside, residents frantically cleared away the debris throwing rubble, bricks and stone into the back of trucks to search for bodies or salvage damaged possessions. Zacharia found it hard to watch and turned away.

Further into the city notable landmarks that once stood proud with pristine white façades were charred and blackened from smoke. Glancing over his shoulder, his cramped family who had previously been moaning about the tight squeeze suddenly fell silent as they witnessed the scene. The journey took longer than usual and Zacharia hadn't allowed for the diversions due to blocked roads; he kept checking his watch. Lim calmly altered their route and turned the car around where roads were impassable. It was nothing short of a grim sightseeing tour and Zacharia was unprepared for the number of casualties lying in the streets. Suddenly, the piercing sound of the air raid siren screamed out again, filling him with dread. Within minutes, the streets became chaotic with people running to take shelter, forgetting there were cars on the road—an older man in a ripped shirt bearing a haunted expression cut across in front of them. Lim slammed on the brakes, launching Zacharia into the dashboard, and the girls slipped forward and screamed. The disorientated man slapped the vehicle's bonnet and shouted '*maaf, maaf!*' and raised his hand in apology and staggered on.

'That was close. Is everyone alright?' Lim asked, checking his passengers in the rear-view mirror before setting off again. A few hundred yards ahead, the approach to Keppel Harbour was nothing short of apocalyptic. Vehicles in various states of abandonment, either on fire or upturned on their roofs and some were crushed completely. Destruction and death surrounded them. With the car park congested, Lim skilfully steered around the obstructions to get closer to the dock entrance. Zacharia wiped his hand across the steamed-up window to reveal row upon row of ships lined up in the harbour, ready to take Singapore's precious cargo away from the conflict. It was quite a sight to see so many imposing vessels in the dock at once and something Zacharia had never seen in all his years here. Lim's path was blocked by hordes of people, forcing him to pull over.

'I can't get any closer sir.'

'It looks like half of Singapore is trying to leave today,' said Anthoula.

'This is fine. We can walk the rest. Come on, girls, we need to move quickly,' instructed Zacharia, swinging the car door open, mindful that it would only be a matter of time before planes swarmed the skies, so he hurried his family out of the car and helped Lim unload cases. Despite the early hour, the smoke from burning fires had darkened the sky, ash floated and danced on the breeze and the acrid fumes caught in their throats making them cough. Thousands of people from all directions made their way to the harbour, mothers carrying babies, dragging reluctant little ones and elderly relatives trying to keep up in the crowd of bodies. The evacuating mass of people swamped them in their panic to get by, knocking into the family with their baggage. Zacharia knew it would be impossible to go any further, this was the end of the road or else they'd get caught up with the swathes of people trying to escape.

'It's too crowded. We'll say our goodbyes here and go,' Anthoula shouted over the racket of screaming children, sirens and ship engines. Hugging her husband tightly, she told him she loved him and would write as soon as possible to tell him they were safe. The urgency of the situation didn't lend itself to long-drawn-out goodbyes, and for that, he was grateful.

'Stay strong, my love. I'll be waiting for you.' Next, he hugged each of his daughters in turn and, last of all, Thalia. When he leaned in to embrace her, she pulled away abruptly, and he was confused; what was she doing? Turning to her mother, she yelled.

'I'm sorry. I'm not coming with you.'

Anthoula's head shook in disagreement, her features crestfallen. With a trembling hand, she touched her youngest daughter's cheek.

'Please, Thalia, don't do this. Why won't you come?'

'I want to stay with Pappa. Please don't be angry.' Thalia kissed her mother on the cheek, and Anthoula nodded. Zacharia was sure at that moment a brief exchange of mutual understanding flickered between them and his wife knew she was powerless to change Thalia's mind. Anthoula accepted the news with a weak smile, confirming she was resigned to losing another daughter.

'Take care of your father for me. Make sure he eats properly. You know what he's like. I wish you'd come, but I understand.' She kissed her youngest daughter and turned to her husband for one last embrace whilst Thalia hugged her sisters and wished them a safe journey.

'We'll miss you, Thalia. I can't believe you changed your mind at the last minute.' Thetie held her tight. 'Take care of yourself.'

'I'm not sure I ever decided to leave. Look after Mamma,' she replied, handing her case to Lim to reload in the boot.

With all the farewells covered, Zacharia kissed his wife one last time and feeling awkward, thrust his hands deep into his trouser pockets. The girls picked up their cases and joined the heaving mass of people. He called out after them. 'Safe journey, write soon,' but they couldn't hear him over the noise. Zacharia watched them go with a heavy heart. The ache in his chest grew, and he bit down on his lip. Through his blurred vision, he tried to focus on their shapes being swallowed up by the crowds whilst furiously blinking away his tears. Bolstering him on either side, Terpie and Thalia linked their arms in his, and he was grateful for their presence keeping him upright. Eventually, he couldn't make out his family in the swarm of bodies merging as one in the distance. There was no going back now, and they were gone. Lim interrupted the moment.

'Sir, we must go now. Look!' he pointed to the sky on the horizon. Zacharia felt his blood turn to ice. Black shapes headed straight for them through the cloud and smoke.

'We need to go now! Girls, get in the car,' Zacharia shouted, feeling panicked. The three remaining family members slid along the back seat with Zacharia wedged in the middle. His palms were sweaty, and he wiped them on his trousers before linking hands with his daughters.

Chapter Nine
Anthoula

Saying goodbye and leaving half her family behind tore deeply at Anthoula's heart, she felt numb and disconnected from reality; like this was happening to a character in a story and not her life. She couldn't cry as her focus was fixed solely on getting through the next stage of this nightmare, with the haunting sound of the siren raising her already anxious mind to another level. As they merged into the mass of passengers waiting, aside from her heartache, the discomfort of her current surroundings began to rise; she hated crowds. Walking away from Zac was so unnatural. The tug of an invisible force pulling her back to him was overwhelming. Moving forward required immense effort, with each step she was pushing against an imaginary tide. If Ino hadn't been holding her hand and dragging her onward with Thetie and Clio forming a barrier behind her, she might have faltered in her resolve and run straight back to him. Since the age of seventeen, she knew he'd be the only man she'd love. He was her protector and always had been. Throughout their marriage, they had only been apart for a few nights on the odd occasion Zacharia was away on business. He managed everything and now she had to face the biggest test of her life without him. With a challenge of this magnitude, she couldn't afford to doubt her ability to cope, and must remain strong for the girls, they relied on her now. Thalia's last-minute decision to stay behind was not unexpected; she'd always been closer to her father than any of her sisters. Knowing Thalia was taking care of him, brought Anthoula some degree of comfort.

The scene at the docks was utter chaos, a mass exodus of bodies fighting to escape the island at the last hour. The sirens stopped, and all around, shouting and screaming burst her eardrums, but worse to bear were the cries of confused and distraught children. Desperate and terrified passengers barged and shoved each other in a bid to register for a place on a ship out of this hellish situation.

From what she'd seen so far, it was primarily women, children and a few men seizing the opportunity to escape. Realising that many of the women were like her, alone with no husbands for support she experienced an overwhelming sense of unity with them; they were in this together. The crowd pushed and jostled against them, swallowing up any whisper of space as it became available. The proximity of strangers was far too close and personal for Anthoula. She never coped well in confined spaces and recognised the signs of discomfort, tight chest, dizziness and shortened breaths. The last thing she needed was a full-blown panic attack. Concentrating on her breathing, Anthoula's focus landed on a young mother beside her, swaying and pacifying her infant in her arms. Breathe in… breathe out… Anthoula was grateful for small mercies; at least her daughters were adults. She couldn't even begin to conceive how she would handle this situation by herself if they were all little ones, and her heart went out to all the mothers. Breathe in… breathe out…

At that moment, the mother caught her staring, and Anthoula smiled back hoping to convey some empathy for this awful predicament they now shared.

Gradually, the sense of rising panic eased, and just as she had begun to feel less agitated, a new wave surged forward almost sweeping her off balance. To hold herself steady, she latched onto Ino, and her other hand gripped her case so tightly she couldn't feel her fingers anymore. A sea of heads bobbed in front of her and she stood on tiptoe to get a glimpse of the arched entrance to the docks and was relieved to see they were caught in a bottleneck and their destination was only a few hundred yards away. Beside her, Ino leaned into her.

'I'm so scared,' she whispered, tightening her hold on her mother's arm.

'Me too,' said Thetie from behind.

'We'll be okay,' she nodded. 'It won't be long now,' she said reassuringly, acknowledging her daughter's anxious faces.

'I wish people would hurry. What if there is no room for us? There are thousands of people here,' said Clio, bouncing on her toes.

'The harbour's full. I'm sure they'll be squeezing as many people as possible,' Ino replied.

'Once we get through those gates it won't take too long. We'll get a place don't worry,' Anthoula said with conviction despite having no idea whether that was true, but she couldn't afford to panic them at this stage and hadn't even considered a plan B. On the periphery of the disorderly crying and wailing Anthoula registered the recognisable hum of aircraft engines whining on their approach. In the commotion to get here and after the distressing farewells, she forgot the air raid siren sounded and what that meant. Her blood chilled and she turned around to see whether her girls had heard it too. The noise of the crowd intensified, and couldn't bear the panic-stricken look on her daughters faces. She was powerless to protect them.

Within minutes, fighter planes circled overhead and the red spot ensign was visible on the underside of the wings. Next, a high-pitched whistle filled the air. To her absolute horror, the planes dropped bombs onto the ships waiting in the harbour. Defenceless to do anything, exposed and vulnerable with nowhere to hide, Anthoula thought she would die here in the crowd, without her husband. The blast of an explosion nearby shook the ground and through her core. The frenzied crowd screamed in terror, hustling harder to drive forward through the gates for cover. The family were hemmed in amongst the throng of fearful bodies shoving from all sides.

'Oh God, have mercy,' she muttered, firmly gripping Ino's hand so hard she might break a bone. Behind her, Clio and Thetie linked arms and huddled tightly together, heads down. Grey and black columns of smoke billowed upwards and out, filling the sky to their left. The unpleasant smell of pungent burning rubber assailed their senses, making them cough and cover their noses. Another surge of movement drove them forward, and now they were beneath the archway entrance to the dock; they were almost there. Above them, planes continued to circle, releasing more bombs and deafening explosions rang in their ears.

'Listen,' Anthoula called over her shoulder to Clio and Thetie right behind her. 'We have to stay together. We mustn't get separated, okay!'

'We'll stick right behind you, Mamma, don't worry about that,' Thetie said.

Clio grabbed the back of her mother's skirt to maintain contact. Another massive blast hit its target and they all jumped out of their skins screaming. In the distance, a fierce ball of orange fire rose majestically into the air. The bombers hit an oil tanker along the harbour. Thick black plumes funnel upwards, spreading their ink far and blotting out any patches of blue sky and the acrid stench of burning oil clung to their hair and clothing. Eventually, rows of registration tables came into view with naval officers manning the desks hurriedly taking names and details of boarding passengers and rushing them through as quickly as possible. The docks were crammed with all manner of vessels lined up, one behind the other, merchant ships, naval frigates, minesweepers, and auxiliary steamers. Any available boat or ship in the area had been called upon to assist with the evacuation effort. Shuffling forward it soon became their turn and the family stood before the next available officer in his starched white uniform, eyes wide with alarm. There was no time for niceties. The balding officer snatched their passports and added their names to the list before handing them each a departure pass.

'You're on the SS Kuala, dock D27. It's the white one down there on the right, blue funnel,' he said pointing towards the rows of vessels waiting patiently before shouting 'Next!' to the people behind them. Picking up their cases, the women barged through the crowd and ran as best they could, heading in the direction the man had pointed to find D27. Anthoula struggled to keep up; she was terrified of losing her girls, and her adrenaline kicked in fuelling her to pick up speed. Her momentum was short-lived. Her sixty-year-old body wasn't up to running and she didn't get far before her lungs tightened and she found herself gasping and coughing from the smoke-soiled air catching in her throat. Finding it impossible to breathe and unable to run further, she bent forward struggling for air. Anthoula forced herself to keep moving but her cumbersome case had become a ton of weight to carry, she was tempted to abandon it altogether to make it easier. The gap had widened between herself and the girls, and now they were out of sight. Other passengers and swirling smog blocked her view. Consumed by rising panic at being left behind, her legs refused to budge. Thankfully Ino looked back and realising their mother had fallen behind, stopped, and shouted ahead to the others to wait.

'Come on, Mamma, we're almost there, keep going,' Ino called desperately as fighter planes swooped down for another attack. Unbelievably they had opened fire with machine-gun rounds directed at the innocent crowds below as they ran for cover. Anthoula fell to the ground twisting her wrist on her case handle as it slammed into the concrete. A sharp pain shot up her arm, and she howled in agony. Exhausted and out of breath, she rested her head on her case for a moment, willing herself to get back on her feet. *Come on. You can do this. You're not dying here today.* Frantic bodies sprinted around her, and through a thicket of legs, she was relieved to see Ino and Thetie running towards her.

'Mamma, are you hurt? We have to move,' cried Thetie. 'Here, give me your case.'

'I'm all right. Help me up, would you.' Anthoula held out her hand to Ino, who pulled her up.

'Come on. We can make it. Lean on me,' said Ino, wrapping her arm around her waist in support.

'I've hurt my ankle too.' Anthoula winced as she put weight on it.

'It's not far now. See, it's right there.' Thetie pointed with a sense of urgency.

Flying bullets pinged and ricocheted off the metal hulls indiscriminately claiming victims in their path. Anthoula's ears were ringing from the noise. Limping along with her daughters by her side, she stared straight ahead and tried to focus on where they were headed, but it was impossible. Around them, misshapen bodies lay sprawled out on the ground, their life liquor pooling on the concrete before her eyes. Enemy fire struck these innocent people down in their prime as they ran for safety and for what? Ahead of them, a mother on her knees screamed hysterically over the limp body of a small child lifeless on the ground, her husband sobbing and tugging her jacket to prise her away. Anthoula's stomach churned and revulsion caught in her throat, her heart ached for those poor parents, but there was nothing she could do.

With her daughters by her side, she kept moving but it didn't feel like she was gaining ground. The marker with D27 came into view. It felt achievable now. A couple of men overtook them running with cases held aloft above their heads as shields from the onslaught raining down. Anthoula and the girls caught up with Clio but came to a grinding halt, their path to the gangplank blocked. On the ground lay the motionless body of a woman dressed in a pale blue suit laying on her side, her arm prettified with bracelets stretched out as if reaching for help, her cold eyes staring blankly into the distance. Her suit jacket pooled with blood; it was too late to save her.

'What shall we do? Can we help her?' asked Thetie.

'Keep going, Thetie, she's dead,' Clio stated bluntly.

The girls awkwardly sidestepped around the woman and Anthoula stumbled, glancing back over her shoulder, unable to take her eyes off the woman's fallen form.

'We made it!' yelled Clio sprinting up the steep gangplank.

'Oh, thank God,' Anthoula gasped. With shaky hands, she grabbed the railings, and with all her remaining strength she dragged herself up the steep incline. Ino and Thetie were chasing at her heels, encouraging her to keep going. Anthoula's heart pounded fiercely, and her lungs felt like they could explode at any minute, but she had made it.

The Kuala was probably an impressive ship in its heyday, but it appeared aged and forlorn today. Dwarfed by some of the larger ships, the hull of the auxiliary vessel was grubby grey rather than pearly white and the tall blue funnel had faded with only flecks of its original bright colour remaining. Relieved to have reached the top Anthoula swayed grabbing the railings the captain greeted her warmly, and she handed over her boarding pass, now crumpled from her fall.

'Welcome aboard, ladies,' said the friendly-looking captain. His welcome sounded like they were about to embark on a luxury cruise rather than a frightful evacuation and his level of normalcy felt out of place. His professional and cheery manner put Anthoula at ease. Still out of breath from the climb, Anthoula smiled and patted his arm as a way of thanks. Thetie guided her mother along the deck, following Clio leading the way. Although they were still in danger, it was a massive relief to be one step closer to getting far away from here. Anthoula followed keeping her gaze downward to concentrate on where to put her feet as the woefully overcrowded deck was full of families sprawled on the floor or sitting on their luggage all along the walkway. Anthoula unsteadily stepped over pairs of legs, bags and small children as they fought to find a space. Halfway along Anthoula smiled at a mother breastfeeding her baby whilst comforting a young child under her other arm. The whimpering of the child cradling her bedraggled stuffed toy was too pitiful to bear and Anthoula looked away. Further along the deck, any nurses on-board tended to the injured the best they could, and Anthoula couldn't help it; she began to weep silently. It had been an emotional day already and the shock of what she had just seen overwhelmed her. What have these innocent people done to the Japanese? Why had they attacked women and children as they tried to get to safety? It was brutal and cold-blooded. All along the walkway, she was greeted by an endless supply of terrified and tortured faces, crying children and hopeless mothers in every direction. Clio stopped and asked if they should go down to the lower deck.

'If no one objects, I'd rather be in the fresh air. Remember, I don't travel well,' Anthoula replied, holding her stomach as she swayed. Even in the harbour, the gentle pitching made her feel queasy.

'We should stay together. Let's see if there's more room around the other side,' Thetie suggested.

Thankfully, the starboard deck was less congested, and they found a space midway along for them to rest.

'Come here, all of you.' Anthoula beckoned her girls towards her. 'Are you all okay? None of you is hurt, are you?' she said, patting their faces like they were porcelain dolls.

'I'm fine. I honestly didn't think we would make it,' said Ino.

'That was the most terrifying moment of my life. When they started shooting at us, I thought, this is it!' said Clio.

'We've been lucky. I was so scared. Are you hurt, Mamma? You're bleeding,' said Thetie, pointing to her leg.

'Let's get you comfortable,' Ino offered, setting down her mother's luggage for her to sit on. Clio and Thetie guided her to a seated position and supported her leg on one of their cases. The leather creaked beneath her weight, and her aching bones were grateful for the rest.

'Let me see. It probably looks worse than it is,' Thetie said, pulling up her mother's skirt to inspect her injury.

'Just leave it,' said Anthoula dismissively, twisting her hand to ease the pain, noticing it had already started to swell and bruise.

'I can try and clean it up for you,' offered Thetie.

'Honestly, don't worry. I'm fine. Sit down and catch your breath.'

The girls assembled along the deck and sat beside her in quiet reflection. Anthoula dabbed the worst of the blood off her leg using her skirt, cursing that it was one of her favourites, ruined now as the stain would never come out. And she promptly laughed at herself for having such a ridiculous concern under the circumstances. Her leg throbbed and was painful, but she kept it to herself as she didn't want to make a fuss. In her relief at reaching the ship, it hadn't registered that bombing was still happening around them, adding a fresh wave of fear to her fragile nerves. She reasoned they could do nothing about it and rested her head on the wall behind her, feeling the reverberations as each blast found its target. With nothing else to do, Anthoula observed their fellow passengers. Beside them a flustered woman sighed, unable to constrain two lively boys. Anthoula wasn't good at gauging ages but guessed they were about six and eight. They appeared unfazed by their surroundings, leaning over the railings and waving to the neighbouring occupants on another ship. Being hemmed in by other vessels meant it was impossible to see any part of the horizon and the deck was overshadowed and gloomy. Anthoula read aloud the name emblazoned in white on the black hull of the ship next to them *H.M.S. Giang Bee*; she liked the sound as it rolled off her tongue. It was slightly larger than theirs but no less crowded.

'Do you think we're going to Australia?' asked Ino.

'Not a clue, but I don't care. I want to get as far away from here as possible,' said Clio.

'We should count ourselves lucky. So many poor souls never made it,' Anthoula said, shivering, replaying a vivid flashback of the fallen lady on the dockside.

'Why aren't we leaving?' asked Ino.

'I expect they'll wait until the planes have gone. It's probably safer in the docks,' suggested Anthoula. She closed her eyes and thought of her husband. She missed him profoundly and prayed he and the girls made it home safely. Already it felt as though she had been away from him for days. Recalling his face from last night, his excitement and plans for their future made her smile. It wouldn't surprise her if he'd forgotten his ludicrous plan to sell the shop. She wouldn't mind betting that he would have changed his mind by the time they returned. Sensing movement, she opened her eyes to see more passengers piling onto the deck, and the increased volume of distressed children and crying infants drowned out the booming explosions. Hours passed before the ships were permitted to leave the harbour and by early evening they were on their way.

Once the "Giang Bee" set off and its hulk no longer overshadowed the smaller vessel, the deck flooded with light, and Anthoula was grateful to see the horizon again. A few hours had passed without planes stalking the skies and now the vulnerable flotilla of evacuee vessels tentatively headed out into open waters. After sitting for a long time, Anthoula called Ino and Thetie to help her stand. She was seizing up like a rusty old bike. Supporting her on both sides the girls levered her up to lean on the railings.

Anthoula savoured the warm air against her face and her skin felt taut and dry. She breathed deeply to conquer the nausea swirling in her stomach only to fill her lungs with smoke-polluted air adding to her discomfort. Since arriving in Singapore all those years ago, she had never left the island and now mournfully watched the angry flames devour it from a distance. From all directions, she saw ships, boats and trawlers thrusting through the waves as if in a race, except they were not competing against each other; it was a race away from danger. Snippets of conversations from the last twenty-four hours replayed like a loop in her head.

She couldn't shift the niggling concern that they made the wrong decision. It felt so wrong to leave Zacharia and her girls behind and doubt plagued her thoughts.

Gazing across the choppy grey ocean, she started a mental argument with herself: *What have I done? I should have fought harder to make Zac and the girls come with us. What was I thinking, leaving them behind? Damn Terpie and her stubbornness!* She clutched the railings tightly. *If only I had been firmer, Zac would be here with me now. I can't do this.*

The exhaustion and emotion of the last twenty-four hours came tumbling out. Hot tears streamed down her face, and she abruptly wiped them away before her girls noticed. She had promised Zac she would be strong and get through this. They had barely left the island and she was falling apart already. *Get a grip,* Anthoula said to herself. But the voice wasn't to be silenced and repeated the same message: "*This is all Terpie's fault. Zac would be here if it weren't for her.*" Anthoula ignored the voice. The resentment towards her daughter threatened like an ugly storm cloud. Anthoula would have to guard against that. This was the decision they had agreed, and it was too late now.

Thetie joined her and stood by her side. 'What are you thinking about?'

'I miss your father already, that's all.'

Chapter Ten
Zacharia

Lim turned the ignition and the car chugged into life once again. Setting off slowly, they meandered through the vehicle graveyard returning to the main road to take them home. The back seat was brimming with tension, and Terpie launched her attack.

'I can't believe you did that at the last minute.' She scowled at Thalia in disgust, slapping her hands into her lap for dramatic effect. 'You were so cruel to spring that on Mamma after everything you said last night.'

'It makes no difference to you, so I don't see why you're so uptight about it,' Thalia retorted, leaning forward to speak over her father wedged between them. 'When it came to it, I couldn't go. I wanted to stay with you, Pappa.' Thalia clasped her hands together to stop them from shaking.

'Did you see Mamma's face? She was devastated. You're such a hypocrite,' Terpie snarled.

'What? You have no right to criticise me. If it weren't for you, we'd still be together. You caused all of this, and we should've left you here on your own. I'm here for Pappa because you won't look after him,' Thalia spat back.

'Girls, girls. What's done is done. Your mother will understand. She'll be fine Thalia. I'm glad you stayed if I'm honest.' Zacharia placed his hand over hers.

'That must have been so hard for you. Saying goodbye,' said his youngest daughter, briefly catching Terpie raise her eyebrows and shake her head before she turned to the window.

'It wasn't easy, but it's what your mother and I agreed.'

The car fell silent and each of them sunk deep into their thoughts. Zacharia couldn't bear to look at the ravaged streets anymore. The city was haemorrhaging, and he had seen more than enough. He let his head fall back and closed his eyes. Although his eyelids twitched and flickered refusing to stay shut, so instead he stared into the footwell to admire his highly polished brogues. It was true, he'd found it tough saying goodbye to Anthoula and the girls, but like ripping off a plaster it was done and over with.

Naturally, he would miss them and worry constantly until they were safely back in his care. He reassured himself he would feel better when he got home, everything felt better at home—moments passed before it became impossible to ignore the deep droning from above demanding his attention. He leaned forward beyond Thalia watching planes swoop like vultures firing bombs and bullets on the harbour. His eyes widened in shock; he couldn't believe what he was seeing. An explosion to his left, propelled fire, water, and metal debris hundreds of feet into the air followed by another and another. Zacharia's heart pounded against his ribcage competing with the explosions a few hundred feet from the road.

Please, God, protect my family. Zacharia thought. With the intensifying fear for their safety, he was sorely tempted to order Lim to turn around so he could run to the dock, find his family and bring them back. He knew that was madness. They were gone, and he'd allowed them to leave. Thalia twisted in her seat.

'Why are they firing at the docks!' she yelled.

'Because they're evil. That's why,' said Terpie icily.

Bombs fell in quick succession like apples shaken from a tree and the billowing blackness merged into the already smoke-clogged sky. Feeling helpless, Zacharia slid his arms around his daughter's and pulled them close. Cradling them one under each arm, their heads buried in his chest. A pitiful attempt to protect them, but he could only shield them from the horror outside. Their childlike whimpering pulled at his heart, and he held them firmly, wishing he had the power to make this awful situation disappear.

'Stay down. Don't look. It'll be okay,' Zacharia soothed. 'Everything will be alright.'

Lim drove with great concentration, his shoulders hunched low over the steering wheel. His bony elbows stuck out like crab claws, and he alternated between keeping his eyes on the road and peering upwards through the windscreen at the planes directly overhead. Zacharia's steely eyes remained focussed on the road ahead, searching for danger with such intensity that he wondered how the glass didn't shatter under his glare—four days of intense bombing left a detritus of glass, metal and stone littering their route. The city was now a war zone, but Lim maintained his composure, avoiding burning cars, abandoned buckled rickshaws, concrete slabs and stacks of rubble causing obstructions. Dotted along the pavements lay small, misshapen bundles and naïvely, it took Zacharia a moment to realise these were human bodies. As if the situation were not harrowing enough, the predators in the sky opened machine-gun fire on the innocent souls running for cover, casting shrapnel and stone in all directions. Right before his eyes, a man collapsed on the pavement, taken down by a bullet in the back as he ran for cover. Recoiling in his seat, he swallowed hard and crushed his precious daughters closer to him.

'Pappa, what's going on? I'm scared,' Terpie wailed, trying to sit up to see what was happening, but Zacharia tightened his hold.

'Stay down. Both of you,' he urged firmly.

His whole body tensed, and beads of sweat ran down the back of his neck. Paralysed by crushing fear and anger, it was as though his heart was being squeezed in a vice, and he found it hard to breathe. The repetitive chugging of machine-gun fire trapped them in the middle of a bullet storm. If only Lim could drive faster and get them out of here, Zacharia knew he was doing his best.

Bullets skimmed past the car, and Lim ducked.

'Takut! Takut! I'm afraid, Sir.'

'I know. Me too. You're doing great,' Zacharia said feebly, his mouth suddenly dry.

'Please Lim, get us out of here!' Thalia squealed from beneath her father's armpit with her hands over her eyes.

'I'm trying my best, Miss.'

Zacharia twisted in his seat and did a double take because he didn't trust his eyes. Through the rear window he saw hovering low, tailing the car, a single fighter plane bearing down on them, chasing them along the street. It was so close that he could almost see the hatred in the pilot's eyes from the cockpit.

'Lim. Have you seen what's behind us?'

'I see it. What shall I do?' cried Lim in panic.

'Take a side road if you can. Find some cover,' Zacharia instructed calmly. The pursuing aircraft swooped lower, and a torrent of gunshots rained down, narrowly missing the swerving vehicle. Beside him, his girls screamed, and they all slid further down in their seats. Buffeting against each other, the three family members were suddenly thrown sideways as Lim steered hard to the left, and the car tyres screeched in protest. As instructed, he'd taken them down a narrow passage with tall buildings on either side shielding them from the open sky.

Zacharia had never been so terrified; his stomach flipped somersaults, and he trembled from head to toe. He braved a glance out the rear window, searching what limited sky was visible, and was relieved to see their airborne pursuer had gone.

'I think you lost him, Lim!'

'Are you sure? Shall we stop or keep going?' asked Lim shakily.

'Pull over here,' Zacharia replied.

Lim pulled up to the kerb; the car idled jumpily, awaiting further instruction. The spooked chauffeur leaned forward, collapsing in a mumbling heap over the steering wheel.

'Is everyone all right?' Zacharia asked, releasing his grip on his daughter's shoulders.

'Are they gone?' Thalia squeaked, raising her head from beneath her father's arm.

'I'll go and check,' Lim replied breathlessly as he left the engine running and shakily removed himself from the vehicle. Zacharia and the girls watched their driver intently through the window as he paced up and down the street, surveying the thin patch of sky overhead. After a few minutes, Lim returned and leaned over the front seat to reassure his anxious passengers.

'It all looks clear. They've gone.'

The three family members unfurled themselves from their hunched-up positions. Zacharia flexed his aching arms and realised the girls had red indent marks on their arms from his harsh embrace. Suddenly his head weighed heavy on his shoulders, and he collapsed forward with his head in his hands, taking slow deep breaths to steady his heartbeat back to a normal rhythm. Beside him, Thalia and Terpie wiped the tears from their blotchy faces and swept their unruly hair from their eyes where they had been sheltering beneath their father's rigid embrace. The girls were shaking, and their faces had turned grey. The sound of distant bombs pounded like fierce thunder behind them, but at least they appeared out of immediate danger. Zacharia reached forward and patted Lim firmly on the shoulder.

'You were amazing back there, my friend. Thank you.'

'I was so scared, Sir. I thought we were goners for sure.'

'I feel sick.' Terpie's voice sounded strained, like she had swallowed a bag of marbles. She shakily wound the window down to let in some air. With the combination of fear and the stench of burning oil, she flung the door wide and vomited in the gutter. Zacharia rubbed her back soothingly.

'Take deep breaths. You'll feel better in a minute. We all need to catch our breath.'

'I can't believe they were shooting at us and bombing the harbour like that. Why would they do that?' Thalia asked.

'This war's not only about gaining control of the island, Miss. Many eastern cultures don't agree with the white man in the east. They feel they have no business being here,' said Lim.

'Well, it's barbaric. It makes me so angry, all those innocent people. Do you think Mamma and the others made it out safely? They must have been so frightened.'

Zacharia lifted his chin off his chest and sighed before offering his answer.

'I don't know Thalia. But I know there's nothing to be gained by thinking the worst. We must believe they're safe and made it to one of those ships. Besides, your mother wouldn't want you worrying.' Zacharia wouldn't allow himself to think the worst, knowing from experience that brooding on negativity wouldn't help. The image of his family waving goodbye floated before him, and he choked down his anguish, praying that wasn't the last memory he would have. Regardless of his concerns, he must be strong for his girls. He couldn't expect *them* to be brave if he was falling apart. It was essential to show them he wasn't scared and believed his family were safe and on their way to a better place.

'I'm sure they're absolutely fine. I expect they'll be making their way out to sea very soon, and your mother is probably feeling sick already, bless her,' he said with a convincing smile.

'Can we go home now?' pleaded Thalia.

'Yes, Lim, are you ready to drive?'

'I think so, Sir. When Miss Terpie is ready,' replied Lim, waiting whilst Terpie wiped her mouth and closed the door. 'I'll try to take the back roads if I can get through, Sir. In case there are more planes,' he added, glancing in the rear-view mirror.

'That's fine, Lim. There's no rush, and I'd rather we got home in one piece.' Zacharia mopped his brow with his handkerchief.

Thankfully, the return journey was uneventful, and the battle in the sky had ceased for the now. Approaching the street where they lived, Zacharia felt in his gut that something was wrong. He couldn't grasp it, but something didn't look right. The trees seemed to have shifted, and he spotted rising smoke behind the treeline. Tension rose in his chest again as the car slowed and turned into their driveway.

'Oh no, Sir,' said Lim, his voice barely audible.

Zacharia lunged forward, gripping the seat in the front, and the vision before him sucked the air out of his lungs; he gasped in shock.

'What on earth…Pappa, the house!' shrieked Thalia beside him and with eyes wide Terpie smothered her mouth with her hands to silence her scream. Zacharia struggled to comprehend what he was seeing. His cherished home, his haven, gapped vulgarly like an open wound with their belongings and happy memories bleeding out into the driveway. The roof at the front of the house had blown off completely, and hungry flames licked their way up the remaining wooden frame spouting sooty fumes into the sky. The veranda had collapsed over the front concrete stairs and split in half, smashing the urn pots below and crushing the bright pink bougainvillaea Zacharia had grown from seeds. His neighbours had come to the rescue, valiantly battling with hoses and buckets to control the flames.

When the car stopped, Thalia jumped out. Zacharia's heart weighed heavy and he stumbled from the vehicle. The shock was too much. Halfway up the driveway, his legs buckled beneath him. He collapsed onto his knees with his head in his hands to comprehend the ghastly sight. He couldn't care less that the filthy soil and ash water mixture was soaking into and staining his cream linen trousers on its path trickling down the driveway.

'No, no, not my home!' he yelled, beating the ground with his fists. He sobbed with his chin on his chest whilst thinking of all the precious memories they'd shared in that house and the years of hard work it had taken to provide it. He was vaguely aware of a hand on his shoulder consoling him. Desolate and angry, he had no clue what to do for the first time in his life. He'd stepped into a terrible nightmare and begged for the rollercoaster of disasters to stop. This couldn't be happening.

In disbelief, he viewed the scene. Book pages, bits of material and remains of household objects strewn everywhere, much-loved homely treasures dangled from nearby tree branches like grotesque Christmas decorations flapping in the breeze. Forty years of memories, keepsakes and belongings were destroyed in one swift blow. Zacharia didn't know what to do with himself and searched the sky for answers. The shock thumped him in the chest, and like a wounded animal, he howled. Thalia crouched down beside him and hugged him tightly.

'Pappa, it'll be okay. It's only things, and the house can be fixed.'

Her arms around him briefly brought him comfort, but all he could focus on were the accumulation of losses: his family, his home and no doubt his business too. Staring at the ground, dazed and confused, he assembled his thoughts. He must pull himself together, he couldn't change events and the house was gone. A terrifying thought occurred to him, making him shiver. Less than an hour ago his family would've been sheltering under the table had they not decided to leave and the outcome could be much, much worse. The harsh realisation bought him up sharp. By putting the situation into perspective, he realised that there was nothing to gain by wallowing in self-pity; it wouldn't rebuild his home or turn the clock back. They had been incredibly lucky. Sharp tugging on his arm dragged him back to the present.

'Pappa, Pappa, please get up,' Thalia begged.

Once on his feet, he hugged his daughters with grateful relief. Their being alive was the most important thing.

'We've lost everything,' Terpie snivelled.

'No, not everything. Although, I'm glad your mother's not here to see this. It would break her heart.'

'Thank goodness we weren't in the house at the time,' declared Thalia, running her hand through her tumble of hair.

'I was thinking the same. Come on, let's help and see if we can salvage anything.'

Together with Lim, they joined the rescue effort, grabbing buckets to douse the flames until eventually the remains of the house groaned and smouldered. Zacharia picked his way through the wreckage; there was nothing much remaining of the family room and dining room which had taken the brunt of the blast. He shuddered. Only yesterday they shielded here but it wouldn't have saved them. The sight of the charcoal frame which was all that remained of the piano in the corner brought another wave of sadness. Luckily, the quick response from the locals prevented the fire from spreading, so the bedrooms at the rear were untouched. Although the whiff of stale fumes and loss clung to their belongings.

'Terpie you'll need some things, so pack a case if you can. I don't think there's anything else worth taking out of this wreckage.' Zacharia glanced around slowly, scratching his head.

The girls coughed and covered their mouths as they headed through the fog cloud to their room and he dragged his weary body to his bedroom. He found some clean clothes and changed out of his wet and stained trousers. It was impossible to stay here. Using what little strength he had left, he tugged on his case, firmly wedged under the bed and opened draws and threw in randomly selected clothes. He grabbed some toiletries, a razor and his toothbrush from the bathroom and took a wedding photo from his nightstand. He smiled and traced his finger over his wife's young face.

Looking around the room, there was nothing else worth taking; none of it had meaning without Anthoula. Running his hand through his ash-filled hair, he sat on the bed he had shared with his wife earlier this morning. Her pillow still indented with her shape and her scent lingered on the ruffled sheets. He half expected to see her there. The last few hours had been a whirlwind of change and he could only keep moving forward. Pinching the top of his nose to stem the tension, he sighed heavily and turned his back on his home.

Thalia and Terpie were waiting outside for him and he was pleased to see they had been able to retrieve some of their belongings. Thankfully, Lim's house was untouched, Shi Min was unharmed and they'd gathered on the garden bench.

'You can stay with us, it's small, but we'll find room,' Shi Min offered as she walked towards them carrying a tray with cups of green tea.

'Thank you for the offer. I couldn't bear to see this every morning.' Zacharia gestured towards the charred carcass of his beloved house 'Besides, there's no room for us all and I'll not impose on your kindness.' He accepted his tea and began to drink.

'I got Lim to rescue your old trunk of photographs from when the girls were little. I know Anthoula would want them,' said Shi Min.

'That was so thoughtful of you. Sorry, my head is all over the place. You're right. Out of everything, they would be her most prized possession,' Zacharia replied.

'We'll keep them safe until you return.'

'One good thing at least, my wedding dress is still in one piece. Shi Min will keep it safe for me, although I doubt I'll be getting married anytime soon,' said Terpie sadly.

'It's all such a mess. I'm so sorry, my lovely girl.'

'It's not your fault, Pappa. As much as I want it, realistically a wedding is out of the question. We don't even have a home. If we aren't staying here, where are we going to go?' Terpie asked, clasping the china cup with both hands.

Zacharia groaned as he lowered himself to sit on the concrete step.

'Give me a minute, I need to think.' His head felt fuzzy, and the grinding headache had returned pulsating behind his eyes. He closed them and caressed his brow, trying to concentrate and hoping a solution would make itself known.

'The convents and churches are taking people in,' Lim offered.

'That could work, girls. It'll be safe.'

'The convent, really? I hate it there,' Thalia grumbled, slumping down beside her father; concern written all over her face.

'But Papp…' Terpie started to protest but he raised his hand to cut her off, clarifying that this was not up for discussion.

'Please don't argue with me. It's the best solution in the short-term.' His primary concern keeping them safe; the convent was their best option under the circumstances. 'None of this is easy for any of us, so please do this for me.' He didn't like the tone of his short-temperedness; these new emotions he was experiencing felt alien to him. His daughters conceded to his request with a curt nod and tight lips.

'Your father's right. The convent is probably one of the safest places in the city. Who knows how bad it will get once their soldiers get here,' said Shi Min gently.

'I wish we could stay here with you.' Terpie hugged the elderly lady.

'It's too dangerous. The Japs will come through here before they reach the city. The convent is our best option,' said Zacharia.

'Well, if it's too dangerous, how can we leave Lim and Shi Min behind?' asked Thalia. She had a valid point and the question made him feel uncomfortable.

'I promised your mother I'd look after you and that's what I'm doing. Lim and Shi Min are welcome to come to the convent if they wish.'

'We have a home, my dear. You need a roof over your head. Don't worry about us. We'll be fine here. Right, I'll not see you leave before you have a good meal inside you.' Shi Min bustled off to prepare them some food. Zacharia turned his back on the smouldering remains.

When the food arrived, Zacharia picked at his meal and couldn't eat, his stomach was still tied in knots. He apologised to Shi Min who dismissed it quickly saying it wouldn't go to waste. Thankfully, the girls managed to eat, so that was something less for him to worry about. Later that afternoon, Lim agreed to drive them to the convent. After exchanging tearful hugs and more goodbyes, they left their Amah standing alone once again. The return journey was less traumatic without bombs and planes overhead and Lim knew which roads to avoid, so in no time at all, they were back in the centre of the city again. The high whitewashed walls of the convent came into view and Zacharia knew it would take more than bricks to protect them, but it looked like a fortress and was the best assurance he had. Having said goodbye to Lim and watched him leave, the three remaining family members stood with their cases before the black iron gates on the dusty street. Terpie pulled the well-worn rope and rang the bell. After a short wait, a nun appeared. She greeted the visitors with a thin smile, her pale skin as white as the wimple surrounding her face. As succinctly as he could whilst holding his emotions together, Zacharia explained their situation and with clasped hands, the sister nodded with empathy listening to his story. When he finished, the sister apologised and explained that the convent was housing women and children only, but he could try the churches and hospitals taking refugees in. Zacharia scratched his head.

'I understand. Please take my daughters,' he replied and turned to the girls. 'Don't worry. I'll stay with Emily. Her apartment is just around the corner. She'll take me in,' he smiled, hoping they wouldn't make a fuss. 'I'll visit you tomorrow to check on you. You must promise me you'll stay strong and look after each other. It could be months until we get news from your mother so, please try to put it out of your minds for now. It's the only way. Now hug your old pappa and get going.'

One after the other, he scooped them into his arms and crushed them with affection until they could hardly breathe. With a degree of reluctance, the girls picked up their cases, approached the iron gates and the sister ushered them in. Left alone on Bras Basah Road, he'd never felt so empty and lonely. Picking up his case, he walked briskly and headed for the Capitol apartments. It wasn't far, but, it could just as well have been a marathon in his exhausted state. Surrounded by so much destruction, he kept his head down and concentrated on the pavement ahead. At the junction of North Bridge Road, he turned right. Ahead of him, two drunk soldiers staggered arm in arm down the road towards him and he watched with curiosity as they tossed their guns into the river. He kept tight to the wall and avoided eye contact with them as they passed, stinking of whisky. The last thing he needed was trouble. It didn't fill him with confidence that the forces enlisted to protect them were admitting defeat.

Further on, he crossed Stamford Canal and contemplated briefly whether he'd the energy to walk another few blocks to the High Street; he was so close. He agonised for what felt like hours to come to a decision. His wife's voice echoed in his head; *what is the point? You can't do anything.* Suddenly he laughed at himself as he didn't have the keys anyway; they'd been hanging in his jacket pocket back at the house or what was left of it. If he found it in ruins, he couldn't deal with that too and thought better of it. There was only so much misfortune a man could take in one day. Besides, he needed to sit down as his hips were grinding in their sockets. With the decision made for him, he crossed the deserted road and approached the majestic, ivory stone entrance of the Capitol building, which dominated the corner of the street. This modern complex housed a cinema and luxury apartments and whilst he could appreciate the architecture of this splendid building, he could never see himself living somewhere like this. Locating the buzzer for Emily's flat, he pressed it and leaned his forehead against the cold stone whilst waiting for an answer. He prayed he was right and that she hadn't evacuated and with relief, the door catch released to let him in. Emily and her husband Bill befriended them shortly after Zacharia and his bride arrived in Singapore and over the years became like family. Anthoula could only speak Greek in those early days and struggled to settle in a foreign land. Being a kind and patient soul, Emily taught her to speak and read English and they has remained friends. Sluggishly scaling the flights of stairs, his knee joints grated with each step and he quickly became out of breath. He wondered what Bill would make of all this drama and was thankful his friend wasn't here to see the demise of the city he had loved so much. On reaching apartment 203, the door was ajar. He pushed it and Emily was waiting on the other side with outstretched arms. He realised he must look a dreadful sight. He honestly didn't know how old she was but assumed she must be in her mid-seventies. Impeccably dressed as always, she greeted him with a friendly face and a warm smile. His dishevelled appearance was a glaring signal that something was wrong. In a split second, Emily's welcoming smile slipped from her face and concern replaced it.

'Come in, come in. What's happened?' she asked, ushering him into her sitting room. 'Would you like a cup of tea?' she offered, but he declined with a wave of his hand. He found it amusing how British people always resorted to a cup of tea as the antidote to any crisis. She patted the sofa next to her and he collapsed into the soft cushions; the tension of the last few days weighed heavy.

'Oh, Emily,' was all he managed before the day's emotion came tumbling out. His eyes welled up again and Emily passed him a box of tissues noting his discomfort. She left the room briefly, returning with a glass of water and placing it on the coffee table in before him. She waited.

'I'm sorry to turn up unannounced like this.'

'You're welcome here anytime. You don't have to talk, but if you think it will help, I'm all ears. Whenever you're ready.' She patted his knee and sat back clasping her hands. Bluish veins protruded through her paper-thin skin and the spattering of liver spots was a tell-tale sign of her age. Taking a moment to gather his thoughts he took a sip of the water and sensed his presence made the room untidy. Zacharia sighed, staring at the colourful spines of books on the bookshelf whilst deciding where to start. Keeping his voice steady, he apprised her of all the facts from the night they decided to leave, up until half an hour ago. She didn't speak during the retelling, but her expression changed throughout from concern to shock, to horror and finally sympathy for his misfortune.

'So, there we have it. My whole family are gone. I don't know if my wife and daughters have escaped to safety, whether they are alive or dead. Our beautiful home is destroyed all in one day and here I am. All alone.'

'Oh my goodness, I'm so sorry, Zac. This is just awful. Those poor girls and Anthoula,' she said tearfully. 'I know I can't help much, but you're welcome to stay here as long as you need.'

'Thank you. I appreciate that.'

'I know you must be consumed with worry, Zac, but you can only take it one day at a time.'

'Yes, that's all I can do. Forgive my bad manners. I haven't even asked how you are. It must have been terrifying for you with the bombing raids. I guessed you wouldn't evacuate.'

'No, I'd never leave this place. I took myself to bed and hid under my covers. Not much a silly old lady like me can do. I laid there thinking, I've had a good life. If it's my time to go, then so be it. I'll get to be with my Bill again.' Her cornflower-blue eyes glossed over and for a moment she disappeared to another place. 'But I'm still here, helping you. I've not set foot outside the apartment for over a week, so tell me what is going on out there.'

'Believe me. You're better off not knowing.'

'I've been listening to the radio reports, so I know things aren't going well. Do you think it's safe to go out? Are there any places to get food as I'm running low?'

'There's a state of panic everywhere, so I don't know. I'll go out early tomorrow. I did say I would call in on the girls anyway.'

'I was about to make myself something to eat. You must be starving.' Emily launched herself off the chair, she was still sprightly for her age and Zacharia wished he had an ounce of her energy.

'Thank you. I don't want to impose.'

Popping her head around the doorframe, she said, 'Nonsense, Zac, you're my dearest friend.' And she disappeared again.

Zacharia approached the window and pushed the net curtain aside, mindful not to disturb Emily's neat display of elephant ornaments she'd collected on her foreign travels with Bill. Usually, Stamford Road was a hive of activity and colour with a constant stream of traffic and bustling with people, but not today. The road was deserted except for a marching platoon of soldiers looking deflated as they passed. From here, he could make out the spire of the convent and hoped his girls were settled.

The events and emotions of the day had sapped his energy and his mind was disturbed. Emily was right; he could only take things one day at a time. The comfortable seating called to him and he flopped onto the floral cushions and rested his head to the sound of clanging pots, running water and the rhythmic sound of chopping, and drifted off to sleep.

Chapter Eleven
Thalia

The iron gates to the convent in much need of lubrication squeaked and groaned on their rusted hinges as they closed behind them. The key turned in the lock, the latch hammered home with a resounding clunk and Thalia knew with certitude they were no longer free. The final glimpse of her pappa waving goodbye through the bars and walking away filled her with sadness. Throughout her life, she had never known a time when they faced such hardship. Her pappa had done everything in his power to provide them with a privileged life and seeing him looking so dishevelled filled her with concern. She had an overwhelming desire to protect him and to make everything all right. The nun introduced herself as Sister Mary Benita. She was petite, with a childlike frame and Thalia suspected she was older than she looked. Her thin lips barely opened when she spoke and her compassionate words almost triggered Thalia to start crying again as she reminded her so much of Thetie. The boundary walls contained a cobbled courtyard with a path looping back on itself around a small fountain in the centre. Thalia tuned into the gentle burbling, instantly soothing her nerves. It was a little haven of tranquillity and she could almost forget what madness prevailed on the other side of the wall which separated them from the outside world. Sister Mary Benita gave them a brief tour of the grounds and convent, guiding the girls through white stone corridors and narrow staircases. Thalia didn't recognise this part of the building when they attended here years ago as they never entered the dormitories for the borders. Her time here wasn't always a happy one, although she loved learning, she found the rigidity of the regime difficult to handle and some of the other girls teased her for that amongst other things. The religious sisters were extremely strict and unforgiving and their harsh authority strangled her spirit. Her sisters all attended here and her parents would never consider breaking tradition to send her to an English school, so she stuck it out. The convent culture didn't beseem her tomboyish nature or mischievous sense of humour as she found out to her cost. Disobedience was a sin and whilst she wasn't badly behaved, (she would never disappoint her father like that) her tendency to be outspoken got her noticed. On numerous occasions, her defiance resulted in periods of isolation to contemplate her behaviour. The familiar earthy scent of frankincense and myrrh seeped through the walls, transporting her back in time and making her feel eight years old again. The cold white concrete walls gave Thalia goose bumps making the hairs on her arms stand to attention. They followed Sister Mary Benita up a narrow spiral staircase, one behind the other and her suitcase ricocheted against the wall leaving chalky white dust on the edges of the battered old leather.

'As you can imagine, we've received the call from many refugees and as a result, we're becoming overcrowded. This is our last available room. Also, bombs destroyed the top floor dormitories so we had a move around.'

'I hope the children weren't hurt,' said Thalia in alarm.

'No, no. Thankfully, our border children were already evacuated out of the city to a convent in Bahau.'

They reached the top corridor and the sister showed them to a small but functional room.

'I hope this is comfortable enough for you. There's a shared bathroom along the corridor and supper will be served in the dining room at six p.m.'

'We're grateful for your kindness and allowing us to shelter here for the time being,' said Terpie.

'Yes, thank you. I was wondering. Is Sister Martha still around? We used to attend school here and she was my favourite,' Thalia asked hopefully.

'No sorry. She transferred to a convent in India two years ago.'

Thalia was disappointed but thanked her for her time. Sister Martha made her time here bearable, and she would have loved to see her again.

'I'll leave you to get some rest. To get to the dining room there is a staircase at the other end of this corridor, it's down on the left. You're welcome to join us in our evening prayer after supper. There's no obligation of course. The grounds are yours to roam and lights out at ten p.m.'

'Thank you, we'll see you at supper,' Terpie replied.

The sister scurried down the corridor, her dainty feet tip-tapping on the concrete as she went. Thalia entered the stuffy room first and placed her case on the metal-framed bed along the wall, opposite an identical bed under a small window. Ripped mosquito nets which had seen better days hung above the beds, but the crisp white bedding looked clean. The sparsely decorated room showed signs of neglect where the pastel green paint peeled from the walls, and flimsy floral curtains framing the window hung precariously from a loosely secured pole. With one tug, they could come crashing down. Between the beds hung a wooden crucifix and on the other side of the room was a large painting of a saint holding a small child in his arms set in a heavily embossed, dark wooden frame. Thalia stepped closer to read the inscription and learned the image was of St Anthony of Padua. Quite fitting she thought to herself as she remembered from her lessons that he was the patron saint of lost things which was precisely how she was feeling. Between the beds on a table sat a lamp with a shabby shade and two copies of the Bible. As for furniture, storage was minimal with one wooden chair and a single wardrobe they'd have to share. Thalia jolted in surprise when Terpie dropped her case making a loud clonk on the tiled floor, her disdain for the accommodation was blatantly clear by her upturned nose and the snippy way she ran her finger along the bedstead checking for dust. Although she would never admit it, Terpie had a penchant for the finer things so it would be interesting to see how her sister adapted to such basic surroundings. Thalia smirked at the thought of her discomfort.

'I can't sleep under the window,' snapped Terpie, crossing her arms tightly against her chest. Thalia didn't see the point in arguing and in the big scheme of things, which bed she had was the least of her concerns.

'So, this is home,' Thalia said, slumping onto the firm bed and the springs squeaked in protest beneath her weight. The frame and the headboard weren't securely attached and with any movement, the loose headboard slammed against the wall. No doubt that would become annoying during the night but luckily, she was not a restless sleeper. Terpie sat on her bed across from her and they sat in silence.

'I'm worried about Pappa. At least we have each other,' said Thalia.

'He'll be fine. He has Aunt Emily, she'll look after him, you know she will,' Terpie replied confidently.

'What if her apartment was bombed? He'll have nowhere to go.'

'Pappa's an intelligent man. He'll find somewhere and he could always go back to Shi Min and Lim if he had to. You worry too much.'

'Did you see his face as he left us? I've never seen him like that before, so downhearted,' Thalia asked, but Terpie shrugged in response and repeated that he would be fine, which annoyed her even more. Thalia knew being away from their mother would be tearing him apart. He adored her.

'Do you think the ships have left the docks yet? I hope they made it out safely. We don't know the name of the ship they got on, so how will we track them?' Thalia's mind whirred with questions.

'I know you're worried. We have to accept we won't know they're safe until we receive a letter from Mamma to say they've arrived which could be weeks away,' Terpie said, unpacking her case.

'And what if we don't hear from them…' Thalia's voice was a whisper.

'Thalia, I don't know all right! We mustn't think like that. There's every chance that they're well on their way,' Terpie replied sharply.

'I don't know how he'll cope without Mamma around. He dotes on her.'

'Are you trying to make me feel guilty?' Terpie asked angrily.

'No! I was saying, that's all. Why do you? You don't seem upset or bothered about them,' Thalia challenged.

'Of course, I'm bothered. I don't see the point in going around in circles asking questions we won't know the answers to. It's been a long emotional day and I need some rest.'

Thalia hadn't intended to rile her but clearly, she had struck a nerve, —and perhaps Terpie did feel some responsibility for their current situation. Her stubbornness would never allow her to admit it though. Of all her sisters she had the least in common with Terpie and already doubted how they would fair with only each other for company. They shared a room at home purely because Terpie refused the alternative which was to have Thetie's room that was more like a cupboard. Not because they got along.

Thalia opened her case and placed her copy of *Gone with the Wind* on the table, the narrative of the story was now becoming a little too close to home with war and lost loves, but she was determined to finish it. Tucked in the corner of her case she found the little package given to her by Shi Min. She unwrapped it carefully to reveal five coins linked together with a red ribbon inscribed with Hanzi lettering—a Chinese good luck charm. Shi Min was a significant person in her life and would be missed as much as her blood relatives. With the charm in both hands, she kissed them for extra luck and hung them on the bedpost.

Looking around at the scant furniture, she decided *not* to unpack her things; in her mind, she wouldn't be staying here long enough and already couldn't wait to leave. Confident her pappa would find a solution to their problem she kicked her case under the bed. With nothing better to do, she removed her sandals and lay on the bed to read her book. Terpie fussed around, hung up her clothes and commandeered the only chair in the room as her own, but Thalia couldn't care less. Time passed, and Thalia was restless, she'd tried to concentrate on reading, but the words floated around the page, and she'd read the same paragraph twice and not retained a word of it. Dropping the book by her side, she listened to the foreign-sounding noises in the street outside. The modest room was stifling, the only source of fresh air came via a small and ineffectual window.

Thalia stood on the bed and tried to open the window further, but it was as wide as it would go. She glanced at Terpie sitting on her bed writing, the nib of her fountain pen scratching on the paper. Another letter to Benny no doubt. Lying on her back Thalia gazed at the ceiling. Thalia was bored. Terpie's nettlesome scribbling began to irritate her. Terpie was so infatuated with Benny, it was like nothing or no one else mattered and her constant writing irked with every stroke of the pen. Unable to sit still any longer and craving some time to be alone, she propelled herself off the bed.

'I'm going for a walk,' Thalia announced. Terpie's eyes remained fixed on the paper and replied half-heartedly.

Stepping out into the dingy corridor Thalia instantly felt cooler, she swept her fingertips along the stone walls and headed to the courtyard. Stepping out into the bright afternoon sun she squinted until her eyes adjusted to the brightness and regretted not bringing her hat. Other than two sisters strolling by on the opposite side, she had the garden to herself. The stones crunched underfoot, and the sweeping path steered her through neat flower borders and around the fountain until she reached the inviting wooden bench. She was surprised to find at the rear of the garden a raised bed of fragrant herbs and neat horizontal rows of leafy green vegetables. She sat under the shade of a tree and the tranquil space felt as good as she imagined it would. The late afternoon sun cast dappled shadows on the cobbles and secluded in this sanctuary she almost forgot the chaotic world outside except for the acrid fumes wafting on the breeze.

All the awful events of the day raced around in her mind, including worries for her family, the loss of her home and leaving her pappa all alone and she tried to process how she felt. Empty and melancholy. No amount of replaying events or wishing circumstances were different could change the point she was at now. She could only influence the future which looked bleak, scary, and out of her control.

Relaxing back on the seat she closed her eyes listening to the gurgle of the fountain and her thoughts drifted to Charlie. It had been almost a year since she last heard his voice, and she imagined what conversation they would have if he were here now. She desperately tried to conjure the image of his face, but it was impossible. He was slipping away from her. *Why is my mind doing this to me? My memories are all I have left!*

Recalling the conversation with her father, she realised it was probably time to let Charlie go. She was in love with a ghost. Too much time had passed. A tear trickled down her cheek and she wept for the loss of her first real love, mourned the future that wouldn't be theirs and for the unfairness of it all. Once the floodgates were open, she laid her head on her elbow on the arm of the bench and cried for all the losses and loved ones she cared about. Absorbed in her misery, she hadn't been aware of the presence on the bench next to her.

'Sorry, my dear, I didn't mean to startle you,' said a voice.

Raising her head sharply, she saw an elderly lady in a white flowing dress with a friendly smile and her charcoal hair tied in a bun. The lady perched on the other end of the bench, and Thalia hastily wiped her face brushing the tears away.

'I didn't hear you, that's all. I was saying goodbye to someone.'

The woman nodded and the look of empathy on her face told Thalia she understood. 'Where are you from? Do you live in the city?' Thalia asked.

'No child, my family and I fled from Malaya in December. Such brutality, we had no choice.'

'Soldiers?'

'Yes, I've never seen anything like it—looting, mindless killing and taking whatever woman they fancied for themselves. Trust me, they're animals. We hid in the forest for three days and made our way here as we have nowhere else to go. They burnt our house down.'

'I'm so sorry. That must've been terrifying for you. Are your family with you?' Thalia was horrified. This stark description of the enemy was very different from the generalisations spread around that the Japanese were an inferior army and posed no real threat. Hearing this from someone with personal experience frightened her and bought home the gravity of their plight and what was to come.

'Yes, my daughter-in-law and my six-year-old grandson are here with me. My son went to the refuge in the church around the corner. I thought we wouldn't make it, but a farmer also trying to escape picked us up in his truck and brought us here.'

'You must have been so scared.' Thalia noticed the slight tremor in the old lady's hand.

'I've never felt so terrified in my life. They're not good men,' said the woman and her eyes began to water.

'I don't understand why they're attacking innocent families and homes. I don't know much about war, but it doesn't seem right. Where are our soldiers? Why aren't they defending us?'

'Oh they are my dear, but the Japs are too strong and clever. Anyway, what's your story?'

'My sister and I got here today because our house got bombed, our mother and three sisters have evacuated, and our father is taking refuge with a friend. We too have been lucky so far.' The woman studied her face with a frown.

'Why aren't you all together?'

'That's a good point and a long story,' Thalia replied.

'Well, I've nothing to do and I like a good story,' said the woman, settling back on the bench.

Chapter Twelve
Anthoula

After a bumpy start, the SS Kuala had been at sail for several hours, gliding east through the waters of the Riau Archipelago in the South China sea. The shock and anguish of the evacuation were far behind them, and with each mile, they travelled away from the island the atmosphere eased, and passengers began to relax. Despite her injured leg and swollen wrist, Anthoula rested a little, her tension and fear had subsided, and she was relieved to have overcome her nausea. She felt surprisingly hopeful for the first time since leaving the docks; who knew she could enjoy being at sea? Her husband would be proud if he could see her now. *Don't think about Zac, don't think about Zac.* She pinched the skin on the back of her hand. It was still too painful for her to think of him. Consumed with worry for his safety, she refused to let her mind wander into that territory. To pass the time, she read a little, chatted with her daughters and dozed with her head resting on Ino's shoulder. After endless hours of travel, there was nothing to do so she observed with interest the peculiar behaviour of her fellow passengers crowded on top of each other in such a confined space. Her attention was drawn to a fractious man standing with his chest puffed out and his hands resting on his hips just a few yards away. It was difficult not to notice him with his loud booming voice continually barking orders at his children to sit still and behave. Anthoula felt sympathy for his meek wife, clearly flustered as she pleaded with the wayward youngsters to comply. On the other side to her left, a young mother bounced her distressed baby on her hip, and her desperate coos to stop her child from wailing were to no avail.

All of a sudden and startling her already fragile nerves, three children, old enough to know better zoomed past, jumping over cases, legs and any other obstacle in their path. There wasn't enough room on the deck for their boundless energy. Feeling protective of her injured leg stuck out in front of her, she observed them with a steely glare. The children ran back giggling loudly and leaping over bodies like hurdles and she shouted a warning, wagging a stern finger at them.

'Hey, you three, stop running and jumping around. There's no room for silly games, and you'll hurt someone in a minute. Do your parents know where you are?' Anthoula growled in a voice she hardly recognised. The children stopped in their tracks, stared at her blankly and walked sensibly along the deck back to their parents, she presumed. She sighed, sat back again, and wondered when she became such a cranky old lady.

'Can you hear singing?' Thetie asked. 'Listen.'

The family stopped what they were doing and listened to a chorus of voices floating through the evening air. Anthoula strained to hear, but couldn't make out the tune above the chatter around them. Gradually the volume increased as more people joined in. Clio and Thetie began to sing along—the soothing ripple of voices spread along the deck. Anthoula couldn't participate because the song was unfamiliar, so instead, she swayed side to side as the melody washed over her. The atmosphere was magical, and she became lost in the moment. Even the babies stopped crying. When the song ended a tremendous cheer erupted, and passengers clapped. Anthoula was amazed by the spirit of human beings and their ability to find joy in the worst of circumstances.

Another song began, a more up-tempo number this time. Again, she didn't recognise it, but her daughters did. Anthoula savoured watching her girls sing and laugh together, reminding her of better times at home around the piano. A lump formed in her throat for her absent family members, and she averted her gaze before the power of emotion overwhelmed her. She'd cried more in the last two days than in the previous two years. The future was too difficult to think about because she couldn't picture a time or place when they'd all be together again. To distract herself, she watched the young children dancing on the deck holding hands. The singing continued for almost an hour until they either ran out of ideas or verve and the deck fell silent again. The spell of reprieve broken, and the dark cloud of despair nudged its way back in.

'That was fun, but now I'm hungry. Can we eat please?' Clio asked, standing over her mother with hands on her hips like a petulant child. Crouching down beside her mother, Thetie beckoned her sisters to gather around.

'These people are hungry too. I say we share our food with them. What do you think?' she looked around to gauge their response.

'I don't mind. It's a good idea. I'd feel bad eating in front of them without sharing,' Ino said.

'Fine with me. I've lost my appetite anyway. What a kind soul you are,' said Anthoula, brushing Thetie's cheek with the back of her hand, relishing the softness of her youthful skin.

'Umm, shouldn't we save our food for ourselves? We don't know how long it'll be until we get another meal. If we share it, we'll be hungry, won't we?' Clio questioned and all eyes turned to her as she bit her lip.

'Clio, I never raised you to be selfish.' Astonished by her daughter's uncharitable attitude, through gritted teeth (she didn't want to entertain the other passengers with their family disagreement). 'What would your father say? No, don't answer that. I'm glad he's not here to hear it. Give my portion away, and you girls do what your conscience tells you to do.' She glared at Clio in disgust, hoping she had made the right choice.

'I was just being practical. It could be days before we get somewhere with food, and I hate being hungry,' replied Clio.

'I'm sure these families are just as hungry. Let's think of the greater good, shall we? We have plenty to go around,' Thetie said calmly.

'Ok, ok. I'll share mine but don't forget this conversation when you're starving,' replied Clio, as Thetie divided the food into equal portions. Ino offered a package to a mother with her daughter about two years old curled up on her lap, sucking her thumb for comfort wrapped in a tired-looking but cherished pink blanket. The girl's dark brown eyes widened as Ino approached. The mother graciously accepted the gift, broke off titbits, and handed them to her daughter one at a time. Thetie approached the two young blonde boys who had become irritable and rowdy; their mother was at her wit's end. Thetie squatted down beside them.

'Hello. We have food our Amah made for the journey, and would like to share it with you. Would you like some?' She smiled at the family and held out a cardboard package.

'I'm starving!' the older of the two boys yelled, snatching the box from her hand.

'Edward! That isn't nice. Apologise at once.' The mother flushed red with embarrassment. 'I'm so sorry; he's not usually bad-mannered. Thank you so much. You're a lifesaver. I didn't have time to pack anything in our hurry to leave.'

'We're all feeling the pressure. It's understandable. Are you travelling alone?'

'Yes. My husband's still on the island. They wouldn't let him leave as he works for the government. I can't thank you enough for this.'

'No problem at all. It must be so hard for the little ones.' Thetie watched the boys devour the bread, cold chicken and fruit with fervour; it was gone within minutes. Their mother relaxed her shoulders, and the boys were already climbing on the railings.

'It must be hard leaving by yourself. If you need help, just ask.'

'That's so kind, thank you,' said the mother, lowering her voice. 'I'm terrified and exhausted. These two are a handful, as you can see. Boys, get down from there!'

'How about I read them a story?' Thetie suggested pointing to a book poking out from the mother's bag. 'It'll give you a break for a little while.'

'Are you sure? That would be wonderful. Boys, this lady is going to read to you. Come and sit here.' The mother patted the deck, and the boys obediently sat cross-legged in front of Thetie, she read the *Jungle Book,* and they became transfixed. Clio stood up and brushed the crumbs from her linen dress.

'I'm going for a walk around to see if there's anyone on-board I know.'

Before anyone could answer, she vanished. After hours of sitting around, torpidity set in with nothing to look at but the sea view or stranger's faces and Anthoula had no desire to contribute to conversations with these people. She wouldn't see them again once the journey was over and didn't see the point in befriending them. Many families on-board she recognised from the upper classes of colonial society, the hoity-toity women she had no interest in getting to know. Their raucous laughter and booming voices grated on her fragile nerves. Anthoula was dozing, resting her eyes and listening to Thetie read when she was disturbed by Clio giggling and another voice. Opening her eyes she found Clio standing in front of her, arm in arm with her friend. The other girl was Angela Steading. She lived in the next street with her parents Hugo and Maria who were an innocuous couple, but Anthoula kept them at arms-length all the same as she did with most people.

'Look Mamma, I found the Steadings on the lower deck.'

'Hello, Angela. Are your parents well?'

Anthoula didn't wish to appear impolite but wasn't in the mood for meaningless conversation. Ino glanced up from the pages of her book and continued reading.

'Yes, thank you, Mrs P. They're holding up under the cramped conditions. Isn't it exciting? I can't wait to see where we end up.' Angela giggled.

'Exciting is not a word I'd use for it, Angela,' said Anthoula flatly.

'Anyway, I came back to tell you I'm going to sit with Angela's family for a while,' Clio announced.

As Anthoula watched them bouncing through the crowd she felt relief they were going, quickly followed by a pang of guilt for feeling that way. Remarkably she could tolerate the sound of crying children, but the girl's excitable and squeaky, high-pitched voices and giggling irritated her ears, and she wanted to do nothing but rest. The light began fading and nightfall was sneaking around the corner. With little room and an unforgiving wooden deck, Anthoula did her best to find a comfortable position to get some sleep.

By morning, the SS Kuala cut the engines and the captain gave orders to anchor down in the waters they were told was Pom Pong Island. Anthoula had no idea where that was in relation to Singapore, and never heard of it before. The morning air was chilly, and Anthoula pulled her cardigan tighter around her; she had been awake for hours already. Despite the early hour, the boat was already a carnival of noise with children and babies crying. She called out to Ino and Thetie deep in conversation next to her.

'Girls, help me to stand, would you? My legs are so stiff, and I can't move. I thought it might help if I moved around a bit.'

Willingly the girls obliged and helped steady their mother to her feet. Anthoula ached all over; she winced in pain as she put weight on her injured leg. Once standing, she leaned on the railings for support, it felt so good to be upright for the change of scenery alone, and she stretched. Each vertebra felt out of line, and she cricked her neck. The ship had anchored about three hundred yards away from the lush jungle island, and Anthoula was relieved to be close to solid ground. Listening to the sound of birdsong reminded her of home. Close to the green haven with golden sands, she saw another ship anchored by the coastline. Straining her eyes to read the name of it, an arm slipped around her shoulders, and Ino embraced her warmly.

'How are you doing, Mamma? Did you have a rough night?'

'It wasn't the best night's sleep I've had, but I did sleep at least. Did Clio come back?' she asked, looking around for her other daughter.

'No, we've not seen her. She must've stayed down with the Steadings.'

Anthoula raised her eyebrow.

'She's a live wire that one.'

'What do you think they're doing?' said Ino, pointing to the crew lowering the lifeboats. 'Do you think they will get us all off the boat? It will take ages.'

'Let's watch them and find out what they are up to. It's not like we've anything else to do, is it.' Anthoula stared across the waves, watching the lifeboats with interest. With nothing better to occupy her time, her thoughts drifted back to her family, wondering where they were and what were they doing. With the ship gently swaying beneath her, it was easy to imagine Zacharia by her side, sipping cocktails on the final stretch of their journey to Italy. Yes, one day when this nightmare was over. For now, though, it would remain a distant daydream.

After a few hours of observation, it became apparent what the lifeboats were for. The Kuala and the nearby ship had deployed men to row to the island to collect tree branches and foliage to camouflage the two vessels. Anthoula stayed on her feet, walking up and down the deck as far as possible without disturbing people, improving her mobility and easing the boredom. Returning to the spot where her daughters were sitting, she became aware of a commotion brewing on the other side of the ship. Passengers began screaming, and she grabbed the railings. Anthoula listened. Planes.

'What's going on?' Ino asked.

'I'll go around the deck to see. I'll be right back,' announced Thetie, jumping up.

'No! Come back, Thetie,' Anthoula shouted after her, but it was too late. She watched her daughter's head of black curls weave through the crowd and disappear. Inside her chest, her heart grew heavy with a familiar sense of unease. The sound of planes couldn't be a good thing. The chances they were friendly were slim. She had no idea where Clio was, and now Thetie had left her side. They were supposed to stay together, for goodness sake. Why didn't her daughters listen to her and do as they're told?

Suddenly, an explosion rocked the ship, and it was a direct hit. Anthoula crashed against the railing, grabbing hold to keep herself upright. Another deafening explosion shook the floor. Panic pulsed through her whole body. The ship instantly became a maelstrom of emotional passengers launching themselves into the sea. Ino was by her side, shoving a life jacket into her chest.

'Put this on. The ships on fire! We have to get off. Look!' Ino pointed further down the deck, where the captain and another officer struggled to lower the gangplank. Behind them, a crazed group of passengers pushed and clawed each other to find an escape. Anthoula pulled the puffy white jacket over her head and fumbled with the ties; her fingers wouldn't cooperate, she couldn't concentrate, and the smell of burning only intensified her panic.

'Where's Clio and Thetie?' she cried, looking around but only saw the faces of terrified strangers. Ino grabbed her shoulders and shook her.

'Mamma, we have to save ourselves. They'll have jumped into the water. We need to do the same and get to the island.'

Anthoula looked into the sea, and all around her desperate passengers were throwing themselves overboard. Anthoula watched in fear as they floundered in the waves.

'Ok, but I'm not jumping. I'll go down the gangplank.'

Ino grabbed her hand and led her to the multitude of mothers and children preparing to jettison into the unforgiving waves below. In front of her, a brave mother entered the water with her children. She floated on her back, supporting her baby in one arm and a toddler in the other, keeping their heads above the waves. Anthoula thought, if she can do it, then so can I. Whilst waiting her turn, anxiety bubbled, she never liked the sea, and now, she must swim for her life. She quickly became next in the queue and briefly, looked back to Ino for reassurance.

'Do it, Mamma. You can do this.' Ino nodded, prompting her forward.

The captain took Anthoula's hand and guided her onto the gangplank, and she noticed he had sustained an injury of his own, blood seeping through his shirt on his torso. A voice behind her yelled out, 'Hurry please!'

She was holding people up and had to move. The gangplank wobbled beneath her. Feeding her hand along the railing, she tentatively reached the edge. She silently counted to three in her head and fearlessly plunged into the sea. The cold engulfed her and salty water splashed in her eyes and mouth, but the life jacket prevented her from going under. She spluttered and gasped for air. Kicking her legs wildly, she looked around trying to locate Ino, but she just spun around in circles. She believed Ino was right behind her, but she was nowhere to be seen. The life jacket puffed up around her ears and blocked her vision and despite tugging, it refused to budge.

Bodies flailed and thrashed in the water, some had found rafts to cling to, and lifeboats were rounding to rescue the drowning survivors. Looking back at the ship she saw it was now ablaze, a fiery orange burning beacon. The enemy in the sky was not done with them yet—the survivors who could swim headed towards the shore beneath machine gunfire targeted at them. Anthoula was paralysed, allowing the undulating waves to lift her up and down in their natural rhythm as she treads water. The planes above circled for another round of fire, and Anthoula swallowed hard. Her only option was to make a dash for it and swim as hard as she could.

She couldn't see Ino and was wasting time, she had to get to safety. The area ahead was pretty clear with few people in her path, but there was a rocky coastline ahead rather than sand. It was her shortest route, and although the jagged rocks looked daunting, she couldn't afford to spend too much time and energy in the water and would have to take her chances. The fabric of her skirt clung and wrapped around her legs, so before setting off, she hoicked it up around her waist, tucking the surplus into her underwear. Anthoula took a deep breath and swam. Within seconds, her legs and arms burnt in pain, and the seawater stung her eyes. The force of the waves propelled her forward, and all she could hear was muffled screams and gunfire, providing the impetus to swim harder and faster.

With her eyes closed, she swam for her life until a searing pain shot up her big toe and she screamed, somehow her shoes had come off and she had scraped her foot on a jagged piece of rock. Opening her eyes, she saw, looming tall, the boulders were getting closer as the waves carried her at speed towards them. She feared she would be crushed against them with the tide and braced herself for the impact. The waves slammed her into the rocks and she scrabbled to grab hold, her feet found solid ground. Her chest heaved as she gasped for air, but she'd made it. A glance upwards told her it was not safe to clamber over the rocks yet with the enemy circling above like a bird of prey waiting to pick off its next meal.

Clinging to the rock, she sidled her way around to take cover. Bobbing in the water with her chin just above the waterline, she allowed her forehead to rest against the cool slimy rock, and she waited. Wedging her fingers in the crevices of the stone she clung on and took a chance to look out to sea. The Kuala was gone; in no time at all, it had sunk beneath the waves, and the other ship was on fire. The sea was awash with makeshift rafts, lifeboats and swimmers making a mercy dash to the shore. One thought played on a loop in her mind. *My girls, please, God, let my girls be safe.*

Chapter Thirteen
Benny

Benny lay on the ground daydreaming, his arms folded behind his head, as he watched the wisps of cloud drifting across the cerulean ceiling above. Since being woken by the first splinter of dawn, he watched the sky morph from indigo, burnt amber to pink through powder blue. He suffered another restless night with little sleep on the unforgiving ground, unable to get comfortable with a head laden with worry. In the peaceful blush of daybreak, an idea swam into focus and had gnawed at him ever since. It was crazy and reckless, he knew, but now it had taken hold; he had to act on it.

After days of running scared, awaiting enemy attack and seeing horrors no one should ever see, he was compelled to follow through on his plan. It had to be today. A mixture of excitement and fear buzzed through his veins, and he rehearsed his plan repeatedly until he felt his brain would explode with the pressure of it. Over the last few days, the enemy had gained ground at an alarming rate, and against all odds, crossed the causeway from Malaya onto the mainland, forcing allied units to retreat.

Last night, his unit received a wire confirming that the Japanese were closing in at Tanglin Halt, about five miles from the city. The fact they'd breached the line of defence so quickly was staggering, given the British advantage of more men outnumbered them three times over. The mood amongst the military was mixed with despair and a foreboding sense of defeat spreading through the ranks, and others were resolute to keep fighting until the bitter end to defend this country. During the last twenty-four hours, some of his comrades conceded defeat and abandoned their posts. These were not cowardly men; they knew they were fighting a war that couldn't be won and weren't prepared to lose their lives in vain.

Benny rolled over onto his side and hauled himself up to a seated position with his knees drawn into his body, his arms wrapped around his legs. Jimmy lay beside him, and to stir him from his sleep, Benny nudged his shoulder. It had been a late night on patrol, so the rest of the men were still sleeping.

'Jimmy, wake up,' he whispered.

'What is it?' Jimmy said sleepily.

'Listen, I have to go. Cover for me. I don't care what you tell the commander.'

Jimmy rubbed his eyes. 'Go where? What's going on?'

'I'm looking for Terpie. I have to do it now, or I'll miss my chance,' he said with determination, and he couldn't care less about this blasted war anymore. Singapore was lost with or without him, and it was a priority to find her before it was too late. Besides, he was not a real soldier; what had he been thinking? He didn't owe his life to the cause.

'You're crazy. The Japs will be swarming the city any minute. You'll get caught or shot.'

'I don't care, I'd rather die trying to see her one more time, and to me, that's worth it.' Benny gathered his things and laced up his boots.

'I'm not letting you do this alone. I'll come to cover your back. Two sets of eyes are better than one.'

'No, I can't allow you to do that! It's too dangerous, and you have a family who needs you. This is my problem.'

'Polak, honestly, the way things are going, we'll wind up dead somehow, and I'd rather die helping a friend than waiting for the enemy to claim me. I'm coming with you. So tell me, what's the plan?' Jimmy sat up and put his boots on.

'You're a good friend. I was thinking of checking the refugees first. That's going to take some time. If she's not there, then make my way out of town to her house.'

'We'd better get a move on then.'

Benny watched his friend roll up his blanket and wondered if their paths would ever have crossed if it hadn't been for the war. Benny glanced around the camp and felt a slight stab of guilt for abandoning his unit, but his allegiance was not to them. Slinging their backpacks over their shoulders, the two friends crept away from their post on Serangoon Road and headed towards the nearest church. Benny planned their route to hit as many refuges as possible; he was fully aware of the monstrous task he had set himself as it would be like looking for a needle in a haystack and could take a week to cover them all. A week he didn't have. The Japs could be here within days, so they had much ground to cover. He didn't care; he'd keep searching until he found her. All he thought about was Terpie, day and night. He was driving himself crazy with worry, and the "what if" questions rolled around in his head, chipping away at his sanity a bit more each day. A pungent smell assaulted their senses, on reaching the city, making them wretch and gag. They crossed a bridge and Benny noted the grimy colour of the water and floating debris.

'What's that smell? It's revolting,' Jimmy asked.

Benny gagged, covering his mouth. He took a handkerchief from his pocket and tried to create a makeshift facemask. He fumbled with the square patch of material, too small to tie behind his head; instead, he held it over his mouth and nose to filter out the stench.

'It's from all the dead bodies, decaying out in the sun,' Benny replied. Beside him, Jimmy coughed as the fumes caught the back of his throat. He leaned over, the bridge and vomited into the water without warning.

'That's foul.' Jimmy took a swig from his flask, wiped his mouth on his arm, and continued walking. On every street, a familiar scene played out with families searching for food, wandering up and down or desperately calling out the names of missing loved ones whilst they could, before the arrival of Japanese soldiers. By midday, they'd made good progress. The friends found ten refuges so far by crisscrossing the city. On the approach to each one, the familiar bubble of anxiety rose for what Benny might find. Each time the scenario played out the same, he hesitated before knocking on the door with sweaty hands, his stomach tied in knots, and he became paralysed by fear as he waited whilst they looked for Terpie's name on their list.

On each occasion, he walked away deflated but determined to continue his search. Naturally, it crossed his mind that he may never find her, and there was also the chance she could be injured, or worse. Forcefully he pushed the dark thoughts out of his mind; he mustn't give up hope. After walking miles through the broken city, Jimmy requested a rest, and although Benny was keen to keep going, he couldn't deny his friend a break. They stopped close to the Fullerton Building on the quayside, and Jimmy hoicked himself up to sit on the wall overlooking the river. Benny slid his cumbersome backpack to the ground, stretched out his arms and twisted his head to ease the tight knot in his neck. If only he could do the same for his stomach. He'd not eaten since last night and although food was the last thing on his mind, he took out his haversack rations and ripped open a tin of bully beef.

Joining his friend on the wall, he chewed on the tough snack and looked around; a memory stabbed like a knife, just around the corner was where he gave Terpie the news that he had signed up, which felt like centuries ago. He should never have volunteered and would be with her now. Their last day on the beach would be forever imprinted in his memory. Terpie wore a lilac summer dress, and both agreed to enjoy their time, putting the impending separation to the back of their minds, and filling the day with laughter instead. They ate fresh mango and sipped white wine before dipping together in the crystal blue sea.

Today, it was grey and choppy waves curled into arches before crashing against the harbour wall. Smothering the sky a dark wall of threatening clouds gathered, and the stormy weather reflected his mood. On a typical day, this area would be bustling with small trading boats and sellers, but now it was an eerie ghost town. Empty vessels remained tethered to the walls, bobbing on the tide surrounded by floating crates and lost cargo. Benny held his head in his hands.

'I've been so stupid!' Benny said, hitting his forehead with the heel of his hand as if knocking sense into his brain. 'Why didn't I think of it before? I think I know where she would've gone. If you were hiding out, wouldn't you go somewhere familiar, somewhere that felt safe?' Benny asked, waving his arms around like an excited cartoon character.

'I guess. Where do you think she is?' Jimmy said, with a mouth full of biscuit.

'She used to go to school at the convent. I don't know why, I have a hunch she might be there,' he said, with a renewed sense of vigour and jumped down off the wall his legs liked coiled springs and began fumbling with the straps on his backpack. He was convinced that's where he'd find her. He paced up and down, mumbling to himself.

'You're sure you don't want to try her house? She could be tucked up safe and sound,' Jimmy suggested.

'I don't think she'll be there. Her father wouldn't have wanted them to be in the path of rampaging soldiers, and I've got a feeling he would've bought them into the city. He would protect them at all costs.' A shiver ran down his spine. Until now, it hadn't even been a consideration, but what if the family evacuated completely? All this searching would be futile, and suddenly his heart felt like a ton of weight in his chest. He may never find her. The excitement he had felt previously drained away like water down the drain. 'Or they could have evacuated.' He slumped against the wall. 'I hadn't thought of that option. Would they, though? I'm so confused! I don't know what to do. Terpie, where are you?' Benny shouted at the clouds in frustration.

'We could try down by the docks. If anyone's still there, they must have a list of passengers. At least it will rule it out, and you would know for sure,' Jimmy suggested.

'I don't know. This is insane. I'm sorry to drag you on this wild goose chase. The dock is miles away, but it would give us some answers as you say.'

'It's a few miles, but if we get a move on, we could be there in under an hour. Let's get going, come on.' Jimmy shovelled the last bite of food into his mouth, launched himself off the wall and slung his backpack over his shoulder. 'We will find her Polak.'

After walking at a pace with Jimmy wincing from the pain of his blisters, they made it to the docks around two o'clock. Benny felt exhausted, his body was running on pure adrenaline. The scene at the harbour was much like everywhere else they had seen. Fires still burnt, debris strewn across the streets and cars were abandoned in their path. The place was deserted.

'I hope someone's here after all this,' said Jimmy, as they walked under the archway. The two men approached the harbour office, the door was open, and the floor creaked as they stepped inside.

'Sorry, you've missed all the ships. There are no more evacuations,' said the harsh voice of a naval officer without looking up from his paperwork.

'We don't need a ship. I need to know if someone was on-board. Can you help me?' Benny asked.

'Name?' asked the man.

Benny waited whilst the officer scanned the clipboards in front of him with thousands of names. This wasn't going to be a quick solution. There must have been over thirty lists piled high on the desk. Benny felt his insides bubbling with frustration.

'Listen, we don't have much time. Can we help? It would be quicker.'

'Help yourself,' the officer said, gesturing to the pile of clipboards beside him. Benny grabbed a stack of clipboards and handed them to Jimmy and then took about ten himself and sat on the floor, furiously flipping over pages searching for the names he was desperate to find. The lists were not in alphabetical order and Benny scanned the scribbled handwriting and realised this would be a painstaking task. Selfishly, part of him hoped they wouldn't find anything because if she left, she was out of reach and he might never see her again. After an hour of searching in silence with only the sound of turning pages and the hum of a small fan blowing, Benny stretched and rotated his head; his neck was stiff and crunchy. He only had two more clipboards to check and was losing hope of finding anything, and this whole exercise had just wasted their time. Jimmy leapt up from his chair, waving a list over his head.

'I think I found them. Well maybe. Look.' Jimmy handed the clipboard to his friend. 'There's the name Pattara, but Terpie's isn't there.'

Benny stared at the list of names. Three of the family were missing, and deep dread spread through his veins. What happened to the others?

'I don't understand…why wouldn't they all evacuate together?' He dropped the clipboard and rubbed his forehead. 'Maybe they didn't survive and make it to the ship.' He looked at the two blank faces, and the naval officer shrugged, unable to offer any help.

'That's one option, but maybe they didn't leave at all?' Jimmy placed the pile of clipboards on the desk.

In a daze, Benny stood up, thanked the officer for his help, and stumbled out of the office. He needed some air. His legs trembled, and the blood drained from his face. Leaning on the wall outside, he felt bile rising in his throat, and scenarios flew around his mind like a swirling hurricane. This wasn't the news he hoped to find and only confused him more. Jimmy joined him outside and shook his shoulder.

'Stop thinking the worst. You know Terpie better than anyone. Would she have stayed behind? Think.'

Benny took a deep breath and looked to the sky. It could be possible she stayed behind. She was stubborn like that, and if that were the case her father would not leave her alone. Thinking through other possibilities lifted his spirits a little and kept the spark of hope alight.

'We still have time. Why don't we try the convent as you said? This isn't over yet,' said Jimmy.

Benny dragged himself off the wall, and they walked in silence. Their roles had reversed and now Jimmy was encouraging him to pick up the pace; Benny felt his despair heavy in his legs and had lost his passion for the search, fearing it would only lead him to heartbreak. Jimmy reminded him to stay positive and his enthusiasm for the search returned. In less than an hour, they had reached the quayside overshadowed by the government buildings—every step he took set off a firecracker of hope in his belly. Striding along St Andrews Road, Benny restrained himself from breaking into a run. Standing tall before him, he saw the cathedral's spire ahead, so the convent was just around the corner. Walking past a shop window, he caught sight of his reflection and did a double take; he didn't recognise the grubby vagabond he had become. He approached the glass, rubbed the rough stubble on his chin, and ran his hand through his matted hair. His skin was filthy and bloody, and he smelled of death. Feebly he wiped the streaks of dirt from his face.

'Come on, pretty boy, she won't care what you look like.' Jimmy laughed.

They rounded the corner, and the high white walls of the convent were straight ahead. The friends stood side by side facing the archway, and Benny took a deep breath to steady his racing heartbeat. His palms were sweaty, and he was almost too afraid to ring the bell.

'You can do this. If she's not here, we'll keep searching.' Jimmy gave Benny a supportive pat on the shoulder. 'Go on, ring the bell.'

Jimmy stayed back and leaned against the wall out of sight. With a shaky hand, Benny pulled on the rope. His legs wobbled, and his heart banged like a drum. After a short wait, a nun appeared behind the bars. He registered the flicker of concern that crossed her face as she scanned him up and down.

'Hello. How can I help you?' she asked, looking between the bars and keeping the key to the lock firmly in her pocket. The words Benny had been asking all morning were wedged in his throat, rendering him speechless. He cleared his throat and tried again.

'I'm looking for members of the Pattara family. I wondered if they were here. They have dark hair, they're sisters and their father too?' The nun didn't answer immediately, eyeing him with curiosity. 'One of the daughters is my fiancée and I need to find her before the Japs come,' said Benny in desperation and he saw the nun's features soften.

'We've two family members staying with us. Wait here.'

Before he'd a chance to find out more, she scuttled away. Relief spread through his body like wildfire.

'Jimmy, they're here! We've found them!' he yelled to his friend wiping the wetness from his eyes.

'Oh thank heavens for that. See, you were right.'

Waiting for what seemed like forever Benny kicked at the ground with the toe of his boot and brushed his fingers through his unruly hair. For some reason, he felt nervous with dancing butterflies in his stomach. He remembered the nun said *two* of the family were here and his previous elation started to evaporate. Pacing in circles he heard footsteps and approached the iron bars. The nun unlocked the gate and beside her stood Terpie, looking radiant. The monster who had been hitching a ride on his shoulder for weeks dissolved, and he felt giddy with happiness. The gate opened and before he could say a word, Terpie launched herself into his arms. He held her tight; she smelled so fresh and sweet and thought he may crush her in his embrace.

'I can't believe I found you!' Benny frantically kissed her hair, her face and her nose.

'I thought I was never going to see you again! How did you find me?' Terpie asked as Benny cradled her face in his hands.

'I've been so worried. I was terrified you'd been injured. I've been going mad. We've been searching across the city looking for you. We went to the docks but then I had a hunch you might come here.'

'You went to the docks?'

'I thought you might have evacuated but when your name wasn't there, at first I thought you were dead. Then I had a feeling you'd come here. What happened?'

'The plan was for us all to leave, but I refused. I was never going to leave you here alone. It caused a bit of a family argument as Pappa wouldn't let me stay by myself and Thalia changed her mind at the last minute. Our house is gone.'

'You stayed for me? Oh no, your house, I'm so sorry.'

'Of course, I stayed. I wouldn't leave you,' Terpie said, slipping her hands behind his neck and kissing him. When they parted, she asked how he was.

'I'm fine, well I'm now. Come and meet my good friend Jimmy. He helped me track you down and I couldn't have done it without him,' he said, taking her by the hand.

Jimmy wiped his filthy hands on his shorts. 'It's a pleasure to meet you at last, not sure my blisters could have taken much more traipsing around,' he laughed.

'Thank you for helping him. I'm so grateful,' said Terpie.

'He might cheer up now.' Jimmy thumped his friend on the arm. 'Anyway, I don't want to get in your way, you have things to catch up on.' Jimmy stepped back. 'I'll wait by the Municipal Building, on the steps. I'll meet you there. Bye Terpie, look after yourself.' He sauntered off with a backward wave.

'Jimmy seems nice, he didn't have to go.'

'He's one of the best. He kept me going. I think he's struggling a bit, missing his wife and daughter. Seeing us together probably made that harder for him. We don't have long. Let's take a walk.' Benny felt a cool drip on his arm, followed by another on his face, then his head. Typical. Rain.

'Come with me.' Benny grabbed her hand and they ran around the corner, giggling taking shelter under the stone parvis of the cathedral. Benny savoured the feel of her dainty hand in his and the warmth of their entwined fingers. He couldn't believe that after all this time, she was here, by his side and couldn't take his eyes off her. With a clap of thunder, the clouds unleashed a mighty storm and huge raindrops bounced off the ground with ferocity.

'I imagine I look worse for wear since I last saw you,' he smirked, ruffling his hair.

'You're still my Benny under all that dirt. I don't care. I'm just relieved to see you. I've been worried sick. I thought the bombs were never going to stop.' Terpie stroked his face.

'I was scared you'd left the island and I might never find you. But your family, they're all ok?'

'Pappa couldn't stay here so he's with Emily. Thalia's with me and the rest you know. I don't suppose you remember the name of the ship my family left on, do you? Thalia's been stressing about it.'

'No. Sorry, I didn't take any notice of that. I was more concerned that your name was missing.'

'That's ok. I just wondered that's all. Aren't you going to be in trouble for looking for me?'

'Jimmy and I deserted our unit. I'm not a soldier Terpie and to be honest, I'm scared out of my wits. I won't be going back.'

'Where will you go?'

'I don't know yet but don't worry, we'll keep our heads down. I'm just relieved you're safe.'

He didn't want to leave Terpie, but remembered the clock was ticking. Terpie's safety was compromised the longer they stood there. Behind the sound of gushing rain, he swore he heard gunfire, bringing him back to his senses with a jolt.

'Listen, I have to go, and you must get back. Now that I know where you are, I'll come to see you again although things might get trickier. The Japanese are just outside the city.' He gripped her shoulders and looked deep into her eyes. 'Don't come looking for me, stay in the convent, do you understand?'

'Do you have to go? We haven't had much time,' Terpie replied, her eyes glistening.

'I was never going to be able to stay. The streets will be dangerous soon and as long as I know you're in the convent, I'll know you're safe.'

'I won't look for you I promise,' she answered in a whisper.

'Listen. Do you hear that?' he asked, pointing into the street. Barely audible through the rain, they heard gunfire in the distance. She nodded. 'I need to get you back. The Japs are coming.'

They ran down the cathedral steps and into the street. The rain saturated Benny's shirt within minutes. Terpie's hair had flattened around her face and her summer dress was soaked through. Outside the convent gates, he rang the bell. Standing face to face, water droplets dripped off their noses, and they laughed. Whilst they waited Terpie wiped smudges of dirt off Benny's face with her thumb.

'Don't leave it too long. Come back soon and be careful,' said Terpie.

Benny didn't see the gates open but heard the squeal of metal on metal. Terpie reluctantly stepped away from him.

'Wait!' she turned back with her hands behind her neck and removed her gold locket which contained a photograph of them and placed it in his hands 'Take this.'

Quickly he returned the gesture and removed his small silver crucifix. His wet fingers fumbled with the clasp slippery in the rain. He placed it around her neck and kissed her once more before she returned to the safe enclosure. Once safely locked inside she waved and blew him a kiss and then she was gone. He walked away not caring that he was soaked through, he felt nothing but bliss. As promised, Jimmy sat on the top steps sheltering from the downpour. Benny bounded the steps with celerity feeling the anxiety he had been carrying for months had lifted. He shook the rain from his hair like a shaggy dog and combed it back with his fingers before sitting beside his friend.

'I feel amazing now,' said Benny, with a soppy grin. Jimmy stared into space looking serious.

'Jimmy? Are you ok?' Benny felt that rope in his stomach knotting up again.

'Some soldiers came through here whilst you were gone. They told me some terrible news. We can't stay here. The Japs pushed back our troops at Pasir Panjang. The Indian soldiers were overwhelmed and were forced back and took cover at the Military Red Cross Hospital.'

'The Alexandra?' Benny asked.

'Yes. According to this Sergeant, the Japs stormed the building. When they entered, the medical army captain approached them with a white flag. They shot him at point-blank range, went on a rampage and massacred the patients, doctors and nurses. He said the hospital was overcrowded with over nine hundred patients, they couldn't say how many survived, but I suspect many did not.' Jimmy rubbed his hand back and forth over his mouth. 'What kind of army does that, Benny?'

'One who wants to win this war at all costs. We need to get out of here.'

Chapter Fourteen
Anthoula

Anthoula had no idea how long she'd been marooned clinging to the rocks, and her only gauge was the sun's position in the sky and the rumbling in her empty stomach. She regretted not eating when she had the opportunity, but hunger was way down on her list of concerns. Squinting against the glaring rays, she guessed it must be early afternoon and if so, a good two hours had passed since she reached the shore. To keep her head above the lapping waves, she wedged her feet into crevices to prevent her slipping and her slight frame from being pummelled against the rocks.

When planes attacked the survivors, aiming their guns at the shore, rock splinters exploded, flinging shards and fragments in all directions. Cowering under the protection of the boulders was her only option which had been enough to shield her. Tragically, the poor souls stranded on rafts between the ship and shore had nowhere to hide from the deluge of bullets and owed their survival down to luck. During the onslaught, she tentatively peered around the rocks, watching bullets scoot across the water. Amid the gunfire were the desperate cries of women and children, arms flailing, trying to stay afloat.

Anthoula had closed her eyes tight and wished she could turn the volume down on the harrowing screams. Gradually, the cries for help dwindled until only an unnerving silence remained. There was no one to save them. Sweltering heat and exhaustion made her sleepy. To stay awake, she imagined travelling with Zac all over Europe and to Volos to see the family they hadn't seen for years. Moving her fingers one by one, bent in a clawed position for so long, her digits were stuck rigidly. Her exposed skin sizzled like meat on a griddle under the extreme sun. She feared it would be impossible to muster the energy to save herself if she stayed here much longer.

With the skies clear of fighter planes, she decided now was the time to move. Slowly cranking each of her limbs like a robot seized from rust, she looked across the rocks for the shortest route to shore. She faced the prospect of climbing over jagged rocks in whichever direction she headed, and doubted she had the strength at her age and fear kept her pinned to the rock. Tears welled in her eyes, and she felt overwhelmed by the obstacles ahead. What was her alternative? She would rot here if she didn't move as no one would come to her rescue. She had no choice. The thought of her daughters who would surely be looking for her on the island was enough to fuel her into action. She wasn't going to wither and die on these rocks. Zac needed her to be strong. There was no rush, and she could take her time, whilst there were no planes in the sky, she was safe and if she procrastinated any longer, there was a chance they could return.

Taking it slowly, she edged along the ledge, using cracks and fissures in the rock to grab hold. Slowly she clambered up the first peak, her feet slipped on the slimy rock, losing her purchase and she slid back into the water. Spluttering for air she gripped the rock, groaning as she hauled herself back up. Taking her time, she heaved herself over each bolder; her breaths were short and desperate, and her muscles protested, but she kept going. The golden sands of the shoreline shimmered, a welcoming beacon guiding her on. Steadily she hauled herself over the last boulder and unable to propel herself any further, collapsed face down on the beach. The warmth and soft spongey sand against her skin felt like a pillow of the finest silk, and she felt herself sinking and an overwhelming desire to sleep. Her eyes closed, and everything turned black. After a brief time, she heard voices above her. Dazed and confused, she felt hands on her body, rolling her over onto her back. The dazzling sun shone on her face but her eyes remained firmly closed. A firm hand slapped her cheek, and her eyes pinged open.

'Hello. My name is Diane. You're ok. We need to get you out of the sun. Do you think you can stand?' said the lady with a thick Australian accent kneeling beside her with hair flopping forward. Anthoula shielded her eyes from the blinding sun and croaked "yes". The woman smelled of cocoa butter, and Anthoula felt a hand support her head, and someone on the other side pulled on her arms until she was standing. Her legs were as shaky as a new-born foal, and she leaned on the arms of her two rescuers. With embarrassment, she realised her skirt was still tucked up, and her underwear was on show. She blushed and quickly tried to untuck the tangled mess, but she couldn't work it free. The material had dried and set solid, and her fingers were so stiff they wouldn't cooperate. She was disorientated and let out a groan of frustration.

'Don't worry about that. No one cares. We're glad you're alive,' Diane said, smiling.

To her left, a young man in shorts and a ripped shirt supported her by the elbow. His floppy blonde fringe fell across his face and all she thought was that he needed a haircut.

'Can you walk a little? We can take it slowly,' Diane said.

Anthoula coughed and wiped the dried sand from her lips. Her throat was sore, and she was desperately thirsty. She shuffled her feet along.

'That's it. Take your time. Lean on us,' Diane encouraged.

'You did well to survive on the rocks for so long. What's your name?' asked floppy fringe and she answered weakly.

'Let's get you out of the sun, Anthoula,' said Diane, and the rescuers guided her to the shelter of the forest. Each step felt clumsy, and it took all her effort to concentrate on putting one foot in front of the other.

'Was anyone on the ship with you?' Diane asked.

Anthoula focussed on Diane's young face with a spattering of freckles across her nose, spreading to her rosy cheeks. Bright auburn hair framed her attractive heart shape face.

'Yes! My three daughters,' Anthoula croaked.

'Well let's get you settled, and we'll see about finding them for you. Are you injured at all?'

Anthoula took time to consider the question as every part of her body throbbed, and she was confused.

'My toe, I caught it on the rocks, I think. My legs, my wrist. I don't know.'

'Just a little further, we're almost there. I'm a nurse. I'll take a look,' said Diane.

The razor-sharp stones, shells and sticks were uncomfortable beneath her bare feet, and she winced with every step. As they entered the shade, Anthoula instantly felt the relief of cooler air on her burnt skin. Gradually her eyes adjusted to the light change, and she saw movement through the bushes. People were drifting in and out of the trees ahead. The strained moans and cries from the wounded and bereaved became clearer.

'It's not far now. We've tried to gather all the survivors together. What are your daughter's names?'

'Ino and Clio, they're twins and Thetie. They're in their twenties, and all three have black curly hair. They're wearing pastel summer dresses.' She figured the more details she could provide would increase their chances of being found. A sharp pain tightened across her chest, and the air was too thick to inhale. She was struck by a terrifying thought which stopped her in her tracks. What if they never made it? She stumbled, and Diane steadied her.

'Almost there, and we'll get you some water. I expect you're feeling dizzy and dehydrated from being out in the heat so long,' said Diane.

'Are there many... survivors?' Anthoula asked tentatively, scared of the answer.

'Not as many as we'd hoped, but we know there's another group further along the island.'

'We've counted about sixty people so far,' said floppy hair man.

'Sixty! Is that all?' Anthoula shrieked, remembering there were about five hundred souls on-board. With those odds, she had to prepare for the worst but refused to accept that her girls didn't make it. They were young, strong and fit, and they could swim.

The trio reached the camp and Anthoula scanned all the faces she passed, desperately searching for her loved ones. Diane guided her to a space beneath a tree for shade.

'Just here will be fine, Tom, thank you,' said Diane.

'Tom, is it? Thank you for helping me. You remind me of my daughter's fiancé, longer hair but the same kind heart,' Anthoula said, as Tom helped ease her down to the ground.

Anthoula looked around the clearing and amongst the bushes saw dishevelled injured survivors in ripped, blood-stained clothing, all tormented and trying to make sense of what happened. None of the faces was familiar. Beside her a young woman wrapped her arms around herself, rocking and whimpering, her messy long hair pasted to her face and a battered teddy in her hand. Anthoula's heart ached for her. Those without injuries collected as many salvageable items as possible from the shore. She watched them and felt utterly useless. Other survivors were sitting or lying around with haunted expressions, and she noticed hardly any children here compared to all those she had seen on the ship.

'Let's make you comfortable and take a look at your foot.' Diane knelt before her and lifted Anthoula's foot, cradling it in her lap. 'The men are scouring the

131

island and collecting supplies before we move to higher ground. Once everyone has rested, we'll make a move. We're not safe here if the planes come back. We're too exposed.' Diane examined her patient. 'Tom, please get some water for Anthoula and a bandage.'

'Please don't worry about my foot. There are needier people you could be helping, I'm sure.' Anthoula brushed her away with a swatting motion.

'It won't take two minutes, and we need you to be fit to walk soon, so let me take a look.' She inspected her toe. 'Can you bend it?' Anthoula felt a searing pain shoot up her foot. 'It looks like it's broken, and you've ripped the nail clean off, so I'll clean and bandage it as best I can. All we have is some ripped clothing but it should be enough to allow it to heal.'

Tom returned with a flask of water, knelt beside her and held it out for her to take.

'There's not much clean water, but we found three flasks on the lifeboat, so it's rationed between us.' He handed her the flask, and she gripped it tightly in her shaky hands. 'Go ahead. You need to drink.' He nodded.

Anthoula took a sip, savoured the wetness on her cracked lips, and returned the flask to Tom. He chuckled, which was a lovely sound amongst all this chaos.

'It's ok. You can have more than that. Take a few good gulps. You're dehydrated, so this will make you feel better.'

Anthoula smiled and drank as instructed. The refreshing liquid glided down her rough throat, and she swept her tongue across her chapped lips.

'There you go, that's better.' Tom grinned at her.

'Thank you, Tom,' she said, and he waved a salute before disappearing through the bushes. Anthoula flinched as Diane washed the sand from her wound with a tin of seawater and patted it dry. With the bandage wrapped tightly around her foot and secured with a knot, she instantly felt more comfortable and less exposed.

'Thank you for helping me, Diane.' Anthoula admired the make-do dressing and shuffled backwards to lean against the tree. The jagged bark dug into her spine, but she was too tired to hold herself up and ignored the discomfort. If she were younger, she would be up on her feet and scouring every inch of the island for her daughters, but debilitating exhaustion pinned her down; simply breathing and blinking took a considerable effort.

'You need to rest up, Anthoula. I'll keep an eye out and ask around about your daughters.' Diane stood and brushed the sand off her shorts. 'I'll be back for you when the party leaves for the hills. It won't be for a while, so get some rest.'

Anthoula attempted to wave, but her arm barely left the ground. Where were her daughters? She replayed the last conversations with them and remembered the last time she spoke to Clio, and guilt crept in. With no distractions, her emotions rolled in like a tornado filling the gap, her stomach churned with regret, her heart ached, and tears drenched her sunburnt cheeks, and she wished she'd never left her husband and boarded that blasted ship. She cried, letting it all out, and didn't care who heard her. With no sense of time, she sat and waited, and as promised, Diane returned. The survivors were preparing to move, and Diane helped Anthoula to her feet. She was wobbly at first but could stand with support, and the bandage on her foot felt cumbersome.

'Have you found my girls?'

'Sorry, not yet, but I believe other survivors will join us, so they could be in that group.'

Next, a loud voice boomed out, addressing the group. A military officer, Anthoula presumed by his manner.

'Can I have your attention please, ladies and gents? We must move from this area as it is too dangerous should the Japanese return for another attack. We'll climb up into the hills for cover and should set off before we lose the light. I appreciate that many of you are wounded or have young children, so do your best and take your time. No one will be left behind and I urge you all to support and help each other. Some Royal Engineers, aboard the Tien Kwang, have built a camp, dug a natural spring, and found clean water. So far nothing edible has been found. The island is small and uninhabited, so our reserves must be used sparingly. I'll brief you again when we reach the camp. Thank you,' said the man, stomping off with purpose.

The weary survivors followed as instructed and climbed the steep incline battling through the foliage. Without shoes and her toe injury, each step on uneven ground was painful and slow. The more able overtook her. Anthoula clung onto branches to drag herself up, stumbling on twisted tree roots, vines and stones. Every muscle in Anthoula's body throbbed. The higher she climbed, the tighter her chest became, and she struggled for air and willed her shattered body to get to the top. She would never know if her girls made it, if she didn't get there, she had to go on.

After hours of walking, the ground plateaued and the makeshift camp came into view. Anthoula leaned against a tree to catch her breath and surveyed the camp. The men had been organised and built a canopy of wooden trunks and thick leaves to shield them from the elements.

'Are you ok, Anthoula?' asked Diane.

'Yes…I need … to sit down.'

'No worries, let me help you.' Diane eased her to the ground against a wide trunk and left her to rest. Anthoula licked her lips. She was desperately thirsty again. Leaning her head back on the bark, she gazed up through the tall canopy of flora, watching the sunlight dance and sparkle as it filtered through the waxy leaves. The flickering of the light was mesmerising, and she found she couldn't look away until her eyelids became heavy eventually, the urge to close them was too strong and she fell asleep.

Sensing pressure on her shoulder, her eyes fluttered open. To her joy and relief, Ino was beside her.

'Oh, thank god you're alive. I was so scared!' Anthoula cried, hugging her daughter tight.

'I've been searching the island for you. I didn't think I was going to find you. Are you hurt?' asked Ino.

'Not really. I caught my foot on the rocks. Let me look at you. You look pale.' She noticed the blood-stained cummerbund around her waist. 'My darling, you're hurt! What happened?'

'After you got into the sea, there was another explosion and a chunk of shrapnel hit me. The force blew me into the water, and a lifeboat picked me up. Some people dragged me into the trees and a nurse pulled it out and bandaged me up. It's sore, but I'm ok.'

'My poor girl. And the others? Please tell me you've seen them,' Anthoula asked, desperately searching Ino's face.

'Clio is fine, she's with Angela.'

'Oh, Thank God! What about Thetie?'

'I'm sorry, Mamma. No news on Thetie yet. I was hoping she'd be here with you.'

Anthoula pulled her daughter into a tight embrace, not wanting to let go.

'Get some rest, Mamma and I'll keep looking for Thetie.'

'Don't leave me again, Ino. Please.'

'You need rest anyway. I'll be back before you know it. Let me do this. I need to find her.' Ino pecked her mother on the cheek and headed off through the trees.

Chapter Fifteen
Anthoula

Thunderous cast iron clouds hovered over the island unleashing a heavy torrential downpour. An electrical light show played out overhead, and an orchestra of thunder cracks sounded like the earth was splitting in half. Anthoula never liked storms and huddled close to Ino with the gushing rain battering the canopy of leaves above them which protected them slightly from the onslaught but not enough to keep them dry. Ribbons of water trickled down the leaf spines onto their skin and matted her hair to her face. She wiped the water from her eyes, grateful to have Ino and Clio by her side. This was their third day on the island, and Anthoula had almost lost all hope of finding Thetie alive. Ino had volunteered for the unenviable task of accompanying Diane to the burial ground to see if she could identify any of the fallen as her sister. The whole time Ino was gone, Anthoula pulled at strands of hair until she accumulated quite a clump in the palm of her hand. Thankfully Ino returned without a positive sighting. The only possibilities remaining was that Thetie had been lost at sea or picked up by a passing trawler and taken to safety. The latter option she knew had slim odds, but a mother never wanted to give up on her child, and she would always be hoping and searching. After days without food and only small amounts of water to drink, Anthoula sensed her battered body was shutting down. It was the same for everyone. Each day the survivors grew weaker without food. Conditions on the island only added to their discomfort with intense heat, extreme rainfall, lack of sleep and a profound grief for lost loved ones. During the day, survivors hid from the Japanese bombers flying overhead, and the number of dead kept rising as more bodies were found and disposed of around the island. But despite all that, many of the younger survivors remained in good spirits and hopeful of rescue. Men were sent out to forage the island for anything edible, and others were directed to the beaches to keep watch for passing ships. To add to

Anthoula's discomfort, the skin across her shoulders and arms had broken out in bulging orange blisters the size of strawberries from sizzling in the sun days before. She was ratty from the pain, the constant itching and the frustration of not touching them to allow them to burst on their own. Beside her, Ino winced as the wound in her side was not healing, blood seeped through her bandages, and Anthoula was worried she had an infection. As helpful as ever, Diane checked it regularly and reassured her that there was no infection that and Ino was feeling perfectly well other than the hunger they all suffered from. She checked Anthoula's blisters and suggested that Ino place cool leaves on the worst ones to soothe the burning and ease her mother's distress. The rain stopped almost as suddenly as it started, the sunlight returned, and people began to move around. Despite the lack of sustenance, Clio had bags of energy and bounced around the camp, talking to people and laughing with Angela. She returned to her family and announced she was going with friends to the other side of the island to look out for rescue ships.

'You can't go. You need to stay here with us, Clio.'

'I can't sit around here, Mamma, it's been days, and I need to keep moving. I have to find a way off this blasted island. Angela and I are together, so don't worry.'

'I won't know where you are. Can you do as I say for once in your life?' said Anthoula, exasperated from arguing with her daughter, her arms flopped by her side. 'It's not safe. We need to stay together. Look what happened last time you went off and left us. I can't bear it, Clio. I've lost Thetie, and I'll not lose you too.'

Clio crouched down brushing her wet fringe off her face.

'Look, I'll be fine. You don't need to worry about me all the time. Ino is here to keep you company.'

'But I *do* worry. It's not that I need your company. I've lost one daughter. I don't want to lose another. Can you at least understand that?' Anthoula snapped in frustration. 'Tell her, Ino. She has to stay.'

'I can't make her Mamma. If she won't listen to you, she sure as hell won't take it from me.'

'I'm going now. Nothing bad will happen, and I'll be back soon.' Clio knelt to kiss her mother on the cheek before wandering through the forest, giggling like a schoolgirl with her friends. Anthoula watched her leave, and anger flowed through her veins.

'That girl's so headstrong she drives me crazy. How is it that you two are so different? I don't know what I did to raise such a defiant daughter. I haven't done a very good job of keeping us all safe. I don't know how long I can do this,' she said to Ino, leaning back against the tree.

'Clio made her choice, she's an adult. None of this is your fault, you know. We have to hang on, Mamma, and stay strong. Think of Pappa, Terpie and Thalia. They need you, and so do I.'

'I think of them every hour, and it's not helping. I miss them so much. I'm so sorry. I made a terrible mistake making us leave.'

'You have nothing to apologise for,' she said softly and held her hand. 'You were doing what you thought was best. You didn't know this would happen. We have to keep going.'

'I'm not sure I can, I feel so weak…so sad.' Her voice didn't sound like hers and she didn't recognise this shell of a woman she had become in a few short days. Where were her positivity and her zest for living? She left them on the dock back in Singapore with the man she loved. The situation seemed impossible, and she would never get back to her family. 'It's because of me Thetie is gone. It's all my fault. My beautiful angel.'

'Mamma stop it. Don't talk like that. We don't know yet what happened to Thetie, don't lose hope. I need you to try.' Ino moved to sit in front of her to gain eye contact, but her mother stared upwards into the trees. 'It's the hunger and exhaustion talking, this isn't like you at all.'

'I failed all of you. Even Clio doesn't want to stay with me.'

'Mamma, that's enough,' said Ino, raising her voice. 'You're scaring me. Clio's doing what she always does. Her own thing with little thought for anyone else, and we don't know that Thetie hasn't made it. It's a big island. She could be here, and we haven't found her yet. She could have been rescued from the sea. Don't give up. Please.'

'It's all pointless anyway if we die on this island.'

'We're not going to die on this island, Mamma. Think positively,' Ino replied.

Anthoula nodded with a delusive smile.

'Ok, I'll try.' But in her heart, she knew the truth, and no amount of hope or positivity would bring her Thetie back or undo all her bad decisions up to this point. She had allowed her family to disintegrate, and was terrified of dying alone on this island without Zac. She noticed the military spokesman was standing on a log in the centre of the clearing, his voice boomed out to call the survivors together for an announcement shortly. Gradually people started moving and assembled around him. Anthoula too weak to move, stayed where she was, leaning against the tree where she had remained for days. She didn't see Diane but heard the crunch of her approach; she brought their daily water ration with her.

'How are you doing, Anthoula?' she asked, crouching beside her and offering her water. Anthoula shakily placed her lips on the edge of the container and sipped. Her stomach began to growl in the hope of receiving some nourishment.

'I'm tired, Diane. So very tired.'

Diane smiled weakly and was about to answer when Ino interrupted.

'Diane, can I have a word?' Ino steered Diane off to the side and the two women turned away from Anthoula and spoke in hushed tones. Anthoula strained to make out what they were saying but it was no good. She surmised that Ino was telling Diane what a lousy mother she was and that they'd be better off without her. As Ino returned and before Anthoula could ask what they were talking about, the spokesman on the log began his announcement.

'Good morning, everyone. I know this has been a tough few days. Everyone's hungry and weak and some of you are in pain from injuries. My men extensively searched the island, and there's nothing we can safely eat to keep us sustained. To survive, we need to move back down to the shoreline for any hope of rescue. I know this will be a difficult journey for many of you so take your time. Now that the rain has stopped, the hillside will be slippery, so we need to keep it steady. We'll begin our descent within the next hour.'

'We shouldn't leave without Clio. Just leave me here. I don't think I can make it,' Anthoula said stubbornly.

'Don't be ridiculous. I'm not leaving you here. You can make it, and I'll help you.'

'What did you say to Diane? I suppose you told her I'm a terrible person.'

'What? Mamma, no. I said I was worried about you and told her Clio had gone off to the other side of the island.'

'Hmmm, I thought you were trying to get rid of me.'

'Oh Mamma, why would I do that? Look, I think the heat, the hunger and your injuries are making you a little… paranoid. This isn't like you at all.'

'I feel like I'm losing my mind.' Anthoula hit her forehead with the heel of her hand. Ino grabbed her hand to make her stop.

'Mamma, listen to me. You're just exhausted, that's all. We're in this together. Let me help get you ready to walk, and things will feel better once we are down by the sea. We'll find help and get out of here.'

'Is Clio coming?'

'I expect she is, yes. I imagine she's already there.' Ino assisted her mother off the ground and they linked arms. The group slowly made their way to the edge of the clearing to begin their descent. Going down was more treacherous than the climb up. The rain had made the glassy rocks slippery, and Anthoula lost her footing several times. Ino battled to keep her upright. As before, the roughness of the ground pierced and punctured her bare feet. The weary procession of survivors snaked down the hillside as they moved tentatively, hanging on to branches for support. In the distance, crystal-clear waters shimmered, and the gentle waves rippled like diamonds below, and she could see the curve of the vanilla bay, but its beauty was difficult to appreciate.

To Anthoula, the island represented nothing but death and loss and had an overwhelming desire to leave. To go home, to the place she should never have left to be with her husband. Feeling light-headed and dizzy she clung to Ino, gripping her arm like a vice. Their trek downwards was slow and steady with the blazing sun on their backs, but after a few hours, they'd made it safely to the beach, where the group gathered like lost property waiting to be claimed. Some survivors gorged ravenously on bugs and insects to ease their starvation, but Anthoula couldn't even though her stomach ached. Her whole body throbbed from some kind of pain. Finding a place in the shade to sit, Anthoula stared along the empty horizon. She tugged at Ino's arm convinced she'd seen something in the distance. Only to be told there was nothing there. Her mind played cruel tricks and she began hallucinating visions of boats, large ships on fire, and ships sinking. What was this madness? She shook her head and felt unable to trust her vision she lay down and closed her eyes to end the torment with her arms clamped over her head. Ino stroked her back whilst she focussed on something she knew to be real which was the tide lapping and rolling on the shore. It became cooler as the sun disappeared on the horizon; the sky turned salmon pink with streaks of purple before the darkness came. The survivors clustered together in various groups and the low murmur of their conversations drifted. Anthoula had no wish to join them. Clio had not appeared and Ino had paced up and down the beach looking for her until the sun faded and without luck re-joined her mother. The celestial night sky was clear and bright, and with no trees to obscure the view or artificial light to dilute it, the expanse was breathtaking. Enchanted by the magical ceiling above, Anthoula lost herself in the glistening silver stars sparkling brightly against the deep indigo sky. The large disc of the moon cast its milky whiteness on the waves below. A memory surfaced of when she was a young girl, sitting on her father's lap on the porch of their home in Greece. She heard his voice as if he were right by her side telling her the story of Selene, the Greek goddess of the moon who had the power to bring sleep to the night and control time. Each night Selene dragged the moon across the heavens with her chariot providing light in the night sky, and in the morning, her sister Eos, the goddess of dawn, opened the gates of heaven for the sun to rise. Anthoula remembered as a child sitting by her window staring so hard at the moon to see if she could see Selene in her chariot. Her father would find her asleep and put her back to bed. Anthoula missed him. Anthoula could never remember the names of the constellations but recognised the familiar southern cross and silently prayed to the universe and hoped it was listening to her pleas. The stars appeared to have received her message and blinked back at her. She felt insignificant against the expanse of space stretching on and on indefinitely. Still, she felt comforted, knowing her family were sleeping under the same sky on this lonely planet wherever they were. The following day Anthoula woke with a start and sat bolt upright. She was shivering and took a minute to remember where she was. The sun hadn't yet breached the horizon, but she could make out the silhouette of Ino lying beside her, and her panic subsided. Whilst the sun clawed its way into the sky, she remained curled up in a tight ball hugging her legs into her chest and rocking to comfort herself until Ino woke up. Another long day stretched ahead, with no purpose, no food, and only a slither of hope left her hollow. The stabbing cramps in her stomach had her doubled over in pain and she groaned. Suddenly Ino shook her shoulder.

'Mamma, get up. Look,' Ino screeched with excitement. Anthoula rolled her aching body to a seated position and looked at where she was pointing. The sound of exuberant cries and whoops of joy could now be heard as other survivors jumped and danced in the wash of the sea. She looked beyond them and was astonished to see a fishing trawler heading their way.

'Oh thank heavens. We can get out of here.' She leaned heavily on Ino to stand and the women crossed the soft sand arm in arm and stood at the water's edge. The fishing trawler was a small steamboat with the words "Kofuku Maru" emblazoned on the hull in white cursive text. It had a small teak wheelhouse, a brown sail fluttered in the breeze, and a cream tarpaulin canopy sheltered the deck. Clearly the small vessel wouldn't carry all the survivors in one trip. It was decided amongst the group that the injured would go first together with as many of the women and children as possible. The trawler anchored down off the shore, and the only way to make it aboard was to wade into the sea. The first group of forty survivors were selected, and Anthoula and Ino were chosen. This should've pleased her, but it didn't. Anthoula became unsettled, shuffling from one foot to the other. She tugged at her grubby skirt and felt light-headed.

'Mamma, what's wrong?' Ino touched her mother's arm, and Anthoula flinched.

'I can't leave Clio…not without Clio…what if we sink? What if we get hit again? I must find Thetie.' She knew she was rambling, her voice shrill and panicked and people stared at her. She moved away from the huddle of people, turned towards the island and screeched for her daughters with all her strength.

'Clio! Thetie!' She paced up and down. 'Come on, Clio, we have to leave now.'

'Mamma. Come on. This is our chance to escape,' Ino said gently, wrapping her arm around her waist. Anthoula struggled against her.

'No. We can't leave them here. Clio!, Clio!' Anthoula shouted, but her desperate, empty cries floated in the air.

'Anthoula, I know this is incredibly hard for you, but we must go now.' Diane joined her and linked arms. 'You're so brave, but you can't stay here. Save Ino and get back to your husband and other daughters. They wouldn't want you stuck here on this island now, would they?'

'Please Mamma, come on. I'll look after you. Clio will be on the next trip.' Ino stroked her mother's greasy, matted hair. Anthoula yielded to their requests with a weak nod and allowed the two women to guide her into the sea, and the trio waded to the rescue vessel. The lapping waves against her legs made her unsteady, and she pushed against them with each stride; the seabed was soft and her feet sunk into the doughy sand.

Hanging against the boat's hull was a flimsy rope ladder. Ino climbed up first, and now it was Anthoula's turn. Diane helped her get her footing on the first rung.

'You're there now,' Diane said. 'Up you go.'

Anthoula forced herself upward, the coarse fibres of the rope grazed her sensitive hands, and her legs trembled with each tentative step searching for the next rung as the ladder swayed beneath her. She felt like a clown scaling the high wire despite being only ten rungs high. Above her, Ino offered encouragement, and she heard a male Australian voice.

'That's it, one more, and you're there.'

The ladder wobbled too precariously for her to chance a look to see whom the voice belonged to, and she was conscious of holding up the other survivors behind her waiting to board. She concentrated on her steps until level with the side of the boat.

'You made it, well done. Let's get you on-board. Can you take my hand?' asked the man. Beneath his white sun hat, his rugged face looked grubby brown, and creases and folds told the story of a life outdoors. Anthoula nodded, her hands quivered on release, and she was shaking until she felt the grip of a solid warm hand. With his help, she heaved her weary bones over the side.

'Well done. Welcome aboard, my name is Bill Reynolds, and I will get you out of here.' He beamed at her.

'Thank you so much.'

Ino led her to space towards the rear of the boat, and another one of Bill's crew took Anthoula's hand and supported her as she lowered herself on the rugged plank seat.

'You've had a bit of an ordeal, haven't you? You're safe now. How long have you been stranded here?'

'Four days, I think. I've lost track of time, to be honest,' said Ino.

'All we've done for the last few days is pick up evacuees. This will be our fourth rescue.' He smiled. Anthoula scanned the sky for aircraft. 'Honestly, you're quite safe. This little boat is our secret weapon. She's registered as a Japanese fishing trawler. The Japs leave us alone.' This titbit of information filled Anthoula with hope, and she relaxed a little.

'Where are we going?' asked Ino.

'We'll stop at Sumatra first for supplies, but it's unsafe there now. The Japanese are swarming the island, so we'll head to India.'

India! Anthoula baulked at the thought of being so far away from home and in the opposite direction she thought they would be heading. It would be such a long journey. The small boat rocked as more passengers came aboard, and the badly injured on makeshift stretchers were kept at the front. Anthoula scanned them looking for familiar faces but her girls weren't among them. Anthoula and Ino wedged tightly between mothers clinging to their babies and children. The young ones were eerily silent, too hungry to cry. The stench of loss and exhaustion clung to them like lichen. The fishing vessel full of passengers carved through the waves and left the island. Anthoula's heart weighed heavy knowing she left Singapore with three daughters, and now only one remained by her side. She berated herself mentally for leaving Clio and Thetie behind. She'd failed as a mother to protect them and would carry the shame of abandoning them for the rest of her life. Her thoughts turned to Zac and he'd never forgive her for losing them. She knew this pain was now a part of her, an open wound and she'd be locked in misery until her family were reunited.

Although it was clear the boat had not been used for its intended purpose for some time, the stench of fish guts ingrained in the woodwork from years of trawler nets slapping on the deck still lingered. The unpleasant seeping scent, along with the undulating movement, made Anthoula nauseous. Needing to feel close, she looped her arm in Ino's, closed her eyes, concentrated on breathing and wished they were going home.

Chapter Sixteen
Zacharia

Zacharia had become like a caged animal within the four walls of Emily's flat, and his narrow view of what was going on made him crotchety. He offered to leave the apartment in search of food because her cupboards were bare, and he'd been consumed with guilt for giving her an extra mouth to feed.

'I'll see what I can find Emily but the last time, shops were running out.' Zacharia leafed through his slender wallet for some cash revealing a couple of notes. 'I won't get much with this.'

'Wait here, I've some money stashed away.' Emily disappeared, returning with some crisp notes. 'Here, take this. Get what you can.'

With the banks closed and no idea for the foreseeable future when life would resume any sense of normality, they needed to be mindful of not spending too much.

'Don't be long and come back if it's too dangerous,' Emily instructed before closing and bolting the door behind him. Braving the abandoned streets Zacharia found many shops destroyed or empty, and the few places still trading only had limited supplies. After roaming the streets for an hour, he eventually found an open shop and joined the queue, stretching along five shop fronts and snaking around the corner. He stood in line for two hours for a kilogram of rice, some greens which looked past their best, two bags of mixed nuts, three bananas and four eggs. The seller offered him some small cuts of fish and pork, which he declined. Out of his comfort zone, having never shopped for a meal in his life, Zacharia felt sure the slimy grey film on the meat he was being offered wasn't a good sign. He trudged back to the apartment with his bag of groceries, his head down, deep in thought, and let himself in with the key Emily had given him. As soon as he knocked on the apartment door, Emily was behind it.

'Zac, I've been so worried. You were gone for so long.'

'It took ages to find anywhere open and when I did, the queue took hours.'

'I'm glad you're back in one piece. Did you go to your shop?'

'No. I don't see the point in torturing myself more.' He relayed his conversations with the people in the queue and apologised that the food he brought back was pitiful. Emily assured him she could rustle up a few meals to keep them going. With nothing but empty time, he paced around the coffee table with no purpose, occasionally stopping to gaze out the window where the scene was a repeat of previous days. The only change was increased military presence, battalions of soldiers marching through, and the sound of rapid gunfire. The Japanese soldiers were closing in.

When he grew bored from pacing, he spent the vacant hours reading from Bill's extensive library. Throughout the day, he and Emily tuned in to the radio at regular intervals in the hope of hearing an update about the evacuation ships. Any news felt empty and inconsequential without knowing the name of the vessel his family escaped on. Specific details were unsurprisingly patchy at best, but there had been confirmation of some evacuees making it to Sumatra and Java, which brought him a degree of hope. Too many reports were coming in about attacks at sea, and confidence that his family could have escaped unharmed was ebbing away. He reminded himself daily that he would keep believing they made it out safely until he received hard evidence to the contrary. One thing he knew for sure was that he must stay positive for his family, wherever they were. At some point in the future, they would rely on him to find them a new home and thoughts of how he could make this possible occupied his mind, preventing the darker shadows from nudging their way in. There was no use trying to make solid plans when uncertainty hung over them, and he'd have to be patient, a characteristic he lacked. Sleep was his only respite from the worry. After one uncomfortable night on the sofa, sweating, tossing and sinking between the gaps of the cushions, he decided he'd be better off on the hard floor. When it did come, sleep was sporadic, and his disturbed mind deprived him of decent deep sleep, keeping him suspended below the surface, so he felt unrested when he woke. The next day, he paced up and down the same area of carpet, nibbling on a jagged fingernail, as a frenzy of thoughts bounced around as he struggled to come to terms with the empty void, he found himself in.

'Zac, sit down, would you? You're making me dizzy,' Emily pleaded, placing her knitting onto her lap. 'What's troubling you?'

'Sorry, I'm finding the boredom hard to deal with. I don't see where this is going or how it ends.'

Zacharia stopped pacing and sat down. They'd not long had breakfast and the thought of the whole day ahead with nothing to occupy him was prickling at his skin. 'I've lost track of the days. What day is it today?'

'The day of our good Lord, Sunday,' Emily resumed her knitting, and the click-clack of the needles filled the silence. Zacharia glanced at the clock, and a smile spread across his face. 'What has changed your mood all of a sudden?' Emily peered at him over her glasses.

'I'm going to church.'

'Will there be a service today?'

'I'm certain of it. People need their faith more than ever,' his grin spread wider as it dawned on him that he'd be granted another opportunity to see his girls. 'I expect Thalia and Terpie will be there, and I'll get to see them again. I can't keep turning up at the convent. The nuns aren't happy about visitors coming all the time. The last time I visited the Mother Superior made it quite clear she was displeased. I felt like a naughty schoolboy,' he laughed, and after a pause, he said, 'Do I look smart enough to go to church?'

Zacharia smoothed down his short-sleeved cream shirt, and Emily laughed at him. He only packed a few items of clothing and was trying to be economical in the rotation of his shirts, and this one was the cleanest of them all. He didn't want to trouble Emily with his laundry, and besides, water had become a precious commodity since the Japanese took control of the reservoirs and the supply to homes had stopped. All residents were urged to conserve water for emergencies only. Before they lost their supply, they filled pots, pans, jugs and bottles for drinking and washing, so keeping clothes clean was not a priority, and he would have to eke out his soiled shirts a bit longer.

'The country is in chaos, I don't think anyone will care. If you don't mind, I'd like to join you. I could do with getting out for some air, and I'd like to see the girls.' Emily knitted to the end of the row and lay down her needles.

'I'll be glad of your company.'

When Emily emerged from her bedroom half an hour later, she'd changed into a dark green skirt and jacket and styled her hair. For all her admonishing, Emily made sure her attire was "Sunday best" worthy, which made Zacharia smile. Together they ventured down the stairs slowly arriving in the lobby.

Zacharia placed his hand on the door handle and hesitated. Emily hadn't been out of the building since the bombing started, and he felt duty-bound to warn her.

'Emily. The city's not how you remember it. It might come as a shock,' he said gently.

'You're a thoughtful man. Do you think it's safe to go out?'

'I wouldn't be going if I thought otherwise. The church is only around the corner. I'm damned if they're going to prevent me from going to pray as well as everything else.'

They stepped out into the sunlight and casually walked arm in arm along the street. Zacharia saw a flicker of shock sweep across Emily's face as she reacted to the ruination of her much-loved home. He remembered the wretchedness he felt the first time he saw it. Fires still smouldered and ash drifted around buildings, the air thick with fumes. A putrid smell in the air he couldn't identify made him almost vomit. Walking side by side, they passed other people scurrying along the pavement with their heads down. He was surprised by Emily's stoicism, she hadn't uttered a word since leaving the apartment. The occasional sigh was all.

Zacharia realised that if he were to keep walking, he would eventually reach the High Street. During breakfast, he toyed with the idea of stopping by out of curiosity, knowing there was nothing to be gained by doing so, the magnitude of his recent losses altered his priorities. Something had shifted within him. All that mattered was reuniting his family. The peal of the church bells filled the streets, bringing people out of hiding and finding solace in their prayer. He approached the steps and leaned back to admire the five-tier ivory spire and the delicate stained-glass windows. He nodded and greeted others good morning as he usually would, although today, a sombre atmosphere hung in the air and people looked fearful.

On arrival, he asked Emily to wait outside whilst he sped inside and searched the pews, looking for the familiar shape of his daughters. Satisfied they weren't already inside, he returned to Emily. She was conversing with a well-dressed lady about his age and he hung back until they were finished. From this distance, he couldn't hear but whatever was being discussed caused Emily to dab her eyes, and she embraced the lady before they parted.

'They're not here yet,' he informed her, glancing at his watch. 'Do you mind if we wait out here a while? We're early, and the service doesn't start for another fifteen minutes. I want to sit with them if I can. Emily? You've gone a bit pale.'

'No, Zac. I've just heard something terrible. That poor woman. Her son was a doctor at the Alexandra Hospital, he was gunned down when soldiers stormed in. I'm not sure it's safe to be here, Zac. Not safe at all.' Emily's eyes darted along the street, looking for threats, and she gripped the handles of her handbag tightly close to her chest. 'I can't make sense of it, Zac. The world has gone mad.'

'That's awful. I don't know what to say.' Seeing Emily's agitation, he offered for her to go into the church and wait. 'If you feel safer, go inside. We're here now, but I promise you, we'll head straight home as soon as the service is over.'

Emily disappeared into the gloom of the church. As he expected, it was not long before the procession of nuns appeared with their flock of refugees trailing behind them. Zacharia spotted his girls strolling at the back of the line and his heart swelled. They looked well. He'd been so worried about how they were coping and dealing with the fact they had nowhere to call home but seeing them looking so nonchalant, chatting and laughing with ease, those concerns melted away. Thalia noticed him and nudged her sister. The brightness of her smile healed some of the pain he'd been feeling in recent days. He removed his hat before wrapping them both in a bone-crushing hug despite only seeing them two days ago.

'Pappa, this is a surprise. You look well.' Thalia kissed him on the cheek.

'I had to get out of the apartment, and I guessed you would attend the service today. Emily's here too, but she's inside.'

The trio entered the church arm in arm. His eyes took a minute to adjust to the change of light, and he spotted Emily in an empty pew. As the church filled with worshipers, the air became suffocating and stuffy. Beads of sweat formed on his neck, and he loosened his shirt collar. It was joyous having his daughters by his side, and with sly glances towards them, he couldn't keep the stupid grin from his face. He reached for Thalia's hand and held it tight.

'Are you ok, my little bird?' he said, in a hushed voice.

'Yes, Pappa. I've said goodbye to Charlie. It was time to let him go. Don't worry. I'm fine. I've met some good friends in the convent and keep busy.'

'That's good to hear. You look well, which is the best your old pappa can hope for under the circumstances.'

After days of separation, being close to his daughters restored his sense of belonging. The last few days on his own left him bereft and unhinged, and with an unpredictable future, he grasped these brief moments and clung to them like a drowning sailor. He couldn't remember a time when he needed his faith, being surrounded by others in a shared union reset his internal equilibrium and restored his strength. After the service, Zacharia squinted in bright sunlight, leaving the dimness behind, feeling lighter than when he entered.

'Pappa, can we stay with you a while?' Thalia suggested with excitement.

'I'll walk you back. The reason you're there is to keep you safe. I'll not have you wandering the streets with Japanese soldiers about to descend on the city.'

'Your father's right, girls. The streets aren't safe anymore.'

'Pappa, there's no need to walk us back. We'll go back with the Nuns. It'll be quite safe. We shouldn't be out here longer than needed,' said Terpie.

'But it's ok for you to leave the convent to meet Benny, I suppose?' Thalia challenged. Terpie's mouth gaped open and looked to her father for his reaction. Zacharia frowned.

'It was once, Pappa,' replied Terpie quickly, sensing her father's scorn. Thalia cleared her throat as a warning. 'Ok, it was twice, but I was perfectly safe.' Terpie glared at her sister. 'He came to find me, so we walked and talked briefly. Ten minutes at most.'

'I'm glad Benny is ok, but I'm most certainly not happy to be wandering around out here. What have I told you? Please don't do it again,' Zacharia said sternly. 'Right, you need to go. They're making their way back. I wish we could talk for longer, but maybe next time.' He nodded towards the bevy of nuns lining up on the pavement.

'I wish I could come back with you and Emily.'

Zacharia hugged Thalia and whispered in her ear, 'I wish that too, but her apartment's overcrowded just with me being there. Trust me. You're safer where you are. Please, ride it out until I can think of something else. Besides, I need you to keep a grip on your sister and stop her from doing anything foolish.'

'I'll try, but she does as she pleases, you know that.' Thalia stepped away from her father.

'Terpie, hug your pappa. Now no more of this leaving the convent nonsense. I know it's hard, but your safety is the most important thing now. Promise me.'

Reluctantly, she agreed, and the girls said goodbye and joined the back of the convoy to return to the safe walls of their refuge. Thalia turned back and pulled a funny face which made him laugh. He missed her company. With an ache in his chest, he watched after them. The sniping between his daughters didn't go unnoticed; he supposed too much time in each other's company was taking its toll. He and Emily hastily returned to the apartment to get off the streets. To his surprise, Emily talked openly about missing Bill. She said it was nice to have some company in the apartment for a change, and enjoyed having someone to look after again. The couple never had their children, and her family lived in England. She was alone. As bad as things were for him, he at least had his family to keep fighting for.

Later that day, another bombing raid came and the apartment rattled. It didn't last long, and the skies fell silent after an hour. Zacharia kept looking out the window, checking the view outside across the convent; he could see burning close but couldn't be sure. He was all for running around there to investigate, but Emily used all her powers of persuasion and talked him down. The idea of his girls being left alone if something happened to him was enough for him to see sense. In the evening, the pair settled into their usual routine to listen to the evening news broadcast at six o'clock. The crackling broadcast was like no other.

It is with great sadness that we report that Lt Gen Percival and the British surrender party met with Lt Gen Yamashita at their headquarters at Ford Motor Factory this afternoon. A declaration was signed despite Churchill's instructions to fight to the last man standing, and Britain surrendered unconditionally to the Japanese. Therefore, there will be a ceasefire at eight-thirty this evening and all soldiers are to put down their weapons.

Chapter Seventeen
Zacharia

Zacharia rolled over and stretched out, jolting awake and banging his leg on the coffee table. He groaned, remembering he wasn't in his bed, or indeed a bed at all. The dull ache in his neck and hips bore testimony to that. As happened every morning, his first thoughts were always for his wife. His heart ached for her and waking alone was alien to him. He never wanted to get used to it. Forty years of sharing a bed, feeling the security of that familiar body beside him was so natural, and the emptiness without her was crippling. Being without Anthoula, his family or purpose, he felt as redundant as a clock with no tick. Zacharia lay on his back, wondering where his wife could be in the world. If it were possible to hone a superpower, telepathy was a strong contender. He was desperate to sense her thoughts and emotions, which seemed achievable when she lay beside him but impossible across the cruel void that separated them. With no celestial signs of communication from his wife, his mind turned to more pressing matters. The realisation he'd woken in a scary new world under Japanese rule. Worrying about that could look like was pointless. Zacharia lay for a few minutes longer before getting up and packing his bedding away before Emily woke up. She'd been so generous in offering him a roof over his head, and he was conscious of invading her space; the least he could do was to keep things tidy and clear up after himself. Soon after, Emily appeared, she prepared a breakfast of crackers, scrambled eggs and a pot of tea. Emily sat across from him at the small dining table, crumbs scattered on her pink cardigan as she bit into the dry cracker. She was brushing them onto the plate with a delicate sweeping motion she reached for her cup and saucer.

'I was thinking. We should be brave and go out today See what's going on. Are you up for that?' Zacharia asked.

'I suppose so. Sitting here won't tell us anything; at least the bombs and guns have stopped.'

'They've shut the radio stations down, so it could be days before we hear any news. I tried this morning, and it just crackles.'

The pair finished their breakfast and left the apartment a little after nine. Zacharia was nervous, he wasn't sure what they'd find when they stepped outside. Could anything have changed overnight? The habitual sound of bombs and gunfire they'd become used to had fallen silent, the peace and stillness were eerie. They wandered through the streets without a particular destination in mind until they noticed swathes of people heading towards the Municipal Building and decided to follow. The pair joined the jostling crowds, and the atmosphere oozed with tension.

En route, they passed hundreds of curious locals, hanging out from windows or standing on rooftops, who, like them, were intrigued to glimpse their new masters. It was evident by the checkpoints and roadblocks on every major street that the Japanese had swiftly seized control. You didn't venture far before coming face to face with an armed guard. Their overbearing presence changed the landscape and Zacharia thought he was in a foreign land. Emily slipped her arm through his and stayed close. Seeing the enemy up close for the first time, Zacharia's pulse began to race and, contrary to popular belief, the Japanese soldiers were fierce and robust.

The couple reached a checkpoint at the end of St Andrews Road where four rigid soldiers wearing dark uniforms guarded their post. Beneath jet-black beards and peek caps their faces were barely visible. Zacharia and Emily approached the queue, but he couldn't bring himself to look at them. These monsters took his home, family, city and innocent people's lives, so he was angry. Also, their intimidating presence made him uncomfortable, so he looked everywhere other than at them. Reaching a short queue, they waited. Zacharia's skin prickled with rage thinking of all the suffering this army caused, but he must control his emotions and thrust his clammy hands deep into his trouser pockets. A glance towards Emily confirmed she was terrified. Clutching his arm tightly, her face turned pale like sour cream.

Edging forward, they'd reached the checkpoint, Zacharia kept his eyes locked straight ahead. A soldier approached pointing a rifle at his stomach instructing him to step forward, raise his arms and proceeded to pat him down. Zacharia's body stiffened as if his blood had turned to set concrete. He hoped the soldier couldn't hear his furious heartbeat. The soldier's hot sour breath and touch on his body made his skin crawl and Zacharia stopped breathing. Beside him, Emily received an instruction to open her handbag. Indignant at having a soldier rifling through her things, she remained tight-lipped until the bag snapped shut and he handed it back. A soldier to their left eyed them suspiciously before waving him through with his rifle. They were free to continue, and Zacharia could breathe again and his heartbeat returned to its normal rhythm.

During the final radio broadcast last night, Churchill made a sullen address to the nation; he called it *the worst disaster and largest capitulation in British military history.* Zacharia wholeheartedly agreed, but what about the people? They deserved better; throughout the campaign, they were told time and time again that the island was safe from attack, and the British forces severely let them down. It was a feeling shared by many, judging by the disillusionment reflected in the faces around him. The big question on the minds of every citizen of any nationality was what life would look like under Japanese rule.

When they arrived at the Municipal Building, the pavement overflowed with onlookers awaiting a procession of some kind. Zacharia and Emily jostled to find a space and settled within the anticipating crowd. Emily padded her glistening eyes with a tissue. They were about to witness a piece of history. Murmurs circulated, and the crunch of marching boots carried on the breeze together with the revolting smell of war and victory. Thousands of triumphant soldiers fresh from the battlefield marched past with weapons raised above their heads in victory. The hushed crowd were dumbfounded, and Zacharia shuffled from foot to foot looking at the ground as they passed. Following in procession came a convoy of tanks cruising by with caterpillar tracks thundering on the tarmac, vibrating his bones. From the open turrets, stern faces stared ahead, and red sun ensigns flowed behind them.

Everything about this procession demonstrated to any doubters, the show of strength of this new, supreme power and they were to be feared. After the tanks a string of black cars arrived, delivering commanders and new government officials to the podium. Once assembled, the sound of trumpets blared out the Japanese national anthem. It was a sombre moment for the city, and Zacharia lowered his head, his shoulders sagged from shame and disappointment. He still couldn't fathom how for all their promises the British had given up in just seven days, rolling over in defeat.

In the distance, a Japanese commander approached the podium to deliver his speech. It was difficult to hear, but it was obvious Singapore was no more. With new leaders came a new name and from today the island would be called "Syonan". Ending over one hundred years of colonial rule, the forlorn-looking Union Jack lowered and the blood-red sun on a white background took its place, fluttering above them with a sense of dominance. The successor's victory roar broke the silence, thrusting their rifles into the air and shouting 'Banzai, Banzai, Banzai!' Their cruel, twisted faces were etched with glory.

Zacharia was finding their jubilant celebration hard to stomach. Because his attention was focussed on the parade, he hadn't noticed behind him in the Padang area by the cricket club, thousands of captured troops were assembled to watch the spectacle. To the Japanese, there was great dishonour in surrender and now, the new junta ceremony was over and another procession was about to begin. Weary allied soldiers drenched in defeat must suffer the humiliation of walking through the streets under the scorn of the people they had failed to protect. They began the eighteen-mile walk of shame to Changi prison. Zacharia couldn't tolerate it anymore.

'Shall we go to the convent? I've seen enough,' he whispered, and Emily agreed, together they pushed free of the crowds. On the walk back through the streets, Zacharia noticed bright yellow posters plastered on various shop doors and windows. They must have just been put up as he hadn't seen them earlier. He stopped to read one and raised an eyebrow. In thick black writing, he read. *All British citizens of European descent are hereby ordered to report for internment to the Kempeitai—North Bridge Road before 17th February.* It appeared the Japanese were not wasting time organising their new realm by discarding unwanted citizens. Emily looked blankly at him and admitted she couldn't read without her glasses, so he read it aloud.

'What's internment, Zac? I don't understand,' she asked, looking confused.

'It means prison, Emily.'

The next morning, Emily and Zacharia left the Capitol apartments for the last time. When they reached the Pandang area, it was heaving with people waiting under a clear blue sky. Having reported to the Kempeitai, which Zacharia now knew to be the Japanese Military Police, they were herded to the checkpoint where a stern-faced guard directed them to the grassy area with no instruction other than to wait which they had, for almost two hours now. The air weighed heavy with expectation as families gathered with their most valued and essential possessions.

Zacharia only had the items he'd scrabbled together from his flame-ravaged home and two flasks of water from their tin pan reserves. With nothing to do, Emily picked at blades of grass, her face obscured by her wide, floppy sun hat. Wisely, he wore linen shorts, a white shirt, sandals and his Panama hat, as judging by the temperature already this morning, it was going to be a sultry day. He couldn't speak for Emily but became more agitated as time passed and his concerns for their future increased. Like a Jack in the box he stood, he sat and stood again, but there was nothing to see other than a sea of people. He sat down again, realising he was getting on Emily's nerves by her tutting and eventually a stern word from her to settle came his way.

'Zac, sit down, for goodness sake. I'm sure when there's something to see, you'll know about it.' She fanned her face with her hat.'

'Sorry, Emily. I want to get going to wherever they are taking us.'

'Changi prison. That's where we're going,' interrupted an older man to his left, leaning into their conversation.

'Are we? How do you know?' asked Zacharia.

'Word filtered through from the front. It could be wrong, but I can't see where they could house this many people,' said the white-haired man.

'Really? But haven't they already taken the British soldiers there? How on earth will there be room for all of us too?'

'I've no idea, and I don't suppose the Japs care much. They'll pack us in like sardines and leave us to rot, I expect. If we're lucky, they'll shoot the lot of us. I'm more worried about the journey in this heat. It's a good fifteen miles and I'm no spring chicken anymore, and it could kill me. One less mouth to feed, I guess,' the man laughed and turned back to his family group.

'We won't get shot,' Zacharia reassured, seeing the panicked look on Emily's face. If Changi were their destination, it would take an entire day of walking in intense heat, and Zacharia had concerns about Emily and how she'd cope. Whilst she was tough as old boots mentally, for an elderly lady, a walk of that distance in scorching temperatures could be fatal. Before arriving here, they detoured to the convent to say goodbye and sitting here now, he felt sure it was the best place. His daughters were safe and spared this indignity.

Before parting, he told them in no uncertain terms to remain hidden and insisted again on how important it was for them to stay within its walls. They mustn't alert anyone to their presence and he hoped they grasped the seriousness of their predicament and heed his warning. This was more for Terpie's benefit than Thalia's. She was a good girl and would never go against his word. He knew Terpie could be reckless and impetuous so he strongly doubted anything he said would make a difference, but he could do no more. It agonised him to walk away without knowing when they'd be reunited. He couldn't be sure what happened first, but suddenly the noise level increased with chatter, and families around them stood up and gathered their belongings.

'Looks like it's time to go,' Emily brushed the grass cuttings from her skirt.

Zacharia helped Emily to her feet, picked up his case and braced himself for the long walk. The crowd shuffled forward, and once the bottleneck cleared, they were out on the road, following each other like sheep.

'Emily. Let me carry your case for you,' he said, slipping his hand around the handle, but Emily stubbornly pulled it away and refused to let go.

'You have your own to carry. I can't allow you to do that but thank you.'

'Ok. All you have to do is say the word,' he sighed in defeat.

Japanese soldiers with rifles walked amongst them along the route, keeping them in line and watching for absconders. The civilised procession wound its way through the empty streets as if the participants were on a sunny stroll, but the atmosphere hummed with fear of the unknown around him. Locals gathered on the pavement along the route to watch the bizarre procession. It was the oddest convoy Zacharia had ever seen with mothers pushing prams creaking under their children's weight and heavy-laden loads, and trolleys piled high with as many supplies as they could carry. To protect their heads from the blazing sun, people carried umbrellas, hats made from newspaper and towels swirled into turbans and even lampshades. Zacharia wondered what Anthoula would make of all this. He pushed thoughts of her away. This had become his new coping mechanism as it was too painful to think of her.

After a few hours of walking, they'd reached the city's fringes and lost shade protection from the tall buildings. His shirt stuck to his back, and his hat did little to keep his head cool. Along the way, he made polite chit-chat with families walking beside him and found the inevitable questions painful to answer. But however difficult it was to talk about, he soon realised everyone here had their own story of tragedy and loss. Theirs was shared grief and no family had escaped unscathed. Emily was flagging in the heat, with laboured breaths, her steps shorter and slower. He snatched the handle of her case and her fingers released quickly, allowing him to take it from her.

'Let me take this now. You've carried it for long enough,' he said forcefully. She offered him a weak smile and thanked him. A little further along, he stopped again to give her a drink of water from the flask.

'It's so unbearably hot, Zac. I'm melting like a candle.'

'You're doing great. Here. Have more water.'

Zacharia watched her drink and was mindful that their supply had to last the journey. When it was his turn, he only took a small sip to make it last. As much as his thirst was barely quenched, he needed to ensure Emily had plenty. With two cases weighing him down, his shoulder muscles burnt, and his fingers were swollen and stiff in no time. Sweat trickled down his back, and his underarms sodden. He trudged ahead steadily, observing his fellow walkers struggling with stooped shoulders and heavy feet. Girls in their twenties reminded him of his daughters. They'd started the journey in high heels and now walked barefoot on the boiling tarmac. Up ahead the melody *"It's a long way to Tipperary"* lifted morale. By early afternoon, they passed a signpost indicating they had eight miles remaining which was demoralising as according to his feet, they'd walked twice that distance. The convoy turned off the main road where potholes and loose stones created a greater challenge. Beside him, Emily shuffled along, tripping now and then and he observed her with concern. An open-topped army truck crawled along the route to collect the stragglers and those who couldn't keep up.

Knowing she wouldn't readily accept help, he would have to intervene and decide to act before she hurt herself. Zacharia approached the nearest soldier walking alongside and ignored the terrifyingly sharp bayonet he carried. Standing in his shadow, with a shaky hand, he reached out and tapped him on the shoulder. The soldier glowered at him with contempt. For a split second Zacharia regretted his boldness, but she needed help. Zacharia pointed to Emily and the truck and hoped this would be enough to convey his request. The soldier snorted, tipping his head to the side to observe Emily and then shouted in Japanese to the driver. Zacharia sighed with relief when he saw the vehicle come to a stop. Emily was stumbling along, staring at the dusty road lost in her own world.

'Emily. This truck will take you the rest of the way.'

Her pale eyes gazed blankly at him from beneath the brim of her hat.

'But what about you, Zac?'

'Don't worry about me. I'll be right behind you.'

With an arm around her waist, he guided her to the rear of the vehicle, where a guard swiftly grabbed her arms, hauling her tiny frame aboard like a rag doll. Zacharia passed up her case and was glad she would have the company of other elderly passengers and a pregnant mother for the journey. He waited until she was settled before giving her a wave and wondered whether he would see her again. The truck shuddered into life and rolled on, and a wave of loneliness hit him. He could almost hear his aching hip joints grinding in their sockets. His sandals were unsuitable for this kind of mileage, and his sweaty feet rubbed on the leather across his big toe and the back of his heel. He braved a look down and wished he hadn't. Angry red blisters protruded from beneath the straps. Gasping with thirst, he gulped the last of the water and savoured the moisture as it trickled down his throat. He stopped to stretch out his back and envied the vitality of the younger generation, unaffected by fatigue, striding along. The welcoming verge of soft grasses beckoned him to sit and rest awhile. Losing momentum had temporarily paralysed him, and his head felt dizzy. He bent over, resting his hands on his thighs and took deep breaths.

'Move!' yelled a soldier, digging him in the ribs with his rifle.

The force almost toppled him, but he corrected himself and stood up straight. Feeling bruised, he picked up his case and hobbled onward, his body groaning under strain. A voice beside him took him by surprise.

'Are you ok? Bloody animals,' said a tall man with slim features and concern furrowed on his brow.

'Just winded me, is all.'

'Barbaric the lot of them. Let me take your case for a while. My hands are free with this backpack. I'm Peter, by the way,' he said, turning around to show him the bag strapped on his back and holding his hand out to take the case from him.

'Maybe for a short while. Thank you. I've lost the feeling in my fingers.' With his free hands, he shook them vigorously willing the numbness away. 'I'm Zacharia.'

On closer inspection, Peter was much younger than he had previously thought, a clean-shaven chap in his thirties. He wore khaki shorts, a pale shirt and a wide-brimmed white hat. Peter pointed to the truck ahead and waved.

'That's my wife on the truck next to your friend. I've been trying to keep up to keep an eye on her.' He nodded towards the truck. 'Martha. We're expecting our first child in two months.'

Zacharia felt instant pity for his new acquaintance. Becoming a father is tough at the best of times, so under these circumstances, Peter must be full of worry and fear for the future. He could easily recall that anxious wait until the baby's arrival and the never-ending feeling of overwhelming protectiveness for his wife and child. He wasn't sure how to respond. Congratulations seemed inappropriate under the circumstances.

'I feel for you both. I'm sure this wasn't in your plans. How's Martha holding up?'

'She's a strong character and takes most things in her stride, but the last few days have taken their toll. We've no family here, so it's been quite isolating for her. I'm terrified of what comes next. Do you think we'll be imprisoned for long?'

Zacharia hadn't considered lengths of time, although he'd been eavesdropping on conversations along the way. There was already presumptuous talk banding around like gospel truth; some said one month and others said no more than three. Generally, he didn't get involved with gossip, he wanted to give the poor man some hope. Peter's face was gaunt from worry, so he shared the second-hand information.

'I don't know what I'm scared of most. My child not knowing who I am, or my wife doing this alone.' Peter stared towards the truck avoiding eye contact.

Zacharia dug deep for some words of wisdom, but in the end, just agreed it was an awful situation. They continued walking side by side, slowly on account of Zacharia's blisters, but Peter generously said he didn't mind. The conversation flowed easily between them on the last few miles, and Zacharia welcomed Peter's company. Talking became a distraction where he didn't register the pain quite so keenly and before long, they had both exchanged their life histories.

He learned that Peter was originally from a place called Bromley in England. He and Martha met at university whilst studying civil engineering, and she was training to be a nurse. An opportunity arose for him to be involved with the construction of the naval base on the island, and they moved here almost ten years ago. Lost in conversation, Zacharia had been oblivious to his surroundings and only just realised they had reached the outskirts of Changi village, where houses, huts and barns came into view.

A huge cheer rippled from the front of the procession, a further indication that they had reached their destination. Every inch of his body throbbed, his mouth was dry as sawdust, and his exposed skin was raw from sunburn. Although Changi was now in sight, he knew it would still be a while until he could rest, but he was surprised that what he yearned for was a nice cup of British tea.

Chapter Eighteen
Thalia

A couple of months had passed since the girls arrived at the convent as refugees. It surprised Thalia that she liked being here; the trepidation from her childhood trauma had become a distant memory. Since the British surrender, some of the fear had eased although, on the last day a mid-afternoon bombing raid struck the convent creating anxiety and panic. Luckily it caused minimal damage to the outer walls and one of the classrooms, which thankfully had not been occupied at the time and no one was injured. When the siren wailed its warning, the Mother Superior well-practised in the evacuation drill chivvied everyone to shelter in the basement until it was over.

Thalia would never forget the sound of the children's screams and their tortured little faces as they clung to their parents and anyone with a spare pair of arms as the bombs hit, shaking the building. That evening, their meal was interrupted by a soulful bang on the table with a wooden spoon and an announcement that the British had surrendered. Stunned silence followed and the blades on the old ceiling fan circulating stale air pulsated noisily above her head. At the time, Thalia fixated on pushing her last remaining grains of rice around her plate, refusing to accept the gravity of the situation. The next day, news reached them that not only did Singapore have new rulers, but from now on, it would be referred to as Syonan meaning "light of the south". The Singapore she knew was changing and becoming a thing of the past.

A month on and living under the Japanese regime was appalling. Food was scarce, they had a small daily allowance of water to drink and none to wash in. Thalia was accustomed to the hunger now, but for a few long days, her insides hurt and she was plagued with memories of the meals back home and Shi Min's cooking; tormenting her ravenous belly. Even in her sleep, she dreamt of tables laden with food which she gorged on until she felt sick. In the morning, her empty stomach still groaned and remained a cavernous pit of emptiness. Worse than the emptiness of her belly, she felt hollow without her father. The memory of seeing him that last day before he was taken to prison would stay with her forever.

As she watched through the gates, he looked frail and old, lumbering away from her with Emily by his side. By a stroke of good fortune, she had found a way to communicate with him and this morning she had arranged to meet Goh for the exchange. With her letter tucked away safely in the waistband of her skirt, she flew down the stairs with a bounce on her way to the kitchens. Goh, a young Chinese man working for his father's cleaning company, collected dirty towels and bedding every Wednesday. Thalia met him by accident but preferred to think of it as fate.

Last week, she had rushed around the corner and they had collided. The basket of towels emptied and she apologised, helping to pick them up. Realising she was British, he lowered his voice and asked her if she had anyone in Changi. Thalia was instantly interested and Goh explained he could get a letter to the prison and to meet him here the following week. During their brief exchange, he revealed that the locals had established an underground network of couriers in the city, keeping people connected to their loved ones under the radar of Japanese scrutiny. Brave delivery men and medical staff had found ingenious ways to smuggle letters and goods in and out of the prison alongside genuine deliveries under the guard's noses.

Goh stressed that absolute discretion was required as it was risky for all involved if they were caught. Thalia heeded his word of warning and didn't even share the information with Terpie. She stole a piece of her sister's writing paper and scribbled her letter in secret whilst Terpie was at Mass one evening and sensed the secret letter pressing against her skin as she waited patiently for Goh to appear. All was quiet in the kitchen once the breakfast shift was over and the sisters were in morning prayer. She hadn't long to wait before Goh appeared with his empty baskets. Thalia felt awkward and wasn't sure how to behave. Should she hand over the letter and leave, or would he speak to her? She was terrified of getting him into trouble or getting caught. He put his basket down and greeted her with a wide grin easing her nerves.

'Hi Thalia, good to see you again. Do you have a letter for me?' he asked.

'Yes, it's here,' said Thalia, looking around to check that no one was listening, before lifting her blouse to retrieve the crisply folded paper and handing it over.

'Don't look so worried. It wouldn't matter too much if we were seen here. This is the safest part of the transaction, believe me.'

'Thank you. I appreciate this and I'm so grateful to you. I can't believe people are willing to take such risks to help us.'

'You'd be surprised what goes on outside these walls. Nobody agrees with what's happening and people want to help,' said Goh, placing the letter in a deep pocket inside his jacket. 'I would say though, don't get your hopes up of getting a reply anytime soon. I've heard it's harder to get stuff out of prison.' Thalia couldn't help it. Her face fell as she desperately wanted to hear back from her father.

'Oh, I hadn't thought of that.'

'It's still early days remember. It will get better. Anyway, I'd better get on. Don't worry. Your father will get this letter, Thalia, don't lose hope, ok,' Goh said, patting his jacket. He bent down to pick up his basket, whistling as headed down the stone steps to the laundry room. It was exciting to think of her father receiving her note and hoped it would bring him peace of mind.

With a lighter heart, she went to the garden to plant some seeds. The heat of the sun scorched the back of Thalia's neck as she attacked the soil with her trowel and sifted seeds into the trough she had prepared. The perforations in her straw hat cast shapes on the dirt before her as powerful sun rays shone through. Kneeling on the hard ground, she removed her hat and wiped her brow on the back of her hand. Whilst observing her handiwork, she fanned her face; it was hot today.

Spending time in the garden was her favourite pastime. For a short period of her day, her mind calmed, shutting out the noise and focussed on the task at hand. Soothing birdsong, trickling water and distant choral voices from the chapel all served to relax and transport her to a peaceful place. Gardening was also a hobby she shared with her father and she felt closest to him when she was up to her elbows in mud with dirt beneath her fingernails. Watering can in hand, she doused the neat rows of new seedlings, which showed signs that life goes on. Without a water supply she relied on rainwater and dribbled the last drop in the watering can over the spiky pandan leaves, bayam spinach, sweet potato and tall wispy lemongrass in the raised beds.

Cultivating produce was now essential to supplement their paltry meals. The convent was a popular refuge and feeding so many mouths was a challenge on the pitiful rations the Japanese allowed per person. In her heart, she hoped she would not be here to see the fruition of her labour, but the future was so uncertain. Without a home to return to, she couldn't begin to envisage what her future would look like. She carried the ache of missing her family like a backpack she never took off; some days it weighed her down, and tears were never far away. Keeping busy was her saviour, dulling the pain for a short while. She hardly thought of Charlie these days since saying goodbye to him in this garden. Her heart had only so much room to carry loss; compared to her nearest loved ones, he was a passing light that had faded away.

Grabbing the yard broom from the shed, she swept the path thinking about what she would give to have a refreshing shower right now. In the distance, she heard a bell ringing. Whoever was at the gate was insistent as the bell rang continually until it was answered. Hearing raised male voices, she peeked around the door. Soldiers. Whatever they were here for couldn't be good. Even at a distance, they appeared menacing and cruel. Her heart raced and she did the best thing she knew how to do. Hide. She slipped into the garden shed and closed the door. Once her eyes adjusted to the darkness, the light shining through the cracks allowed her to navigate around the garden tools, and she sat in a tight ball in the corner behind a large wooden planter.

Time passed slowly and she wondered how long she would need to sit there. As a child, she often used this tactic to avoid the reprimands of the sisters and kept them guessing for hours about her whereabouts. Her favourite spot was under the church altar until Sister Martha cottoned on. She must have nodded off at some stage and woke with a start when she heard Terpie calling her name. Her limbs were stiff when she tried to move and leaned on the planter to stand up. The shed flooded with light when she opened the door and saw Terpie pacing around the garden, calling her name.

'I'm here,' she called.

'I've been hunting for you everywhere. I was terrified you'd been taken.'

'Taken? What's been going on? I saw the soldiers come and got scared, so I hid.'

'Probably a good job too. They've gone now. The sisters took some of us into the basement to hide as soon as they saw them at the gate. I was worried about you.'

165

'Why? What were they here for?'

'They were looking for British or Europeans and rounding them up to take them to prison. We're safe again for now. I've only just stopped shaking.' Terpie led her sister by the arm to sit on the bench. 'The soldiers will come back so we have to be alert.'

'I'm glad I hid now! I don't want to end up in that place.'

As much as the convent felt like a prison at times, if she was honest with herself, Thalia was happy here and felt protected. She had met some good people and had structure to her day, which made her feel useful. Prison sounded like a terrible place to exist and she vowed she would do everything in her power to avoid being sent there. Thalia noticed her sister's legs were jittery and she couldn't keep them still. She really must have been spooked.

'I need to go now, so I'll see you later for dinner,' said Terpie, checking her watch.

'Go where?'

'Umm, just out to the market. I offered to help the sisters with collecting groceries.'

'Are you sure that is a good idea knowing the Japs are hunting us down? I don't think that's wise. Let the sisters go.'

'I'll be fine, honestly. I need to get out of here for a bit. I'll wear a headscarf and be as quick as I can.'

'Pfft. Do you think wearing a scarf will outsmart the Japanese? You're crazy. Well, I'm not letting you go alone. I'll come with you. I'm sure you will need another pair of hands for the groceries.'

'No! You can't do that,' answered Terpie firmly.

'Why? If it is ok for you to go then why not me?'

Terpie stared at the floor. Thalia smelled a rat. Something wasn't right here and Terpie was acting very strangely and not making eye contact with her.

'Terpie, what's going on? You're keeping something from me. I know it.'

'Ok, ok. I didn't want to tell you because I knew you'd give me grief. On a Wednesday at three o'clock, I wait on the cathedral steps. Benny and I came up with this plan to see each other. He would meet me just for a few minutes, but it's been weeks now, and he hasn't shown up. I'm terrified something has happened to him. I have to go, to check.'

'I can't believe you've been so stupid. What was the one thing Pappa said?'

'Is that all you're worried about? I broke Pappa's trust. You're so immature, Thalia. I just told you my fiancé is missing, and that's all you can say.'

'I'm surprised at Benny for allowing you to take such a risk.'

'I knew you wouldn't understand. He's everything to me and seeing him for a few minutes has kept me going. I've been perfectly safe, haven't I? Nothing bad happened.'

'Yes, but it could have. I'd be left alone, had you thought of that? God, you're selfish sometimes. Terpie, please. I know you love him but don't go. He won't be there. I'm not saying anything bad has happened but if he's not shown for weeks, there's a good chance he won't be there today. It's not worth the risk. This time you might not be so lucky.'

'The soldiers did scare me today.'

Thalia reached for Terpie's hand. 'You're all I have now and I don't want you to end up in prison and leave me here. I know we fight sometimes, but we should stick together.'

Terpie agreed that she wouldn't leave the convent again to her relief. Until now, she hadn't realised how much she needed her older sister and the thought of being separated and alone filled her with dread. It dawned on her that her father endured a solitary world, a life separated from all his loved ones which must be unbearable for a man who dotes on his family. Thalia raced up to their shared room two days after their conversation in the garden. On entering, she found Terpie on the bed with her back against the wall, and her knees pulled under her chin like a child. Thalia sat on the end of her bed, it was apparent Terpie had been crying.

'Whatever's the matter?' Thalia asked, reaching out to touch her sister's foot which she quickly retracted. Terpie didn't answer. She stared blankly at the wall ahead and handed her a crumpled dirty piece of paper. It was a scruffy letter that appeared to have be written hastily.

Terpie my love. I've been captured by the Japs. I don't know where I'm being taken. I'll write when I can. Try not to worry. Stay strong. I'll find you. All my love forever—Your Benny x 17th February 1942.

Thalia smoothed out the worn letter Benny had sent almost a month ago and laid it on the bedside table. Kicking off her sandals, she climbed onto the bed beside her sister and wrapped her arms around her, pulling her close.

'I'm sorry, Terpie.' Her sister leaned into her and sobbed.

'I just knew something was wrong and there was a good reason why he didn't show. I felt it. He could be anywhere by now.' Terpie sniffed.

Thalia didn't know what to say. No words would take the pain away or make her sister feel better. Benny was a prisoner of war. He would be at the mercy of the Japanese and no doubt Terpie was well aware of the danger he was in. All she could do was comfort her as she sobbed on her shoulder. They sat like that for a few hours, crying and talking so much they had missed supper and the light was fading. Thalia's shirt was damp from Terpie's tears and she unravelled her arms from around her sister's shoulders.

'Terpie. I know it's easy to say but try not to think the worst. Sorry, I have to move. I have a cramp in my leg,' said Thalia, peeling herself away and shuffled from one foot to the other to entice the feeling back into her limbs.

'I might never see him again,' she mumbled, twisting and rolling the chain Benny gave her through her fingers.

'You mustn't think like that.'

'Do you know, this has made me realise I haven't been a good sister. I never understood what you were going through with Charlie. I haven't been there for you at all.'

Thalia was stunned for a moment by her sister's confession. Despite being close in age, their relationship had always been turbulent with a history of boisterous arguments, spiky squabbles, and long-held grievances. Thalia had never understood why they wound each other up so much. Yet, there could be times when they got along, but these were usually short-lived. Terpie showing her compassion was a remarkable event, so she found her response awkward and clumsy.

'Yes, well, don't worry about that now.'

'We've missed dinner too,' Terpie croaked.

'I wouldn't worry. It would only be rice, soup or potato. We could go and see if there are any leftovers?' Thalia sat on the bed waiting for her response. Out of the silence came a light tapping on their door. They exchanged a glance before Thalia got up to open it. Sister Stephanie apologised for interrupting their evening.

'Mother Superior has asked me to summon you both. She would like to see you in her office.'

'Can you tell us why? Is it my father? Has something happened?' Thalia's insides began a familiar simmer of unease, something she hadn't felt for a few weeks.

'I'm afraid I don't know any details. I was just asked to send for you.' The sister offered a weak smile.

'We'll be right down,' Thalia confirmed, pushing the door closed and resting her head on the wooden frame. Her mind was racing with scenarios, perhaps her father had suddenly fallen ill, or maybe there was news of her mother and sisters. Terpie stared back at her vacantly.

'Terpie, we need to go, did you hear?' Thalia slipped her feet into her flip-flops and gave her hair a quick run-through with the brush. 'Terpie, get up.'

'You go. I'm staying here,' Terpie replied, rolling over to face the wall.

'Oh no, you heard her. We both have to go. Come on.' Terpie didn't move. Thalia's pulse quickened. 'Terpie, please. I know you've had some terrible news, but I'm not doing this without you,' Thalia said, scrabbling under the bed for her sister's shoes and placing them by her feet. Terpie slid off the bed and wiped her face.

'I don't think I can deal with any more bad news today,' Terpie said, putting on her shoes.

'It might be good news, but we won't find out by dilly-dallying. Come on.'

The girls reached the Mother Superior's office and found the door closed when they arrived. Thalia rapped three times before the voice within told them to enter. Hunched behind an old mahogany desk the elderly Nun peered over her glasses, she was partially hidden by piles of neatly stacked folders at one end, an intricately carved box in the centre and two hefty books collecting dust on the other. In the dreary space, two oil lamps and a few church candles provided the only light, Thalia inhaled the musty odour and looked around. The room hadn't changed much from her memory. Along three walls, identical tall bookcases sagged under the weight of dusty, ancient tomes and the large stained-glass window with the image of Jesus bleeding on the cross stirred the same disturbance it had as a young girl. She welcomed the girls with a bland smile, gestured for them to sit in the vacant chairs opposite and firmly clasped her hands on the desk. Thalia swallowed the lump in her throat. Sitting here took her back to feeling six years old. The nun's authority always unnerved her and Mother Superior looming over the desk did nothing to relax her jitters.

'Girls, I'm sorry to disturb you, but this really couldn't wait. Terpie, my dear. There's no easy way to say this, so I'll just come out with it. I've received notification from the new authorities that you've been reported to them for meeting with a British soldier,' she said, pausing for a response. Terpie remained silent eyes to the floor, so she continued. 'Terpie, my dear, did you hear me?' she asked, Terpie nodded slowly. 'Is there truth in this accusation?'

'Yes. He's my fiancé,' replied Terpie softly.

'Well, I'm a little shocked by your actions, but I'm sure you had good reason. Now that the authorities know you're here, must hand you both over. We did our best to protect you but it's out of our hands.'

'I can't believe this. I don't want to go to that dreadful place. Do we have to go?' Thalia pleaded.

'I can't do much about that now child. But there's more. So you're in no doubt of the severity of this situation you must know that the Japanese officer informed me that Terpie's name was on a list.'

'What kind of list?' Thalia asked, looking across at Terpie, still showing no sign of being interested.

'Forgive me girls, I've never been in this situation before and I'm finding this difficult. The list is an execution list.'

Thalia gasped in shock and hid her face in her hands. Did she hear correctly? Execution?

'Just for meeting up with her fiancé? That's madness. It can't be true!'

'I hope indeed that it's not true, for Terpie's sake,' she continued, speaking directly to Thalia as Terpie refused to engage in the conversation. 'The Japanese are renowned for their brutality and scare tactics. I assure you we appealed on Terpie's behalf and pleaded for mercy to spare your sister from such atrocity. After some negotiation, the officer agreed to remove Terpie's name from the list but only on the condition that I hand you both over immediately to be interned in Changi prison. Hopefully, that will be the end of it.'

Thalia slumped deeper into the chair as the news sunk in and glanced across to her sister for her reaction. Terpie continued to stare out of the colourful window beyond, her features blank. Thalia wondered whether she heard anything at all. Feeling uncomfortable, Thalia squirmed in her seat and suppressed the boiling anger bubbling in the pit of her stomach by gripping the arms of the chair until her knuckles were on the verge of popping out of her skin.

She didn't want to cause a scene. A scream brewed in her chest, so she kept her mouth shut.

'You'll be collected at ten tomorrow morning. So please be packed and ready to go.'

A warmth rose in her cheeks and Thalia apologised whilst her sister remained a static statue, staring into space. She wanted to slap some sense into her.

'We'll be ready. Thank you for everything you and the sisters have done for us. We're truly grateful,' said Thalia, standing up to leave. 'Terpie, it's time to go.' Her sister didn't move. 'Terpie! Come on let's go.'

Terpie rose from the chair like a zombie and silently headed out the door. Thalia was enraged by her sister's nonchalance and wanted nothing more than to bawl in her face for spoiling everything, but quickly concluded there was no point. The relief gained from offloading her anger would be short-lived and besides, Terpie couldn't care less. She was so wrapped up in her own emotion that she couldn't acknowledge anyone else's feelings. Thalia couldn't trust that what came out of her mouth wouldn't be hurtful, so the girls silently walked the corridors. Thalia wanted her sister to take some ownership and apologise for the predicament they now found themselves in, but she knew from experience, that Terpie was too stubborn for that.

Back in their room, Thalia dragged her case out from under the bed and packed her possessions away. She took the lucky charm coins from the bedside table and tossed them into her case; any protection they offered had run its course. Terpie flopped down on the bed, curled into a foetal position and hugged her pillow. Thalia's skin prickled and she couldn't bear to breathe the same air as her for one more minute, so she grabbed her books from the bedside table to return them to the library and couldn't resist slamming the door on her way out. Alone in the library, she ran her fingers along the spines of well-thumbed books, books she would never get to read. In a matter of months, her life had turned upside down and she grappled to make sense of the jumble of emotions jostling through her body. She'd tried so hard to remain hopeful and to make the best of the situation; once again, it was all slipping away. Anger and bitterness gnawed at her skin. Lately, she had started to feel more like herself having settled into a good routine, but life must change again because of Terpie's selfishness. Of course, she loved her sister but couldn't stop herself from despising her at the same time. If it weren't for her, the family would be on a ship together somewhere on the Indian Ocean sailing to safety. Returning her borrowed books to the shelves, she decided not to go back to their room to spend the evening simmering, and the last person she wanted to see at the moment was Terpie. To clear her head, she visited the garden where the moonlight shimmered on the bright white walls and the cool breeze gently ruffled the leaves. Sitting on the bench with her hands under her legs swinging freely, she surveyed all her hard work and wished her father were here to see it. He would love this garden. It was funny to think that when she arrived here, she couldn't wait to leave and now desperately wanted to stay. She couldn't begin to imagine what life in prison would be like, but tomorrow she would become a prisoner. She remained in the garden until she heard the clock on the tower strike ten, silently said goodbye to her plants, and headed to bed on her last night of freedom.

Chapter Nineteen
Terpie

Terpie stared at her packed case on the ground beside the bench and found it incredible that its contents and the clothes she wore were the only possessions she owned in this world. Deep in thought, she massaged Benny's crucifix on the chain around her neck. Thalia sat tight-lipped with arms folded across her chest beside her; they had barely spoken since last night. She was acutely aware of Thalia's anger and hadn't found the words to bridge the gap between them. Terpie knew the blame firmly sat with her for their current plight, but she had no regrets.

Listening to the burbling fountain, it seemed impossible that within the next ten minutes, they would be torn away from these tranquil walls, which had become a safe home to face an unknown fate as prisoners. She rubbed her clammy hands on her shorts and tucked her legs under the bench to control her jitters. Last night when Mother Superior delivered the news, at the time, her concern and worry for Benny were all-consuming.

Nothing else had mattered, but now, in the cold light of day with their departure imminent the seriousness of the situation was beginning to sink in. When she heard the word "execution", she went into a trance. Her father warned her and she hadn't listened. Her life hung in the balance, and she could only hope the Japanese guards honoured their word. She couldn't undo her reckless actions, the damage was already done.

This morning, she woke with nausea and anxiety battling in her stomach, preventing any hope of eating breakfast and felt guilty for being so wasteful. Of course, she was remorseful that her actions had resulted in expulsion, but she didn't like the idea of prison either. Thalia would never forgive her even if she apologised and every time she tried to speak, Thalia gave her the cold shoulder and turned away. She would wait until she calmed down and try again. The sound of a truck pulling up outside the walls signalled the end of their safe confinement—time to go.

Terpie glanced at her watch; as promised, the guards had arrived precisely at ten o'clock. Thalia stood first, grabbed her case and walked to the gate to say goodbye to Sister Benita. It struck her as a curious twist of fate that she was the nun who opened the gate to shelter them and now she would be the one to send them on their way. Terpie forced herself off the bench and dragged her feet. Two fierce-looking Japanese soldiers wielding weapons approached the entrance, their heavy boots kicking up dust as they walked. Sister Benita unlocked the squealing gate and with a timid wave closed it behind them. The two girls shuffled out and stood before their captors.

'You bow to a soldier!' yelled the taller of the two, ramming the butt of his rifle into the ground. Terpie glanced at Thalia and, with hesitancy, they both bowed as ordered. It felt unnatural and clumsy. Having to perform for these tyrants made her cringe, but she decided it was better to suck it up and blank it out to get through this ordeal unscathed. Her heart beat a little faster in their presence, sweat emanated from every pore. Up until now, the behaviour of Japanese soldiers had been nothing but gossip and rumour.

Standing here in their shadow, she was in no doubt of the accuracy of the stories which had filtered through to the convent of the atrocities they had inflicted on innocent people caught up in this terrible war. The other soldier was stout, with a thin black moustache. He bellowed in their faces 'Papers!' and held his hand out expectantly. Startled, Terpie fumbled in her bag for her passport. With a shaky hand, she retrieved it and handed it over. The guard scrutinised her picture and glared at her with such piercing eyes, she looked away. He stood so close she could smell his oniony breath and sweat.

With a grunt, he handed back her passport. He turned to Thalia standing before him with confidence and her eyes sparkled with defiance. Out of nowhere, Terpie saw his arm whip through the air and the back of his hand slapped Thalia's face, creating a loud smack with such force that her head twisted violently. Crying out in pain, Thalia recovered quickly and stared down at the dirt, blinking hard to fight away the tears, her hands clenched into tight balls at her side. A surge of fear coursed through Terpie's veins, but also protectiveness for her sister, and she wanted to reach out and hug her. But she kept still, like a statue and focussed on the ground in front of her feet instead. Terpie was horrified by the angry red blotch appearing on Thalia's cheek and silently willed her forthright sister to hold her tongue for once, fearing she would escalate the situation making things a whole lot worse. The atmosphere was so tense that she forgot to breathe. To her relief, Thalia kept quiet.

'No look soldier in eye. It forbidden,' the soldier scolded Thalia in his stunted English and handed back her passport. Next, he signalled for them to climb into the truck and gave them a shove between the shoulder blades to hurry them up. Once on-board, Terpie reached her hand down to Thalia and helped pull her up. A slight acknowledgement passed between them. Eight pale-faced women were already seated in the truck with their belongings by their feet. At a glance, they appeared middle-aged by their clothes, hairstyles and soft wrinkles. Two of the girls closest to them looked younger and about their age. Terpie slid along the bench seat, clutching her case between her legs. Awkwardly, she offered a friendly smile to the blank faces staring at her. Thalia sat opposite, nursing her burning face. Terpie was sure the humiliation in front of an audience was more painful for Thalia than the slap.

'Are you ok, Thalia?' she whispered, leaning over to comfort her.

'I'm fine. Don't make a fuss,' replied Thalia curtly.

The truck engine rattled into life and pulled away from the gates. The passengers lurched forward grabbing the side rails to keep them upright as they swerved down the narrow city streets. Terpie's instinct was to comfort Thalia, but her negative body language made it clear she was in no mood to talk and definitely not to her. Her sister sat sideways, avoiding eye contact and stared out the back of the truck rather than make conversation. The young woman sitting next to Thalia shuffled beside her and placed a warm hand on her shoulder now that the soldiers were upfront and out of sight.

'Hi there, I saw what that brute did to you. Are you alright?' Thalia turned around. 'I'm Carol,' said the young woman, sliding the skinny strap of her sundress back onto her shoulder. Terpie guessed with her bronzed skin that she had been on the island for many years and was surprised by her American accent. Long brunette curls cascaded down her back, tied loosely in a red ribbon and her round face reminded Terpie of the cartoon character Betty Boop. With wide saucer eyes, long lashes and neat pouty lips. Terpie felt dowdy and old-fashioned in comparison to this cosmopolitan beauty.

'It hurts like hell, but I wasn't letting him see me cry. I'm Thalia, and this is my sister Terpie,' she said, gesturing towards Terpie, who appreciated that she hadn't disowned her completely.

'That's the spirit, girl. You don't look like sisters.'

'We get told that a lot. We have three other sisters, but they've evacuated with our mother,' Thalia said, and seeing the confusion briefly flash across Carol's face, she interjected before she had the chance to question her again. 'Don't ask. It's a long and boring story, isn't it, Terpie? We'll save that one for another day. How come you're here?'

'We got rounded up from one of the temporary hospitals. We're nurses Betty and me,' she said, tipping her head towards Betty sitting behind, smiling brightly. 'The swine's stormed into the building and marched us out. Luckily, we were prepared with our cases packed, or else we would be sitting here in our uniforms and have nothing to our names,' Carol said, scrabbling around in her floral tapestry bag and pulling out a small white pot with a silver lid. 'Here, put this on your cheek. It might help with the sting. I carry it around with me everywhere. It's a lifesaver,' she handed Thalia a small pot of pond extract cream. 'It's got witch hazel in, so should cool it down at least.'

Carol lit a cigarette and blew smoke rings in the air. Thalia unscrewed the lid and sniffed the creamy flowery scent before dipping her finger. Whilst she dabbed the cream on her tender skin Terpie asked Carol what bought her to Singapore. She had confidence about her that Terpie admired, vivacious, the type of girl who was not afraid of anything. Terpie experienced a curious stab of envy and wished she could be self-assured and comfortable in her skin like Carol.

'When I was seventeen, my parents moved out here from Durham, North Carolina, but I never quite lost the accent.'

'This cream is helping, thank you. It feels better already,' said Thalia handing it back. 'Do you miss it? America, I mean?'

'Not really. Nothing much happens where I'm from, and I love the vibe in Singapore. I don't think I'd ever go back. Your face looks better already. I told you this cream is like liquid magic.'

'What about you, Betty, where are you from?' Terpie asked. Betty wore a navy blue and white polka dot dress with a white scalloped collar and canvas daps. Her styled blonde curls were held tight with bobby pins and a navy headband with a bow on top. She looked so stylish with her bright red lipstick and looked dressed for a day out rather than being transported to prison.

'I was born in England but moved here when I was young. My father works in the rubber industry, but I have plans to travel.'

'Oh, me too! There's so much of the world to see,' Terpie said. 'My fiancé and I were supposed to marry, next week actually and we had plans to travel to Europe. None of that can happen now.'

'You poor darling. That's ghastly. Where's your fiancé?' asked Carol. Terpie glanced at Thalia just in time to see her roll her eyes.

'He volunteered for service and I just found out he's been taken, prisoner. I don't know where he is,' Terpie replied, trying not to cry and she saw Thalia scowling at her and thought better of saying any more. 'Anyway, I don't feel like talking about it.'

'That's such a sad story. I don't think I have met anyone who hasn't got some awful story to tell,' said Betty. Taking them by surprise, Carol jumped up on the seat and stuck her middle finger up towards the cab.

'Bloody Japs. They can all go to hell!' she yelled, collapsing in a heap next to Betty giggling, making everyone laugh. The girls continued chatting, filling in the time and Terpie found them easy to get along with. Thalia was fully engaged in comparing the best night out in Singapore, allowing Terpie to sit back and take a break from the conversation. She stared absentmindedly at the passing verdant scenery. She yawned. Sleep was fitful last night, with constant tossing and turning. She got stuck in a loop of visions of Benny being held against his will, all alone and she sobbed into her pillow which was still damp by morning. Wallowing in pity and overthinking did her no good at all.

The thought of facing weeks, months and God forbid years without contact from him had played on her mind since yesterday. She knew she needed to toughen up, be more robust, and be more like Thalia. She would always love him and keep hope in her heart that they would be together again, but her survival depended on living and she couldn't do that in a perpetual state of mourning. So, from today, she chose to put the thoughts of Benny aside. It wouldn't be easy, but she must try. The musical sound of laughter around her as the girls all poked fun at their jailors, safe in the knowledge they couldn't be heard from the cab upfront, made her realise that at twenty-four she was far too young to become a miserable old maid. The war had already stolen so much from her that she was determined it would not take her joy too.

The truck began to slow and pulled up outside the prison's grim, six-meter-high concrete walls topped with barbed wire. With the engine idling, she looked up at the depressing tower and the intimidating tall black gates that would keep them incarcerated. Guards opened the gates the truck slowly rolled into the inner courtyard with another lower perimeter wall and gate. Once through the second gate, which closed with a resounding bang, the truck came to a halt, the cab doors slammed, and Terpie watched the guards strut round to the back to let them out.

'Move!' the tall one yelled. Picking up her case, she jumped, and her legs jarred as she hit the ground. Thalia followed and one by one the women lined up beside each other, clutching their belongings with tense expressions and stiff bodies. The guard ordered them to follow him and they traipsed behind into a large administration office. A sense of foreboding had returned with a fluttering in her belly. The office interior was bare except for an enclosed reception desk with a sliding glass window, a row of shabby wooden chairs and a bench. Their footsteps echoed as they entered. The stuffy room felt damp and had an unpleasant musty odour like stagnant water, which twitched in her nose. White paint flaked from the walls revealing a pale avocado shade underneath and patches of black mould spread across the ceiling. On the wall was a large noticeboard with a label in the centre that read "Changi Prison Information" and a couple of worn and ripped notices beneath it. Only the reluctant shuffle of their feet across the floor and tapping of typewriter keys from somewhere in the back office could be heard over her rapidly thumping heart.

The guard instructed them to sit and he approached the front desk, his boots stomping on the concrete. Terpie's legs jittered up and down and goosebumps appeared on her arms. After a short wait, the guard beckoned her and Thalia to come forward. Leaving their cases, they approached the desk where behind the glass, an Indian man with kind eyes in a crisp white linen shirt welcomed them with an unexpected smile. In front of him were two large leather-bound books. He selected the thinner of the two and flicked through the pages until he reached the most recent entry. The pages were divided into columns and with his pen poised, he asked her politely for her name, age, occupation and nationality, which he wrote in the neatest handwriting she had ever seen. The list of names seemed endless. Thalia stepped forward and confidently reeled off her details. The Indian official thanked them for their information and just as they were about to move on, Thalia asked a question.

'Please, can you help me? I think our father has been interned here. Can you confirm he's on your list?' she asked, offering him a gleaming smile. He hesitated and nodded.

'One moment, please.'

Terpie nudged her and whispered, 'What are you doing?' but her sister remained silent and chewed on her fingernail. The officer picked up the thick heavy book and flicked through the pages until he arrived at the "P"s. He scanned down the long list with his finger. Terpie wondered if she should enquire about whether Benny was here too. He wouldn't be too hard to find with a Polish surname. Glancing at the guard, she could see his irritation in his tapping foot and a deep frown forming, so she decided against it. She was sure there would be another opportunity to find out.

'Is this him? Zacharia Pandazzi Pattara, aged sixty-six, merchant?'

'Yes, that's him. Thank you so much,' she said, placing her hand over her heart and stepping away from the desk.

'Why did you ask that?' whispered Terpie as they sat back down.

'I don't trust these monsters. I wanted to make sure he got here safely. I heard thousands of men were taken to the jungle and were beheaded, Chinese men, I think, but I had to be sure Pappa was here,' she said in a hushed voice.

'How did you know about that?'

'I read the news. You should try it sometime.'

Terpie ignored her comment but recognised the dig behind it. She knew recently she had been consumed with her relationship and had shut the rest of the world out. Reflecting on her behaviour had been a revelation and now she felt enlightened and was prepared to make amends. As soon as everyone had been registered, the women were taken to another dank room full of empty tables. With a violent thwack from a baton against the wall, the guard instructed them to place their cases on the table and open them. Terpie stood behind the table and reluctantly unlatched her case.

A guard stepped forward and rooted through her belongings in a thorough search. He held up items for closer inspection, flicked through books looking for hidden objects and tipped out the contents of her cosmetic bag. All the women's cases were searched and guards confiscated anything they felt like. Terpie was instructed to remove her watch and hand it over. Too scared to question it, she obeyed the order and the guard snatched it from her hand. Another of her belongings was gone and she rubbed her bare wrist, missing its familiar presence. Another woman from the truck had a camera seized and removed.

'Hey, that's mine. You can't take it. Give it back,' the woman yelled, reaching out to reclaim her property. Without hesitation, the guard slapped her twice across the face, left and right for challenging him. Terpie's back stiffened and she protectively folded her arms across her body. The ordeal was degrading, with a Japanese guard touching her underwear and personal belongings. With his filthy hands, he held up a pair of her knickers and swung them around on his finger, jeering across to his comrade. He ogled her with a lewd grin which made her feel sick. Her cheeks flushed red hot with embarrassment and she stared steadfastly at the floor.

At the next table, the beefy guard in front of Thalia with a pitted face shouted in Japanese, ranting until the blood vessels in his temple looked fit to burst. In his chubby hand, he clutched the coins that Shi Min had given her as a gift and with a tight fist, he shook them in front of Thalia's face. Without warning, he launched them across the room, narrowly missing a woman's head where they slammed against the wall and clattered to the ground. He spat in Thalia's face and walked away. Terpie trembled and placed her hands on the table to keep herself steady, suddenly feeling light-headed. She couldn't understand his overreaction and could only surmise that the Japanese didn't tolerate the Chinese.

To her surprise and relief, Thalia remained unruffled and calm as if nothing had happened. Terpie proudly watched her calmly wipe her face, collect her things with a graceful coolness and repack her case. Terpie respected her courage, knowing full well that if it happened to her she would have dissolved into a flood of tears. Terpie's parting gift from Shi Min had been a black writing pen which didn't offend anyone. When the guard had finished, she was left with a messy jumble of clothes and belongings to swiftly pack away before they were directed to follow yet another guard through bleak, dark corridors through the heart of the jail. This guard was agile and fast. He had a slight frame, a skinny chiselled face and wire-framed glasses, and the girls had to walk quickly to keep up with him. On the way down the rabbit warren of passages, she noted various signs for the laundry room, hospital annexe, dispensary and operating theatre, dining rooms, kitchens, and general stores.

The prison even had a mortuary which gave her the chills. It occurred to her that it was eerily quiet for a building housing thousands of people. Eventually, the corridor opened up to an external walkway, and she could now see the vastness of the buildings within the walls. Straight ahead was a vast one-storey building nestled between two long concrete blocks stretching left and right as far as she could see. Each grubby, grey block stood three storeys high with rows of tiny windows secured with vertical bars and additional mesh. It was sinking in that this was real, she was a prisoner, and there was no way out. Her chest grew tight, and she concentrated on steadying her breathing to avoid panic overcoming her.

Behind her, Carol muttered, 'Well, this is grim.' And the other women only tittered for fear of the backlash from the guards. The leading guard took them through a metal door in the right-hand block. They walked past door after door belonging to cells, some closed, some open with women chatting casually to each other across the corridor who retreated quickly like scuttling mice when they saw the guard coming. Terpie glanced inside an open cell as she passed and was horrified by the tiny space; there was barely enough room for one person, and these cells housed three or four women. No beds, just a slab of unforgiving concrete.

In the corner, a hole in the ground, which she could only assume was the toilet facilities. The heat inside was like an inferno despite the cold concrete walls, the small windows offered barely any fresh air, and the stench of body odour snagged her nostrils. Bugs the size of bottle tops scuttled across the floor, and she felt she would be sick at any moment, and her legs itched just at the sight of them. Her cotton blouse felt damp against her skin from the sweat seeping from every pore, and her hair hung lank and greasy.

'This is disgusting. You wouldn't keep animals locked up like this, let alone humans,' Thalia said, swatting flies out of her face.

Terpie's chest ached when she realised that young children were sharing this space too, curled up on their mother's lap or huddled in corners with pale faces and terror in their eyes. The guard stopped abruptly, and the line of women concertinaed against her. She forced her feet into the ground to centre herself and prayed she didn't fall forward against him and feared he would be crushed.

'This block is full. Follow me,' he ordered, turning on his heels and marching forward.

'I'm quite relieved it's full,' said, Thalia.

'Yes, although I think this is all there is,' said Carol.

'Oh, I didn't think of that.' After a pause, Thalia said quietly, 'Poor Pappa is stuck in this hell hole. I hope he's alright.'

'He is strong-willed. He'll be ok,' said Terpie reassuring her, and they continued walking until the guard opened another heavy door. Another one of his comrades stood guard on the other side. The women assembled in a huddle awaiting further instructions.

'Bow, bow, bow! How many times do you stupid women need to be told?' The guard yelled, launching at the nearest person to him, Betty, and whacked her across her back with his stick. She cried out and stumbled but stayed upright. The skinny guard screwed up his face and gripping his swagger stick hit them all for their disobedience. He swiped at Terpie, landing a blow to the back of her legs. She yelped from the sting on her bare skin. Thalia received a whack across her shoulders. With reluctance, the women bowed.

'I hate them already,' Thalia whispered once they were out of earshot. The guard marched them up a set of iron steps to the next level. This floor was a repeat of the storey below. Rows and rows of cells with open doors lay before them. With a shove, the guard pushed the sisters, Betty and Carol, into the first cell. Terpie's stomach flipped. The room was a sweatbox with a tiny window, and their accommodation came with sitting tenants. The floor was crawling with insects and flies. The girls stood in the cell designed for one person and looked at each other in horror.

'I can't believe they're keeping people here in conditions like this. It's barbaric,' said Carol, 'I need a cigarette.'

'It's the bugs that concern me the most and look at that toilet!' screamed Thalia, stamping on as many crawling insects as she could.

'I don't even want to put my case on the floor,' said Betty, surveying the filth.

A young woman appeared in the doorway and swung on the doorframe.

'Good morning, ladies, welcome to hell. I see you've checked out the facilities. They are not great, but believe me, you get used to it. My name's Sue, and I'm in the next cell.'

The girls introduced themselves, and Sue explained she had been there for a few weeks and offered to show them around. She ran through some of the daily routines of the prison and the dos and don'ts. 'Leave your cases and come with me.' The girls followed Sue down the corridor, and she talked over her shoulder as she walked. 'Each floor has been assigned a representative so any issues, speak to them. Josephine Foss is our superintendent and is on the committee and has meetings with the authorities on our behalf, she's trying to get more food, medicines, and stuff like that.'

'There's a roll call every morning at eight. It's a bind, and everyone has to troop outside and line up to be counted. That's when they tell us the notices and instructions for the day. You'll be assigned jobs to keep the camp running, and everyone has to do their bit. Just avoid the latrine cleaning if you can. That's a shit job, excuse the pun.' Sue laughed at her joke and kept walking. She led them outside. 'This is the exercise yard and where the roll call is held. The men are on the other side of that wall. Are any of you married, got husbands here?' she asked.

The girls all shook their heads. 'Good, because you'll never get the chance to see them if you did. The Japs are very strict about that. No mixing with the men. I know, I know. It's all a bit much to take in at first, and I'm rambling. When I got here, there wasn't even running water. There are outside showers and other toilets, so I'll show you those later. You may have noticed we have to look after ourselves around here. The Japs are here to keep us in order, and that's about it. If you keep on the right side of them, your life will be a whole lot easier, believe me.' And she nodded towards the guards standing at their posts around the yard. 'You're all very quiet. Does anyone have any questions?'

'Only one that you can't answer. When will we get out of here?' asked Carol.

'Well, that's the question we've all been asking,' said Sue and continued with her rapid tour of the prison. Once they had been shown the facilities, Sue left them to it.

'I need some air. I'm going back out to the yard. Are you coming?' asked Thalia.

'Yes, this place makes my skin crawl,' said Terpie, rubbing her bare arms.

'Well, get used to it. This is home.'

Chapter Twenty
Benny

The view from his elevated location across the city was nothing short of apocalyptic. The expansive window allowed Benny to witness the horror with a panoramic view. In the distance, black towers of smoke roiled skyward, blotting out the evening sun from the burning oil tanks on the harbour hit days ago, their fury still raging. The home he and Jimmy had found refuge in three days ago belonged to an accommodating Chinese family with two teenage boys. After finding the two starving and bedraggled soldiers hiding in the bushes in the street nearby, they offered them shelter. The deserters had been hiding out with them ever since.

Benny looked down at Lin Chow, the elder of the two boys, leaning against the chair Benny was sitting on, the boy's eyes laser-focussed on the street below on the lookout for danger. His mother was not too happy about him hanging around with Benny and tried several times to enlist his help in the kitchen, but stubbornly he stayed put. Lin Chow had been fascinated by the English soldiers and quickly became a shadow, following them around, asking questions about the enemy and grilling them about what they had seen. Benny's response was the same each time he asked. You are too young.

Benny yawned. Since early morning, he had kept watch whilst Jimmy slept off the night shift. On the windowsill before him, his unused rifle lay like an ornament. He had lugged this weapon around for weeks but knew he never had the heart to use it to shoot someone and take a life. Benny was under no illusion that they had no hope of evading or outsmarting the Japanese should they appear, but his training had taught him one thing which stuck, and that was to be vigilant at all times. Benny hadn't thought much about what to do when the enemy arrived. Surrender seemed the only option if they were given a chance. Secretly, he was more scared than he had ever been. With pockets of gunshots and explosions rallying back and forth, the Japs were rampaging the city below, but there was no saving it now. It was clear the enemy was a formidable strength. He and Jimmy figured they stood a better chance if they retreated to the leafy suburbs on the hill, which is how they came to be here. Did he feel like a coward? Yes, but he was a regular schoolteacher and not trained for war.

'Are they coming?' asked the boy.

'I can't see any signs, my friend, anyway, you're not meant to be with me. Your mother doesn't like you being here,' Benny said, ruffling the boy's silky black hair.

'I'm almost sixteen. She worries too much.'

'That's what good mothers do.' Benny laughed.

Then something odd happened. The skies fell silent. After half an hour, Benny nudged Jimmy sleeping on the chair beside him.

'Wake up. The guns have stopped.'

Jimmy rubbed his eyes and levered himself off the chair to join him at the window. They listened. The air, which up until now had been perforated with constant gunfire and explosions day and night, had become unnervingly quiet. Lin Chow left the room and returned a few moments later with the rest of his family traipsing behind, carrying a walnut brown Bakelite radio. With the cable stretched across the room, he placed it in the centre of the coffee table. The household crowded around to listen. The boys eagerly sat on the floor directly in front of the speaker. There was only one news report playing on a loop. Benny knew this didn't sound good, and his insides twisted whilst he listened to the crackle between broadcasts. The message when it came was clear. The British had surrendered. Lin Chow's father turned the radio off.

'This is terrible news,' said the boy's father as he slumped backwards in his easy chair. This news was no surprise to Benny, as the British only had enough provisions for a few extra days of fighting. It was only a matter of time before this inevitable outcome was announced. The allied forces were overrun from the start, and their opponents were too strong, intelligent, and diligent in their pursuit of victory. The Japanese military had outwitted them every step of the way, and now Singapore would pay the price for the British commander's folly. Graciously the homeowners agreed that Benny and Jimmy could stay with them for the time being. Jimmy and Benny discussed their options and decided to remain in hiding for as long as possible and in the days that followed, the atmosphere in the house had become strained and fearful. The father left the house daily and returned in the evening with shocking reports of Japanese soldiers raiding homes and beating families. After hearing terrible stories of brutality, the family decided to lock down and stay close to home and Benny and Jimmy agreed to keep watch.

The boys grew restless, having been away from school since January. Benny used the time by helping them catch up with their school subjects as some small compensation for the family's generosity. Providing lessons served as a reminder of how much he missed his old life, his pupils and how much he had lost. Two days after the surrender, Benny was in the yard chopping wood with Lin Chow when Taoi, the younger brother came speeding up the hill on his bike shouting in a frenzied panic. The boy skidded on the gravel; his bike clattered to the ground, and sprinted into the woodshed.

'The Japs are coming! I saw them,' he blurted breathlessly. Benny stopped chopping and set the axe on the workbench.

'Slow down, Taio, tell me exactly what you saw,' Benny asked calmly. The boy panted, his face florid and he needed a moment to catch his breath before speaking. Hearing the commotion, his mother and father came rushing to see what was wrong and began ranting in their native tongue, arms flailing. Taio looked terrified as he pointed down the hill. His words came in breathless gasps.

'There are soldiers… marching up the hill. I saw them… some were coming out of the houses. They have guns.'

'It will be ok,' Benny said, crouching to his level. 'How far away are they?' The boy thought for a moment.

'They're about halfway, but they're stopping in houses along the way.'

'Did you see how many?'

'Umm, I'm not sure. Maybe ten or twenty? Hard to tell.'

There was no time for hesitation. Benny turned to Jimmy, who had appeared from the garden and whispered.

'We have to go. Being here puts the family in danger.'

'I agree. We have no choice. Freedom was good whilst it lasted, huh?'

Benny turned to the couple with concern written all over their faces.

'We'll leave. We can't be here when they arrive. You've been so generous and kind to let us stay, but we won't put you in danger. Do you have somewhere you and the boys can hide?' Jimmy asked.

The couple exchanged a confused glance.

'As soon as we leave. Take the boys and go deep into the woods and wait until the soldiers pass. Don't come out until you are certain they've gone. Ok,' Benny said forcefully and the couple nodded.

'Where will you go?' said the man of the house, his wife behind him twisting a cloth nervously through her hands.

'I think our best bet is to turn ourselves in.' Benny looked across at Jimmy to gauge his reaction and supported his suggestion with a nod.

'I don't rate our chances of escape, and we'll be caught sooner or later,' Jimmy said.

'We don't have long.'

'I'll get our things,' said Jimmy, sprinting back into the house.

'No, you can't go! Pa tell them to hide under the house. They'll be safe there,' screamed Lim Chow.

'They can't stay, son. Let them go.'

'Please, I don't want you to leave!' Lim Chow's eyes began to pool with tears. Benny placed his hands firmly on the older boy's shoulders.

'Listen, we'd love to stay, but it's too dangerous. The soldiers are not good men and will punish your family for having us here. I can't let that happen. You're nearly a man now, and I need you to be brave. I need you to look after your family and take them deep into the woods. You must hide.'

He could see the pain in the boy's eyes and how he was trying so hard not to cry. Benny thought the boy might consider himself almost a man. However, his emotion revealed his immaturity. Benny's mind was racing. Turning themselves in guaranteed they would become prisoners at best and corpses at worst. With his fate unknown, he had to get one last message to Terpie, and an idea formed.

'There is something you could do for me. If you can.'

'Yes! What is it?' the youthful boy's skin crinkled around his eyes when he smiled.

'If I write you a note, could you take it to the Convent of the Holy Infant Jesus on Bras Basah Road? Only when it is safe though. In a few days when the soldiers have gone.'

'Yes, I can do that. I'll go on my bike through the back streets. Who is the note for?'

'It's for my fiancée. I need to let her know what's happening. Do you think you could do that?'

'No problem, I'll get you some paper and a pen.' Lim Chow ran off and when he returned, Benny leaned on the wooden bench; pen poised. What should he write? He had no idea what was about to happen and didn't want to scare her, so he kept it simple. He folded the note, handed it to Lim Chow, and hoped it would not be the last letter he would write.

'Thank you, my friend. I'll never forget you.'

Benny and Jimmy thanked the family for their kindness. Benny handed over his rifle and box of bullets to the father, should he need them to defend themselves and hoped it wouldn't come to that. He stressed again to the family that they must hide deep in the woods until the soldiers were gone. With a raft of handshakes and manly hugs, the goodbyes concluded, the two rooky soldiers slung their backpacks on and headed down the hill to face their fate.

'We're doing the right thing, aren't we?' asked Jimmy.

Benny looked over his shoulder again and gave a final wave to the bereft family on their driveway.

'Leaving, most definitely. Handing ourselves in…I'm not so sure.'

As they rounded a bend in the road, they encountered the enemy coming towards them. As Taio had said, at least ten soldiers on foot with a military truck coasting slowly behind them. With raised hands above their heads in surrender, Jimmy and Benny cautiously approached. Benny's heart thumped against his ribcage, the sound of blood pumping in his ears. The Japanese hollered an order, and four of them broke from the pack and accelerated towards them, guns and bayonets thrust in their direction. Sweat trickled down Benny's neck, and he compelled his reluctant legs to keep moving forward and prayed.

'Here we go. If this gets messy, it was nice knowing you, Polak, you're one of the best,' said Jimmy through tight lips.

'You too, my friend, it's been an honour to know you.' Benny didn't recognise the strangled voice that left his parched mouth. Seeing the soldiers running at him with guns raised filled him with terror, and he was ill-equipped to fight, and the odds were not in their favour as they were outnumbered. Confused about what he should do, he stopped short and froze. The ambush happened so fast. The soldiers were on top of them, and somehow Benny found himself on his knees in the dirt. Jerking bodies and raised voices surrounded him, and he could not focus. A sharp stab from a rifle butt pierced his shoulder blades, and he yelled out. Followed by a swift blow to the face but with what he could not tell.

First came a loud crack, his nose throbbed, and his mouth filled with a salty, metallic tang. His kidneys exploded from a solid kick from an army boot, again and again. He swayed like a buoy buffeting in rough seas until he toppled over. With no time to react, his face hit the gravel, which felt warm from the sun. Winded, he gulped for air but inhaled a mouthful of dry grit and dust instead. Kicks from what felt like one hundred men pummelled his body whilst he choked and spluttered helplessly on the ground. Closing his eyes and tensing for the next blow, he was helpless to do anything. Pain radiated through his pathetic limp body and another strike jerked his head awkwardly, rattling his skull and a guttural groan escaped his mouth.

His eyes flickered open enough for him to make out Jimmy's fuzzy body slumped beside him, his features drowning in crimson liquor. Everything happened quickly, his mind was playing catch-up and had no time to feel afraid. The savage thumping in Benny's head forced him to close his eyes, and darkness came like a slow-rolling cloud, welcoming him to sleep.

The next sensation he became aware of was the cold rush of air licking his open wounds. Was he dead or alive? The solid metal surface beneath him vibrated, rattling his brain. The rumble of an engine filled his ears, and as he came to, he knew he was in the cargo bed of a military truck. With effort, he peeled his heavy lids open, which were held shut by a sticky substance and to his surprise, it was dark. He must have been out cold for hours and certainly didn't remember getting into this vehicle. Blurry spots floated across his vision until his eyes adjusted to the dimness; he could see shapes of other bodies tightly packed around him. They appeared stony grey in the moonlight like irregular tombstones in a graveyard on the lean or collapsed, unable to hold their weight any longer.

He searched for Jimmy, but from this awkward angle, slumped against the back of the cab, he could not make out anything other than the mass of tangled limbs. Recalling his friend's blood-soaked face, fear rippled through him that he may not have survived. He would have to sit up, which was easier said than done. His limbs felt as heavy as lead. Every inch of him felt bruised, and it was impossible to tell which part of his body hurt the most. Running his tongue over swollen lips, he could taste dried blood mixed with earthy grit. With no room to manoeuvre and too exhausted to move, he gave up the idea and lay on his side watching the transitory night sky above and the myriad of stars glinting down at him.

Grateful to be breathing, his thoughts turned to Terpie. The pain of missing her overshadowed his physical wounds. It was strange to think they were making wedding plans only a few months ago, excited for their future as husband and wife. That possibility was ebbing further away and on a trajectory beyond their reach. Imagining her floating around the convent lifted the corners of his sore mouth. There was no use trying to think about the future. Things were what they were, and wishing they were different wouldn't help anyone. His thoughts then turned to his hard-working parents, whom he'd not seen for five years. They would be so worried about their only son, but he knew they were so proud of him for making a new life in a foreign land. When war broke out in Europe, they were forced to abandon their bakery business in the town and hid deep in the country with his younger sisters from the Germans. He hoped with all his heart that they were safe, and alive.

Benny had no idea how long they had travelled or where they were headed. The visible scenery around him changed gradually from open skies and tall shady trees to concrete buildings, and the cool breeze carried with it the saltiness of the sea. Edging himself onto his elbows and straining his neck, he saw the truck was part of a convoy heading towards the docks where a large Japanese cruiser loomed. The truck began to slow. Was this their destination? His fellow travellers started to stir as if sensing the change of pace, cranking up lifeless limbs from their comatose state. A mixture of groans rattled amongst the men as they moved for the first time in hours. The back of the truck became a writhing mass of bloodied bodies. Beside him, a lump of a man leaned on Benny's shoulder for support whilst easing himself up, setting off sparks of pain down his arms.

'Arghhh,' Benny cried and painfully levered himself into a sitting position.

'Sorry fella. I'm Duncan, but everyone calls me Big D.' The ruddy-faced man held his hand out for Benny to shake in greeting. His broad Scottish accent was not what Benny expected. 'Nice to meet ye.' His grip was firm, and Benny fought the urge to flinch.

'2nd Battalion of the Gordan Highlanders,' announced the big Scot.

'I'm Benny, Volunteer Force, not a soldier at all, to be honest.'

'Nowt wrong with that, big respect to a man who comes forward to fight for his country. Failing means yer playing!'

Benny wasn't entirely sure what he meant by that and just nodded and smiled.

'Are you here on yer own?'

'I'm not sure, to be honest, my friend, Jimmy. We were together when caught, but I can't see him here,' Benny said. The truck turned a sharp corner into the harbour and pulled up alongside the towering grey battle cruiser.

'Where in God's name are they taking us now?' grumbled the big Scot. The truck engine idled loudly, and Japanese soldiers began yelling whilst the tailgate was lowered. The men practically fell out the back, stumbling on their feet. Benny's legs buckled when he hit the ground and looked around frantically for the familiar face of his good friend, but strangers surrounded him. He felt so lost. He shouldn't be here. This is not where he belonged. The Japanese soldiers rounded up the men and marched them towards the gangplank to board. Their destination was unknown.

Chapter Twenty-One
Thalia

Thalia's morning routine was always the same. The only changeable feature was whether the conditions outside were hot or cold, dry or wet. Life in prison was more repetitive than she could ever have imagined but there were always chores to do. Thalia always woke early with the sun on the rise when the prison was peaceful and shrouded in darkness. With her towel draped over her shoulder, she stepped over her cellmate's sprawled limbs with the precision of a cat in the semi-darkness and tiptoed out and along the corridor, avoiding the scuttling cockroaches and bugs in her path. This was the only time of day when the concrete block felt cool before the searing rays turned it into a furnace again; skimming her fingertips along the walls, she silently exited the sleeping block. The guards on patrol took little notice of her, although she bowed to them anyway to avoid being thwacked.

Later today, she planned to visit Emily who had malaria and was admitted to the hospital wing. Thalia felt a stab of guilt that she had not been able to visit Emily as often as she would have liked. The work regime was such that she had little time to herself in the camp. The last time she saw Emily when she had been well, they sat in the sunshine whilst she reminisced and shared memories of her time with her parents before they had children. Thalia had listened intently and loved hearing what her parents were like when they were younger. Her mother was timid and unable to speak English back then, and Thalia could not picture it. Her mother had been such a strong and forceful woman throughout her childhood.

On her way, she had not seen a soul, and for that, she was grateful. This was her favourite time of day as it was a rarity to find a pocket of solitude in this overcrowded hell hole. As she rounded the corner, two older women approached her on the path. Their long grey hair scrunched behind their heads, and they shared the same bedraggled look of peasants in tatty dresses stained with sweat and manual labour. These women likely came from the once glittering high society and were now forced to endure poverty they had never known. Thalia said good morning, and they greeted her with a smile and grumbled in reply about the blocked latrines as they passed by.

The rudimentary toilets in the cells got blocked frequently. With the heat, the stench became unbearable, so they were hardly used now. The women now preferred to use the latrines outside, which were not much better, often overflowing and swarming with flies, but at least, they were out in the fresh air. Set behind a flimsy screen, wooden planks cover the deep holes in the ground, and she kicked off the circular cut-outs which covered the stinky void below with her flip flop, which sent a flurry of flies up into her face, which she swatted furiously, gagging as one entered her mouth. She cursed herself for forgetting to keep her lips firmly closed.

Having no such luxuries as toilet roll, she grabbed a square of newspaper skewered on a nearby metal spike. The only newspapers available in the camp were American tabloids which were months out of date by the time they arrived, and much of the content was of no relevance, so toilet roll was a perfect use for it. Rolling her skirt up around her waist, she squatted over the hole and immediately her presence attracted insects who came to feast on her bare skin landing on her face, arms and shoulders. Despite the uncontrollable urge to swat them away to stop the incessant tickle and itch of their tiny feel crawling all over her body, she had learned it was futile to try. It only made the uncomfortable process more drawn out in the long run. Thalia kept her mouth firmly shut to do her business. Once finished, she kicked the lid back over the stinky void.

The only luxury she relished was a shower, water cleansing her from the outside in. There was no such thing as privacy anywhere on camp, and the washing facilities were no different. The external showers comprised a crude row of pipework attached to a wooden frame with a row of ten showers. There were no screens and Thalia quickly overcame her bashfulness of being naked and exposed to others. No one here cared. They were all the same now, starved, scrawny-boned women with their dignity in tatters trying to survive. There was already a young woman with long jet-black hair under the shower. Thalia hung up her towel on the nail and removed her shabby clothes. The girl was turned away from her, and as Thalia reached to turn the tap, she couldn't help but notice the raw markings on the girl's back. She didn't like to stare, but the girl had not noticed her and was intrigued. Across her shoulders and back were a series of raised crisscross laceration scars, and the sight of the made Thalia shiver. What had happened to this poor girl? She turned away. Both girls stepped out and grabbed their towels at the same time. Thalia wrapped her towel around herself, turned to the girl, and introduced herself.

The dark-haired beauty replied, 'I'm Meena.'

'I hope you don't think I'm being insensitive, but what happened to your back? I couldn't help but notice in the shower. I wasn't staring, I promise. Sorry, I shouldn't have asked. That was rude,' said Thalia in a fluster. She felt embarrassed and wished she had just kept her mouth shut. Why was she always so inquisitive? Meena pulled her long hair over her shoulder and squeezed out the water.

'No, it's ok. I come to the shower early to hide my scars. I imagine they are pretty unsightly.'

'They look sore, are they?'

'Not anymore, although the pain of how I got them will never leave me.'

'How did it happen?' Thalia asked, and Meena tightened her towel around her body. 'Sorry, you don't have to talk about it if you don't want to.' Thalia raised her hand by apologising and batting the question away.

'I'm ashamed, and it's not something I talk about, to anyone.'

'Not a problem. I'm sorry to make you feel uncomfortable. I shouldn't have asked. Forget I said anything.' Thalia reached down to pick up her clothes. Other women were now approaching to use the facilities.

'I like to sit on the bench and let the sun dry my hair. Do you want to join me?' asked Meena. Thalia agreed and the two girls sat side by side. With the morning sun now risen, they bathed in the warm glow and the girls closed their eyes and sucked up its golden honeyed warmth. After about ten minutes of sitting in silence, Meena spoke.

'If I tell you my story, don't judge me.'

'I'm a good listener. Only tell me if you feel comfortable, and I won't judge you, I swear.' Meena looked down into her lap as he told Thalia how she and her husband would throw rocks with messages to each other on the other side of the wall. They got caught.

'Oh my god, you poor thing. They did that to you just you for that?' Meena nodded, and a tear trickled down her cheek, and she brushed it away.

'It was worse than that.' She looked up to the sky, searching for the strength to continue. 'I got off lightly. The Japanese beheaded my husband as a warning to others and made an example of him.' Tears trickled down her bronzed cheeks, and Thalia's heart cracked a little. She had never met this woman before, but instinct made her reach out. She flung her arms around her.

'You poor sweet thing. I don't know what to say. I've heard rumours about this sort of thing but thought they were scare tactics. I'm so, so, sorry this happened to you.' Meena cried on her shoulder and Thalia comforted her until she was ready to talk again.

'Thank you. I can't shift the guilt. I'll live with it for the rest of my life. My JoeJoe died because of me,' she sobbed. Thalia grabbed Meena's hands.

'No, Meena, don't you dare, none of this is your fault, and you shouldn't feel guilty for anything. Your husband wouldn't want that. The Japs are evil,' Thalia exclaimed forcefully. 'You did nothing wrong, you hear me?' Meena wiped her tears and solemnly nodded.

'I'm still in shock that they would do something so cruel,' said Thalia.

'They have no hearts. Are you married? Do you have family here?'

'Not married, no, I'm here with my sister, and my father is on the other side.' Thalia didn't feel like explaining the whole story about her mother and sisters and left it at that.

'I have no one. My parents died in the bombing.' At that moment, Thalia realised how lucky she was. This poor girl had lost everything and didn't know what to say. Everyone had a story of pain and suffering.

'You're so brave Meena. Well, you have me now. If you need anything, come and find me—anything at all! I'm on the top floor. We have to stick together, and we'll get through this.'

Meena smiled. 'Thank you. I don't feel brave. Don't tell anyone what I told you.'

'You have my word. I won't tell a soul. Sorry I have to go as I'm helping to serve breakfast, but we'll meet again, I promise,' said Thalia. The girls carried their clothes and headed back to the block and before going their separate ways Thalia hugged Meena goodbye agreeing to meet the next day. As she climbed the stairs, she could not get the horrific story out of her head and felt such sadness for Meena and nothing but hatred towards the guards. She remembered that not long ago, she had considered ways to get a message across to the men's camp to her father to let him know they were ok.

Hearing Meena's story, she realised it would be a more formidable challenge than she first thought. Her concern for her father grew daily, and she knew he must be worried about why she had not written to him again. For all he knew, they were still in the convent. It pained her to think of him alone in the men's camp, having no idea whether his family was alive or dead.

By seven o'clock, a line of scrawny women and children queued before her with whatever receptacle they could find to collect their small portion of porridge in. Today they were lucky. Half a banana or slice of pineapple was available as an extra. With the breakfast ritual out of the way, the women hurried the children back to their cells before heading outside to the rose garden for the morning roll call at eight o'clock. The rose garden was too grand a name for what was essentially a large dusty square area surrounded by a twelve-foot wall on each side so named because of a straggly dog rose with pale pink flowers surviving against the odds in the corner.

The scorching sun was already burning down as the women lined up in rows. Even though she knew it was coming, Thalia jumped slightly at the sound of the gong, which was their cue to bow to the east. This act still turned her stomach. As she lowered at the waist, she glimpsed the red circle flag hanging limply on its prominent pole. It stood out, the only flash of colour amid the bland surroundings. Somewhere along the row, a woman cried out in pain, and flinched. It was not uncommon for the guards beat the women for not bowing quickly enough, low enough, respectfully enough or just because they felt like it.

This morning, Thalia stood between Carol and Betty with her sister in the row in front. When she stood upright again, Sargent Sokomoto stood before them on the wooden, raised platform with his usual stern expression. He addressed them briskly, his voice booming over their heads.

'Good morning, ladies.'

Whilst he unrolled his daily notices to read, the other guards, Sato, Tanaka and Yamato, strolled up and down each row, counting and checking the women.

'Firstly, the petitions submitted by your committee for regular authorised meetings between husbands and wives have been denied. However, meetings will be granted under exceptional circumstances only.' Pausing for effect, he frowned as he looked across the crowd. 'And for the record, wedding anniversaries are not sufficiently strong reasons. You'll apply through the usual route by your camp representative, and the High Commander will review your request.'

Sokomoto ignored the light murmur of disappointment that rippled through the crowd and continued. He looked down to the next point on his list. Thalia felt herself swaying, and she found these announcements dull. Rarely was there any news which bought them joy. She switched off as he continued.

'I remind you that there will be no music or singing other than the allotted one-hour time on a Wednesday. Anyone caught playing music will be punished.'

Blah, blah, blah, Thalia thought. After Sokomoto rattled on through more rules he eventually rolled up his paper and tucked it under his arm before striding out of the yard. Most women dispersed in all directions as soon as he was gone, but some mingled in groups to discuss the day's notices. Terpie caught her by the arm.

'Are you going to see Emily today? Give her my love, won't you.'

'Yes, I'm heading there now. See you later.'

Thalia did not hang about. She carved her way through the dawdling women, striding at pace. Terpie had been the previous day as the number of visitors was limited. Thalia entered the small reception and waited for someone to come. A young nurse carrying blankets stopped and asked if she could help.

'I've come to visit a friend. Emily Walters.'

'If you wait here, please, I'll get the doctor to come and speak with you.' And she hurried off down the dimly lit corridor. Thalia paced around the small reception area, and her stomach griped. She didn't have to wait long before a grey-haired doctor arrived, hands buried deep in his long white overcoat pockets. Seeing his blank expression like a man about to deliver bad news, Thalia braced herself for the worst. He motioned for Thalia to sit on one of the two wooden chairs in the small room and sat beside her. Before he began speaking, she knew what he was going to say.

'I'm afraid, Emily passed away during the night. We did all we could to make her comfortable, but the combination of old age, malnutrition and malaria was too much.'

'Thank you, doctor. I wish I could've seen her one last time to say goodbye. She was like an aunt to me.'

'She passed peacefully so wasn't in any pain. She didn't have any family, is that correct?'

'No, only her husband, and he died years ago. I appreciate all you did for her. Thank you.' Thalia got up to leave, wiping a stray tear from her eye.

'There will be a burial in a few days so that you can pay your last respects. If you ask your camp representative, I'm sure you will be allowed to attend. Oh, I almost forgot, please take these. I'm sure she would have wanted you to have them. It amazes me how she didn't lose the rings. They were so loose on her slender fingers. We found the rest in this pouch she'd pinned into her underwear—canny lady. I thought I'd seen it all. I'm always surprised by the lengths people will go to, to stop the Japs taking things that are rightfully theirs.'

The doctor reached into his pocket and placed a pouch overflowing with jewellery into her cupped hands. Thalia looked down at the haul of gold and silver. First to catch her eye was a sparkling garnet stone nestled in a ring of dainty diamonds, a wedding ring, a topaz stone ring, a tangle of necklaces, bracelets and a gold watch. She looked up to thank the doctor again, but he was already halfway down the corridor, striding back to his patients. Thalia felt self-conscious carrying the haul, so what was good enough for Aunt Emily was good enough for her. She undid her shorts, wedged the pouch in her underwear, and hurried back to the cell trying to think of a safe hiding place where the guards wouldn't find it. They had taken so much already that she was damned if she would let them get their sordid hands on it. The only person she wanted to tell was her pappa. He was incredibly fond of Emily, and he would be devastated. In a way, it was a blessing that she was unable to pass on the news. Her eyes began to well up; she took a deep breath and strode on through the maze of corridors. Emily had reached a good age, but she was sure she had more years in her. What upset Thalia the most was that she died here, in this place all alone. The urge to sit under a shady tree, and cry in memory of Emily was huge. Thalia pined for the rustle of a lush green canopy overhead and craved the opportunity to rest her head against the wizened bark of a familiar friend. In her old life, which was becoming a distant memory, she would always head for the outdoors whenever she felt her emotions taking over to help keep her grounded. There was no bloody privacy here, no space to call her own, and she felt suffocated by the concrete barricades and bland greyness. She missed trees. This place was slowly choking the life out of her. A frustrated scream balled in her chest like tangled string. Walking with her head down, she didn't notice loud Margery coming towards her.

Chapter Twenty-Two
Zacharia

Zacharia was finding prison life and keeping track of time a challenge. Only the day-to-day rigid routines of working, eating and sleeping kept the days revolving around, however being a numbers man, Zacharia had been counting since day one. Today was day one hundred and ninety-four, the eighteenth of September. One hundred and ninety-four days of monotony, misery and emptiness of every kind. Enough time to become accustomed to the noise of men, their fruity and overpowering body odour, the squalid conditions and having no privacy at all.

Sitting on the rice sack he used for his bed, with nothing to occupy him, he became mesmerised by the nonsensical path of several flies circling above his head. He glanced around the grubby concrete walls of the eight-by-twelve-foot cell he shared with two other strangers who had since become his friends. Each man had an area to call his own with their few belongings pushed against the wall. Walter slept on the concrete slab in the centre, and Micky had graciously taken the opposite wall next to the toilet pit. His cellmates sat cross-legged on the slab and played gin rummy with a set of cards Walter had brought. Zacharia swatted at the flies buzzing around his head and was puzzled why they didn't leave.

With a small open window a few feet away, they had a choice to be free, to escape but chose to stay in this godforsaken cesspool. With his back pressed against the wall, his knees bent under his chin, and his head rested on his folded arms, he felt hollow, a gaping black hole in his chest. Leaning against the dismal grey concrete he wondered whether the walls would absorb him until he disappeared into nothing. Would anybody notice or care?

Zacharia stretched out his legs, and his old joints groaned. For over an hour, he had sat hunched up in the same position, his only movement being the rise and fall of his chest, and somehow even that was exhausting. Since he arrived in

D Block, Zacharia fought hard against his crippling dark thoughts from swallowing him up, and he had never experienced sadness like this before. He felt so alone and ached for his family. With too much empty time to think, he questioned his worth; who was Zacharia Pattara if he wasn't a husband, a father or a shopkeeper? He did not know himself anymore and had lost his tethering, come adrift. And how was it possible to feel the constant ache of loneliness when he had no privacy at all and shared a building crammed with thousands of men?

With so much time dedicated to his negative thinking, he could examine everything he did wrong; it was an easy downward spiral to the pit of despair. In his mind, he was a lone wolf, the alpha who failed to protect his pack. His internal voice had only one thing to say; he was a terrible father and worthless husband. The words played on repeat and prodded him during his waking hours. In these solitary moments, he battled with an incessant regret of not evacuating with his family. He would be forever haunted by guilt for not protecting his girls and being a stronger man. He had developed a stoop from the crushing weight of it.

He should have insisted, not taken "no" for an answer and taken none of Terpie's stubborn nonsense, and he could have avoided all this misery. It hurt, every second, every minute, every hour. No matter how much he tried, he could not find peace with his decision to stay. Hindsight only acted as a torment to his troubled mind. How he wished he could go back and do things differently. It took all his mental strength to find hope in a scenario where Anthoula and the girls found safety in a new life in Australia and imagined that any day now, he would receive a letter, and his heart could rest easy.

The only letter he had received was from Thalia which arrived four months ago. It was joyously uplifting at the time, but as the weeks and months passed without another, it troubled him deeply; why had she not written since? Surely, by now, she would have written again. This led him to only one conclusion. Something catastrophic had occurred to prevent his little bird from putting pen to paper, and it caused him such profound sorrow. As the authorities had banned newspapers, he had no clue what was happening in the world outside other than snippets of gossip and hearsay which were smuggled in via the locals on the other side of the walls. He functioned on the most basic level to survive each day, but his mind kept him captive. A prison within a prison.

He often thought back to those first few weeks of his internment when prisoners were kept in the houses on the edge of Changi village, which upon reflection felt like a cruel tease, lulling him into believing that being "interned" at the hands of the Japs might not be so dreadful after all. They had all been allowed the freedom to roam around the camp; his time was his own and, compared to the meals now, he was well fed, and had somewhere comfortable to sleep. What he would give to walk freely in the open air around the gardens again. Conditions then were relatively pleasant until the Japanese soldiers rounded up the prisoners a few weeks later. The melancholy cohort marched another five miles onto the main prison with their humble belongings on their backs on another sweltering day. A horrific sight greeted them on their arrival which he would never erase from his memory.

Along the high walls of the prison, a savage display of rotting, decapitated heads speared on tall poles came as another stark warning that the brutality of the Japanese was to be feared. The tortured men were of Chinese descent, and he silently prayed for the poor souls. To his surprise, as the prisoners approached the tall gate, in a final act of defiance and staunch patriotism, the group began to sing at the top of their voices, *there'll always be an England*, which hovered on the breeze long after the singing stopped. The guards looked on, nonplussed. Zacharia walked through those gates hoping that the imprisonment would be short-lived and, in a few months, they would be released and permitted to go on with their lives.

Six months on and with no signs of change, his hope of a release ebbed away. The early days were chaotic and disorganised, and conditions were terrible. As the weeks passed, men took it upon themselves to form a committee with a commandant assigned to each block and four representatives with roles and responsibilities to keep order and routine. The Japanese soldiers left the day-to-day running of the prison to the internees, and were there purely to guard, punish and supervise working parties outside of the camp. Due to their irascible nature, they appeared to thrive on the cruellest treatment and beatings, often for the slightest infraction. Only a handful of decent guards were not so heavy-handed with the beatings, but they were few and far between.

Zacharia found himself amongst men of all professions, and his fellow prisoners came from all walks of life; government officials, doctors, university professors, clergymen, miners, business owners, and engineers and all were reduced to the title "prisoner" with a name and number, stripped of any title or hierarchy gained from the outside world. Physical and mental suffering held no regard to titles, rank or wealth. The military prisoners were detained in various outbuildings or huts with civilians in the main block. In addition, over a thousand soldiers were held at the Selerang camp a mile away. The women and children lived behind a dividing wall and had no contact with the men on the other side.

The numbers boggled his mind, three thousand civilians in a prison built to house six hundred, and he had heard the military numbers were far worse. Around April, the Japanese added tougher restrictions to prevent the mixing of men between the blocks as their paranoia of inmates conspiring against them grew. The only opportunity to meet other inmates was in the exercise yard, snatched conversations on the lorries which took the men out of the camp to work or in the communal areas for laundry or cleaning. The Japanese soon set the prisoners to work and loaded men into trucks each morning to carry out manual labour and rebuild their destroyed city. Zacharia didn't work every day, and to combat the boredom, he volunteered for "fatigue" duty when the list appeared on the noticeboard in the block. He was tasked with cleaning the communal stairs and walkways every evening.

Fatigues wanted:

Clean and empty bins daily at 10:00 from each cell.

Kitchen staff and cooks wanted on a rota for breakfast, lunch and dinner (full medical required).

Chop wood.

Clean septic tank each week (additional rations available)

Various cleaning duties. Sweeping the exercise yard.

Dig and empty latrines daily.

Laundry workers.

Camp maintenance—requires plumbers, electricians & carpenters.

Roles will rotate every month, and extra rations will be provided as payment. It is forbidden for additional rations to be sold.

The violent clanging of a wooden spoon against a metal pan further down the corridor signalled it was mealtime and snapped him out of his daydream. Mickey stood over him, sweating profusely and swatting the swarm of irritating flies away from his face.

'Zac, come on, time to eat. Got to keep your strength up.'

Zacharia was grateful to be sharing his cell with good people. Micky, a motor mechanic and Walter, the owner of a small family-run hotel on the western side of town, were two of the finest characters you could hope to meet.

'Time for a bowl of delicious, sloppy rice and a cup of tepid, watery tea. Who can't be tempted by that? Come on, my friend,' Mickey said, holding out his hand to help him to his feet. 'You've been quiet for hours, are you ok?'

'Just the usual, lost in my thoughts. I'll feel better once I have eaten.' Zacharia took his friend's outstretched hand and stood up.

'You want to watch that thinking, it's not good for you.'

Zacharia grabbed his shallow metal tin and a cracked mug he used for mealtimes, and they shuffled out of the cell. The hunger and a diet of rice for breakfast, dried bread for lunch and more rice took some getting used to. It didn't help that in the early days the British kitchen staff had never cooked this type of rice before, giving everyone constipation and stomach cramps. When it was served, the rice plopped off the spoon as a waxy ball of gelatinous grey pulp, and desperation made him eat the repulsive mixture, and he worried about the gut ache later. Thankfully, since seeking advice, they learned the rice needed to be soaked before cooking so that it was palatable.

Occasionally, there would be some vegetables or fish on the menu, and a biscuit would be considered a special delicacy. As he walked, his filthy clothes clung to his sweat. The heat inside the cells was like an inferno, and most men only wore shorts, but Zacharia refused to walk about bare-chested despite the oppressive temperatures and always wore a linen shirt around the camp. The combination of physical work, which he wasn't used to, and a reduced diet meant he had lost two stones already. All the men were weighed regularly, and records were kept as evidence to support the issue of poor rations with the Japanese authorities in a bid for more food. So far, he had seen no improvement. The meals were still meagre and lacking in essential nutrition.

He rubbed his ravenous tummy, which no longer protruded over the waistband as he stood in the queue for his bland and unsatisfactory ration. Feeling the familiar ache in his hips, he leaned against the railings on his forearms and glanced down to the ground floor below. The crammed central corridor below was full of make-do beds out of blankets, jute matting and old bits of carpet. Men lived side by side with barely a shoe width between them. Recognising a friendly face, he called down to his friend Peter.

'Hey Zac, good to see you,' he waved.

'Any news on Martha?'

'Yes, can you meet me in the exercise yard after?' he smiled, which was a good sign.

'I have cleaning duty to do first but can meet you after, say seven-thirty?'

'Great! I'll see you there.' Peter waved, and he disappeared from view under the mezzanine floor. The queue shuffled forward, and Zacharia arrived at the front and held out his tin, ready for filling. A rotund guard named Chiba stood behind the servers to oversee the proceedings. His main job was to ensure portions were distributed fairly. No man should have more than his allotted ration. Having spent months with the same faces, most inmates in the block were now familiar, and Father Oswald, the round-faced priest on serving duty, slopped his five ounces of rice allocation into his tin and greeted him with a wide smile.

'We've been blessed with some variety this evening, my friend.' Father Oswald nodded towards the slop of rice and Zacharia followed his gaze.

'Is that carrot I see? What a treat.'

'Here, don't forget your bread, you earned it.' Oswald handed him a small white roll. Zacharia accepted the bread, an additional ration and only given to the prisoners who carried out fatigue duties. Hardly a fair payment, but he was grateful for the extra sustenance all the same.

'You know I always have to ask, any news on the family?'

'No nothing, no letters or word from Thalia and Terpie.' he shuffled along the line where Joe, a plumber by trade, stood poised with a jug of tea.

'I'm sorry to hear that, but small miracles do happen. Don't give up hope, my friend.'

'I'm trying not to, but not so easy.' Zacharia watched as Joe poured the tepid, dishwater grey tea into his mug and nodded to him as a way of thanks. He had forgotten what a decent cup of tea tasted like. He thought of Emily and how much she loved her tea and hoped she was surviving without it. As he wandered back along the walkway, squeezing through the crowd of hungry men waiting in the queue, Zacharia looked at the measly bread roll on the side of his tin. Was the extra hard work worth it for the small reward? He had been thinking about it for some time but decided to hand over his duty to a younger, fitter man. The physical labour was too much for him now. Bread or no bread, he was too old for scrubbing and climbing stairs. He would finish the week and then get his name taken off the rota. He saw a man hovering by the door to his cell on his approach. He recognised him as one of the block representatives, Gerrard, who usually carried out the morning roll call. He was a gangly specimen, and his bald head with combover strands looked too big for his body. Behind his wire-rimmed glasses, his small brown eyes looked like shiny buttons and beads of sweat bubbled on his forehead.

'Ah, Mr Pattara,' said Gerrard in plummy tones. He carried a worn notepad in one hand and the other, a pen-raised in the air like a conductor ready to lead his orchestra. 'I won't keep you long as you are about to eat.'

'Zacharia will do.'

'Super, well Zacharia, I've some good news for once. We're co-ordinating a list to establish monthly family visits between relatives from the women's camp. The authorities have only permitted each family with one half an hour slot a month, but we're grateful for any small show of leniency on their part. Sadly, visits will not apply to husbands and wives. The Japs are quite obdurate on that arrangement, so visits are strictly for relatives only at this point.'

Zacharia frowned in confusion as he could not understand why Gerrard was canvassing at his door whilst his meal grew cold. The rice was unpalatable warm, let alone cold. He was not up for committing to more responsibility and was already mentally preparing his excuses. With a swift movement, Gerrard flipped open his pad, peered over his glasses, and scanned the list on the page.

'Ah, here we are, I have a request from the women's camp from a… Thalia Pattara to see her father. As you are the only Pattara on record in the men's camp, I presumed this must be your daughter?'

Stupefied, Zacharia's heart raced, his legs gave way a little, and he slopped some of the insipid tea on the floor. He steadied himself against the railings trying to find some words, and his jaw hung open in shock.

'You did know she was in the women's prison. I take it?'

'No, I had no idea.'

His mind sprinted in all directions, wondering how she became imprisoned, but it wasn't important. She was alive, and he could see her. 'Can you give me a minute?' Turning slowly, he entered the cell to set his meal on the raised concrete slab. He rubbed his face with his hand and squeezed his cheeks to check he wasn't dreaming. 'Sorry, this is a bit of a shock. The last I knew, my daughters were safely hidden in a convent. I've not heard from them in over four months. Is Terpie here too? Do you know how long they have been here? Are they alright?' Gerrard raised his hand to silence him.

'I understand. It must be difficult. I'm afraid I don't have any details. I can check the intern lists to see whether your other daughter is here too and come back to you on that. This is the only name I've been given.'

'Yes, if you could, I'd be grateful,' Zacharia trembled.

'This is good news, and I'm so glad we can reunite you both. God knows we need some good news around here.'

'It's incredible. When can I see her?'

'October. Meetings will be held on the first Wednesday of the month. Once confirmed, I'll let you know the time slot, and you will meet in the admin blocks. Supervised, of course, the Japs are suspicious creatures, think we're all plotting a mass escape or something,' he snorted.

'I can't believe it. I'll get to see my little girl. I never expected this.' his eyes welled up. 'Thank you. This is the best news.'

'My pleasure, I'll be in touch nearer the time with the details and will get back to you later in the week about Terpie. Now, enjoy your meal before it gets cold.' Gerrard tucked his pen in his breast pocket and his pad under his arm and strode down the walkway. Zacharia watched Gerrard's gangly frame weave through the queuing men whilst he let the news sink in. For the first time in months, he felt jubilance and a reason to wake up in the morning. Knowing his little bird was just the other side of the wall warmed his soul. Surely Terpie was here too, though, wasn't she? He couldn't imagine they would have separated, even though they sometimes got on each other's nerves. Unless…What if Terpie had been reckless and met up with Benny again? Her defiant streak was a concern, and he couldn't trust that she hadn't defied him and got herself into bother. For now, all he could do was put his worries to the back of his mind and hope his daughters were together. He returned to his cell, and Mickey and Walter were hunched over their tins with crossed legs, beaming at him.

'Couldn't help overhearing your conversation. That's great news. I wish they let married couples have visits, but we can hope, eh?' spluttered Mickey with a mouthful of rice. 'I'm pleased for you.'

'I can't quite believe it,' Zacharia said, picking up his meal and easing himself onto the concrete slab to eat. After a few spoonsful, he acknowledged his friend's comment, which had struck a nerve. He stopped eating and flicked the remaining rice around the tin. 'I feel guilty. I can see my daughter, but you can't see your wives. It's so unfair.' He stared down into his half-eaten meal.

'Good God, man, you have nothing to feel guilty for. We're made up for you, aren't we, Walt.'

'Definitely. You grab this opportunity with both hands. Don't worry about us. Eat up and look forward to your visit.'

'Maybe I can pass on a message via Thalia for you?'

'That's a kind gesture, but no. I wouldn't put either of you in danger on my account. Who knows what those evil bastards would do to you both if you got caught? I couldn't live with myself,' said Mickey. 'Besides, I've at least seen Sheila once on the "Dustbin Parade".'

'What's the "Dustbin Parade"?'

'It's a duty reserved for married couples only, that's probably why you haven't heard of it, and those involved are sworn to secrecy.' Mickey got up from the floor and stuck his head out of the cell to check the corridors, satisfied they would not be overheard. He sat next to Zacharia and lowered his voice.

'A nine o'clock at night the pre-selected men, about twelve of us wait behind the doorway in the brick wall on the southside of the yard. Have you seen it?' Zacharia nodded despite having no recollection of ever the seeing the door. Mickey continued. 'Anyway, the superintendent of the women's camp selects the married women to take with her. Somehow, please don't ask me how. She has got word to her male counterpart before the meet who she's selected so he can arrange for the husbands of those women to be there.'

'So do you get to spend time with them then?'

'No, not exactly. The guards open the door, and two women detach from the group and bow to the sentry guard. He lets them through with the rubbish bags, and two men step forward to meet them. The women place the rubbish bags on the ground, and the men pick them up and take them away. This gets repeated until all the rubbish has been handed over. It's all over pretty quickly.'

'You don't get much time then. Can you speak to each other?'

'Only a quick whisper, but what can you say of relevance in a few seconds? Not much. I was just grateful to see Sheila's smiling face again.'

'How often can you do this?' asked Zacharia, genuinely interested in the operation.

'It's on a rota, so about once every seven weeks. It's my turn next week,' grinned Walter, glancing at his wife's photo propped against the wall.

'I'm sorry you are both reduced to a few seconds with your loved ones. It isn't much, is it? I don't understand the cruelty of it all.'

'No, but it's better than nothing, and we must be grateful for small mercies,' said Mickey.

'It's all about control and punishment, keeping us down to break our spirit, well it won't work,' said Walter.

Zacharia shovelled the last few forkfuls of his meal down, keen to get through his duty so he had more time catching up with Peter.

'I better get going for my cleaning duty.'

'Leave your dish. I'll clean it.'

'Thanks, Mickey. I'll see you both later.'

Zacharia bounded towards the stairs feeling buzzed with energy. Knowing he could see Thalia couldn't have come at a better time. Zacharia attacked his cleaning duties with gusto, completing them in half the time and couldn't wait to share his news. With his tasks finished and his brushes put away neatly in the cupboard, he made his way to the yard. As soon as he arrived at the dusty square area enclosed with dominating high walls, he saw Peter immediately with a broad grin on his face. They began walking around the yard, conscious of the guard in the corner with his beady eyes following them.

'You look the happiest I've seen you since we got here. I take it you have news?'

'Oh Zac, finally, after weeks of grovelling and nagging, the guards have brought me news of Martha and the baby. I have a son! Jacob. They're both doing well.'

'That's fantastic news, congratulations. How did you persuade them?'

'Well, I couldn't have done it without the committee's help; they have weekly meetings with Lt. Okasaki, the camp commandant and requested news on my behalf.'

'You must be so relieved.'

'I am but it breaks my heart knowing I'll not meet my son and don't even know what he looks like. For now, I'm just grateful to know he made it safely into the world and that Martha is doing well.'

'You're a stronger man than I, Peter. Poor Martha, having her baby in prison. I can't imagine how awful that was for her.'

'No, she was lucky. All the expectant mothers were taken to Kandang Kerbau maternity hospital, that's why it has taken so long to get any news. She's only recently been moved here, So near and yet so far. I can't believe my son is almost four months old, and he doesn't know who his daddy is.'

'Oh, he'll know who you are, don't worry about that. Martha will tell him every little detail, I'm sure.'

'I know she'll be a great mum. I wish I could help her. I don't like to think of her doing it alone.'

'I imagine it's quite the community on the other side of the wall. You know what women are like. They'll all rally around her. She won't be alone, I can assure you of that.'

Peter scuffed at the dry dirt with his sandal.

'I've had some unexpected news too.' Zacharia shared the information with Peter about the relative family meetings and how Thalia, now a prisoner, had requested a meeting with him.

'That's great news. Have you heard anything about your family who evacuated?' Peter asked.

'Not a dickie bird. I wonder if I'll ever find out what happened to them.'

The friends made a few more laps of the yard as the light faded, enjoying the outside air before returning to the stuffy confines of their cells before lights out at nine-thirty. After months of darkness, Zacharia found that the day's events had given him a glimmer of light to hold on to. He truly felt like he had been granted a miracle, which was enough to keep him fighting, surviving and getting through the next day.

Chapter Twenty-Three
Thalia

'Thalia, so glad I bumped into you,' Margery said, her face taking on a look of concern. 'Is everything alright? You don't look well.'

Thalia rubbed her temple and felt the onset of a stress headache or maybe from lack of fluids.

'Hi Margery, I visited an old family friend in the hospital, but she passed away last night,' sniffed Thalia, fighting off the urge to cry.

The two women briefly discussed the tragedy of suffering in the atrocious conditions here and how no one should die alone. Margery said she was sorry for her loss, and Thalia was grateful for her kindness. Margery had inherited the name Loud Margery because she was just that. Loud. Thalia suspected she was a little deaf, and the reason she shouted all the time. The fifty-something brunette was pleasant enough, though, and Thalia had met her whilst on fatigue duty doing the breakfast shift. Margery was one of life's organisers and liked to rally people together. Having no children of her own, she gravitated towards the younger girls in the camp and took on the role of surrogate mother to the lost lambs. Thalia liked her.

'Strange, I should see you. I was going to pop up and see you later anyway. Is this an ok time for me to talk to you about the sewing club?'

'Yes, of course, I could do with the distraction, to be honest. I was on my way back to my cell, so you can walk with me if you like?'

The two women climbed the black iron stairs, their steps perfectly in sync with each other. Thalia's head was pounding and she had to concentrate on the long-winded story Margery was telling her about a lady in the camp who had set up a girl guide group to keep the younger ones occupied. According to Margery, for the lady's birthday, the girls collected material between them and sewn her a beautiful quilt with off cuts and old clothes. The quilt was seen by a Red Cross representative who was so impressed, that she thought the women who had loved ones in the military camps could undertake a similar project. She had the idea that they could each embroider a square personal to them and sew them together to form a quilted blanket to send over to the men's camp with messages of hope. When Margery finished speaking, Thalia replied saying that was a lovely idea.

'I wondered if you and your sister would be interested in getting involved. I know you're not married but your father is in the camp, right? Also, it does help ease the boredom, and the ladies are a lovely bunch.' Margery oozed enthusiasm, so it was hard to say no. 'So, you'll give it a go then?'

'I would love to. I'm a bit rusty and have not done any embroidery for a while, but I'll give it a go. Count me in.'

'Come along this afternoon if you like? Our group meet on Tuesday and Thursday afternoons in the small dining hall. Bring your sister too and anyone else. I have to go, and I'm sorry to hear about your friend.'

Margery clattered back down the metal stairs. Thalia continued along the corridor and felt the jewellery pouch digging into her thigh. When she entered the cell, she found Terpie leaning against the wall with her journal resting on her bent knees, and she looked up as soon as Thalia entered.

'How's Emily today?' Terpie stopped writing and sat tall. Thalia shook her head.

'She passed away last night.'

'I can't say I'm surprised, she was weak yesterday, and I could barely get two words out of her. I'm sorry you never got the chance to say goodbye.'

'She's at peace now. Pappa will be heartbroken when he finds out.'

'The chances of that happening are pretty slim at the moment. Who's going to tell him? Are you ok? You look a bit flushed.'

'I've got a bit of a headache. I need to drink more I think.'

'What's that in your shorts?' Terpie asked, pointing to the bulging material. Thalia loosened the drawstring bag and tipped the jewellery onto the floor between them.

'Oh yes. I completely forgot. The doctor handed it to me. Emily had this stash hidden in her knickers. Look at it all. It's beautiful.'

'This must cost a fortune,' Terpie said, holding the jewels up to the light.

'How can we hide these? The guards would easily find them if they searched our room. I did wonder about burying it somewhere only we know where it is, but I think we should carry it like Emily did. What do you think?'

'It'll be pretty uncomfortable, but I guess we could.'

'It won't be so bad if we split between us. I'm not letting the Japs take this away from us. Emily would turn in her grave if she knew they got hold of it.' Thalia trickled the necklace chains through her fingers like water. 'I met Margery earlier. She's invited us to the sewing club this afternoon to make a patch for a quilt. Do you want to come?'

'You know sewing's not my thing besides, I have to finish this short story for the creative writing competition, the closing date is tomorrow.'

Thalia grabbed her ratty-looking sunhat; its edges were beginning to fray. She fanned her face vigorously.

'I don't know how you can stay cooped up in here for so long. It's claustrophobic. I need to get outside for some air. I'm so hot. I'm going down to the yard for a bit.'

'With Betty and Carol out all day, it's the only place I can get some peace and be alone. You can leave this lot with me if you want as I'm not going anywhere,' Terpie said, scooping the jewellery into a pile and filling her pockets.

'See you later,' Thalia said. The heat was getting to her today and her head pounded behind her eye sockets. Thalia was not surprised Terpie did not want to join her this afternoon. The two sisters were like chalk and cheese and did not share many interests, but they seemed to be getting on better lately since Terpie had dropped her obsession with Benny. Terpie hardly spoke of him anymore, and Thalia never felt comfortable bringing the subject of him up. She assumed that if Terpie wanted to talk about him, she would.

Occasionally, she would catch her sister staring wistfully into space, holding his cross firmly against her lips, and she wondered if he was on her mind, but she never asked. When she reached the yard, a group of children about eight years old were playing chase, scuffing up the dirt and barging into people strolling at a leisurely pace. Shielding her eyes from the bright sunlight, she recognised a group of people she knew and went to join them.

Dotty, Stella and Tina greeted her warmly and invited her to sit on the bench. They talked excitedly about the concert they had enjoyed on Tuesday night. The men from the camp orchestra were permitted to come over to perform a set of classical pieces which offered some light relief. Thalia and Terpie had sat side by side, the music had reminded them both of evening's at home in the family room, listening to the gramophone whilst their Mamma sewed, and Pappa read the paper. How she wished she could turn the clock back to those innocent times.

212

The women's conversation jumped rapidly to camp news and gossip, which naturally occurred with nothing much to entertain them.

Stella, a stern woman in her sixties who lost her husband a couple of years ago when HMS Repulse was attacked, lowered her voice before regaling them with a tale of a wealthy merchant risking his life to smuggle supplies into the camp. Stella knew practically everyone here, so when there was gossip, she was the first to know and could be relied upon to fan the flames to spread it like wildfire. If you had a secret, you didn't share it with Stella.

'How did you hear this, Stella?' asked Tina.

'Now, you girls no better than that. I can't reveal my sources.'

'I heard the committee repeatedly asked the Japs for more food because people are starving to death. I assumed they listened as we have had more variety lately. I don't know about you, but I've been grateful for the improvement in our diet!' said Dotty.

'Oh me too, the biscuits we had last week were divine,' Tina said.

'You do realise they were dog biscuits?' giggled Dotty.

'Were they! I don't care; they were heavenly.'

'Can I continue with my story?' Stella interrupted, slapping her hands on her lap theatrically. 'Thank you. Where was I? Oh yes. You're right, the committee did approach the authorities, and the camp commandant granted permission for a few women to leave the prison to shop for food in the local market. But that wasn't the end of it. A merchant on the first stall slipped a wad of dollars into the pocket of one of the women as she passed and told her to buy all the pumpkins on the next stall. They thought it was odd but did it anyway. It wasn't until the pumpkins were safely stashed in the dungeons of the camp that the women found they were tightly packed with high denomination dollar bills! Right under the noses of the Japs.'

'You mean we're rich?' said Tina.

'Shhh, keep your voice down, will you,' Stella urged, looking around nervously. 'The money won't go far with so many mouths to feed and we don't know how long it has to last.'

'That's an incredible story. We better hope the Japs don't find it,' said Thalia.

'You see, the strength of human kindness is still very much alive. Thanks to those brave and generous locals, we can have eggs, powdered milk, tins of sardines and fruits! I'm grateful for anything to keep my old bones going for a bit longer,' said Stella.

'And there was me thinking the Japs had finally developed a conscience and were feeding us better,' said Dotty.

'Pah,' Stella scoffed. 'You need to be human to have a conscience, and the Japs are monsters, the lot of them.'

This was just one of many stories circulating the camp that Thalia had heard of acts of defiance and goodwill to help the prisoners survive. Any support from the locals came with considerable risk and anyone caught doing so would be shot or tortured. Thalia struggled to keep track of the conversation and suddenly wasn't feeling well. Dull, pulsing aches began in her stomach, radiating through her body until she could not concentrate. She excused herself and returned inside to rest before meeting the sewing group. By the time she reached the second floor, climbing the stairs had become a herculean effort with legs as heavy as lead. Her progress was slow as dark blobs blurred her vision. Holding tight to the handrail she wheezed her way up the last flight of stairs. The headache had intensified, and she imagined a thousand men with hammers beating against her skull, and just wanted to lie down.

'You look terrible,' said Terpie, watching her sister flop onto her jut rug mattress like a marionette puppet whose strings had been cut.

'I feel awful. Can I borrow your blanket, please I'm freezing?' Thalia drew her knees in tightly. Terpie covered her with the blankets from both beds and touched her forehead with the back of her hand.

'You're burning up. I think we should get you down to the hospital wing.'

'Not now, please let me sleep awhile. I'll go down in the morning if I still feel bad. It's probably just a chill,' Thalia mumbled. 'Could you let Margery know I won't be able to make the sewing club. They meet in the dining hall.'

'You'll stop at nothing to get me to that sewing group.' Terpie laughed. 'Get some rest, and don't worry about it.'

Thalia slept right through until morning and knew she was no better the instant she woke. Her body shivered and ached all over, and immediately regretted opening her heavy eyelids as the room span before her. Nausea bubbled in her stomach, and she knew whatever was swirling around down there was not going to stay put for long. With effort, she clambered over Betty's feet to reach the toilet in the corner of the room. Fortunately, Carol was on duty in the hospital, so there was more room for manoeuvre. Leaning over the hole in the floor, she placed her hands on the walls to steady herself. With her eyes closed, she moaned from the pain. Her stomach was cramping now, and beads of sweat dripped off her face. She retched, acid burnt the back of her throat, and a stream of vomit splattered down the hole. Wiping the drool off her chin on back of her hand she felt the soothing cool hand of Betty rubbing her back.

'God, you're boiling. We should get you down to the hospital.'

Thalia was too weak to argue and nodded. With one hand leaning on the wall, and the other cradling her painful abdomen, she swayed with her eyes shut.

'Terpie, wake up. We need to get Thalia down to the hospital. I'm pretty sure she has malaria. She has all the signs,' said Betty.

'Thalia, can you hear me? We need you to stand so we can walk you down,' said Terpie, patting her face.

'There's no rush, and we can take our time. I know you're feeling pretty rotten, so we'll go at your pace,' said Betty.

Betty and Terpie bolstered her on either side, keeping her steady to make the long slow walk.

'She'll be ok, won't she?' Terpie asked.

'She's young and fit. A few doses of quinine, and she'll be right as rain.'

Chapter Twenty-Four
Zacharia

Zacharia stared at the floor, wedged against his fellow inmates in the back of the workers truck ready for another gruelling day. Being over sixty meant he fell into the "mature" category and was only required to do manual labour three days a week, which was a slight relief as the work was physically challenging. Still, Zacharia embraced the opportunity to escape the confines of the prison and it relieved some of the boredom. Wearing dead men's boots, workers from the prison travelled in convoy each day except for Wednesdays and Sundays to various locations around the island to carry out repair work, to lay new roads and rebuild the city the Japanese bombers destroyed. All workers performed under the discernible gaze and harsh scrutiny of guards. Today they were headed to the docks to load munitions onto ships headed for Japan. The sky at this hour had a warm peachy glow and if only the temperature remained at this level throughout the day the work might be more bearable.

When the prison gates opened and the truck cruised along the once familiar streets, he averted his gaze and looked upwards to watch the birds soaring gracefully and envied their freedom. Conversations happened around him, and he felt isolated without the energy to contribute anything of interest. As the truck neared the docks, Zacharia stared blankly at the houses and buildings baring the scars from the air assault from months before. Returning to the last location where he belonged to a family stung in his heart, he replayed visions of their hasty parting and goodbyes. Savouring the last kiss he shared with his wife and fleeting embrace before she walked out of his care was bittersweet. When he reflected on that time six months ago, he realised how naïve they had been to believe that their separation would be brief, and that life could continue as usual. There was no such thing as everyday life under Japanese rule and he was scared that he would never experience normal again. When the truck stopped, the workers dismounted, and guards led them to their workstations along the dockside, where a stack of large crates awaited them ready for loading onto a conveyor belt. Zacharia had no idea what they contained and did not much care. All he knew was that they weighed a ton and moving each one shortened his life expectancy a little more. A whistle blew, signalling the start of his long day, and as slave, Zacharia began work. The first hour usually passed quickly, but as the day wore on and the sun reached full-strength baring down on his back like a laser, he slowed and struggled to grasp the crates. Sweaty hands, aching limbs and general malaise slowed down his productivity. Wiping the sweat from his forehead, he took a quick breather. A wall of pain radiated in his lower back, sending shooting pains down his legs, and standing became unbearable. A young, keen eyed guard close by noted his lack of pace, and Zacharia did not see him coming but felt the harsh thwack across his back. With a howl in agony, and the air whipped from his lungs he collapsed on the ground. He couldn't remember falling but sensed the smell of oil and dirt in his nostrils and his body crushed and broken beneath him. Above him, other workers rallied to his aid.

'Get this man a stretcher. He shouldn't be out here. Get him back to the hospital,' shouted a man at the juvenile guard looking panicked, and he ran for help. Zacharia felt someone roll him from his side onto his back.

'You'll be ok, my friend. You're going back to camp. Do you think you have broken anything? Can you move?' said the voice.

Zacharia groaned. He wasn't sure as his whole body throbbed from the top of his head, down the tips of his toes. The only break he knew for sure was deep in his chest and beyond repair. He moved each limb in turn, and with help, he managed to sit up. Nothing appeared to be broken, but his body and pride had taken a bruising. With his arms flung over the shoulders of two men, they lifted his fragile form, loaded him on the truck, and he was transported back to camp. Riddled with exhaustion, he nodded off to the rhythmic rumble of the engine. On arrival, two unsympathetic guards walked him at their pace to the hospital wing, where he was grateful to sit down to receive a thorough once over.

'Mr Pattara, you have no broken bones, which is good news. How old are you?'

'Just turned sixty-seven,' replied Zacharia, sitting on the hospital bed with his legs dangling off the edge like spindly branches of a tree.

'I expect you were in good health before coming here, but like so many, the conditions are taking their toll, and you, my friend, are no exception. I'm concerned about your heart. You're not a young man anymore, and this manual labour is too much for you.'

'Thanks for the reminder, Doctor,' Zacharia laughed. 'I looked after myself and suffered the same aches and pains as most my age before Changi, but since being here. I feel I've aged ten years.'

'I'm afraid you'll have to stop the manual labour. I'll write you an exemption certificate so there will be no more hard work for you in the future.'

'But you can't do that! I won't get any food. You know the rules, doctor. No work, no rations,' said Zacharia in alarm. This was how it was. He did not want to become a burden to the other men for them to have to share their already limited rations. 'I have to work to earn my meal.'

'If you continue working, Zac, you'll not be around to worry about meals. It's that serious. You have a family?' the doctor questioned and Zacharia nodded. 'I strongly suggest that you look after yourself as much as possible. The other men are used to sharing with the sick. They'll see you are alright.'

'What will I do with myself all day?'

'I'm sure you'll find something to occupy your time. There are plenty of chores around the camp you could help with, nothing too strenuous, of course. You're well enough to return to the cells but have internal bruising so take it easy for a few days.'

In a daze, Zacharia slid off the bed. The hospital corridors were overflowing with patients on temporary beds and Zacharia asked the doctor if it was always like this.

'It's worse at the moment due to an outbreak of dysentery caused by a contaminated water supply and a higher number of malaria cases than usual.'

Zacharia's attention was drawn to the sound of screaming, and he turned to see the man in the adjacent bed flailing his arms around and kicking his legs in distress. Rooted to the spot, he couldn't help but watch as nurses restrained him and calmed him down. The poor man was delirious and confused. Shocked and a little repulsed by the look of the man's skin, Zacharia had never seen anything like it. The poor man's arms, hands, face and neck, were covered with dry brown scaly patches which resembled burns or scalds. Zacharia looked along the row of beds to see that others had the same affliction. The distressed man was now calm and lying still.

'What's wrong with these men?' Zacharia whispered to the doctor.

'It's an unusual illness called Pellagra, caused by a deficiency of vitamin B. Causes the skin to blister, dementia in the brain, confusion and delirium and diarrhoea. It can be fatal if not treated. Once the patient's levels of the missing vitamins are rebalanced, they should be right as rain. We are treating him with marmite. It'll be a long road to recovery. As you can imagine, marmite is hard to get hold of. With the poor diet provided, we see the return of some diseases not seen for many years. The lack of thiamine, niacin and riboflavin from the vitamin B complex is causing these deficiency syndromes, all very unpleasant for the patient.'

'So what you're saying is that this can be avoided then? All this suffering,' Zacharia asked.

'Oh yes, most of the problems we treat are caused as a result of a poor diet. The rice supplied is polished white rice and has very little nutritional value. The body doesn't run efficiently and becomes susceptible to disease because of the lack of meat, fish, vegetables, eggs, milk and cheese. I've never seen some of these conditions in my medical career. Anyway, I hope you will heed my warning and take things easy. I mean this is the nicest possible way, I don't want to see you back here.'

'I understand doctor. If nothing else, I'll do it for my girls as I'm all they have left.'

'Good man,' said the doctor, slapping Zacharia on the shoulder.

In addition to his concerns over his health, he considered himself a strong man, being a provider, and he despised relying on others. He knew he should feel relieved as the work was killing him, and the doctor was right. To survive and get out of here alive, he had to stop working. He had noticed pains in his chest recently but dismissed them as anything serious, thinking it was muscle ache from all the lifting but the thought of having no purpose was equally frightening. He had to keep busy and motivated to stop despair from creeping in. On reaching the main body of the prison, he stopped at the information board for inspiration. With so much time on his hands, he decided he may as well put it to good use, learn something, a new skill. Posted on scraps of paper were lists of lectures and classes run by the professors and teachers. If nothing else, he could sit in one of those and maybe learn something of interest. Then he saw the perfect thing, a carpentry course.

Chapter Twenty-Five
Thalia

Thalia wiped the sweat dripping off her forehead on the back of her hand and squinted at the harsh afternoon sun. Her arms felt like taught rubber bands ready to snap at any moment. Casting a surreptitious glance over her shoulder, she saw Sokomoto on patrol, walking away from her in the other direction so she could afford a *little* break. She eased up and stretched out her back, moving her head from side to side, the audible creaking of her vertebrae echoed inside her head. As the nurses predicted, she recovered quickly from her bout of malaria and generally felt well, except for tiring easily. It didn't stop her pitching in with the working party of women put to labour around the camp. Thalia would rather keep busy and occupied than sit around with nothing to do but contemplate her existence and have boredom drive her insane. The women had learned to become self-reliant without men around to do things for them. The manual work was tough, but they would not be defeated. Fearing a beating for laziness, she got back to her task. Today she was clearing out undergrowth from blocked drain gullies where it had sprouted wildly. For six solid hours, she had been bending, pulling, ripping and the palms of her hands stung, and her fingers had become so stiff they refused to bend. Crenulated leaves as sharp as knives and razor-sharp grasses ripped her palms to shreds as she yanked the plants from their stubborn roots. With no such luxuries as gloves, she had improvised by wrapping some material from old rags around her hands, which protected them from the toughest vines. Outdoor work was the closest she came to gardening; she preferred the fresh air, which was the only reason she had volunteered for this task. She wavered like an unsteady ship in high winds with her legs spread wide over the deep gully. In front of her, Meena tugging at the weeds, turned and gave her a brief smile. The end of the working day was approaching, and she would be relieved to hear the final whistle. Her back was stiff from bending, and her knees were giving out. Her scrawny legs resembled a patchwork of deep red scratches, old and new, colourful bruises and a peppering of oozing insect bites which kept her awake at night with her ferocious itching. Her shabby dress was sweat sodden, smeared with mud and splattered with stinky drain water stains. For labouring, she wore a battered old pair of men's boots which didn't fit and rubbed blisters, so she was eager to slip on her flip-flops and let her feet breathe. Her hair held no style anymore, which she kept off her face with a headscarf and a straw hat to protect her from the harmful rays. She thought of all the beautiful dresses and shoes she used to have in her wardrobe at home and realised what a privileged life she and her sisters had and taken for granted. For a young woman in her early twenties, she felt more like an old sow, her skin was dry and flaky from poor diet and hours in the sun, and her periods had stopped since she got here, not that she minded that so much. She heard the shrill whistle to indicate they could stop, and her body sagged with relief. Sergeant Sokomoto bellowed an order for the women to stop and assemble into a single file line and followed him like good little soldiers back to the camp. Thalia needed a shower. The thought of cool water cleansing her sunburnt, dry skin at the end of a hard day was the closest thing she had to any kind of pleasure. She said goodbye to Meena and began the climb to the top floor, which ordinarily was a chore and backbreaking after a day in the fields, but the thought of dinner being served soon spurred her on. It would be the usual soggy rice and perhaps some sardines again if they were lucky. She guzzled water from the drinking tap until her thirst was quenched and wiped the dribble from her chin. It had been unusually hot for September with temperatures above thirty-two degrees, and she welcomed the rainy season. She had never sweated so much in her life since being here. On her way to her cell, she scanned the bulletin board to check that she hadn't missed anything important from zoning out in the boring roll calls. A notice on cream paper headed "Family Visits" instantly caught her eye. This wasn't mentioned and she certainly would have remembered hearing news as monumental as this. Her heart thumped and she continued to read. The form offered visits for relatives to meet with family members from the men's camp one day a month. Anyone interested needed to register with their block representative. Only two members of the family could meet at once. The first meetings would take place in October, but in bold capital letters, it categorically stated that husbands and wives were not permitted to apply. Why on earth they made this stupid rule, she could not understand. Her heart soared, and her eyes pooled with happy tears. This was the best news. By October, it would be eight months since she had seen her father, and they had so much to catch up on. More importantly she had to know he was alright. She placed her hands together in prayer and beamed at the idea. She was excited to share the news with Terpie. It occurred to her that she had to remain healthy between now and the visit day. She could not allow herself to get sick again and risk missing the chance to see her pappa. Terpie predictably sat cross-legged writing in her journal when she reached the cell.

'Terpie. Have you seen the noticeboard?' she said, crashing into her sister as she kicked off her boots.

'Hey, slow down. No, I haven't. Why?'

'I hope you've not been sitting here all day. You need to get out of this concrete box once in a while. It's not good for you. You look very pasty and need some sun.'

'Thanks. I do. I mean, I have. I went to choir this morning. You stink, by the way.'

'I've got some fantastic news. You're not going to believe this,' Thalia said, clasping her hands and grinning from ear to ear.

'Are we being freed? That's the only news that would interest me,' Terpie sighed.

'Oh, Terpie, stop being such a grouch. They're allowing monthly family visits. We can see Pappa. Isn't it wonderful!'

'Goodness, that is good news. When can we see him?' asked Terpie, eagerly leaning forward for more. Thalia sat opposite her sister.

'The meetings will begin next month, we have to put our names down, but… there is one problem,' she frowned. It would be ok. Terpie wasn't bothered about Pappa's welfare; she never mentioned or said she missed him.

'What? Tell me.'

'Only one of us can go at a time. So, one of us will have to wait until the November visit.'

'Oh, I see. That is a problem.'

'I have to see him. I need to know he is ok.'

'Why do you think your need to see him is greater than mine? He is my pappa too. I am the eldest, so I'll go first, and you can go next month.'

'Are you joking? You know how much I've been missing him. You don't even mention him, or anyone come to that. You've about as much emotion and compassion as a brick at times. I know you are jealous of our relationship and are just doing this to spite me,' Thalia raged, now up on her feet, showering Terpie below with the steam from her anger.

'Ok fine, have it your way. You usually get what you want in the end, and I can't be bothered to argue with you. But for the record, I do miss him and all the others. I don't feel the need to express it constantly.'

'I can't believe you have the gall to say that after everything that has happened. We wouldn't even be here if it wasn't for you. So don't talk to me about getting my way. You ripped our family apart, and I hate you for it and will never forgive you.' Thalia's face was bright red, and the word "never" spat from her mouth with venom.

'Perfect little Thalia who's never done anything wrong. Always Pappa's favourite. I knew you would never let it go and would hold it against me forever. Don't you think I wish I could change what happened too? I carry that guilt every day.'

'Good, I'm glad. You should feel terrible. People are hurting because of you. Firstly, for splitting the family up, secondly for getting us thrown out of the convent and thirdly for just being a dreadful bore and thinking of nothing else but Benny.' Thalia counted the points on her fingers and mimicked her sister's lovesick puppy voice when she said Benny's name. 'I can't help being Pappa's favourite, hardly my fault. I enjoy spending time with him. You're consumed with your writing and Benny, and nothing else matters to you. Whilst the rest of us have to suffer in your wake.'

'You're just jealous, Thalia because I have someone who cares about me. You need to grow up,' Terpie yelled, jumping to her feet.

'You're the last person I'm jealous of. You're selfish and self-centred, and I'm glad to be nothing like you,' shouted Thalia, pointing her finger towards Terpie's face.

Betty walked in at that moment and stood between the battling sisters. Thalia had not held back and could see Terpie looked defeated and uncomfortable. It needed to be said. Thalia had kept her frustrations held in for too long, bitterness had pumped through her veins for months, and Terpie needed to hear it.

'Hey, hey girls, what's going on here? I don't think I've ever heard you two fighting before. Half the corridor can hear you,' said Betty.

'Yes, well, this is what we're usually like,' Thalia spat.

'Surely whatever it is can be resolved. Do you want me to go?' asked Betty.

'No Betty, it's ok, stay. Thalia, I'm sorry. I was being spiteful. I want to see Pappa, but you are closer to him than me, so go and put your name down and mine down for November. I've always been jealous of your relationship and don't feel like I fit in the family. Let's not fight. It's been nice the last few months of us getting along. I know you're still angry at me for what I did at the convent, and I couldn't find the words to apologise at the time, but I want you to know I am sorry. With nothing but time in here, I've thought about things and agree that it was my fault, and I'm not proud of it. It pains me to admit, but you're right. I was selfish. Please, will you forgive me?'

Thalia's jaw dropped. This was a monumental moment. She was shaking and had to sit down.

'I'm sorry too. I hate fighting. All this time and I thought you didn't care, and I've been so mad at you. Of course, you fit. You're my sister. I'm angry about what happened, but I don't hate you. Actually, I said a lot of unfair things. Let's put it behind us and never mention it again.'

'I've realised how badly I behaved towards you all. I love Benny and miss him terribly, but some reflection time has shown me that I thought of nothing else. It wasn't healthy. I shut everyone else out. I'm not blaming anyone, but I clung to him because I felt left out of the family. I've never been anyone's favourite.'

'I didn't know you felt like that,' said Thalia quietly.

'Why would you? Anyway, I know I can't make it up to the family. I want to forget about it and hope they forgive me.'

The girls agreed to put the past behind them. What was done was done. All Thalia ever wanted was for her sister to show remorse for how her actions had impacted them, and now she had apologised, the balance had been restored. The war wasn't Terpie's fault; the invasion was why they had been driven out of their home. She needed to remember that.

'Phew, well, I'm glad that is sorted. I feel I can leave you both, and you won't be ripping each other's eyeballs out,' laughed Betty, picking up her towel hanging over the door and walking out.

'There is one more thing we need to discuss,' said Thalia. 'Should we tell Pappa that Emily passed away? He was fond of her, and I know he'll have been worrying about her. I'm just concerned it might be too much for him to take.'

'I think he should be told, but he'll be devastated. Maybe when you see him judge what his mental state is like. If you feel it would be too much for him at the moment, then hold back. I mean, what's the harm? Maybe it's kinder to let him believe she is fine. What do you think?'

'I'd hate lying to him. You know I can't. Just think how upset he would be if he found out later and knew we didn't tell him. No, I can't do that to Pappa. If he's very down, I'll say she's poorly, and perhaps you can tell him on your visit that she did not recover. Break it to him gently.'

'Ok, let's go with that. I can't believe we get to see him after all this time. I wish we had some news to tell him about the others,' Terpie gasped and moved awkwardly. 'Ouch. This jewellery. It's digging in today. I wish we could find somewhere safe to hide it.'

'It's alright for you. You haven't been out in the heat working in the fields all day,' teased Thalia, giving her a gentle shove. 'I don't know how you manage to get away with doing the chores that require the least effort, and you never get dirty.'

'What can I say? I like working in the office, plus I can steal paper for my writing,' Terpie laughed.

'It would be helpful if you could use your connections to find out information about the evacuee ships.'

'I am trying. I want to find out what happened to them as much as you.'

Chapter Twenty-Six
Zacharia

'Today's the big day then. I'm so chuffed for you,' said Mickey.

'Yes, it's finally here. I'm so excited to see my little bird I hardly slept,' replied Zacharia, folding his blanket and laying it neatly on the floor.

'That's what you call her? Little bird. Nice. My father just used to call me a little shit and give me a clip round the ear,' laughed Mickey, but his face dropped to the floor, so Zacharia recognised there was hidden pain behind that statement.

'It's just our thing. We like gardening and nature and would sit out on the veranda in the evenings watching the birds come and settle and fly away again. I said she would fly away one day too, and that's how it started, I think. I'm sure he didn't call you that all the time. Did he?'

'My old man wasn't like you, Zac. He had a temper and didn't realise he didn't like children until he had some of his own. My childhood memories involved him ignoring my existence or venting his frustrations on me. He left when I was ten. Your girls are fortunate, growing up with a father who cares so much.'

'Mickey, how awful. Have you seen him at all since being an adult?'

'Not really. Our paths have crossed a few times. He came back into my life in my early twenties, but we were strangers. He knows nothing about me, and I've no respect for him, so there's no relationship to be had there. It would have been easier not to have a father at all in some ways. I remember as a kid always trying so hard to make him like me, but nothing was ever good enough, and in the end, he left anyway. I thought I was to blame for why he left. It took me years to realise it wasn't my fault. He left for another woman he met in a bar,' Mickey said, pushing himself off the wall and dismissed the conversation with a wave. 'Anyway, enough about him. I just wanted you to know it's been good for me to see how it can be different. I know you're a good father by how you talk about your girls. You're present in their lives and take an interest.'

'Thank you, Mickey, that means more than you'll know. I had a bad relationship with my father growing up too. I worried I would become him when I became a father.'

'But you didn't, and I don't think you ever could because you know what it felt like.'

'No, I didn't, but I still have my demons. I worry I've not been a good enough father. I worked a lot when they were young. I missed so much and can't help feeling I've let them down,' said Zacharia, spinning the loose wedding band around his finger. Since losing so much weight, he was terrified of losing it but could not bear to take it off. It felt like a betrayal to Anthoula, so he would keep it on as long as he could.

'I'm sure you're being too hard on yourself,' said Mickey.

'Too much time in here makes you question everything. I suppose the last straw was feeling I couldn't protect them from this. I couldn't keep them safe.'

'No one stood a chance against the Japs. When you see Thalia today, you'll see the love in her eyes, which will dissolve all those silly doubts from your mind.'

'I suppose you're right. Anyway, I'm off to get a haircut to make myself presentable. See you later,' said Zacharia, striding out of the cell purposefully. The promise of time with Thalia this afternoon set off fireworks in his belly, and he couldn't stop smiling. Since finding out she was in prison, niggling questions circled in his mind on a carousel. Round and round they went, driving him insane. Finally, he would have answers to his most urgent questions. Half an hour would never be enough and would pass quickly, so he was mindful not to get too carried away. After a visit to the friendly barber, he took himself for a shower. Standing before the round mirror rusted at the edges, he peered at the gaunt, sallow face staring back at him. No matter how hard he scrubbed, no amount of water would wash away his dishevelled appearance. Slowly he touched his face, the thin skin pulled tight over his bony cheeks, along his angular jaw and thin, dry lips. He barely recognised his reflection and hoped his appearance would not terrify his daughter when she saw him. Zacharia had always enjoyed his food and had a healthy appetite, and who wouldn't with a cook as good as Shi Min, so his figure had always been on the rotund side, but now his potbelly had vanished, and his stomach had more of a concave appearance. He was back on fatigue duties around the camp to earn a little extra, as he didn't want to become a camp statistic. The number of deaths was increasing and had become so bad that coffins could not be made quickly enough, and wood was in short supply, so bodies wrapped in blankets were the best burial you could hope for with a short ceremony and few attendees. There was nothing like being surrounded by death to make you question your mortality, and Zacharia tried not to think his days could be numbered too. He had hours to kill until his meeting, and he needed to keep occupied, so on his way to the main block he scanned the noticeboard for activities he could join. Pinned to the board were various pastimes he could engage in, but nothing on the list appealed to his current mood. Before setting off to the library, a ragged piece of paper pinned to the bottom of the board caught his eye.

'Come and play the King's Game. Chess. Room 141 (by the cobbler's station).'

His mind flashed back to the last time he played, with Thalia under the table, when his family were together. He swallowed down the emotion that took him by surprise and decided that a chess game would be the perfect way to occupy his mind. When he found it, the cobbler's station was a tiny room, more like a cupboard with no door and light flooded in from a barred window. He stepped in and looked around. Along one wall stood a rickety wooden shelf housing a row of repaired men's and women's footwear neatly labelled ready for collection, boots, brogues, sandals and flip-flops, their lives eked out a little longer for their owner. On the wall opposite was a workstation and small wooden stool tucked under, and beside it on a hook hung a grubby apron which had seen many days work. No one was around, so he turned to leave and saw a man standing in the doorway.

'Sorry, the repair shop is only open two days a week. You can leave your shoes with me, and they'll be done by Friday,' said the middle-aged, balding man before he took a long drag on his cigarette. Seeing that Zacharia was empty-handed, the man lowered his voice. 'Or maybe you're here to collect a letter?'

Zacharia had no idea what he was talking about.

'I was looking for the chess game. What do you mean about a letter?'

The man put his finger to his lips, and gestured for Zacharia to follow him into the cell next door.

'You've come to the right place for a game of chess. I'm Robert, but I get called Rob, Bert, and Bob. Call me what you like, I answer to them all.' The man extinguished his cigarette under his shoe, and picked up the butt. Zacharia introduced himself and followed. Inside, two chessboards were arranged on the floor. Two men already sat cross-legged, silently engaged in a game. They nodded to him as he entered. Robert put his cigarette butt in an ashtray on a small table inside the door.

'Do you smoke Zacharia?' asked Robert.

Zacharia replied saying he used to when he had his cigarette business in the town but gave up twenty years ago. He did not want to at the time, but Anthoula was relentless with her nagging about his health. She usually swayed him around to her way of thinking in the end.

'I keep thinking I should give up, but few things keep me going in this place, and smoking's one of my pleasures,' he said, nodding towards the small tin of Players cigarettes and swept up some loose ash from the table placing it in the ashtray. The light in the room was dim from the single light bulb hanging from the centre of the yellow stained ceiling, and there was a long narrow window the length of the wall, which was open, not that the room was any fresher for it. Thick stale nicotine hung in the air interlaced with stale sweat.

'So, you fancy a game, please take a seat,' Robert said.

There were no chairs. Only a tatami straw mattress wedged along the wall with a pillow and a blanket. Thin cushions were placed around the chessboard on the floor, and Zacharia lowered himself to the ground with a groan. Once seated opposite each other cross-legged, Zacharia asked Robert again what he meant by a special letter.

'Can I trust you with this information? Not to pass it to the Japs?' he asked, placing the pieces on the chequered board in front of them.

'Oh, my goodness, of course, I wouldn't tell those monsters anything.'

'I thought so. You look like an honest man,' he smiled, revealing large gaps between his yellowed teeth, 'I allow letters to pass through my cobbler station to the women's camp. See, it works like this. The women write letters, conceal them inside a pair of shoes, and give them to their camp superintendent, Miss Foss. She brings them over for repair and I pass the notes on to their husbands. Then when the shoes are returned, we sneak a note back. Ingenious, don't you think?' Robert grinned from ear to ear. 'If you have a letter, you would like to send over, let me know.'

It was indeed ingenious. Any scheme or plan hatched right under the Japs noses outwitting them, which made life more bearable could only be good thing.

When he saw them next, he was excited to share this new information with his friends.

'I'm sorry about your wife and daughters,' Robert said, placing the last piece on the board. 'I've got connections on the outside because the committee permits me to leave on prison business once a week. They give me an allowance, and I buy food from the local market and other goods. I could ask my contacts to see if they can find any information about the evacuation ships. I'm sure others in here are waiting for news like you.'

'You would do that? It's driving me insane, not knowing.'

'I can't make any promises. I'll ask around though,' said Robert, lowering his voice. 'Singapore's a different place now. Conditions for locals are as bad out there as they are in here. They have food shortages too and are subject to unfair treatment. The Kempeitai have set up their headquarters on Stamford Road in the old YMCA building. They arrest people with little or no evidence and beat and torture them for days to get information. People are living in fear, especially the Chinese. It's not unusual for people to go missing and not return and the young women live in fear of being raped. The streets aren't safe anymore. Any help they give us is putting them in danger.'

'I had no idea it was as bad as that. Don't take unnecessary risks on my account. I'm desperate to know what happened to my family but not at the expense of an innocent life,' said Zacharia gravely.

'Don't concern yourself, Zacharia. The locals like to help. It makes them feel useful. The war isn't over, and people want to fight the only way they know how. Shall we get this game started?' Robert asked.

He had won the coin flip and began the game by moving his white pawn two spaces. The game was intense with both players focussed on the board. Robert was a worthy opponent, he played strategically, no rushing, and each move was made with great concentration. Zacharia had spent the last few moves being chased around the board with only a knight, a pawn and his king remaining. He found himself lost in the battle and appreciated this time when his mind was quiet and the moves on the board were the only concern. Robert confidently moved his bishop in, backed up by a rook and called 'Checkmate.'

'Congratulations, what a great game. I can't tell you how much I enjoyed that,' Zacharia said, reaching over the board to shake Robert's hand.

'You're a strong player. We must play again sometime.'

'I'd like that,' said Zacharia, and he gasped, suddenly remembering his meeting. 'Oh no! Do you know what the time is? My family visit!' The rise of panic rise in his chest made him queasy. He'd been so engrossed in the game; he'd forgotten about the time. Silently cursing the damn Japs, he scrabbled off the floor. They were responsible for all his suffering. He could have kept an eye on the time if they had not stolen his watch from him on arrival. Remembering with fondness the cream faced timepiece encased in gold with a chocolate brown leather strap, his fiftieth birthday present from Anthoula. Another treasure lost. He held his breath. Robert dug deep into his pocket, pulled out a small watch face, and confirmed it was almost four o'clock. Zacharia sighed in relief.

'Thanks for the game. We'll play again. Good luck with your visit and come to see me whenever you need to get a note to your daughter.'

Zacharia thanked him again and promised he would be back. With no time to waste, his galloping heart steered him towards the admin block, his tummy performing cartwheels, and he couldn't decide whether it was excitement, nerves, or both. Ignoring the aching and grinding in his hips he hurried through gloomy corridors, his heart thumping loudly and his sandalled feet shuffled along as speedily as his wasted limbs would allow. He could not afford to miss this meeting, it has been the only thing to bring him any joy for months. Puffing and holding his chest, he approached the back end of a short queue of men and slowed until finally he wobbled and rested his hand on the wall to keep him upright. Gasping for air, he wheezed. He'd made it.

Shortly after his heartbeat regained its regular rhythm, a grey metal door screeched open, and the queue of men shuffled forward. His precious daughter was on the other side. His limbs twitched with excitement, and a fuzzy delight tickled his stomach; around him, he sensed anticipation in the waiting families, desperate to be reunited with loved ones. The line of family members filed one by one into the room. As the last one in, Zacharia scanned the spattering of occupied tables and chairs for the face he longed to see. The dry air tickled his nostrils with the sickly odour of fresh sweat. Inside the walls were shade of grimy white, which provided a backdrop for dark shadows cast by bare lightbulbs hanging from the ceiling. The room was hot and stale. A guard occupied each dingy corner, and another strutted up and down between the tables like a preened peacock. Chairs made a scraping noise as their legs dragged across the concrete, and the room was suddenly packed with noise, filled with emotional greetings and tears of joy as loved ones reunited. Zacharia weaved around the tables, and saw her across the room. His heart swelled like a freshly inflated hot air balloon, and he viewed her through a watery blur due to the quick onset of joyful tears. She was up on her feet now, waving furiously at him, and a bright smile filled her thin face. With his eyes focussed on her, he glided between the chairs and collapsed heavily into the seat opposite her. Every fibre in his body screamed to scoop her into his arms and hold her tight. A sign plastered on the table in thick black writing clearly stated, *No contact other than hands across the table is permitted.* With outstretched arms across the void between them, he clutched her dainty hands so tightly he was in danger of crushing her fingers. His eyes darted all over, looking for signs of miss harm or neglect. Thalia had lost weight, her lank hair grown past her shoulders bleached by the sun, and her skin looked blotchy, dry, and flaky in places. But she looked happy.

'Pappa, I've missed you so much,' squealed Thalia, her eyes awash with tears.

He had so many things he had planned to say, and none of them came to the surface. The emotion of the moment overwhelmed him, rendering him speechless. A few stray tears dripped off his cheeks bleeding into the woodgrain on the table. Thalia entwined her fingers with his, and she squeezed gently.

'Pappa. I'm fine. Terpie's here too. We're ok,' she reassured him.

His brave girl was comforting him, and he had desperately wanted to show her he was strong too, but now sitting across from her, he was a blubbering wreck. Her tales of the last few months filled the space between them, and he was happy to let her words roll over him, so he listened and drank in her every word. He nodded and smiled back at her until he found his voice. She talked fondly about their time in the convent, her gardening, and how she met Goh and could write to him. He was relieved to know that Terpie was safe but could not help but feel cross that they ended up here as a consequence of her actions. He listened to her talk and her voice floated around him; he relaxed and enjoyed being in her company again. He soaked up her energy, recharging his depleted zest for life.

'...and we have made some great friends. I hope one day you can meet Meena. She's my best friend. Terpie is good. Although we share a cell, we work in different places around the camp during the day, so we rarely see each other. The guards leave us alone mostly.'

He noticed her face hardened, and her smile dimmed whilst she talked about Changi, and he had a sense she was covering over the cracks to spare him from the truth. He knew the women were not spared from the brutality of the guards, and he felt nauseous at the thought of one of them with their filthy hands on either of his girls, but he was not sure he was brave enough to ask because he might not be able to cope with the reality. She rambled on and told him about her spell in the hospital wing with malaria and how she and Terpie had argued recently.

'I'm glad you two have made up. I couldn't bear to think of you fighting and falling out.'

'We needed to clear the air, Pappa. Things will be better between us from now on. So, tell me about you! Listen to me rambling on. What do you do with your days here? You look so thin; I hardly recognised you.'

'I needed to shift a few pounds anyway,' he laughed and told her about Peter, Mickey, and Walter and how he filled his time, had joined a carpentry class, and did chores around the camp. He consciously decided not to tell her about working at the docks and the doctors warning, she would only worry. Besides, since he stopped the manual labour, he felt much stronger.

'Terpie will meet you next month if you like? We can stagger the meetings, what do you think?'

'Sounds like a great idea. Have you managed to find out anything about the evacuee ships?'

'No, Pappa, nothing. I would tell you if I knew anything. We have asked for information via our camp commandant, but there's been no news.'

'I'm still hopeful they're out there and they're alive.'

'Someone, somewhere must know what happened.'

'I still can't believe you're here. It's all my fault,' Zacharia said, hanging his head.

'No Pappa don't blame yourself. None of us knew what was going to happen. Terpie and I are fine. We'll survive Pappa, and when we get out of here, we'll find the others and start again. I promise,' Thalia pleaded across the table and tightened her grasp on his hands.

'I question all the time whether I did the right thing and hope the girls and Mamma aren't struggling in a new place and don't hate me for it.'

'Oh, Pappa, you're torturing yourself. We were all there, we had choices, and we made them. Mamma couldn't hate you for anything. We don't have much time left.'

'No, you're right,' he glanced at the clock overseeing the proceedings, and it told him he had just five minutes remaining. How was time going so quickly?

'Have you seen Aunt Emily? We travelled together. I'm worried about her. She's not as tough as she looks,' he said with concern.

Thalia cleared her throat, and her eyes darted around the room; she shuffled uncomfortably in her seat.

'We see her regularly, and she lives in a block reserved for older ladies. The women agreed that the comfortable beds must go to the senior citizens, and no one minded that. She's not been well lately and been in and out of the hospital wing with malaria,' Thalia smiled weakly.

'I'm glad. I thought for a minute you were going to say she'd passed away, and I don't think I could cope with that. She's a special lady. Please pass on my love when you see her and look after her won't you.'

'Of course I will,' Thalia said quietly.

In Thalia's company, Zacharia began to feel like his old self and grounded to who he was. He wasn't an empty shell of a man with no hope or future. In what felt like no time at all, the guard banged on the table.

'Visiting time's over. Say your goodbyes and step away from your tables.'

'Look after yourself, Pappa,' Thalia said, her eyes beginning to water as she stood.

'Give Terpie my love. Seeing you today was just what I needed.' Zacharia gripped his daughter's hand until the last possible moment, and her slender fingers slipped from his grasp, and he turned away.

Chapter Twenty-Seven
Thalia

Thalia could not suppress the giggles as she skipped along the corridors after seeing her father. Yes, he'd lost a lot of weight, but she had anticipated that. Everyone had shrunk a clothes size or two. Knowing how dire the food situation has been, she had fully prepared herself to find him looking sickly and pale, but was relieved to find he looked surprisingly healthy. It was such a relief to know he had the company of good friends, and they sounded like decent people. Her parents, by default, were reclusive and liked to keep themselves to themselves. With a small but trusted circle of friends, they lived a quiet life with limited social interactions. It concerned her that if her father did not make an effort here, he would cut himself off from people, and loneliness would be his silent killer. Hearing about Mickey, Peter and Walter reassured her so she could stop worrying so much. With a niggle of annoyance, she knew she hadn't handled the inevitable question about Emily so well. As predicted, he wasn't ready to hear that news. She would talk to Terpie; perhaps it would be kinder to withhold the information a little longer. As she climbed the stairs to her block the voices of loud Margery and Sue wafted down the stairwell. As they approached, Thalia registered the look of concern on their faces.

'Thalia, just to warn you. I don't know what is going on up there, but there's a bit of commotion going on in your cell,' said Margery.

'What do you mean a commotion? Is Terpie alright?'

'We aren't sure. I think Terpie's ok. She was sitting in the corridor when we left, but the guards are searching in your room. And they seem pretty angry,' said Sue with a sidewards look to Margery, who nodded in confirmation.

'We don't have anything to hide so, what the hell they are getting so uppity about? Thanks for the warning. I better go.' Thalia bounced up the remaining flight of stairs with a nervous niggle in her tummy.

The second she opened the heavy metal door to her corridor, she heard the shouting for herself. Loud banging and shrieks coming from her cell made her fearful. Her eyes widened when she found Terpie curled in tight ball on the floor outside their cell quietly sobbing and she knelt beside her. Inside the cell, she watched the two guards, Sato and Yamato, raging like a tornado, hurling their belongings into the walkway. She dodged a cup narrowly missing her head, followed by a plate that bounced off the wall and smashed beside her on the concrete. The sisters slid along a few paces out of the firing line of the doorway.

'What the hell's going on? Are you hurt?' demanded Thalia, searching for visible signs of injury.

'No, I'm ok. I got a slap, but that's normal. I'm more worried about Carol and Betty,' Terpie sniffed, wiping her nose on her threadbare hanky.

'Why?'

'The guards must have had a tip-off or something. They haven't searched anyone else's cell, just ours. They found a radio under Carol's bed. God knows how she got hold of it. Did you know?'

'A radio? No, I had no idea,' she said, leaning over to see Betty and Carol cowering in the corner of their dismantled cell. 'Where the hell would they get that?'

Sato stomped out and glared at Thalia like an angered black bear on its hind legs. He towered over her with hands-on-hips, his lip curled in a gruesome snarl. His English was pretty good. He ordered her to stand up, which she obeyed and her eye line only met with the breast pockets on his shirt.

'Did you know about this?' Sato demanded as Yamato appeared, waving a small red transistor radio in her face.

'I've never seen that before,' she stated, keeping her voice calm and steady.

'Liar!' shouted Yamato, and the back of his hand met her cheek with a resounding slap.

Thalia recovered and stood her ground.

'Honestly, I've never seen that radio, I swear,' she looked pleadingly at him. Yamato's features were frozen in a scowl. His only movement was the flaring of his nostrils like a raging bull preparing to charge and the quivering bristles of his black beard. Thalia steadied her breathing, secure in the knowledge that she was telling the truth.

'They didn't know we had it, I promise. We hid it from them,' offered Betty bravely from behind them.

Sato grunted, ignoring her suppliant plea and charged the girls anyway.

'You two,' he barked, pointing at the sisters with a stubby finger. 'Your punishment is three days in the pits. Starting tomorrow morning, I'll collect you at nine-thirty after the roll call. I'll make it five if you're not here and ready to go when I arrive.'

'But they're innocent and didn't know we had it. Please, it's so unfair to punish them,' Carol cried out. She mouthed the word sorry to Terpie, who looked up at her disappointedly.

'No, the punishment remains. It'll be a lesson to them both to choose better friends in future. It will also be extra punishment for you to know your friends must suffer because of something you did,' Yamato said smarmily, like he was enjoying this way too much. He spat in Carol's face and an evil grin spread from ear to ear. Sato turned sharply, and the heels of his black leather boots slapped together, grabbing Carol by the arm, he dragged her forcefully from the room like a child's plaything. Her head hung low as she passed. Thalia flinched as Yamato smacked Betty across the shoulder blades with his stick with such force that she almost experienced its sting.

'Move!' he commanded, pushing Betty forward.

He had tied her hands together behind her back and she stumbled, looking up briefly at Thalia with a staid expression before they were both gone. Thalia slumped down on the floor, her heart still racing.

'I don't believe this is happening. How the heck did they get hold of a radio? They know they're outlawed. They never had one when we came in because we were searched,' said Terpie.

'They must have had it smuggled in. I can't believe they had it and kept it secret, I'm glad they did, or we'd be in for a much tougher punishment. I don't understand why having a radio is such a problem. They're not spies. I expect they just wanted to listen to music.'

'The Japs are so suspicious. They think we are all plotting against them. How could they have been so stupid?' asked Terpie.

'I'm scared for them and don't want to think about their punishment,' Thalia admitted.

Together the girls gathered the scattered belongings, picked up the breakages and set the cell straight again. With the drama of the last hour, Thalia had entirely forgotten to tell Terpie about how the visit went with their father until later that day. They sat side by side waiting for their friends to return, and Thalia recounted the visit.

'So, you chickened out then. I thought you said you couldn't lie to Pappa.'

'You didn't see his face. He said he didn't think he could cope if I told him she had passed, so I don't regret my decision. It felt so bad lying to him, but it was the kinder thing to do. We can't tell him. He's not ready,' said Thalia mournfully.

With the conversation about their father exhausted the girls sat in silence, but Thalia felt a low energy emanating from Terpie beside her.

'Are you ok? You've gone quiet,' Thalia asked.

'I suppose in the back of my mind. I held on to a small hope that you'd come back with the news that Benny was with Pappa. It's silly, really, and I shouldn't have gotten my hopes up.'

'It's not silly at all. But now Pappa knows Benny has been taken prisoner, he can ask around. There are thousands of men coming in and out of prison being taken to other places, so there is a chance he may be able to find out something. Don't give up yet.'

To distract them from their concern for their friends, they spent the evening playing cards on the floor below, and when they returned to the cell, there was still no sign of Carol and Betty, and as the girls read their books before lights out, they shared a hope their friends would be back in the morning. Thalia had a fitful night's sleep; she wasn't worried about the confinement. She relished the idea of being alone for three whole days. Knowing what the guards had done to Meena and her husband, she feared for her friends and tormented visions of them suffering at the hands of their captors revolved around in her mind until finally, she drifted off to sleep in the early hours of the morning. As she sat up, it felt like she had not slept at all. With only Terpie to step over this morning, she realised the shakiness in her legs and nausea swirling in her stomach related to the terror she felt for Carol and Betty's welfare rather than her impending punishment. She could not share her concerns with her sister, which would mean breaking her promise to Meena. Thalia took her time in the shower, and when she arrived back at the block, breakfast was being served, and her mind had been so distracted she had no recollection of having showered at all. News of their cell search and punishment had spread like wildfire and was common knowledge amongst the women. Thalia hated the attention and felt like a criminal, but they were innocent and had no reason to feel guilty. Most women she passed gave her a sympathetic smile or offered supportive fighting talk for the injustice of their treatment and words of encouragement to stay strong. Thalia felt confident she could handle the confinement. She has been isolated many times as a young girl in the convent. Surely this would be similar.

As soon as the block roll call was complete, Sato appeared, the girls dutifully bowed, and he escorted them out of the block to a desolate area at the back of the camp. He didn't utter a single word. Walking behind, Sato chivvied them along with a jab of his stick if they were too slow. Thalia hugged her blanket tight to her chest. The ground underfoot was dry and barren, and eventually, they reached the far perimeter wall. It occurred to her as they approached the site was so remote, no one would hear them if they screamed at the top of their lungs. Thalia suddenly felt fearful; what if he forgot they were out here? They would be buried alive. When they reached the row of confinement pits, Sato lifted the wooden lids and ordered the girls to get in. The realisation was now sinking in, and Thalia began to shake, gripping her blanket tighter. The rudimentary pits were the prisoners' handiwork, dugout in the first few weeks of their capture. Strategically placed in full sun and without any supply of water. Sato handed her a small flask of water that would last three days. Before lowering herself in, she smiled weakly to Terpie, and the girls disappeared. Swallowed up by the ground Thalia flinched as the lids slammed shut, and the scrape of the bolt secured the cover tight.

'I'll be back in three days, don't bother shouting. No one will hear you,' Sato sneered and Thalia listened to the sound of his heavy boots until they faded away. At five foot six, she was not overly tall and stooped to avoid hitting her head. The space was hot, dry and dark. It felt like a grave and smelled of urine. Only thin slithers of light shone through the cracks in the wooden lid and around a two-inch air hole.

She called out to Terpie in the pit a few yards from her, 'Terpie. Are you ok?'

'I can't breathe. I've got to get out.' Terpie hammered her fists on the wooden lid. 'Please let me out… I can't breathe. I…need air. Get me out.'

What could she do? Terpie was having a panic attack, she had to try and calm her down. With her back pressed against the earth wall, she directed her voice through the small hole.

'Terpie, listen to my voice. You're ok. You're safe. You need to take slow breaths.'

'I… can't, I… can't…' she gasped.

'You can. You need to focus. It's a panic attack, and it'll pass. I'm right here with you. I need you to close your eyes and breathe in with me to the count to five, hold for five and then breathe out for five.'

'I'll try.'

Thalia started counting and talking Terpie through the exercise. All was quiet so she assumed Terpie was following her lead.

'Good, that should start to feel better. You're doing great. How do you feel?'

'Better.'

'Do you need to keep it going?'

'No, I think I'll be ok now. It's so cramped and hot. I panicked.'

Thalia opened her eyes and gradually adjusted to the darkness. The edges of the mud pit were only an arms width away. The uneven floor revealed the scuttling of the creepy-crawly insects trapped in with her. She flinched and instinctively brushed her arms, even though nothing was there. After a short while her neck began to ache, and she knew she could not remain bent over like this, she would resemble a walking stick handle and be doubled over like an old lady by the end of the confinement. There was only one way to get comfortable, which meant being brave and sitting down amongst the goggas and parasites she feared so much. Sitting down on her folded blanket, she closed her eyes tightly shut like she did when she was a child. Believing what she couldn't see couldn't hurt her. Wearing only shorts and a cotton vest top, she knew the insects would be feasting on a banquet of her human skin and crawling all over her. Her skin tingled and bristled with movement. In a frenzy, she brushed and beat her bare skin, her arms and legs flailing to keep them off her. Ruffling her hair, she squealed. Her fingers disturbed something crawling. She flicked it off her. Her futile writhing had exhausted her, and accepted she had no choice but to tolerate her skittering companions. She curled into a ball and hugged her knees to her chest. It was so quiet out here that the regular pumping of her heartbeat rang in her ears. She knew this would be the longest three days of her life.

Other than the natural circadian rhythm of night and day, the times between were impossible to gauge. Thalia had not spoken to Terpie in hours, or maybe it was a whole day? They had agreed to save their energies, and besides, her mouth was too dry to speak and it was painful to swallow. Her water supply had run dry long ago. Initially, she thought solitary confinement would be a welcome break from the overcrowding in the prison block. She relished the peace and time to herself, but now she was here, alone with only her mind as a companion, she realised it was not the idyll she had imagined. One day had been enough. She invented many ways to keep her mind active to pass the time. She tried to recall every childhood memory in order, which only upset her and miss her family. She tried not to dwell on thoughts of them after that; it was too painful. How much longer? Surely by now, it had been three days? Maybe Sato told them three days but had no intention of releasing them. Panic rose like hot acid in her veins that she had been forgotten and left here to die. How would it feel? Would it hurt? She didn't want to slip away from this world alone. Sobbing for what seemed like hours, she decided enough was enough. She was only torturing herself and had to keep up her mental strength with the remaining time. This is what the Japs wanted, for her to break, and she would not give them the satisfaction. So instead, she made mental lists of her favourite movies, books, and songs. Once she had exhausted these, she retold herself her favourite fables from Greek mythology and recited words to her favourite songs. Anything she could think of to keep her mind from thinking of her family. She tried to imagine what the world would look like when the war ended and what her future might be. Like other young girls her age, she wanted a career and eventually to settle down with a family of her own and for that she had to survive. Her life awaited her when she got out of here and she would make the best of it. In the full heat of the day, the underground cell was like an oven, and she was roasting like a Christmas turkey. She could feel her blood simmering beneath her crackling skin. Thalia's thoughts were sluggish, her brain and body were slowing down, it was harder to concentrate and remember things, the walls of the pit were closing in on her, and her eyes were so dry it was like scouring them with sandpaper every time she blinked. She drifted in and out of sleep. After that, a kind of delirium set in, and she was on first named terms with the scuttling bugs round her. Lying on her side in a foetal position, consciousness faded in and out. She was woken by the sudden brilliance of light blinding her, and shielded her eyes. The pit lid was wide open, and a tall, dark silhouette loomed above her. A wave of relief coursed through her body; Sato had not left them to die. Strangely her relief was so great that she felt like hugging him, forgetting his propensity for violence, and he was the enemy who put her there. He reached down to her and dragged her out, and she collapsed in a tangled heap like a wooden puppet. The natural daylight dazed her, and she repeatedly blinked until she adjusted to her surroundings. The warm breeze on her skin and breathing in fresh air revived her. Yamato thrust a bottle in her hand, and shy she guzzled the water down. It felt like drowning. She gasped, spat and spluttered. With Sato's support, Terpie climbed out of the pit beside her. The guards left them and didn't help them back to the block. For a while, they sat together, their bodies too weak to move, and it took them a few attempts to stand and take wobbly steps like new-born foals. They leaned on each other for support and shuffled their way back. Eventually they arrived at the cell and Thalia's heart sank when she saw that Betty and Carol had still not returned.

'Maybe they've been at work?' Terpie said lowering herself to the floor.

'No, this doesn't feel right. Nothing has moved since we tidied. I don't think they've been here at all.'

'You don't think…'

'No,' Thalia cut in quickly. 'Don't say it. They'll be back.'

The girls slept until lunchtime, and once they had feasted on fish paste and red palm oil cake followed by pineapple, they felt more like human beings. Thalia was still hungry. She called on Meena to see if she wanted a walk around the yard to distract herself. A door in the corridor clanged, and she jumped out of her skin. Any noise seemed amplified compared to the silence she had accustomed to over the last few days. Meena was glad of her company, and they walked and talked until it began to get dark. When Thalia returned to her cell, she received a shock she could never have prepared herself for. Carol and Betty were back sitting beside each other in silence. Instinctively Thalia's hand flew over her mouth, silencing a scream as her friends, as she knew them were barely recognisable. She couldn't help but cry seeing the awful state they were in. Carol and Betty had been beaten and tortured. Their clothes splattered with blood, their arms and legs gouged from lashings. Cigarette burns punctuated their forearms and chunks of hair missing where it had been burnt down to the scalp and their faces contorted from the swelling, split lips and black eyes. Thalia knelt beside them. The desire to fling her arms around them and hug them was overpowering, but she feared they were too bruised for that. The brutality her friends had endured made her three-day confinement seem like a holiday. Her deep sadness quickly became a boiling rage that had nowhere to go.

Chapter Twenty-Eight
Terpie

Standing in the yard, Terpie dreamily gazed at the clock tower whilst waiting for her friend Cathy, a pale, blonde girl with the most striking blue eyes she met working in the admin offices. As she waited, she pondered on the view from the tower and closed her eyes briefly to picture the open fields stretching out to the sea beyond. To freedom. Alerted by her friend's approach she opened her eyes. The girls engaged in light conversation passing the converted dining room, now home to the "Changi school". A chorus of young voices singing rhymes made her smile. The school was a recent addition to the prison only after persistent pressure from the committee to the Japanese authorities for basic resources like pencils, books and paper. The youngsters were becoming feral without structure to their day, and goodness knows when this nightmare would end. Thalia's persistent nagging had finally rubbed off, and today Terpie was on route to the sewing club with Cathy for moral support. Terpie had been in a rut lately, wallowing in the cell, and perhaps Thalia was right. Getting out with others would help. The ladies met in one of the dining rooms, which was repurposed recently as a sleeping area due to overcrowding. As they approached, laughter and chatter echoed along the corridor.

The quilting idea had been a success, and several quilts formed out of small squares with wives' names and a unique embroidered picture had been sent to the men's camp hospital. The women scavenged for material and found it either in old clothes, flour bags or old bed linen sheets, and the authorities provided sewing thread to repair clothing. When Terpie and Cathy arrived, they saw a group of women seated in a circle on the concrete floor with needle and thread in hand chatting easily. The space was stiflingly hot despite open windows on both sides, with fly's zigzagging across the room. Terpie crossed the area carefully to avoid standing on someone's bedding to join them and was greeted by a brunette lady in a pale pink vest top and blue shorts. She motioned for the new arrivals to sit.

'Hi Terpie, come and join us. Thalia said you were coming today. I'm Margery.'

'I've been meaning to come for a while, but I admit my sewing skills are not as good as my sisters. This is Cathy, by the way.'

'You're both very welcome. Oh, I wouldn't worry about that. Half of us can't sew either. This is an excellent way to while away some time in good company. Everyone, this is Terpie and her friend Cathy. I won't introduce everyone at once. I don't want to confuse you with too many names,' she laughed lightly and nodded to the others in the circle. 'Help yourself to materials.'

Terpie squeezed into a space beside a mother in her thirties. Between her crossed legs, her toddler lay curled in a ball, fast asleep.

'She looks comfortable there.'

'She would sleep anywhere this one. Not like her older brother, who never slept through the night until he was five. I blame him for all my wrinkles and the bags under my eyes. I'm Sheila.'

On the floor in the centre, were separate piles of neatly cut squares of material, various colours of threads, a small tobacco tin with needles of different sizes, pencils, and scissors.

'The flour and banana bags are quite tough to sew with. If you're not used to it, I'd go with the linen material,' suggested Sheila, pointing to the selection of materials in front of them. Terpie chose her square, thread, and a needle. She thought for a moment. What design could she sew on her square that would have any meaning? With all her heart, she hoped Benny was being held in the men's camp on the other side of the wall and that one day he would see her name on a quilt. All her attempts to find out so far had fallen flat. On her first family visit with her father, she had tasked him with putting the word out in the male camp, but that was five months ago and still nothing. Her father gently reminded her that the Japanese held thousands of military personnel throughout the eastern region. Terpie hadn't even considered there could be other prisoner of war camps outside of Singapore and felt naive in believing he would be across the wall from her. In the end, she settled on her design, a dove for peace, and in each corner, she would sew dainty hearts and flowers on a vine with her name on a diagonal slant. Terpie reached for a pencil to sketch her idea on the material before sewing.

The women had fallen back into their conversation, so it took a while for Terpie to catch the drift of what they were saying.

'Going back to what Molly said, I agree. Each to their own.'

'Well, I think it's disgusting. No self-respecting woman would lower herself to such behaviour.'

'Oh, come on, Janet, these are hardly normal times, are they. People are pushed to the limit and do what they can to survive. You've no idea what drives them to do it. I don't think it's for us to judge.'

'That's exactly the kind of liberal attitude I'd expect from you.' Janet lowered her sewing and glared at Kathy.

'All I am saying, Janet, is it's easy for you to sit on your moral high horse, but we'll never know what drives a woman to behave like that. They're not doing you any harm, so I don't see why you are getting so het up about it,' Kathy said.

'It reflects badly on all of us. I hope the Japs don't think they can try any of their dirty business on me. I'll soon tell them what's what!'

'I don't think they would go near an old hag like you, Janet. No need to worry.' Laughed a woman with a tight ponytail and sunburnt shoulders.

'There's no need for that, Tina!' Janet protested.

'Ladies, please! I think this conversation's getting a bit personal. Sorry Terpie, I hope you don't have a bad impression of us on your first visit,' boomed Margery.

'I'm intrigued if the truth be told. I've no idea what you're talking about,' she admitted.

'Probably best you don't know. You look like a good sensible girl,' said Janet.

'Before you arrived, we were discussing the topic of comfort women in prison.' Kathy and Terpie didn't like to admit she had no idea what comfort women were and hoped the following few sentences would fill in the gaps. She looked across to Cathy who looked as bewildered as her and shrugged.

'There are women in the block who provide sexual favours for the guards in return for extra rations or an easier life,' explained Kathy.

Terpie cheeks warmed as topics like this were not openly discussed in her circle of friends, and being a virgin, she felt embarrassed.

'One of the ladies across the corridor from me has been seen going off with Sgt Tenak, quite regularly, and we noted she gets extra rations. It's common knowledge other women do it too,' said Margery.

'There's not one decent looking guard among them. You'd have to be pretty desperate,' said Tina.

'I wouldn't let one of those filthy beasts touch me. They make my skin crawl. How anyone could want sex with them is beyond me after all they have put us through,' chipped in another lady from the opposite side of the circle.

'What do you think about it, Terpie?' Margery asked.

Put on the spot, Terpie thought for a moment. She couldn't imagine such a scenario but felt pressure to answer.

'I wasn't aware what "comfort women" were until a moment ago, but I can see how vulnerable women might try to make their lives easier. People living in fear do strange things in extreme situations.'

'I'll never understand it or condone it, no offence, but we are all entitled to our opinions,' said Janet.

Relieved she hadn't said anything too awful, Terpie kept her head down and began sketching her outline on her square, balanced on her knee as the women around her carried on their discussion.

'Are you married, Terpie?' asked Shelia.

Terpie bit her lower lip. She hated these questions. She felt as good as married. They had a date, a dress, and felt married to him in her heart.

'He's a volunteer, and I don't know where he has been taken or if he's still alive.'

'I'm sorry, love, it's so hard. My husband's on the other side of the wall. We've got to stick together. All girls together,' said Sheila.

'My father is next door and I've had the chance to meet with him on a family visit. It must be frustrating knowing your husband is the other side of the wall.'

'At least I know where he is. You have it far harder than me. Absence makes the heart grow fonder they say.' She winked, and they re-joined the conversation.

'We're all being tested in here. It's been over a year now, and no sign of getting out. Who's to say those women just like sex and are missing it? I know that's a foreign concept to you, Janet, but some women have needs too. Do you have needs?' asked Kathy.

'I'm not discussing my bedroom preferences with you,' Janet replied curtly.

'I know I miss it. I never thought I'd say that. I wanted it more than ever for the first few months in here. The human body is cruel sometimes,' giggled Sheila.

'Imagine what the male camp is like then. All that testosterone. It can't be healthy,' said Tina.

'On a serious note, though, ladies. If those women didn't have sex with the guards, they would take it anyway. In the early days, my friend was raped.' The room fell silent. 'I think we must be grateful to the comfort women. They keep those bastards away from us,' said Kathy gravely, and the women silently contemplated her statement and continued sewing.

Terpie found the whole conversation enlightening. This kind of open talk never happened in her household. She couldn't imagine discussing such topics with her mother and sisters; they had led such innocent lives in comparison. She and Benny had agreed to wait until they were married, so honestly, she had no idea what these women were talking about, but she soaked it up like a sponge and made a mental note to relay it all to Thalia. Thalia wasn't in the cell when she returned but she found Betty squashed in the corner, reading her book, who looked up as she walked in. It had been a few months since the radio incident, and whilst the bruises and swelling had gone down, her hair had not grown back fully, and she still had burn marks and scars which would serve as a constant reminder of her ordeal.

Betty had changed. She used to be a bubbly, confident and happy girl but the Japanese stripped away her essence leaving behind a shadow; an empty shell. The girls never talked about what happened during those three days; they didn't need to. Terpie knew Thalia would be in the garden and went to find her. As if by coincidence Sgt Tanaka was on his way up. She bowed, realising she could never look at the guards in the same way again and was sure her cherry cheeks flushed a little. A wall of screams and raised voices hit her as soon as she opened the ground floor door. It wasn't clear what was causing the distress, but further down the corridor, she saw one of the women from the sewing group, Molly maybe, or was it Margery? Terpie couldn't remember, but Thalia would know, standing between a wailing woman and a red-faced Sato.

Sato held a young boy by the arm in distress, pulling against the brute to free himself. Other women poked their heads around door frames of their cells, gawping at the commotion. Terpie stopped and asked a woman leaning on her cell doorframe with her arms folded if she knew what was happening.

'Yeah, the boy is being taken to the men's camp now. Sato has come to fetch the poor lad and he doesn't want to go and leave his mum and little brother.'

'Why does he have to go?' Terpie asked.

'Happens to all the boys when they reach twelve years old. No getting out of it neither.'

'That's awful. The poor child,' replied Terpie.

'Not too great for the mother either. Glad mine are only little'uns,' said the woman before returning to her cell.

Terpie continued her journey, feeling sorry for the boy being ripped away from his mother. There was no humanity to any aspect of prison life and once again, she was glad not to be a parent.

Chapter Twenty-Nine
Terpie

Propping herself up in her hospital bed Terpie was reading a dogeared copy of *Wuthering Heights* hoping to return to the cells soon. There was only one benefit to being in hospital: sleeping on a proper mattress, which felt like a long-forgotten luxury. However, the downside was being surrounded by noisy patients crying out at night, which meant uninterrupted sleep was impossible. The novelty had worn off now, and Terpie had become restless insisting to the nurses when they came to check on her that she felt well enough to leave but they said they recommend keeping an eye on her for one more day. This current bout of illness developed a few weeks ago quite out of the blue. It was memorable because it began on the fortuitous day the women and children escaped the confines of the prison on a bathing party to Changi beach. The uncharacteristic generosity of the guards caused a considerable degree of delight amongst the women and especially the children. There were too many people to escort at once so the timed visits of one hour each, were spread over a couple of days. It took Terpie by surprise to discover how a basic visit to the beach (an activity which she took for granted before all this, had been a regular occurrence that she took for granted) could become such a precious and cherished event.

At two o'clock, several armed guards accompanied the walking party of about a hundred women out through the gates and along a short walk bringing them to a mile long stretch of golden sand and glistening ocean. The simplicity of stretching their legs further than the exercise yard bought joy and they bounded out the gates like unrestrained yearlings having free rein of the paddock. The two sisters linked arms with each other and with towels tucked under the other, Thalia and Terpie skipped along like eager children who had never seen the sea before. Upon arrival, almost everyone made a dash for the sea, brazenly stripping down to their underwear to take the plunge. Thalia, who couldn't swim, was happy to kick about in the surf up to her knees but Terpie couldn't wait and began stripping her clothes off whilst in transit.

'Come on, Thalia, give it a try, it's perfectly safe,' encouraged Terpie jovially.

'It's perfectly safe here too,' replied Thalia.

'You'll never learn if you don't try. I'll help you,' Terpie offered stacking her clothes in a neat pile and laying her threadbare towel down on the sand ready for her return.

'Nope, not for me. I'm quite happy here. You go,' said Thalia burying her toes in the sand.

Shrugging, Terpie turned on her heel and approached the sea, nimble and light on her toes dodging the sharp shells and stones in her path. Without hesitation, she waded through the frothy surf up to her waist, dived beneath the rolling waves, and continued to swim freely, stopping a few hundred yards off the shore. With the exertion of the exercise and feeling energised by the blood pumping around her body, she whooped out loud and smashed the waves with her fists. Treading water in the expanse of ocean and tipping her head back, surrendering to the movement of the undulating glistening waves was the closest feeling to freedom. She revelled in her privet of happiness. With the warm water temperature, she was content to bob in unison with the rhythm of the waves, listening to joyous laughter and the sound of play reaching her on the breeze from the shore until a negative thought disrupted her peaceful state. Snapping her out of her blissful reverie came a distressing image of her mother and sisters in peril, panicking in the confusion and fighting to survive in and angry and undulant ocean. What if their ship had been bombed during the evacuation? Finding the image distressing she rolled onto her tummy and concentrated on her breaststroke motion with the tide back to the shore.

'That was amazing,' she declared as she flopped her wet body on to her towel besides Thalia, soaking up the sun.

'It's pure heaven isn't it. I hope they let us come here again. Have you seen how happy the children are? It's so good for them,' replied Thalia.

'I hope so too.' After a moment, Terpie continued solemnly, 'My last day with Benny was on this beach. We had such a lovey picnic and I miss him so badly.'

Thalia sat up. 'I'm sorry, Terpie. You haven't mentioned Benny in such a long time, I wasn't sure whether I should talk about him or not.'

'Do you know what's awful? I'm struggling to picture his face, I don't have any photographs of him, there may have been a few back at the house but I'm terrified I'll forget.'

'I felt the same way about Charlie. I think I was trying too hard. You'll never forget him. Besides, he could very well be in one of these camps somewhere thinking of you right now.'

'I give myself a headache sometimes trying to visualise his face and all I see is a black blur,' Terpie said, looking away. Not a day went by that she didn't think of Benny. Successfully she fought off the pinprick of tears which stung the back of her eyes but the crushing ache in her heart never seemed to go away. She never spoke about him to anyone. It was easier that way. On top of her yearnings for Benny, she silently carried the burden of her family's suffering and the cause of their separation. It would haunt her for the rest of her life. Even though she had cleared the air with Thalia, the guilt hovered deep in her chest like a storm cloud, and she wondered if her mother (wherever she was) blamed her exclusively for their predicament. Terpie could only hope that one day she would get the opportunity to apologise and seek their forgiveness.

All avenues of trying to trace Benny had been exhausted. The driving force behind her work in the administration offices was so that she had access to the right people and resources to find out information. Any possible leads within the last two years had drawn a blank and she was running out of options.

'As time passes, it's getting harder to believe he's still alive. It's hard to be positive when my gut instincts tell me it's pointless.'

'Listen, Pappa gave me some advice when I hadn't heard from Charlie. It might help you too. He said to have a future date in my mind, a point to reach where I would have to let him go so that I could move on. I think you should so the same.'

'Maybe, it feels so defeatist and I owe it to him to keep searching.'

'It's so hard and only you will know what's right. I don't think you are ready to give up hope yet.'

'I don't think my search for him will begin until we get out of here. *If* we get out of here. I must exhaust every avenue before contemplating letting him go.' Terpie's voice faded out to a whisper.

'I understand that, and you can talk to me anytime you know. If you need to. I know I'm only your little annoying sister, but I understand what you're going through,' Thalia offered gently.

The girls lay side by side to savour the sublime experience and to finally relax with nowhere to be and no walls to confine them. The guards kept their distance knowing that nobody would be so simple-minded to think they could escape whilst they had weapons to take them down if they dared to try. As Terpie lay daydreaming, her stomach began to cramp. She wondered briefly if it might be her monthly's making a return as they had been absent since April, or was it May? This pain was different though. The onset was quick, and she pulled her knees into her stomach and groaned.

'Hey what is it? Terpie, tell me what to do?' said a concerned Thalia kneeling by her side.

'Get help. My stomach feels like it's being ripped open.'

'Ok, ok, stay calm,' said Thalia turning and waving her arms to get anyone's attention. 'I need help over here, my sister's in pain,' she shouted.

Two older ladies who were sitting nearby came over and taking one look at Terpie went to get a guard. Terpie cradled her stomach and rolled in agony.

'You'll be ok, the guards are coming over. Stay calm, I'm not going to leave you,' Thalia reassured, gripping Terpie's hand.

'I feel so sick. I must have caught something. I felt a bit sick this morning but in all the excitement I forgot about it,' said Terpie weakly.

'Well, this is just typical of you, we get a nice day out of the prison, and we have to go back early because you're not well,' teased Thalia, trying to lift the mood.

It wasn't until much later in the hospital that Terpie learned she had contracted dysentery and had never felt so ill. Walking back to the prison was a slow and painful process, flanked on either side by Thalia and one of the guards. She was sure she was dying. Doubled up in pain, she vomited three times and passed out. In the end, a stretcher had to be bought out to carry her back to the hospital, where she spent a week in isolation with a temperature of 106 degrees. Between sweating and shivering, she drifted in and out of sleep and her mood darkened with no visitors to entertain or distract her. Her medicine consisted of a daily quinine tablet and a diet of watery rice mixed with powdered charcoal.

After two weeks of bed rest, she could take on small meals, and at least in hospital, the best and most nutritious foods were reserved for the sick. Bananas, fish, eggs and sweet potatoes were on the menu. It was a shame she was too ill to appreciate but she couldn't wait to get back to the hubbub of the prison. She hoped she had not missed too much of the Christmas preparations. She put her book on the bedside table just as Thalia appeared.

'Hey stranger, how're you feeling?'

'Please get me out of here. I've had enough of these walls. What've I missed?' Terpie said, smacking the bedsheets.

'There's so much activity to make it memorable, especially for the little ones. I volunteered to help sort the Red Cross parcels and wrap the gifts sent over from the men's camp. You wouldn't believe the carvings and toys they've made. Little trains and cars with wheels that turn, soldiers, animals and little houses, the children will love them. There will be a church service on Christmas day but wait for it… The best news is that everyone on camp can meet up for the afternoon. Men, women, families. Isn't that great!'

'That's fabulous news.'

'We can spend time with Pappa together. Oh, and the camp's being decorated, and someone has got hold of some Christmas trees, I've no idea how, so it's beginning to feel restive.' Thalia beamed. 'And whilst I remember, I questioned the Red Cross representative yesterday about the evacuee ships again.'

Terpie sat forwards in interest. 'What did she say? Another string of excuses?'

'No actually she was very helpful. She apologised that it's taken so long. Survivor lists are being put together now and should be available in the new year. She assured me copies would be sent to the camp.'

Terpie's tummy flipped and not through illness this time. 'I'm a bit scared. I want to know what happened, but I also don't want to know if that makes sense? Whilst there's no news, I can imagine them safely living a new life in Australia.'

'I know exactly what you mean. We've got to be brave. I hate this limbo of not knowing whether I should be grieving them or not.'

'Once we know, we'll have to decide whether to tell Pappa.'

'Hmmm. That's not going to be easy.'

'Surely we'd have had a letter from them by now don't you think?' asked Terpie.

'Not necessarily. Mamma doesn't know where we are, so any letter would have gone home first. Shi Min would have sent it to the convent, and we can only assume they'd have sent it into the prison. There are numerous ways a letter could have been lost. Plus, the Red Cross only just delivered eight hundred letters to the men's camp, but they've taken months to get through the system.'

Their conversation was interrupted by a nurse appearing to check Terpie's temperature.

'I'm going but I'll see you tomorrow. She is still being allowed out isn't she?' Thalia questioned the young nurse.

'Yes, I'm happy with her temperature, she's eaten well, and her blood pressure has stayed down so she can go in the morning.'

Terpie beamed and her body relaxed knowing she could once again be part of the liveliness of daily routines and could at last join in with the Christmas preparations.

This was their second Christmas as prisoners, and everyone made every effort to make it a worthy celebration despite their surroundings. As the big day approached, an atmosphere of joy and hope spread around the camp, and even the guards seemed to have relaxed a little. The day began with a service performed in the old dining hall by Rev Jefferson where Terpie and her sister joined in with carols and hymns. No matter how diminished their lives had become, sharing familiar songs evoked happy memories and made them feel good. People throughout the camp exchanged gifts, either hand-me-downs or simple homemade gifts and cards that were treasured much more than traditional presents because of the effort that went into making them.

In various areas of the prison, paper cut-outs of stars, and Christmas pictures drawn by the children had been hung and together with paper chains made from scraps of old newspaper the prison looked festive. The cooks in the kitchen made a heroic effort to make meal worthy of a celebration and produced a menu of soup, pork, rice and vegetables, which was more like a traditional Greek Christmas in the end, but it didn't matter.

By far, the best gift was the opportunity to spend the afternoon together as a family without loitering guards hanging over their shoulder and having time to finish a conversation. Terpie observed her pappa chatting and smiling with Thalia, and despite his gaunt face, his eyes lit up with joy which was the best gift she could hope for on this strange day. They exchanged small gifts they had each made for each other, nothing much as resources were hard to come by. Zacharia presented them each with miniature carvings he made for them in his carpentry class, a cross for Terpie and a little bird for Thalia. Thalia had embroidered a handkerchief with her father's initials in the corner and dainty forget-me-nots around the edge, which he used immediately to mop his tears after reading the poem that Terpie had written neatly on some card she had smuggled out of the office where she worked.

In the darkest night when you're alone.
Close your eyes, remember our home.
The family together is what you will find.
Keep them there, fresh in your mind.
Laughter and love our memories made.
Remember them often, don't let them fade.
Not lost forever, just simply apart.
Until reunited, keep them close in your heart.
When the war is over, and we become free.
We'll be together again. One family.
Stay strong, have hope, come what may.
Our freedom is coming.
We'll embrace that day.

Her pappa's eyes welled up and he gazed into the distance until the emotion had passed. Terpie hoped it would bring her pappa strength when his hope was fading. Words were all she had in her arsenal to combat the dark times.

'Thank you Terpie, I will treasure this. You've always been so good with words.'

Around them, families reunited, fathers played with their children and kissed their wives, and a magical opportunity for all to forget the last two years of hardship for a few hours. The trio sat with Meena who they had invited to join them. Thalia insisted as she couldn't bear to see her on her own and having spoken about him so much, wanted her to meet Pappa and as predicted, they got on swimmingly.

'I was hoping to see Emily today, but I can't see her. I thought she'd be joining us. Do you know where she is?' asked Zacharia, looking beyond at the groups of people milling around.

Terpie wasn't prepared for the question and tried to conceal her surprise with a cough and surreptitious glance in Thalia's direction. Terpie silently berated herself for forgetting about Emily. How could she have not thought of her today of all days? The fact that her jewels were sewn into her underwear should be a constant reminder, but they'd become part of her now. For this reason, she didn't like lies; eventually, they caught you up with you and hurt the people you love. Quick thinking Thalia filled the slight delay in the conversation and hoped their pappa did not notice.

'She wanted to be here, Pappa, but she has malaria again, poor thing. She's in the hospital.'

'Oh really, that's disappointing. I wanted to give her this,' he said, handing a carved wooden elephant to Thalia. 'She had a collection of ornaments in her flat on her windowsill, all elephants, so I made her one. Can you make sure she gets it for me?'

'Pappa, it's beautiful. I'll make sure she gets it,' said Thalia, caressing the small object between her fingers.

'The main thing is she gets better. Oh, there's Peter,' said Zacharia, waving to a man and his family heading their way. Terpie couldn't make eye contact with her sister as she was sure the guilt was stamped all over her face, and deceiving her father felt so dreadful, and she knew Thalia would feel the same. Her pappa proudly introduced them to his friend Peter, his wife Martha, whom he knew so much about but had never met, and their blonde-haired little boy Jacob who clutched his wooden soldier gift the whole time and wouldn't let go. The couple joined them for a while and for some reason Jacob was all over Thalia, showing her his new toy and giggling when she played peek-a-boo with him. Terpie knew that one day she would make a great mother. Peter was explaining to them how it had taken months for the guards to finally agree for him to see his son during the monthly family visits. The little boy would grow up knowing his father, as it should be. After exchanging pleasantries and light conversation, the two families parted ways, not wanting to infringe on precious family time. As the afternoon drew to a close without a doubt, they were all feeling the gaping hole of absence for family members they missed so dearly. A fleeting thought crossed Terpie's mind. Would they ever spend another Christmas together with Shi Min and Lim or were those days a thing of the past? Naturally the day triggered thoughts of Benny, wondering where he was, and she prayed that next year would bring them news of their loved ones. All too quickly, the gong sounded to signal the end of the visit, and they embraced each other in what felt like the most prolonged goodbye. Thalia and Terpie stood side by side to watch their pappa shuffle back to the men's camp until he was out of sight. The New Year celebrations were a low-key affair. The sisters didn't feel like celebrating, although the committee organised a fancy dress ball, so they attended for the first hour to be sociable. And so on to another year. Terpie went to bed clutching her wooden cross and prayed so hard that 1945 would be better for them all.

Chapter Thirty
Zacharia

The prison this morning was particularly quiet enabling Zacharia to behold the cacophonous snoring and gurgling from his cell mates deep in their slumber, whilst frustratingly he had been awake for hours. With his body shedding weight and his bones more prominent than before, sleeping on the hard floor was torture. Luckily, he had managed to salvage an extra blanket for additional padding which improved the situation slightly and prevented the cold concrete seeping into his bones quite as much. The light outside was on the turn, and it would soon be time to begin another monotonous day. He wrinkled his nose in reaction to a waft of pungent body odour assaulting his senses. Feeling numb on one side he turned over awkwardly to get comfortable in the small space with his back firmly pressed against the wall. Mickey's skinny body was barely a foot away. Zacharia watched the rise and fall of his friends grubby stained vest and the fly's using his torso as a landing pad before taking off again to circle the room. Two other sleeping forms in the cell snored and snuffled. Last week two new Dutch inmates, Koen and Lukas, joined them filling the emptiness Walter's absence left behind. A few weeks ago Walter's health deteriorated quickly following a bout of dysentery and he never recovered to make it out of the medical wing to re-join them. It came as a shock to them all. Together with Mickey, Zacharia attended a short burial service with a few others who knew him. Saying goodbye to friends seemed commonplace as time passed, and losing a good friend hit him hard. With Koen lying lengthways by his feet and Lukas on the concrete slab there was hardly any space between them. Zacharia ached for the familiarity of sharing a bed with his wife. Everything about this existence without her felt like a poison, killing him slowly. Nothing was familiar to him anymore, not even his reflection. He was a stranger in his own life. Every morning his first conscious thought would be maybe today it will be over, and we'll be free. Surely one of these days, he had to be right? He'd given up counting the days of his incarceration, once he'd reached the second anniversary, it seemed an inefficient use of his time. With the sun rising, he could see his way to step over the sleeping bodies and eased himself off the floor trying not to disturb Mickey breathing heavily with his mouth wide open. Grabbing his tatty washbag, Zacharia padded to the bathroom to wash. He nodded to the other early risers he met along the way along the corridor. Changi was a mysterious place; the occupants of the prison changed regularly. These days he may never see the same face twice and was left wondering whether they died or were just redistributed around the network of prison camps. He always kept his eyes open in the hope that one day he would cross paths with Benny so he could ease Terpie's agony. It was usual for the Japanese to remove people, soldiers mainly, out of the prison, never to be seen again. Word had it they were taken to Thailand to work on the Burma Railway or to Japan to work in the mines, and new POWs arrived all the time. He kept the poem Terpie wrote him inside a paperback book and read it daily. With nothing new or positive to focus on, he found it hard to keep the blackness at bay from swallowing him whole. Zacharia coughed and noticed a new rattle in his chest as he shuffled along to the grey concrete bathroom and leaned against one of the two sinks standing side by side. His body felt about ninety years old and more often these days, he became out of breath from the slightest exertion. Usually he avoided the mirror; it repulsed him to see the gaunt, unfamiliar face gawping back at him with lacklustre skin and hollow eyes. Leaning forward, he patted his sunken cheeks and let his fingers creep upwards over the ledge of his angular cheekbones. His frail fingers picked at wisps of ivory hair emerging through the grey and mourned his full head of dark locks he was once proud of. All over his body, wafer thin skin clung to his skeletal frame. God, he was a mess. The stress of the last few years had taken its toll in so many ways. Every man shared the same emaciated appearance, no one was fairing any better than anyone else. Young, old, rich or poor. The men looked the same, skin and bone. Today he was meeting Thalia hence his particular concern for his appearance. Due to his recent spell in the hospital with malaria and his general ill health, two months had passed since their last visit. Still, they had at least exchanged letters a couple of times via the cobblers' station thanks to his friend Robert and his covert operation. With one arm supporting him on the sink, he set to brushing his teeth. The nylon bristles of his brush were long gone, so he improvised and fashioned a new toothbrush out of coconut fibres. Overall, it did the job as long

259

as he didn't push too hard, or he would end up with fibres stuck in his teeth and bleeding gums to add to his troubles. Living in Changi made scavengers of them all. After washing with a disc of soap made from fat and caustic soda, not much larger than a Malayan dollar, he returned to his cell to await breakfast.

Later that afternoon, he waited patiently against the wall in the yard, where the family meetings were now taking place. It was a vast improvement from the depressing and gloomy meeting room. It meant they could walk and talk in the fresh air, and thanks to the uncharacteristic generosity of the Japs, the meeting time had increased to forty-five minutes and intervals reduced to a weekly schedule. Zacharia hoicked up his new pair of navy shorts three sizes too big for him but the old familiar saying, beggars can't be choosers rang true. As morbid as it sounded, he was grateful for the new clothes he had acquired as his own were falling apart. Not new clothes, of course. Their previous owners had passed on, and their belongings were distributed amongst the men. Initially Zacharia cringed at the idea of wearing a dead man's clothes, but these were unprecedented times. Today, Thalia wore a checked blue and white wrap-around skirt and a white vest, and he noticed how thin she has become and the numerous cuts and bruises on her legs. She greeted him with the usual embrace, and he latched on, craving human contact. With eyes closed, he savoured holding her in his arms. When they eventually parted, they took a slow walk around the perimeter.

'You look smart, Pappa, new clothes?'

He chuckled. 'Hmm, well, they're new to me. What I wouldn't give for a new silk shirt and smart Panama hat.'

'I swear when we get out of here I'll never take my clothes for granted again,' replied Thalia.

They talked back and forth about his recent hospital admission, and she asked him if he was eating better since the recent arrival of the Red Cross parcels. He had not noticed any significant improvement and rice was still the staple diet. Their delay in boxes getting to Changi was due to the Japanese preventing any ships through their waters stopping the much needed aid from reaching them. Somehow, a limited supply was beginning to filter through, although the Japanese were keeping some for themselves and only one in fifty boxes made it to the prisoners they were intended for. On reaching an empty bench, they sat down.

'There is something else I need to tell you. The Red Cross have provided some information about the evacuee ships. Do you want to know?'

Zacharia held his daughter's hand and stared out across the yard. She hadn't told him anything yet, and his eyes were already welling up.

'Well, I've had plenty of time to prepare for this. I need to hear it.'

'It still doesn't tell us much but I think you should know.'

Thalia squeezed his hand, and he nodded. Two years with no news and now suddenly, to have some answers made him dizzy and nauseous. He wasn't sure he was ready but needed to be brave and hear her out.

'When we left them at the harbour, they boarded the SS Kuala. Many ships never made it out of the harbour, but they managed to get to a place called Pom Pong Island.'

'That's good news. Isn't it?' he looked into her eyes; her features blurry from his tears threatening to spill over.

'It is Pappa, but there's more you need to know. The ship was attacked from the air, and survivors made it to shore. There are records of another ship coming to their rescue three days later. But that ship was also attacked, and the Red Cross are still trying to identify those on-board who are still missing. There are reports of survivors making it to Sumatra and various islands. It could take another year to track everyone down.'

Zacharia's head flopped forward and breathed deeply whilst processing the news. Thalia wrapped her arm across his shoulders.

'Are you ok Pappa?'

'We're still no closer to knowing whether they survived. It doesn't sound too positive, though, does it? My poor girls. I wasn't there for them,' he said, rubbing his brow fiercely.

'Pappa. Don't torture yourself. We still don't know for sure that they didn't make it. What have you always told me? We must have hope. Please promise me that you won't leave today and blame yourself. So many choices were being made that day, and we did the best we could at the time. It was all down to chance,' said Thalia.

'I suppose so. My memory is a bit hazy. It happened so quickly.' Zacharia replied, nodding slowly.

'The way I see it is they could be among the survivors waiting to be found. Thetie and Ino are good swimmers and would have helped Mamma get to shore. They wouldn't have left her side.'

'What does Terpie make of it?'

'She agrees. Until there is news, we must be positive, and I suggest you do the same.'

'Where did you get your positive outlook on life from? Such an optimist.'

'You taught me that, Pappa, you've forgotten that's all. Talking to people and hearing their stories makes me appreciate what we still have. We have to look forward to the future.'

'My sweet child. You're young and have the rest of your life to live, but as for me, I've had my best life with your mother and you girls, but the thought of making a new future without them terrifies me.'

'A life without you terrifies me just the same. Please don't talk about giving up,' said Thalia.

'I'm not giving up. Things just won't ever be as good as they were. That's all.'

Father and daughter sat together quietly until Thalia changed the subject.

'Have you heard the rumours? We're moving to a new camp.'

'I heard something about it, I didn't believe it though. Do you know more about it then?' he asked.

'Nothing officially. Everyone is talking about it though. The facilities are better, with proper beds.'

'Well, I'd pay no heed to rumours. They only lead you to disappointment in the end. Although I do like the sound of a proper bed to sleep on. Keep me posted if you hear anymore. It would be a refreshing change that's for sure.'

The sound of the gong announced the end of the family meeting.

'Same time next week?' Thalia asked kissing her pappa on the cheek.

'Just try and stop me.'

Chapter Thirty-One
Terpie

Within seconds of waking, a rush of anticipation flooded through Terpie's body as she stretched out and yawned with the realisation that she just experienced her last uncomfortable night of sleep in this dank concrete cell. Before moving from her space on the floor, she sensed the buzz of excitement rippling through the block. Laughter and happy chatter wafted along the corridor, a pleasant change from the usual early morning hubbub of children whining and crying from hunger or boredom. Thalia had gone for a shower, so with a clear path to the door, she stuck her head out and peered up and down. A hive of activity greeted her in both directions, and the corridor had already become cluttered with packed belongings, rolled up bedding and bits of furniture made or acquired during their time here. Everyone seemed keen to be leaving.

'Have you seen this out here?' Terpie asked, turning to Carol sitting cross-legged in the corner, lighting a cigarette.

'Yes, it looks like a bring-and-buy sale. I nearly tripped and broke my neck coming back from the ward last night. Some idiot left their stuff across the corridor, and I didn't see it in the dark.'

'I can't believe we're getting out of here today!' Terpie shrieked and did a little dance on the spot.

'It would be better if we were getting out to freedom. I don't see what the excitement's all about. It'll be a different set of walls. That's all. It's still a prison,' said Carol flatly, exhaling the smoke from her cigarette into a perfect ring shape which floated for a few seconds and dissipated like a popped bubble. Terpie hated smoke, especially in the confines of the cell but she had no choice but to tolerate it. With any luck, that would change too and she would have space to call her own and a real bed.

'Yes but it'll be different scenery, and the guards say the camp is much nicer. It's a palace compared to this place.'

'If you say so,' replied Carol, flicking through the latest copy of the *POW WOW* newsletter.

Today they were moving to a new home. The women had been starved of any excitement or adventure for so long the move was a seismic event in the camp calendar. Terpie enjoyed the sparks of euphoria going off inside her, something she hadn't experienced for what felt like an eternity. She wouldn't allow Carol's negative outlook to taint her optimism. Finally, she had something to look forward to, they all did. The reason for the move they were told was because the military prisoners currently being held in Sime Road were to be swapped with the civilians in Changi, but no further rationale was provided for the switch. Whilst the prisoners waited eagerly for news, a melancholy mood descended, and tempers shortened with squabbles and very unladylike fights breaking out over the slightest disagreement. When the women finally received the announcement at the end of a morning roll call, there was a great deal of whooping and cheering that the guards dared not suppress. Terpie had not felt this energised since the "Changi stroll" to the beach many months back. Another short-lived privilege whisked away from them since the new commander on camp put a stop to it.

'Morning. It's wonderful to see everyone so happy,' said Thalia, returning to the cell, dragging her fingers through her damp hair, which was beginning to curl. 'Do we know what time we're moving out?' she asked.

'I heard a rumour the men were going to be moved first,' said Terpie.

'I think we'll get told in the roll call. They can't move all of us at once. It'll be chaos. There must be a few thousand of us at least,' Carol said, forcefully stubbing out her cigarette before jumping up.

'Actually, the number is closer to four and half thousand in both camps combined,' said Terpie knowledgably.

'Of course, you would know that, working closely with the Japs in your office. I don't know how you bear to be so close to them,' Carol scoffed. 'Are they your best friends now?'

'Don't be ridiculous. I'm working for the camp committee, not the Japs. Yes they are in the same offices, but I keep away from them as much as I can,' Terpie protested indignantly. 'I hate them as much as you do,' she replied, trying to overlook the sting of Carol's accusations; it wasn't her fault. She would forever carry an underlying bitterness towards the Japs and understandably so.

'I can't think of one person I've met that doesn't,' Thalia added.

'Anyway, I gotta hit the road,' said Carol, picking up her case as if nothing had happened. 'I'm meeting Betty to help prepare the patients for travelling. See you both on the upside. It's been swell sharing with you, and you better keep in touch.'

The girls hugged before they watched her saunter down the corridor with her tatty suitcase and her ponytail swinging from side to side. Unlike Betty, Carol rarely let it show that she had been affected by the interrogation and appeared to the outside world that she was the same old Carol, but Terpie knew something inside her had changed forever. The human mind can't erase an experience like that so easily and the trauma would catch up with her eventually.

'It's weird to think we won't be sharing with those two anymore,' said Thalia, as she watched Carol navigate around the fully loaded prams and overflowing wheeled carts, ready for the off littering her path.

'I know, I'll miss them. I hope whoever we end up sharing with next time will be as easy to get on with. Can you imagine being lumbered with someone like grumpy old Mrs Forbes?'

'Or drama queens like those squealing Canadian sisters!' Thalia flapped her arms and pouted her lips in imitation. 'I couldn't bear it.'

'Me neither. Well, it has to be better than this dump. I can't wait to sleep on a proper bed. Can I leave you to pack up the rest of our things? I've agreed to help move some boxes into the trucks.'

'That's fine, it's not like we have much stuff. I'll see you at the roll call later.'

Terpie glanced around the cell for the last time. These suffocating concrete walls had been her home for too long, and she vowed never to think of this place again once she was out. Resting her hand on the doorframe, she sighed and quietly mourned the wasted years and made her way to the yard, her feet danced down the steps, and she found herself singing out loud. Later that morning, during the roll call, Thalia and Terpie learned they would be in the third convoy of prisoners to transfer to the Sime Road about thirteen miles away. Due to the large numbers, authorities were transporting groups of five hundred at a time so the relocation would go on into the evening. Even though she was grateful to be amongst one of the first groups, Terpie still found the waiting unbearable, and she twitched with impatience; time dragged sitting around with their baggage in the yard until finally, it was their time to leave. The two sisters stood side by side, waiting to board one of the many buses, trucks and lorries which would transport them and their paltry possessions. Before climbing onto the army truck, Terpie took one final look at the formidable heavy iron gate which gaoled them all for so long. Casting her mind back to when they had arrived over two years ago, she recalled thinking that this imprisonment would be temporary, six months at most. How naïve they had all been and underestimated the Japanese's strength of power in the region.

'Come on, the sooner we get in, the quicker we'll get out of here,' urged Thalia impatiently, chivvying her from behind. The women shuffled along to make room and bewildered children looked vacant, not knowing quite to make of the upheaval. Terpie shuffled uncomfortably in her seat. The pouch of Emily's jewellery rubbed against her thighs as she clutched her case tightly on her lap. Both girls did not want to risk their only asset being found in a potential bag search, so they kept it hidden under their clothes.

'I wonder if Pappa's made it safely to his new home. I'm sure the change of scenery will lift his spirits.'

'I hope so. He's been quite low lately,' Terpie replied. Cheers and whistles rippled through the convoy as vehicles navigated through the camp gates and onto the open road. The route to their new future took them along the coast, and the scent of the sea and rolling scenery stimulated Terpie's senses. She breathed deeply, nourishing herself with the crisp, clean air and relished the pleasant breeze on her skin. Terpie's heart sang with the thrill of change and a new beginning.

As they progressed into the city, Terpie eagerly observed the streets to soak up the surroundings that once formed part of her daily life. A landscape she now realised she had taken for granted. Whilst the roads had been cleared of fallen rubble, the city looked grubby, tainted by battle and a mere shadow of its previous splendour. Slowly but surely the elation she experienced only moments ago began to drain away, replaced by a dense sorrow and a heaviness in her heart. She wondered if Singapore would ever recover. Queues of lean looking locals waited patiently outside stores with tickets in hand to collect their daily rations. No one escaped the poverty and hardship in this new world. Blazoning from the heights of prominent buildings the firm stamp of Japanese control was evident with flags bearing the rising sun hanging limply where the Union Jack had proudly flown before. She forgot this was Syonan now, and the Singapore city

266

she knew no longer existed. The vibrant city had been stripped of its soul with a noticeable loss of cars on the road and colourful locals going about their business freely.

Suddenly the truck turned sharply around the corner where four Kempeitai officers stood in dark green uniforms. Their stern faces and shiny weapons intended to send a message of fear. An icy shiver trickled down her spine. Selfishly she hadn't given much thought to what life was like on the outside, assuming that nowhere could be as deprived as prison life, but it was evident that beyond Changi's walls was equally unpleasant.

'Are you ok?' Thalia asked softly.

'Our beautiful city is gone,' Terpie said quietly.

They continued down a long dusty track, and the landscape changed again with trees on both sides, and the convoy slowed, pulling up outside another set of camp gates. Smaller than Changi but no less formidable. Terpie's spirits lifted again now that they had arrived. The blue sky was barely visible through the dense, sprawling canopy of a majestic rain trees. Suddenly catching Terpie by surprise Thalia abandoned her battered suitcase, and jumped up on the seat grabbing the overhead roll bar where she was exposed to an uninterrupted view across the vehicles snaking down the road. On the street below, hundreds of people on foot like pack mules loitered with their belongings, waiting for instructions. Guards with rifles herded them into a tightly packed group to avoid losing any stragglers. Slowly the black gates opened, allowing the first of the prisoners in.

'What are you doing? Get down from there,' Terpie pleaded, tugging on the hem of her shorts.

'It's so green. So many trees. You'll love it,' Thalia shrieked.

Her enthusiasm spread through the truck like a Mexican wave, and other women stood on the seats trying to get a better view. Terpie remained seated clutching her case. The vehicle rocked and swayed with their eagerness.

'Terpie, stand up. Look at those little huts and all the trees,' Thalia said, grinning from ear to ear.

'It looks idyllic compared to that concrete hell we have just come from,' Terpie said, standing to join her.

'You women, get down!' yelled a guard from the ground, sweeping his gun in a downward motion. Terpie's heart hammered as she caught his steely stare and yanked her sister's hand. Thalia jumped down, and the other women followed her lead. After a short wait, they were allowed to dismount, and with worn shoes and bodies, they strode through the gates with optimism. With their cases in hand, the prisoners meandered along the road taking in the wonder of their new surroundings. They passed a huddle of one-story brick buildings with flaky white paint and tin roofs. Before the invasion, these buildings served as the Royal Air force headquarters, and more recently, the British Army and Terpie strained to read the old tin signs at a distance. 'Restricted Area—Keep Out.' Neatly cut patches of grass separated the buildings and winding paths linked to other areas beyond. Terpie took in the new scenery, which was a feast for the eyes and beside her, Thalia was doing the same.

Thalia tugged at her arm, and for a moment, they stood still. 'Listen.'

Birds. Terpie closed her eyes. It was a sound denied to them for so long. Beautiful melodic chirping and peeps from hidden birds nestling in the branches brought a flood of memories of their home and garden rushing in. They continued and the sight of an eight-foot high chain-linked fence which separated the men from the women reminded her that this was still a prison. Through the fence, she saw male prisoners milling about and trying to catch a glimpse of a familiar female face.

A little further ahead, small brick buildings with corrugated metal roofs in various states of disrepair and ramshackle wooden huts came into view. The stony silent guards escorted them along the route, and as they reached a new hut, they herded women in until the buildings were full. The prisoners continued walking deeper into the camp where the orderly and neat tarmac roads petered out to stone and pebble paths. Terpie crunched along, feeling the unevenness of the stones through her thin sandals, and hoped there was not much further to walk. Eventually the girls were ushered into a long hut resembling a barn for housing animals. The guards shoved them forward and the women stood dumbfounded in the inadequate accommodation. The hut was divided into twelve sections by horizontal wooden planks and had a mud floor covered in hay and old rugs scattered beneath their feet. Scraps of furniture, a milking stool, a wonky chair, a selection of wooden crates, and the odd tatty blanket lay around and Terpie's heart sank with disappointment.

'Tell me they're not serious,' whispered Terpie, through gritted teeth.

'Sadly, I think they are. Take a look up there,' said Thalia, pointing to the roof where slithers of blue sky could be seen through the metal panels and wooden struts.

'That's going to be interesting during the heavy rainstorms. So much for the facilities being better! You lied to us!' Terpie growled, but the guard was at the other end of the hut cramming more women in, so unless he had the senses of a bat, he would never have heard her. She sensed disbelief that the Japanese expected them to live in these primitive conditions on the hard floor in the dirt, exposed to the elements. Terpie didn't know why she was surprised. Overwhelmed by the disappointment, she began to weep. The day had been supercharged with mixed emotions and the promise of something better, and this was most definitely not better. She wiped her face and briefly felt her sister's arm around her shoulders, giving her a consolatory hug.

Thalia stumbled on the jute mat curling at the edges, stained and damp from a recent downpour. The area was no more than five feet wide. Terpie dropped her case and slowly surveyed the horror of their living conditions.

'It could be worse. At least we have a view,' Thalia said, putting her case on the floor and using it as a stool to sit on. Her scarred tanned legs stretching out in front of her. She had a serene and relaxed look, which Terpie couldn't fathom.

'Are you kidding? I can't face another night on a hard floor. I've been dreaming of a soft mattress for weeks. Doesn't it make you mad?'

'I'm not surprised and had no expectations. The Japs lie all the time, so this is nothing new,' said Thalia, resting her chin in her hand watching her aggravated sister pacing like a caged tiger.

'Come on, don't let this get to you. It'll be ok.'

'How're you always so calm about everything?' Terpie sniffed.

'After everything we've been through, it's not worth my time. Why don't we get settled and go and explore?'

Chapter Thirty-Two
Zacharia

Zacharia waited at the previously agreed meeting place by the old wooden tool shed for Peter to walk down the hill together for the family meeting. Even though his eyesight was failing him and generally people were fuzzy shapes in the distance, he could always recognise Peter's form as he approached by his slight, laboured gait as he ambled along wearing his familiar white hat which looked as though it could disintegrate at any moment due to frequent wear.

'Afternoon Peter, you look well today.'

'I'd like to say the same to you my friend but forgive me, you look terrible.'

Zacharia laughed, wheezing slightly. 'Thanks, I can always rely on you to be brutally honest.'

'Do you think you should go to the hospital wing to get checked out?' Peter asked looking concerned.

'I don't feel great but no. I don't want anything to get in the way of seeing my girls. Getting stuck in hospital is too depressing, surrounded by death and illness. I'll be ok and the walk will do me good.'

Zacharia was conscious that he was shuffling along at a snail's pace as his legs were aching today and his back hurt more than usual. The downward slope played havoc with his knees, and he tried not to worry about how he would manage the return journey back up. 'You can go on ahead if you want to. I'm holding you up.'

'No problem, Zac, honestly. Martha's never on time anyway. Jacob runs rings around her, and she takes forever to get ready. Besides, you don't look too steady today, and I wouldn't want to leave you.'

'I do feel a bit wobbly on my old legs. So, if you don't mind taking it slowly, I'd be grateful.'

'Not at all,' said Peter, and they continued walking until he halted abruptly outside the tin smith's hut. 'In fact, can you wait there. Just for a minute. I'll be right back.' He signalled for Zac to stop by raising his hands and bolting around the corner out of sight. Seizing the opportunity for a rest to catch his breath, Zacharia leaned against the hut soaking up some shade beneath the umbrella like canopy of a young rain tree and waited. A short while later, Peter reappeared carrying a gnarled but sturdy walking stick.

'Here, I thought his might help. I remembered seeing it propped up against the wall a while ago and it was still there so clearly doesn't belong to anyone,' said Peter, handing it to his friend.

'Thank you. I am an old man now and look the part,' said Zacharia, hunching over the stick for comedic affect. 'No honestly. Thank you. Joking aside. This will be a great help. See! That's better already,' exclaimed Zacharia, trying out the walking aid and moving with more confidence. It touched him that his friend was so thoughtful. With little news of any consequence, the men exchanged day-to-day minutiae as they continued their slow and steady pace until arriving at the dusty parade square. Thankfully family visits were a more relaxed affair these days, more frequent and finally husbands and wives were free to meet and mingle, usually for an hour. Still, occasionally they got away with longer if the guards were in a favourable mood.

Peter was a changed man since he had seen Martha and Jacob together as a family unit. Following the move, some aspects of camp life had improved but the jury was still out on whether Zacharia preferred this camp to the last but the trees were a welcome addition. Resting both hands on his stick he watched as a squealing Jacob ran to his father with his arms outstretched to be lifted, followed by Martha with a sunny smile. The little boy had the blondest hair he had ever seen, so fine with a glossy pearlescence that made him want to reach out and stroke it. He was thinking what a handsome couple Peter and Martha made when Thalia suddenly appeared next to him, slipped her hand through the crook of his arm, and pecked him on the cheek.

'Pappa, come and sit down. You look exhausted,' said Thalia, guiding him to sit on the log behind them. 'Nice walking stick,' she commented.

'It is, isn't it. Peter just found it for me. I think it suits me,' laughed Zacharia, setting the stick down.

'Here, I've something for you. Put it in your pocket. Don't let the guards see,' she said quietly, surreptitiously passing him a soft, round package wrapped in material.

'What is it?' he said, taking it from her and stuffing it in his breast pocket.

'It's my portion of papaya, I don't like them. You need it more than me. You have to keep your strength up.'

Zacharia patted her thigh. 'Always looking after me. Your mother would be proud of you. Have you heard any more about the evacuee ships?' he asked, aware this was something he queried every time they met, but he couldn't help it. He knew that Thalia would tell him if there was any news, but he had to ask. It was a little ritual between them. She would always say, 'no, not yet, but I keep asking.' And he would nod and say, 'ok, well keep me informed.' He lived in hope that she would have something to tell him one of these days. Good or bad. It had got to the point where anything was better than nothing. He had a horrible feeling that his seasons were coming to an end and couldn't bear the thought of leaving this world and never finding out what had happened to his beautiful family. He wouldn't say that to Thalia and frighten her, but he felt increasingly fragile by the day and wasn't sure how much time was left on his clock.

'I meant to say. We've been allowed to send postcards out of camp. I sent one to Shi Min and Lim. Just a few words to let them know we're ok,' said Thalia. 'I hope they are alright.'

'That's a good idea. Yes, me too. When will Emily be well enough to come out here and visit me one of these days? I think of her often, and I can't believe I've not seen her in all this time. Has something happened to her, and you've not told me?' He paused awaiting her answer and her lack of response set off alarm bells. 'Thalia?' he questioned stiffly. During the awkward silence he searched his daughter's face for a flicker of surety, but she refused to meet his gaze and stared down into her hands on her lap. Her silence spoke volumes and his temper boiled over.

'Something's happened, hasn't it? Why didn't you tell me? I'm not a child, Thalia, you're not responsible for me, and I can handle the truth,' he exclaimed, raising his arm in protest and knocking the walking stick clean off its perch.

'I'm so sorry, Pappa, Terpie and I thought it was better not to tell you. At the time, you were in a terrible place, and we thought bad news might tip you over the edge.' She reached for his hand, but he snatched it away. A horrifying thought crossed his mind if she could lie about this, what else has she kept from him?

'What other secrets are you keeping from me? Do you know what has happened to your mother and sisters? Have you chosen not to tell me that as well?' he demanded, and his voice increased another octave with each sentence. He gasped, unable to catch his breath and dissolved into a coughing fit.

'No, Pappa, please believe me. I don't have any news about the others. I promise. I swear on my life, I would tell you. But with Emily, we honestly thought we were doing the right thing.' Thalia rested her arm on his shoulder.

'When did she pass?' he croaked once he'd recovered and regained his breath.

'She died of malaria and malnutrition back in Changi, July 1943.' Thalia's voice was barely a whisper. 'She died peacefully, and Terpie visited her the day before.'

'What? Over two years ago. You've been lying to me all this time!' Zacharia fumed, staring out into the distance. A tightness spread across his chest, and he breathed deeply, staving off another bout of coughing. Poor Emily. She was like family, and he would have appreciated the opportunity to say goodbye to her and visit her grave. That was never going to happen now. He would never set foot in Changi ever again. Father and daughter sat beside each other in awkward silence for ten minutes or more, watching the other families mingle and children run around the yard with an innocence Zacharia envied. With regards to Emily if he was honest, he'd suspected as much. He wasn't a stupid man, but the confirmation of the truth opened the floodgates for all the suppressed emotion he had kept buried. This unfamiliar sensation of resentment and distrust towards his daughters was something new he must now navigate.

'I'm sorry, Pappa. I made a mistake. Please forgive me,' soothed Thalia rubbing his arm.

Zacharia composed himself and reached inside his pocket for his embroidered handkerchief which he always carried and dabbed his eyes.

'Do you know how it feels to be deceived? I don't feel I can trust you anymore. She was my friend, and I had a right to know,' he said calmly.

'Please, Pappa, I know I let you down. At the time, we thought that men and women would never be allowed to meet in Changi and that you would never find out. Well, until you were stronger, at least. We were trying to protect you,' Thalia snivelled.

'I appreciate that, but I'm supposed to look after you. I'm the head of the family. Not the other way around. I feel so helpless and useless in this place.' He hated to see Thalia upset, which softened him a little. 'So, to make it clear. If you ever find out anything, don't keep it from me. Good or bad. You hear me?'

Zacharia slid his arm around her shoulder and pulled her close. He couldn't recall an occasion when his daughter's behaviour had angered him, and it was an unpleasant emotion. After the initial shock had subsided, he understood there was no malice in their decision. He could only trust that in future they would not withhold information from him again.

'I took the carved elephant you made her last Christmas to her grave,' Thalia said quietly.

'Thank you. Where's Terpie anyway? Didn't she want to see me this week?'

'No Pappa, it's not that. She's doing important admin duties in the office. I've no idea what.'

'What's more important than seeing her pappa? I get precious little time with her as it is,' he said, nodding his head sullenly.

'You know what Terpie's like. Her priorities are not always the same as ours.'

'Well thank goodness I have you.'

Monsoon season had arrived a month later and was about as welcome as hole in a lifeboat. Days of rain followed, with torrents gushing like a waterfall onto the ramshackle huts in Sime Road and turning the paths into streams and puddles into ponds. In the crowded hut, Zacharia was surrounded by men shouting to be heard over the din of water pummelling the tin roof. The men had placed tins and any suitable receptacle underneath the leaks to catch the rainwater runnels. The relentless drips and pings that had a melodic quality were now annoying. Zacharia sat with his knees tucked under his chin reading a battered copy of *Tender is the Night* by F. Scott Fitzgerald, passed around the hut and landed with him. It wasn't his kind of book, and he struggled to sympathise with the central protagonist, Dick Diver and found it a thoroughly depressing read so far. He held the book far out in front of him, it wasn't his indifference making it a slow read. He persevered with it for something to do and as the day grew darker even that wasn't possible. He shared the ten-person hut with thirty others and a host of various body odours and germs. Zacharia believed himself to be the grandfather of the group, but all the men seemed to get along. There was not as much work to be done outside the camp anymore (besides, much of the labour force had either died or were now too weak to work) leaving the inmates struggling with an indefinite tedium and feelings of worthlessness. Some of the younger men sat around playing cards with cigarettes hanging loosely between their lips, wavering up and down precariously as they talked. Others lay on their beds in conversation with their neighbour, or some were silent, locked in their torment, whilst others caught up on lost sleep. Zacharia closed the book and slid it under his blanket. Even though he did not care for the story, he wouldn't let the rain ruin it. He lay on his bed with an unappealing view of rows of damp laundry hanging across the entire length of the roof, which would never dry in this weather. The frowsty air wasn't helping his chest.

'Given up then?' said Tom, lying on his side on the bed next to his.

'Yes, my eyesight's gotten worse in the last year, and it's too dark in here,' Zacharia wheezed.

'I hope this storm passes soon. The boredom's driving me crazy.'

'I never thought I'd say I miss Changi, but at least it was well organised, and there was some structure to the day. And dry!' Zacharia grumbled.

'I know what you mean. There isn't the same enthusiasm for getting things sorted anymore. It's like people have given up. The food situation needs sorting, that's for sure. Do you think they're starving us to death, and that was their intention all along? Let us die a long, slow hungry death?' Tom asked, stretching out and folding his skinny arms behind his head like a pillow.

Zacharia scratched at the stubble on his chin.

'I don't think they'd have gone to all this trouble. If they wanted us dead, they'd have taken us all out and shot us on day one.'

'This way, it looks like they made an effort to keep us alive,' challenged Tom.

Zacharia was losing patience and sighed. 'To be honest, Tom, it's irrelevant. I've spent too much time wondering about the what if's and why's of this bloody war. We are where we are. We must be thankful for each day that passes and I'm just grateful if I wake up every morning. One of these mornings could be the day the Japanese are forced to surrender, and I'll be damned if I'm going to spend my days worrying about things I've no control over.'

'No. I suppose you are right.'

Zacharia had no desire to continue the conversation, so he lay in silence, his hand resting loosely upon his esurient, sunken abdomen, feeling hungry as usual. The food situation had deteriorated further still and this week, prisoners were offered an unpalatable watery soup mixture made with slimy green leaves, morning and evening. Occasionally, the murky fluid appeared to be enhanced with floating meaty chunks which raised Zacharia's suspicions. He strongly suspected the additional sustenance was likely from an unfortunate rat or bird. Much of the food was taken at face value as no one really knew what the ingredients were, but the hunger was so intense it was necessary to pay no heed to the content.

Zacharia was eternally grateful to the younger cohort who generously shared their food rations with him, despite its revolting taste and questionable origin. There had been occasions where his stomach ached so much he had scavenged for bugs, grubs, and insects to eat. Everyone had. It was the only way to survive. Zacharia felt he was growing weaker by the day and some days he never left the hut. To add to his discomfort his skin had broken out in painful boils again despite having them lanced several times, they kept returning. Recently, he found it was easier to point out the areas of his body which didn't cause him pain and he suspected his body was giving up, which was a terrifying thought. He was desperate to be well enough to make the long walk to meet Thalia and Terpie and had now missed three weeks of visits.

Knowing how important these visits were to him, Peter and Mickey had offered to support him there and back and he had thanked them but declined. It was not just the walk which concerned him. Even though he had not seen a mirror in months, he was fully aware he must look dreadful and did not want his daughters to witness how rundown and dishevelled he had become. It would only scare them to see him so frail. Zacharia decided to wait a bit longer until his health improved. Still, as time went on, as it invariably does, he never did feel any better. He soon found himself paralysed by the familiar heavy cloud which had rolled in cloaking his heart and soul in darkness rendering him a prisoner of depression once more.

Chapter Thirty-Three
Benny

Under the intense heat of the day and with a gun focussed on him only a few feet away Benny swung the pickaxe over his head again for about the thousandth time that day. Every muscle in his withered body protested. His shirt tied around his waist was sodden in sweat, attracting insects to feed on his glistening skin. Despite the excruciating pain, he kept on digging. The axe came down on rocks sending a jolt up his arms and rattling his teeth. The frustrating process had minimal impact on the unforgiving sun-baked ground, disturbing only the smallest fragments of rock and mud. Sweat poured out of him, trickling down his forehead, stinging his eyes and blurring his vision. If he dared to stop for a second to wipe it away, a beating would follow which he feared most beyond his discomfort. However short, the Japanese soldiers showed no tolerance for the men taking a break. Benny was one of a long line of men labouring like robots on the side of the road, and the mind-numbing rhythm of swinging the axe and splintering of stone kept the voice in his head quiet. It was too exhausting to think. Enslaved against his will, his existence had been reduced to following orders from guards who hounded him throughout the day and nightmares which tormented his sleep at night. Benny no longer recognised himself as a man or indeed a human being. Following capture, he and two thousand soldiers found themselves in Borneo. They had been sent out in various working parties for the last two years to rebuild the airstrip, aerodrome, and the supporting road structure in Sandakan. Unsurprisingly, camp conditions were appalling, and the men worked from sunrise to sunset on a restricted diet, and there was no medical attention to speak of. To their captors, they were disposable labour, machines, not men with souls. Over the years Benny had lost many comrades to disease and malnutrition and the pain of saying goodbye was hard to bear. None more so than Jimmy. During the voyage from Singapore, they reunited and managed to stay together until an infection from an open wound took hold and without medical treatment there was nothing to be done. Jimmy's death saddened him profoundly, further fuelling his hatred of the Japanese. In his role as a priest, he had witnessed death, but not like this. The senseless loss of a young man in his prime with a family, struck down before his life had barely started was difficult for him to process. Benny remained by his side until the end, ensuring he wasn't alone. Benny made a final promise to his dear friend that should he survive this hell, he'd search for Charlotte to make sure she knew how brave her husband was and that he was the best damn friend Benny ever had.

From somewhere behind him, a whistle blew signalling the end of the shift, and with relief, the axe slipped from his calloused hands and thudded to the ground. He joined the other men shuffling forward in threadbare boots to form an orderly line and together they made the slow march back to camp. The sprawling camp comprised rows of shabby huts housing mostly Australian soldiers, and the sturdy brick buildings were reserved for Japanese military. For the first year, life was relatively good, and prisoners received fair treatment. The variety of food choices were minimal but there was plenty to go round. Back then, Benny had enjoyed the concerts organised by the prisoners and spirits were still high.

How things had changed over the year. Gradually, the influx of hundreds more soldiers, many of whom were sick and desperate for medical attention tipped the balance and resources. Out of desperation some men took risks, thinking they could outsmart their captors by trying to escape, share rations with the sick, or steal extra food. Benny never understood futile attempts which resulted in punishments of the worse kind. Down by the guard's office under a tree, the Japanese constructed cages with iron bars only one meter wide by two meters high with barely headroom to sit. Anyone placed there went without food for the first week and only after day three were they allowed water to drink. If they survived, the victims were released for an hour's exercise in the evenings, followed by a beating.

Food was not a civilised affair and had to be earned by fighting amongst the dogs for scraps from a long metal trough. They remained incarcerated on half food rations until their thirty days of punishment were up and only the hardiest souls made it out alive. The fate of those suspected of spying was no better and they were dragged to a basement, strapped on their backs to a table with a dirty blanket covering their face. Guards laughed as they pumped water into their mouths from a hose, choking them whilst their bellies filled with water, drowning them alive. The few survivors were plagued with mental suffering far worse than any physical pain and were never the same. Lost in a faraway land they became terrified of human contact and huddled in corners with glazed eyes, like zombies.

Some months back, one of the desperate soldiers breached the perimeter, escaping through the wire to scrounge fruit from trees nearby. He was caught and shot on the spot. No cage for him. It seemed the Japs were losing patience. With such abhorrent penalties, Benny surrendered completely to Japanese control and avoided trouble at all costs. Laying on his back, he stared vacantly at the ceiling. He savoured the stillness on a hessian sack for a bed, allowing his aching limbs to recuperate. Benny's sole objective now was to survive to return to his family and Terpie. Only during these quiet times did the blackness lift enough for Benny to entertain thoughts of his loved ones.

'Benny, grub's up,' said a voice above him startling him. Benny hauled himself up and queued for his half ration of rice. As he waited in line it was hard not to ignore the men around him too weak to leave their beds with swollen bellies and raging fevers, staring at the ceiling gasping for breath. He doubted they would last much longer. Benny put his hands in his pockets and took them out again. Unsettled, he was desperately fighting the urge to take food to them. Turning a blind eye to their distress out of fear for his own life snagged at his conscience. His need to survive had overridden his compassion for his fellow man and he disliked himself for it. To share food was an act of certain death.

With a small tin containing his ration, Benny joined his comrades around the campfire to eat. He shovelled the rice down with feverish haste and licked the container clean using his dirty fingers. His body craving more. As the fire crackled and hissed Benny felt isolated listening to the men's conversations as they shared war stories and scenes of previous battles. He didn't belong. Stretching his legs, he rubbed at the dirt, wincing from the painful ulcers on his shins. The man beside him passed the flask of water, and gratefully he took a few gulps, and passed it on. With mealtime over, Benny retreated to the hut. Laying on his bed, he waited for sleep to come.

The following morning, he was disturbed by a distant hum. His heart began to race, and sat up abruptly calling out to the man in the bed next to him.

'Moxy, can you hear that? The planes are coming again.' The man beside him rolled over.

These were not enemy planes. These were Americans coming to attack the airstrip, to thwart the progress of the Japanese. For a split second, Benny indulged the fantasy that their mission was to rescue them. Benny joined others at the open windows to see the sky filled with over twenty bomber planes heading for the aerodrome. Dark shadows dominating the sky. After a few minutes, bombs exploding filled his eardrums, and he began to shake. The memory of the attacks in Singapore still haunted him. Quietly, he returned to his bed and curled up in ball whilst behind him men cheered in triumph.

Their bravado quickly faded when Japanese guards stormed into the hut with weapons, thwacking anyone within their reach to quash their jubilance. Benny cowered with his arms over his head and prayed he had become invisible. Those who could not move fast enough to escape the wrath of the angered Japs yelped in agony and eventually silence descended again. Any hope of troops storming in to save them soon faded once the bombing ceased and no one came. The work schedule had been interrupted, and all they could do was wait. Later that afternoon, the guards returned ordering them outside.

'Everyone up! Get out. Line up outside, now!'

Clearly, the attacks had angered them, and they swarmed into the huts like frenzied wasps pushing and shoving, grabbing men and pulling them to their feet.

'All of you, even the sick. Get a move on.'

With his pulse racing, wondering what was happening, Benny hurriedly slid his feet into his tattered boots and threw on his shirt. With no time to fiddle with buttons, he headed out, his shirt flapping revealing his bony ribs. Benny stumbled outside and marched to the parade square with the other thousand men standing in confusion, waiting for further instruction. Time passed slowly and Benny gazed at the wispy cloud trails making a peaceful journey across the boundless blue sky, his sweaty hands clasped behind his back. Surrounding the parade square guards with guns stood sentry, glaring at them with loathing. Was this it? Were they all going to be shot?

All was still and quiet, except for the rustling of leaves from the jungle beyond the camp. It didn't seem that anything was happening for a long time, and Benny willed his weary legs to hold him up a bit longer. Captain Hoshijima, the camp commander, with four of his aides, made their way slowly up and down the rows carrying out what looked like an inspection but for what was not yet clear. During the excruciating wait Benny could not see what was happening, and his heart hammered against his chest as he waited anxiously for them to reach him along his row. As they neared, Benny realised prisoners were either being rejected or selected for what purpose he had no idea. When Hoshijima finally reached him, he stood uncomfortably close, their noses almost touched, and Benny could not avoid the warm sour breath on his face making him feel sick. Keeping perfectly still, Benny held his breath and stopped himself from blinking. Under the scrutiny of the guards looking him up and down, his skin burnt. A finger jabbed sharply into his chest.

'You,' was all he said, and the captain stepped back to allow Benny to follow the others selected ahead of him. Benny began breathing again and felt the blood rush to his head, and he tripped over his feet in his haste. At this point, couldn't tell whether being chosen was good or bad. The chosen men were led to a large storage building, the black doors wide open, naturally with armed guards at their post. The guard to his left directed him to stand among a group of men assembled with long faces, waiting in silence to learn their fate.

Once his eyesight adjusted to the gloom, he observed that the building was packed to the rafters with large wooden boxes and crates. On the tower of boxes looming over them were the words "ammunition" stamped in red whilst others were emblazoned in Japanese symbols he couldn't identify. To the side were more crates stacked haphazardly and large hessian bags of rice piled high to the roof top, the contents spilling out onto the floor. Seeing all that food made him angry as there seemed to be plenty to go around, yet they were being starved like lab rats.

The pounding of boots on the tarmac drew his attention, and he saw the dark figure of the captain and his entourage of grim reapers approaching. Clenching and unclenching his hands, he looked straight ahead between the heads and shoulders of the men in front and forced himself to breathe slowly. The pungent smell of combined sweat, fear and general uncleanliness stuck in the back of his throat. Supported by his men, captain Hoshijima, climbed onto a pile of boxes to be visible to his awaiting audience. From beneath the peak of his cap, he glared around the room with contempt for the dishevelled cohort before him.

'The air strikes by the Americans have destroyed our work on the aerodrome and it's beyond repair. Another attack is imminent, so we must move our supplies and equipment quickly. Therefore, you will help us take them to our camp at Ranau. You'll be the first of three organised marches and have been selected due to your fitness level. The camp is a hundred and sixty miles away and the route will take us through jungle and marshlands to avoid being hijacked. We expect you to make the trip in nine days, but you'll only carry enough food and water for four. So, it pays to keep moving,' said the captain pausing to pan around the room at the blank faces before he continued. 'Be warned, we have no time for the sick or wounded. If you can't keep up, you'll be left behind. If you slow us down… you'll be shot. Wait here to be sorted into your groups; the first group will leave tomorrow at daybreak.'

When he finished his address, the captain jumped down, nodded to his men and marched purposefully out the door with his legion of black rats close at his heel. Benny's shoulders slumped and he couldn't decide whether he felt relieved or scared. Could walking be less exhausting than digging day in, day out? Could he walk that far? Benny examined his tattered boots, fraying at the edges with worn soles, hoping they would be up to the task. Regardless of how he felt about it, he'd be setting off again on a course which took him further away from Terpie. The following morning Benny learned he had been selected for dispatch in the third group with fifty other men he knew only by sight. By the time they got organised with backpacks, crates fully loaded with supplies and ammunition, it was mid-morning when they were given the order to set off, escorted by armed soldiers. For the next five days, Benny obliviously stumbled through the most inhospitable terrain. His only focus to stay upright and keep moving forward. The Japs pushed them to cover at least eight miles a day through dense jungle, steep rocky inclines, and wading through marshlands. Two days ago, the food rations ran out and the gradually the platoon suffered fatalities through exhaustion and sickness, too weak to continue thus ending their story. With no time for commemoration, the unit ploughed on leaving the bodies abandoned in the bushes or floating in the swamps. His group of fifty men, now reduced to forty-two. The light was fading, and a few times Benny stumbled, losing his footing on the loose rocks, grabbing at branches to save him from tumbling down the deathly ravine below. The Japanese were machines, pushing the convoy to the limits, but they weren't foolish. To continue walking through the night would be suicide, and the men had to rest at some point. After another hour, they reached a clearing near a river, the men slowed, and the leading guard raised his hand, signalling them to stop.

'We'll rest here for the night. You can wash in the river, but you'll be shot if you try to escape.'

Loosening the straps of his weighted backpack, Benny let it slide to the ground. His shoulders sighed in relief, and he knelt on the edge of the riverbank to submerge his head in the cool, shallow water. For those few seconds, he entered a quiet and still world. His heartbeat pounding in his ears. To quench his raging thirst, he lapped at the water like a dog then scooped handfuls into his mouth. He patted water around his face, neck and head and refilled his water flask. With no strength left in his legs, he slid along the ground to find a resting place against a tree and massaged his temple which felt hot to the touch. His head was pounding. It was exhaustion, he told himself, and no doubt he would feel better after some rest. Like those around him, Benny scavenged the undergrowth for bugs, berries, snails, and fern shoots to eat without food rations. He stuffed whatever he thought was edible into his mouth. Benny watched as some of the men stripped off and took a dip in the river to wash off a week's worth of grime and sweat. He had no energy to join them and huddled against tree whilst his mates frolicked and splashed in the water like young boys under the rigid scorn of the guards observing from the riverbank. It seemed such a long time since he had heard laughter and he savoured the magical sound. He laughed along with them briefly before he began coughing. As much as he wanted to join the fun, his body pinned him to the ground. As darkness fell he fidgeted around, turning from side to side trying to get comfortable. The jungle floor was heaving with insects and ants, which seemed to take great umbrage to his being there. In frustration, he slapped and swatted at the insects until he realised, they had the upper hand, so he gave up fighting and resigned himself to being bitten and allowed them to crawl over him, using him as their personal highway. Whilst his comrades spoke in hushed tones, he yawned and could not keep his eyes open, and the overwhelming desire to sleep swept over him, taking him offline into blackness.

At dawn, Benny was shaken awake by someone and his body felt as heavy as lead. Around him the platoon prepared to move off again and Benny levered himself onto his feet, leaning on the tree for support. He did not feel himself. As the day drew on, Benny became one of the stragglers at the back of the group. The heavy bag of supplies crushed against his spine, and he was convinced someone snuck some extra weight on whilst he slept. Breathing heavily on the slight incline left him gasping for air. The sky overhead was thick with grey clouds and soon heavy rain followed, soaking him to the bone. With each step, his boots squelched and rubbed the sores on his feet. The extra saturated weight slowed him down and a stream of raindrops dripped down his face into his eyes, blurring his vision. His slow unsteady steps carried him along the uneven path, his spindly legs crisscrossing, almost tripping himself up. Despite the coolness of the rain, he was burning up, his insides on fire. He needed to stop and rest to get his breath back, but they were nowhere near the end of the day, so he knew rest was impossible for hours yet. He felt a hand on his upper arm.

'Come on, fella, keep going. We'll get a break soon.'

Benny nodded and stumbled on. Glancing at the lime green canopy of oval leaves overhead, a vivid memory flashed before him from when his life was his own. He had arranged to meet Terpie for lunch in the botanical gardens, and a midday torrential downpour had caught them out. She wore a cream linen dress tied at the waist with a bold fuchsia ribbon and a pale pink cardigan draped over her shoulders. Her outfit reminded him of an ice cream sundae. To prevent the rain from ruining her hair, she held her cardigan aloft and laughed as they ran together to shelter under a nearby tree. He missed her with an intensity he never knew was possible. She wouldn't give up, he thought. Terpie would be willing him on to keep going, and he had promised to get back to her. The thought of leaving her alone and full of sadness fuelled him to pick up the pace. He must get back.

Battling on for another two miles through overgrown paths, his body shifted between shivering chills to sweating dizziness. Stabbing pain pinged around his body like a pinball machine hitting every nerve on the way round. He had thrown up a few times, not that he had much content in his stomach to dispose of, which left him light-headed. He walked with his hands outstretched in front of him as he could not see clearly through the hazy blotches that danced around in his vision. After a few more yards, Benny was grateful to hear the guards shout an order to stop. Collapsing onto his knees, his bundle of bones fell heavily onto the mossy jungle floor. His breathing came in rapid rattly gasps. If only he could get this damn bag off, he could breathe but the clasps would not release. Floundering in panic, he fought to loosen the straps, but it refused to budge since the webbing had become damp and swollen. From behind, he felt someone tugging and pulling. His friend Jerry knelt before him and clasped his cheeks in his hands, looking him straight in the eye.

'Benny, Benny. I've got this ok. You just concentrate on breathing. Alright, pal.' Jerry fed the webbing strap through the clasp, and the bag fell to the ground with a thud. Finally, with the burden lifted, Benny's frail body heaved as he breathed big lungs full of air.

'Get the man some water,' someone said.

A tin flask was shoved in his face, and he grabbed it urgently and took three big gulps. Wiping the excess water from his chin, he thanked his aides. This was more than exhaustion, and he knew it.

'You alright now? Hang in their Benny boy. Get some rest, and you'll be right as rain by morning, and you'll be running around Ranau like a spring lamb when we get there. Just got a spot of jungle fever, that's all.'

'Yeah, you get some rest, lad. Don't worry about anything. We'll look after you.'

Benny shook uncontrollably, sweat poured from every pore, but he was so, so cold all over. He wrapped his arms around himself to keep warm and collapsed on his side, his legs drawn in like a child. In addition to the fever, he felt a wave of terror rise and swallow him whole. He recognised that tone, that same pitying look, the words of platitude and false hope spoken many times before to other sick men, dying men who later would not make it. He was not ready to die. Surely, this was not his time. Terpie needed him where they had a life waiting for them. Benny wanted to live, but without medical attention, his body couldn't fight the infection which had taken hold. He was unaware that his skin and the whites of his eyes had turned yellow from jaundice because his liver was failing. He did not realise his coughing was due to fluid build-up in his lungs. He had no idea that a female feeding mosquito at some point in the last few weeks landed on his skin and injected her filthy malaria parasites into his skin along with her saliva, which made a beeline for his red blood cells and multiplied. Whilst he had been trudging through rough jungle terrain, infected blood cells swelled and began to clog up the circulation in his major organs, brain, lungs, liver, and kidneys. Invading parasites dominate his blood cells, making them fragile, so he now has anaemia and not enough red blood cells to pump oxygen around his body. His body was slowly shutting down. Benny curled into a foetal position under the shady fronds of a low growing palm consumed with sadness and fear. Even all his religious teachings seem woefully inadequate when faced with one's mortality and impending death. He tried to draw on them now to comfort him, closed his eyes, and recited some prayers. Dying did not scare him. It was the thought of not having a chance to live the life he had planned first. He wanted to die peacefully in his bed as an old man, having achieved some of his hopes and dreams. At the age of twenty-seven, he had not had enough time, not nearly enough. Sometime later, the men began preparing to move on, and he knew he would not go with them. This was the end of his journey. He reached his arm out to Jerry to get his attention.

'Jerry, please. Tell the guards I can't go on. You know what to do.'

Jerry came down to his level and nodded, gripping his hand tightly. 'It has been an honour to march alongside you, son.'

With his fingers gripping Terpie's necklace, he closed his eyes, and a tear rolled down his cheek.

The crack of a gunshot pierced the afternoon sky dispersing a flock of birds from the trees and they soared freely towards the sun.

Chapter Thirty-Four
Thalia

The wand on the large, round dial didn't have far to go to return to its resting place at zero once Thalia stepped off the weighing scales and sat down. Fiddling with her fingers in her lap, she waited whilst a nurse recorded her results on the application form laying on the desk between them. Could she really be that thin? She checked again where the nurse scribbled down six stone, three ounces. She had never been one to be obsessed about her weight, unlike Clio who was forever dieting and comparing herself to her siblings. Of course, she knew she had lost weight. Her clothes hung from her bony frame, and she'd altered them several times to make them fit. Everyone had. It still came as a shock to see the reality in writing. Thalia missed her soft and curvy figure and despised the skeletal waif she had become. In total, she had lost four and a half stone. Next, the nurse placed the cold disc of the stethoscope against her skin and listened to her heart and chest. If Thalia was allowed to work in the kitchens, she had to pass the medical checks for the hygiene assessment and silently prayed she would.

'You're in good health, Thalia.' The Malaysian nurse smiled, adding her scribbled signature to the form.

'I think the fresh air helps. I feel better here than I did in Changi. I've not been sick once since we got here.'

'I can see from your records you've had several bouts of malaria, but you're young and fit so I would expect you to recover fully.'

'Like I say, I think the greenery here suits me and I feel good. Hungry obviously but aren't we all. So have I passed then?' Thalia asked.

'With flying colours.'

The clattering of trolley wheels along the concrete corridor halted their conversation and through the open-door Thalia caught a glimpse of a cloaked gurney pass by. The nurse shook her head.

'Sadly, we've seen too many pass before their time—good, decent people who are too weak to fight off infections. The numbers have increased since moving here. The men's camp is worse on account of the manual labour.'

'Oh really? My father's sick in the men's camp and he's been too weak to manage the long walk to meet me. I'm so worried about him,' Thalia said, glumly as the nurse popped the completed form into a brown envelope.

'I'm sure you are. The camp committee is always fighting with the authorities to get what we need. Most medicine we get these days comes smuggled in through the black market. But it's all too late. Most of the sick could be cured with a balanced diet, it's as simple as that. Anyway, I'm rambling, and I'm sure you don't want to hear it. I hope your father's situation improves.'

Thanking the nurse, Thalia made her way outside clutching the envelope tightly to her chest until she reached the admin office where she handed it in for review. Thalia had been told that was the last thing she needed to do, and a camp representative would confirm when she could start. Although she enjoyed working outdoors, she had grown tired of doing manual work and fancied a change of scenery. Sheila had informed her the kitchen were short of helpers so that made up her mind. The crunch of heavy boots on the gravel path alerted her to two guards approaching deep in conversation in their native tongue. As natural as breathing, she stood to the side, placed her feet together and bowed. The guards ignored her existence. Thalia was invisible to them and once they had passed, she continued her walk. Thalia enjoyed the openness of Sime Road camp. The huts were overcrowded but the wide-open spaces between them gave the appearance of freedom. Free roaming in certain areas was not permitted, and guards patrolled regularly but the presence of soldiers in recent months had dwindled. Thalia hoped this was a sign that they were losing the war and had been called back to fight. As she walked along, the conversation with the nurse swam around in her head, and without realising she found herself on the road towards the vegetable patch. It was not her day to work but something was drawing her there and besides, she could check how the brinjal she recently planted had faired in the heavy rains. Waving to Meena in the distance she knelt on the damp earth and re-secured the stems to the wooden trellis support. Her mind was whirring and out of the foggy mix of thoughts a clear idea emerged, jolting her. Would it be possible? Could she pull it off? Talking to the nurse about nutrition earlier had set the seed in her mind; now she knew what to do. She must do something to help her pappa, he was growing sicker by the day. Her plan was not without risk and would need meticulous planning. The undertaking was too big for her alone so she would rely on the help of others but would worry about that later. What if she could send him extra meal rations? Once she was in the kitchens it could be possible. During a conversation some months back, her pappa had let slip that he relied on other men to share their meal rations because he was too old to work. When she heard this, it made her furious, and since then it had been a source of constant worry that he was not getting enough to eat. But now she had an opportunity to do something about it and knew she had to take it. The danger was of no consequence. Her mind raced with possibilities. As with all plans, several stages must come together and the question of how to get food over to the men's camp was her first to answer. Thalia headed to the partition fence separating the men from the women and a tumbling ball of excitement expanded in her stomach and for the first time in years she felt alive and purposeful. In this area, husbands and wives would lean against the chain-link fence clutching fingers through the gaps to be as close to their loved ones as humanly possible. The rules had relaxed considerably since Changi, and families could enjoy daily contact, improving living conditions immensely. The area was quiet today with a few family members sharing some time together. Thalia casually walked along the fence line, her hand brushing across the bumps and ridges where the wires crossed. The fence was high and topped with barbed wire so going over the top was not an option. With a quick look around, checking for guards she continued with her gaze downwards, scanning for gaps. A few men paced around on the other side or stood around smoking. She realised she probably looked strange hugging the fence line, but she didn't care, this was important research. The fence bowed slightly in the middle, and she was pleased to find a few points at the bottom where the wires curled upwards leaving a gap deep enough to fit her hand through. It occurred then that she should measure the hole, so she knew how much room she had to play with and whether she needed to bring her gardening tools to dig out more earth. Her pockets were always full of bits and pieces for gardening so after rummaging around she took out a small piece of string. When she came upon the deepest gap, she knelt, held one end on the ground, and tied a knot at the top where it met the fence to measure the gap. With her recce of the area complete and the piece of string held firmly in her balled fist, she cut across the grass and returned to the hut as it was almost mealtime. Thalia couldn't remember the last time she looked forward to a meal. Eating was purely a perfunctory task and never took long. This evening was no different. Tonight's offering was a blob of fish paste served on a spinach leaf, a quarter of their usual ration of rice and a swig of red palm oil. Thalia hated the oil, it tasted acerbic on her tongue, and gagged until she swallowed the last drop. It was important to have it as the oil was rich in vitamin A and antioxidants. So reluctantly she drank it. Shortly after dinner the guards came to carry out a hut inspection. All the women filed out and sat on the mound opposite whilst guards pulled their belongings apart looking for non-existent evidence of spying. The women had grown accustomed to this ritual now and were no longer phased by the search which were becoming more frequent. This allowed Thalia to speak with Terpie without being overheard as they sat far from everyone else on the hill.

'I need to talk to you about something. But you have to promise not to say a word to anyone.'

'Ok, this sounds like trouble.'

'Well, it's not without risk. I've had an idea to help Pappa.'

'Hmm go on,' said Terpie, raising an eyebrow.

'As you know he's not been well enough to meet us, and getting weaker. I can't stand by and do nothing. When I spoke to the nurse today for my medical, she said people are dying because they're not eating properly, and that gave me the idea.'

'How can you help him?' Terpie stared blankly at her.

'When I start working in the kitchens, I'll make extra portions for Pappa. I've found gaps in the fence where I can pass them through. I just need a contact on the other side to take them to him. We can feed him and make him well again.'

'Have you completely lost your mind? You'll be shot if you're caught for sure,' shrieked Terpie, waving her arms about frantically.

'Shh not so loud! Calm down,' pleaded Thalia, glancing towards the guards in their hut.

'You're talking like a crazy person. I understand why you want to do it, but it's too dangerous.'

'Give me a bit of credit would you. I'll plan it carefully and won't take unnecessary risks.'

'Thalia don't be so naïve. After coming close to being on the execution list myself and seeing what the Japanese did to Carol and Betty, I forbid you to do this.'

'Listen, I get it. I'm scared too, but I'm more scared of losing Pappa knowing I could have done something. I just need to find someone in the men's camp to help me. Maybe Peter or Mickey,' Thalia pondered out loud.

'You can't involve Peter. He has a family. If you get caught, think about the other people you will take down with you. No, no, no,' said Terpie shaking her head.

'You're being a bit dramatic don't you think? Trust me. I'll work it out. I'm smart, I won't get caught,' said Thalia confidently.

'Ok, well if you need more evidence. What about what happened to that family a few months back?'

'What family? I don't know what you're talking about.'

'You must have heard about it. It happened outside the Flying Dutchman, the old RAF public house,' Terpie quizzed her but Thalia looked back blankly. 'Anyway. A father was beaten and whipped publicly, and his family were made to watch. They made a spectacle of him because his daughters were caught stealing. It was horrific. The poor man could barely stand once they'd finished with him and I'll never forget the sound of his screams.' Terpie shuddered. 'So, don't you dare go through with this,' said Terpie forcefully. 'Promise me.'

'I never heard about that. As awful as that story is, I can't make that promise to you Terpie. I really can't. After all we've been through here, it seems the right thing to do.'

Just then the guards emerged from the huts empty-handed and waved the women back into their accommodation as their search proved unfruitful once again.

'We'll talk about this another time. Not now.' Terpie glared and Thalia knew not to push it. Over the next few days, Thalia mulled over their conversation and despite the risks involved she felt compelled to ignore her sisters' warnings. So, she told Terpie the biggest lie that she had decided to drop the idea. Thalia's application to work in the kitchen had been approved and she was learning how to peel and chop vegetables, she kept her head down but observed the routines like a hawk. There was one hurdle she had to overcome: who could help her get the packages to her father on the other side of the fence? It had to be someone she trusted, who knew her father, and were willing to take the risk. For days, it had been playing on her mind who she could approach for help and then when it came, she recognised it as divine intervention. Because the women's side did not have a chapel or church, priests from the men's camp provided the only form of

Sunday service on a rota. Today it was the turn of Father Oswald and when she saw him, Thalia knew he could be her answer. Terpie sat beside her, utterly ignorant to Thalia's rising optimism when she saw him bustle over to the table and set out an altar for his sermon. With her mind preoccupied, she fidgeted throughout the service and was not listening. If she were to hazard a guess, she would say Father Oswald was about her pappa's age with a thin dusting of white hair and well-worn wrinkled face. When the service finished, Thalia was relieved that Terpie made a hasty exit, so she didn't have to tell her why she was staying behind. Thalia hung back until she was alone with the priest, and he smiled warmly over his wire-rimmed spectacles as she approached with the armful of bibles she had collected.

Thalia placed the small stack of bibles on the table.

'Father, I need to ask you something of a sensitive nature and you've always said for us to come to you if we need help.'

'Well Thalia the good lord has sent me along this path to help as much as I can, so be brave and tell me your troubles and I'll see what I can do.' He sat on a wooden chair and straightened the golden tassels hanging from his belt.

'It's not for me, it's my pappa. He's sick and I'm desperate to help make him better, but I can't do it on my own. I need help.' Thalia knelt on the ground at his feet nervously wringing her hands in her lap and proceeded to tell him her plan. Father Oswald listened as all good priests do and finally rubbed his chin and frowned.

'Hmm I see your dilemma and your passion to help your father. You're not the first and won't be the last person to come to me with requests of this nature. The strength of human spirit forces us to do dangerous things for the ones we love. Believe me many things are going on in this camp under the radar of the guards. Every day people take great personal risks and not for their own gain. Are you asking me to be involved or give you my blessing?'

'Both. I suppose? I know it's a huge risk and I don't want to put anyone in danger, but I thought you could liaise with someone on your side. If you don't mind of course. I only know Pappa's friend Peter or Mickey. Do you know them? I'm sorry I don't know their surnames.'

'I know them. Tell me, how and when you need help.'

'I finish my kitchen shift around seven and planned to wait until dark to slip the food under the fence. There are no lights along there and I've found several places where the gap is deep enough to fit something through. I would need to show someone the passing point. I've been watching the patrol and there are no guards between nine and ten o'clock because that's when they're doing their lights out rounds. Ideally, I want to send meals over to him every night. I know this is a huge ask but I'm desperate. My pappa is all we have left. He has to survive.' Tears began to bubble to the surface, and she cursed herself for appearing so weak and emotional. She sniffed and wiped them away on the back of her hand.

'You have clearly done your homework. I know your pappa and he would be proud of you.'

Thalia replied quickly 'Oh, I don't want him to know that the meals are coming from me. He must never know. He'll worry too much, and I don't want that. Please don't tell him what I'm doing,' Thalia pleaded.

Father Oswald smiled. 'I understand. I'll not say a word. Leave this with me for a few days and I'll speak to Peter and Mickey. I think between us we can help. If I tell one of them to meet you on the fence line, say eight o'clock on Wednesday? I know most guards will be at the music recital.'

'Oh Father. That would be amazing. I'm truly grateful and I can't thank you enough. Please tell them if they think it is too dangerous and don't want to do it, I'll understand.'

'I know both are very fond of your father so I'm sure they'll want to help. Take care child.'

Thalia watched Father Oswald lumber back to the men's camp weighed down with his two cloth bags and she felt warm inside. Her plan to help her pappa was another step closer to becoming a reality.

Chapter Thirty-Five
Thalia

Thalia skipped back to the hut feeling satisfied and optimistic after the conversation with Father Oswald. She found herself humming a familiar melody. It was a piece of music Thetie used to play all the time while learning to play the piano. Thalia fondly remembered how the repetitive tune drove her nuts as Thetie would play it constantly. The memory caught her off guard and her chest grew heavy thinking of her sister. Since Terpie made it clear she thought the idea was too dangerous and forbid Thalia from taking it any further, Thalia decided that Terpie need never know. And if she ever found out and dared to question it, Thalia would refer her sister back to her own risk taking at the convent with Benny which got them into this mess in the first place. Thalia was keen for Wednesday night to come around. That meant she had three nights to perfect her plan and prayed that at least one of her father's friends would be willing to help. On the first night, she salvaged and cleaned two old sardine tins and hid them on a shelf under the sink amongst the cleaning cloths. They would make the perfect the vessel to transport a meal. During her second shift she made a point of observing the kitchen routines. Who did what and when. Everything was coming together. When Wednesday night eventually arrived, after her shift she crouched down behind the bins until it was time to meet at the agreed location. As predicted, the concert was well underway allowing trumpet and drum harmonies to disguise her thumping heartbeat. When it was time, alert like a predator flushing out its prey, she skimmed across the grass keeping low to the ground under the shroud of darkness and her eyes darted around at every sound. For all her vigilant planning, she had not devised a backup a plan should any guards appear, other than to run for her life. On her approach to the fence, she strained her eyes and to her relief out of the gloom she recognised Peter's lanky form waiting, her heart eased, and she picked up pace.

'You came!' she whispered through the fence when she reached him.

'Of course, I'm worried about your pappa. He's been like a father to me in here, so I want to help if I can.'

'Thank you so much. We don't have much time.' Thalia looked around, scouting for guards. 'How about starting tomorrow night? I'll meet you here, same time. There's a gap just along here,' she said, leading him along the fence and bent down to where she had placed a large stone to cover the gap on a previous visit.

'Yes, of course. Mickey said he would help too. We'll take turns, and I'll let him know the spot. Don't worry. We won't let you down.'

'I'm so grateful to you both.' Thalia's voice started to break, and she blinked hard to prevent tears forming. The pair exchanged hasty goodbyes and slipped away in opposite directions into the darkness.

The next evening, Thalia buzzed on adrenaline whilst pulling on her black overalls ready for her shift. Little explosions fired in her stomach as she peeled and chopped sweet potatoes washed spinach grown and picked from the camp garden. The six women on her shift were all much older than her and had taken her under their wing like a daughter. Thalia enjoyed their company. There were some women in the camp who, if you sliced them open like a piece of seaside rock, would have "bitch" written right through them. Maybe it was hormones, some older women said it was due to sexual frustration, but Thalia didn't understand what that meant.

Whatever the cause, it shocked Thalia that women could behave that way, scrapping and fighting like feral cats. Thalia avoided these pockets of brittle and aggressive women around the camp. She felt fortunate to be surrounded by good wholesome women who showed her nothing but kindness which made her feel slightly uncomfortable for her deceitful behaviour.

Initially, she struggled to keep up on a busy shift and felt clumsy and awkward when her concentration lapsed from her daydreaming, and she dropped things on the floor. She had spent very little time in the kitchen at home and only helped Shi Min with baking on the odd occasion. It was all new to her, and she was learning fast. Sandy, the main cook was a patient teacher, and before long, Thalia was adept with a chopping knife. Once the long shift was over, her chores involved washing up the pots and pans and cleaning the surfaces down. Thalia had never seen such an abundance of food and not contemplated the vast quantities required to feed all the women and children in the camp.

A store cupboard at the end of the kitchen was packed to the rafters with boxes, bottles, and jars of food to be used with the strictest rationing. Thalia found it completely torturous to be working within easy reach of so much food and the cooking smells had her stomach in a constant grumbling state of hunger. Initially, Thalia was horrified to find a guard present to oversee proceedings, standing watch over the store cupboard to ensure that no one helped themselves. Her plan seemed doomed to be a non-starter but to her relief, the guard left his post as soon as the servers collected the food and the store cupboard duly locked. Thalia only had a few more potatoes to peel and chop and was grateful as her wrists ached.

Large stainless-steel pans of rice simmered gently on the stove, filling the kitchen with steam causing rivulets of condensation to trickle down the walls. Thalia carefully slid her chopped vegetables to the bubbling water on the burners, avoiding the splash as they went in. With all the burners on full, the kitchen was a furnace and Thalia sweated profusely in her black uniform which had pasted itself uncomfortably to her limbs, hampering her movement. Taking a breather, she fanned her face with a tea towel and puffed into her fringe.

Tonight, everything seemed to be under control and running smoothly. At one end of the workbench, Marissa and Eileen grated coconuts into two large earthenware mixing bowls, ready to be added to the sago mixture for pudding. At their feet stood a large wicker basket filled with discarded hairy shells. They would not be wasted. Sandy leaned heavily on the other end of the workbench, pen in hand, deep in thought over her trusty recipe book. Feeding two thousand women and children was a huge responsibility and Sandy had the unenviable task of meticulously planning a menu with whatever ingredients were available.

Thalia was fond of Sandy. Before all this nonsense started as she put it, Sandy had been a chef at the Raffles Hotel and Thalia listened in awe to her stories of serving rich dignitaries and famous film stars. The glory days, Sandy called them until the Japanese military commandeered the hotel for their malfeasant purposes. One evening whilst the officers sipped cocktails, the hotel staff secretly buried the silverware and anything of value under the patio in the Palm Court to prevent the sordid intruders from claiming it. Thalia wondered how many of the island's treasures had been squirrelled away, concealed from the Japanese to be revealed at some future time.

Glancing at the clock, she realised time was marching on, and to her surprise, she wasn't nervous at all, her determination stronger than ever. The po-faced guard on duty tonight stood like a silent statue in the corner and would be leaving soon. Thalia filled the sink with water and began her cleaning routine, and as she bent down to get a cloth, discreetly she slipped the two old sardine tins into her front pocket like a kangaroo pouch. Now she just needed to bide her time. When the food was ready, it took four people to lift each of the heavy pans to tip the contents into the deep serving trays and then the discarded pans were ready for Thalia to wash. Beside her, Sandy wiped the sweat from her brow with the back of her hand and gave the call.

Swiftly, a team of servers bustled into the kitchen to collect the hot trays of food to be taken to the awaiting hungry masses and the bored-looking guard strutted out behind them. Thalia used this period of transition to make her move. After a quick visual check over her shoulder to ensure her colleagues were busy, Thalia retrieved the containers from her pocket and placed them side by side on the worktop. She held her breath as she quickly scraped the insides of the large pots with a spatula and topped up the tins. There was always residual food left in the bottom and on the edges, enough to make one meal or even two for her pappa. Thalia did not feel any guilt, she was not taking anyone's ration away, but she knew she could still be heavily punished for it. With the tins full of rice and vegetables, she swiftly concealed them on a shelf between two boxes and began scrubbing the pans.

Glancing around, she was relieved no one had suspected a thing. She had done it! Thalia felt a warm rush of triumph as she continued with her cleaning. Whilst the pans were heavy and her arms ached to lift them, inside, she bathed in reposeful satisfaction and composed herself ready for phase two of her plan. One by one, the other women said goodnight until only Eileen remained.

'I don't know how you can stand to be in here so long,' said Eileen, removing her apron and hanging it on the back of the door. 'It's so hot. I can't wait to get out of here.'

'I don't mind. I hate our overcrowded hut. At least it's peaceful in here and I get some time to myself,' said Thalia, placing the large stainless-steel pot on the draining board. With no luxuries like washing up liquid, she used lemon halves and bicarbonate of soda to clean the worst of the grime and boiling water for the rest. The juice from the lemons stung every small cut and over time, the hot water had dried her skin which had become itchy and raw.

'Well, see you at the same time tomorrow.'

'Bye. Have a good night,' called Thalia.

With the dishes done, Thalia mopped the floor, took the clean pots and pans down from the shelf in readiness for the morning, and placed them on the stove with all the utensils they would need. The breakfast girls were always grateful to her for getting things ready, as it saved them some time. With her chores finished around eight-thirty, she had plenty of time to spare. With shaky hands, Thalia retrieved the small fish tins she had hidden earlier and peeled the lid down, slipping them into the front pocket of her overalls. The containers were warm against her belly. Sitting on a wooden stool, she patiently watched the clock until it was time to go. It was only now that her stomach began churning with nerves and her legs jiggled uncontrollably.

She reflected on the story Terpie told her of the family caught stealing, quickly dismissing it. The girls in that story were younger than her and couldn't have thought out their plan very well. But it set of a series of questions in her mind. Could they pull this off? Was she endangering Peter and, worse, her father? She launched herself off the stool, there was no time to question her actions. Taking one final look around the kitchen she turned off the lights and locked the back door. Even though she had rehearsed in her head what she was about to do many times, the buzz of excitement and nerves overwhelmed her. This was not a dummy run; this was real.

Thalia sidled down the side of the building under the cover of darkness, feeling like a ninja in her black kitchen overalls. She cradled the tins in her pouch to stop them from chinking together and making unnecessary noise. There was no music to cover her crunching footsteps and rapidly beating heart tonight. Thalia's legs felt unsteady beneath her as she crept along the perimeter of the building. With her senses on high alert, she looked around furtively for the familiar dark grey uniforms of guards and breathed a sigh of relief to see the coast was clear, making strides towards the fence where Peter was waiting for her. Seeing his beaming face through the chain-link fence instantly bought her a sense of calm and she smiled back.

'How is he?' whispered Thalia.

'Steady. He didn't leave the hut today.'

'Don't tell him these are from me. Make something up. Who is that?' Thalia's voice rose alarmingly, seeing a dark figure in the distance.

'Don't worry. That's Father Oswald. He's keeping a lookout and will snap the pages of his bible as a signal if he sees any guards coming.'

Thalia grinned. 'I see I'm not the only sneaky one. Thank you again. I couldn't do this without you. I know you're taking a huge risk.'

'It's no trouble. Zac is a special man. Mickey will meet you tomorrow night; same time.'

'Ok, remember, not a word that this has come from me.' Thalia placed her finger over her lips, and Peter confirmed with a nod.

The pair separated, and Thalia crept back through the camp with a smile and a warm satisfaction in her chest.

Chapter Thirty-Six
Anthoula

Years had passed since the refugees from Singapore and surrounding islands had been placed in the rescue camp in India and Anthoula had steadily become mute, refusing to speak or interact with anyone other than Ino. If she were an animal, she would have been put down by now she often thought. Whilst physically there was little wrong with her other than gradual deterioration that came with old age, she knew she was sick. Her mind had become brittle, fractured, and only brought her torment. Her heart blackened by grief was something she couldn't find a way back from. There were no chinks of light to guide her out and the flickering flame of hope had long burnt out.

Years of waiting for news on the whereabouts of her family tormented her fragile mind. The accumulation of loss unravelled her mental state, condemning her to exist in world of regret, bitterness and longing. Anthoula scanned the tent's interior, scrutinising the strangers surrounding her as they sat cross-legged, tucking into their meal from a bowl, using fingers as utensils. A crackling fire in the centre offered a cosy amber glow but she only felt cold, like marble. She didn't feel much like eating.

Being one of the oldest occupants of the camp, she had nothing in common with the younger women with children. There wasn't one face among them she found appealing. They were perfectly decent people and had shown her nothing but kindness over the years, but they were not her family. Most of them spoke Malay, Indian or Chinese and it was simply too much effort to try to communicate when her heart was not in it. She had no interest in anything, least of all new friendships. The group had given up trying to engage with her and now, she spent solitary days staring at the mountains in the distance, watching cloud formations slide from one side of the sky to the other and observing the changing seasons wondering how long it would be before her heart stopped and she could slip peacefully away.

This wasn't how her last years were supposed to play out. She should be travelling around the world with her husband. He would be coming to get her soon, wouldn't he? Why hadn't he come to find her? Anthoula failed to keep a grip on her thoughts as they flipped from one story to another, her reality shifting all the time. Sometimes she convinced herself that Zac couldn't have loved her as much as he said; he had abandoned her. She lost her footing in her memories; the details were fuzzy around the edges, and she couldn't trust her mind to know what was true and what was a fabrication. Perhaps Zac and Terpie had planned this together from the start. Terpie had always been a difficult child, they had never been close and maybe this was her revenge.

Anthoula scowled deeply at the very mention of Terpie's name, and over the years, bitterness and resentment festered and multiplied, until Anthoula blamed her daughter wholeheartedly for her family's demise. Pained from the swirling destructive thoughts she could not switch off exhausted her. Just then, one of the camp helpers crouched beside her and gave her a nudge, pointing to her bowl indicated with her hands that she should eat. Anthoula stared blankly at the woman and ignored her encouragement.

Now Ino wasn't around either, her life was a pointless existence. Timescales were difficult for Anthoula to place. She couldn't remember precisely how long Ino had been gone. However, she recalled how it broke her when her remaining daughter announced she was leaving to get a job in Delhi. Anthoula felt abandoned. When she tried to understand, her daughter was young with her life ahead of her and could start again. Ino wrote, of course, telling her she had met a lovely man in the RAF and had plans to marry once the war was over. With tart resentment, Anthoula found it impossible to be happy for her when, in contrast, she had nothing left to live for.

Chapter Thirty-Seven
Thalia

The months passed quickly in Sime Road, and the first anniversary came and went without celebration. Thalia tarried along the path in no particular rush after her early shower with a towel wrapped tightly around her body, her wet hair dripping onto her bronzed shoulders. Her thoughts were never far from her father and despite not being able to see him, she appreciated the updates from Peter and Mickey during their evening rendezvous. Sadly, their reports indicated his health had not improved as much as she had hoped with her illicit food parcels. Both men reassured her that Zacharia remained in good spirits and expected to be well enough to meet soon. However, she was sure she sensed uncertainty in their statements. Four weeks had passed since the start of her plan, skulking around in the dark, dodging guards, and she had expected to see her pappa long before now. She missed him terribly. She missed her mother and her sisters too. But missing them served no purpose, and she was well-practised at shifting her thoughts. Arriving at the hut, she found Terpie getting dressed.

'I desperately need some new knickers! I can't believe these have lasted this long. Look at these,' Terpie shrieked, holding up the flimsy remnants of material with half the elastic missing. 'Where were you last night? I thought you were coming to the concert. It was good, you missed a good show.'

'It took me longer to clean up the kitchen, and I had a headache, so came back here and went to bed,' replied Thalia, feeling guilty for her lies. She had been making lots of excuses lately to cover up for her absences. Terpie was still blissfully unaware of her clandestine meetings and Thalia wanted to keep it that way. She dressed quickly and chose a grubby pair of shorts and a vest from her select pile of outfits.

'You were snoring your head off when I got back. You could have been part of the percussion you were that loud,' Terpie teased.

'Ha-ha, very funny.'

'Well, you need to stay awake tonight, there is a lunar eclipse, and the moon might turn red at about midnight.'

'I'll probably have better things to do, like sleep,' said Thalia.

'Listen, I nearly woke you last night, but I know how busy you are. When the Red Cross representative came in and I chased her for the evacuee lists again,' said Terpie, and Thalia rolled her eyes. 'No listen. It's good news. The lists have been put together now and said she'll bring them next week. They're not publicly available yet because information is still missing, but I pleaded with her to let me see what they have so far.'

'Finally! I can't understand why it's taken this long. There had better be some positive news. Pappa could do with a boost. Maybe he'll be feeling better this week and can come to meet with us.'

'I hope so too. Are we sure we'll tell him? What if it's bad news?'

'Oh, Terpie, I can't ever lie to him again. You didn't see his face. He was so hurt and angry about the Emily thing. We have to tell him. He deserves to know.'

'He does, but I would rather wait until he's stronger. I'll talk to you about it later. I have to get to work.'

'What do you do in that office all day?'

'Honestly, not much of great interest. I type committee meeting notes and do the filing.'

'I don't suppose you know anything about the planes overhead lately? There must have been about thirty yesterday. It was a bit scary. Are the Americans attacking the Japs?'

'I don't know! I'm only an office assistant you know. I wouldn't know about anything confidential. All that military stuff is top secret. Besides, I couldn't tell you even if I did know.' Terpie laughed. 'What are you doing today?'

'Just the usual, working in the vegetable garden and the kitchens later. Our tapioca crop is almost ready, so I'm excited about that. Isn't that Carol over there?' Thalia recognised her long tanned legs in her linen shorts and the bounce of her long curls with each elongated stride. Terpie turned around on the spot and confirmed it was their friend walking purposefully towards them.

'Yes, it is. What's she doing all the way up here?'

The friends had not seen much of each other since the camp move as they were all so busy, and the sprawling layout meant their paths rarely crossed. Carol's expression was unusually wooden. When she reached the sisters, she took hold of Thalia and Terpie's hands and avoided eye contact—a gesture which caused Thalia to experience a sinking feeling in her stomach.

'I'm afraid there is no easy way to say this. I wanted you to hear it from a friend. I'm so sorry, but your pappa passed away this morning.'

Thalia stared at her and blinked. It took a few seconds to register and realise she meant *her* pappa. She withdrew her hand from Carol's as if she'd been stung. Her legs crumbled beneath her, and she collapsed to the floor. Her whole body began to shake and from somewhere deep inside an animalistic howl found its escape. With her arms wrapped around her body, she rocked backwards and forwards, trying to soothe herself in the black void she found herself in. Her first thought dawned that she never got to say goodbye, followed by the agony of never seeing his kind eyes and the soft creases of his face again. He would never hold her again. Never call her "his little bird".

No, no, no, this could not be true. A vision of his kind, smiling face appeared before her, and her heart cracked open. Her pappa was her world, her special person. They shared a bond; he could not leave her! How dare he die when she risked everything to keep him alive. And for a split second, she felt a flash of anger quickly followed by accusations of self-judgement, *I didn't do enough. I failed him. This is my fault.* Harshly lambasting herself for being stupidly naïve in believing her actions could have made a difference. A relentless stream of tears flowed, and her body ached all over. She was so caught up in her pain, she momentarily forgot about Terpie. Through her tears, she observed Terpie crying silently within Carol's embrace. Looking away, Thalia covered her face with her hands and continued sobbing as the weighty dark blanket of grief wrapped around her.

'How and when?' she heard Terpie ask.

'He was found this morning. Your pappa passed away in his sleep and wasn't in any pain. The doctor examined him and confirmed he had pneumonia. There was nothing that could have saved him. I'm so sorry. I know how much he meant to you both.' Carol's platitudes washed over Thalia. 'There will be a burial service later today. Would you like me to come? I can ask Betty too.'

'Thank you, Carol. It would be nice to have you both there,' said Terpie wiping her tears.

'Ok. I'll come by and walk down with you later. I am sorry,' she hugged the girls once more before saying goodbye.

With Carol gone, Terpie joined Thalia on the grass, and they comforted each other.

'I can't believe he's gone. Can you?' said Thalia, pulling away from Terpie's embrace wiping her raw cheeks.

'No, not really.'

'Peter and Mickey seemed so sure he was making a recovery. They said he was improving. I don't understand it.'

A brief silence hung between them before Terpie responded, 'What do you mean? I'm confused. How did you speak to Peter and Mickey?'

Terpie's question opened the flood gates, forcing Thalia to come clean about her secret contrivance. Surprisingly, when she finished speaking, Terpie's reaction was better than expected.

'I'm stunned you did all that behind my back. It was so dangerous, Thalia, and thank god you didn't get caught. But I'm proud of you for trying to help him. You're far braver than me. Not so much the baby of the family now. You're looking after us,' said Terpie, giving Thalia a rub on the shoulder. 'Mamma will be so proud of you when we tell her.'

'If we ever get the chance to tell her. She might be dead too,' said Thalia bluntly.

'Don't think like that. Come on, we promised to stay positive.'

'I know but I'm running low on positivity right now. I should have done more. I was so stupid, thinking I could keep Pappa going,' sniffed Thalia, staring into the distance. 'You know what hurts the most? Not being able to say goodbye to any of them.'

'Please don't blame yourself, Thalia. You did the best you could. You took huge risk to help him. I did nothing. There are so many things I wish had been different.'

'Will you be ok on your own? I need to be alone for a while,' said Thalia, leaning on the wooden post of the hut as she dragged herself to standing.

'You go. I'll be fine,' Terpie replied, waving her off.

Thalia was unprepared to attend a burial to say goodbye to her beloved pappa but knew she must. Before leaving, she scooped up the little wooden carved bird he made from under the folded blanket she used as a pillow and spent the next few hours wandering around the boundaries of the camp, clutching it to her chest, trying not to unravel. It dawned on her that this morning they had potentially become orphans and could be all alone in the world, which was terrifying territory.

In the present circumstances, she had lost all confidence in the possibility her Mamma and sisters had survived. If by some miracle they were still alive, how would they find the words to tell them Pappa was gone? It was all so hopeless. Thalia expected someone to say it had all been a terrible mistake, they were sorry, but someone else had died and her pappa was safe and well. In this reality however, the facts remained the same. He was gone. It would forever haunt Thalia that their last meeting resulted in him being disappointed with her and she so wished she could turn back time and right that wrong. His trust had been broken and she would never get the opportunity to earn it back which would always be a bitter pill to swallow.

After a few laps of the perimeter to clear her head, her empty shell of a body returned to the hut. As promised, Carol came to fetch them later that afternoon. Thalia wore her most presentable outfit, not that she had many clothes to choose from but wanted to make the effort to look respectable. She owned a half-decent skirt with buttons down the middle, hoping no one would notice a couple missing. Julia who shared their hut was kind enough to lend her a pale blue blouse, and she wore some wildflowers in her hair she had picked from around the camp. Terpie looped arms with her as they ambled silently in the shade of the trees towards the burial ground with Carol and Betty following arm in arm behind.

Thalia observed the rows of fresh earthy mounds, too many to count. Crude memorials of loved ones now at rest. Another stark reminder that the cruelty of prison life had claimed too many casualties. It was a sight that would be difficult to forget. Standing beside the prepared earth was Peter, Father Oswald, Mickey and two men she didn't recognise. It pleased her knowing her pappa had good friends and was grateful to them for attending. Peter reached out and shook her hand.

'I'm so sorry, Thalia. We did what we could didn't we. You kept him going. He loved you girls so much, he was so proud of you. I swear I never told him the meals came from you. We honestly thought he was improving,' Peter said softly with a look of anguish.

'Thank you, Peter. He was lucky to have a friend like you and he thought a lot of you too. I couldn't have done it without you, both of you,' she said, turning to include Mickey.

Next, Mickey stepped forward and embraced her.

'Sorry for your loss, Thalia. Zac was a good man and a great father. He talked about you girls all the time. I wish there was more we could have done,' he said kindly.

'I know. You looked out for him and that's all I could have asked for.'

In turn, the men embraced Terpie standing beside her but something about Mickey's comment grated on her. She never understood that saying. 'Sorry for your loss.' A loss is an act of carelessness, like misplacing a purse or set of keys. You can't lose a person. She did not lose her pappa. He was taken from her before his time. A lost item can be replaced. Her pappa was gone forever. She stood at the edge of the pit unable to comprehend it was her Pappa's body that lay bound tightly in a sheet in the shallow grave. He had been such a prominent figure in her life, and the crumpled, dishevelled heap that lay at her feet did not represent the man she loved and admired.

Father Oswald stood beside her and silently passed her a small bag of his things. Inside the bag was the handkerchief she had sewn for him two Christmases ago, his wedding ring, a photograph and Terpie's poem. Father Oswald performed a short service with prayers and finished with reading. Mickey and Peter each shared a story about their time with Zacharia and what he meant to each of them, despite not knowing him that long. It was interesting to hear their honest insights and memories, but unexpectedly Thalia found herself feeling jealous of the extra time these men got to spend with her father which she had been denied. Slowly Thalia removed the flowers from her hair and tossed them in with her pappa together with his adored tattered wedding photo and her handkerchief. She wanted part of her to lie with him. None of it felt real. It did not seem possible the man she loved, who raised her, who taught her everything and knew her thoughts was gone from her life.

Silently, she said a final goodbye and solemnly promised she would find their mother. The simmering grief she had managed to keep contained up to now bubbled up inside her, forcing her to walk away. A boiling rage stopped her in her tracks and her legs refused to carry her further. Falling to the dry earth she punched the ground grazing her knuckles in a hatred fuelled frenzy. She needed someone to blame, and in her eyes, the Japanese were wholly responsible for her father's needless death. If he had been at home, he would never have got sick and would still be here with her.

The following weeks passed in a blur. Thalia failed to show up for work in the kitchen, in fact, she didn't leave the floor of the hut other than to visit the bathroom for almost two weeks. She knew Terpie was worried about her by her constant checking and fretting. Thalia just needed to work through her grief in her own way. Quietly, without fuss. Over recent months she had accepted it was unlikely her mother and sisters would be found alive, but she never imagined her pappa would die and leave her. With him gone from her life, a darkness smothered her. Terpie adjusted much quicker by returning to work a day after the burial, preferring to keep occupied to take her mind off things. Thalia had no appetite for eating and found it amusing that during her starvation she had thought of little else. Her cravings vanished and for once she wasn't bothered about food at all. All her aches of hunger were replaced by a much deeper visceral pain. Laying on the floor of the hut she watched the wisps of cloud floating on the breeze and she drifted in and out of sleep. Some hours later she hazily sensed the presence of someone sitting down beside her. It was Terpie.

'Thalia, I have some news are you awake.' Terpie shook her leg.

Thalia pushed herself up onto her elbows. 'What is it?'

'Look, I have the passenger lists. The Red Cross finally came through with information,' Terpie announced, waving a large manila envelope in front of her face enthusiastically.

'Have you looked?'

'No, I wanted us to do it together. Plus, I was too scared.'

'Do you think it's too soon after Pappa? I'm not sure I can take any more bad news,' Thalia stated solemnly.

'I did wonder that too. We have to know.'

'I can't believe it. All this time we have been waiting for news and it comes when Pappa is no longer here to hear it. It makes me sad that he never knew what happened.'

'I don't think I can look,' Terpie said tersely, having a sudden change of heart and dropping the envelope on the ground between them as if her fingers had been scalded. 'Since receiving it, it's sat on my desk like a time bomb waiting to go off. I thought I could do this, but now it's time to open it, I don't think…' Terpie choked.

'Come on, we can do this. I'll open it if you can't,' said Thalia, picking up the envelope. She took a deep breath and peeled open the flap and pulled out a wedge of folded paper. Printed on the sheets were rows and rows of names listed by surname under different headings by ship or vessel.

Rifling through the pages, she found the papers relating to the "Kuala" and traced her finger down the list of names, giving a slight flicker of recognition at names she recognised from a time before.

'I've found them,' Thalia said, jabbing her finger on the page and began reading the passage aloud. *Anthoula Pattara boarded the SS Kuala on 13th February 1942 with her three daughters, Clio, Thetie and Ino. The ship was attacked and sunk off Pomp Pong Island...*

'Yes, we know that, what happened to them after that?' said Terpie, chewing her brittle nails.

'Hang on, I'm getting there. *After three days of being stranded, Mrs Pattara and her daughter Ino were rescued by a Japanese trawler captained by Bill Reynolds and taken to Bombay. They now reside in a camp in Nainital, India. Clio was later rescued by the SS Tanjong Pinang which was bombed off the shore of Banka Island on 17th February. There were no survivors. Thetie has not been found, presumed lost at sea.'*

After agonising years of waiting, they now had answers. The girls wept for the loss of their sisters but held onto the positive news their mother and Ino were alive. They were not all alone in the world.

Thalia sat back on her heels. 'If only Pappa had held on, this news might have been enough to make him fight harder and he would still be with us,' Thalia cried, soaking up her tears using the front of her shirt.

'Pappa was ill, and no amount of good news would have saved him. I think he knew he was dying and that is why he stopped coming to see us. He just got sick.'

'I don't understand why Clio wasn't rescued with them. I can't believe we'll never see them again,' Thalia croaked.

'It does seem strange, but we probably won't find out the whole story until we speak to Mamma and Ino.'

'We have to write to them, let them know we're alive. Do you think you can find out from the Red Cross how to get a letter to them?' Thalia asked.

'I'm sure if they're in a refugee camp, it shouldn't be too difficult. We shouldn't tell them about Pappa in a letter though,' said Terpie.

'I agree. We should make contact in the first instance to let them know where we are. The post is slow so it could be months before they receive our letter.'

'Thalia, I know you and Pappa were close and how hard this has been. We'll be alright you know. He would have wanted us to keep going and now with this information, we will find them one day.'

'I miss him every day. He has always been there. Even in this godforsaken place, we have known he was just the other side of the wall,' Thalia said, folding the paper and returning it to the envelope which moments ago felt so terrifying and placed it on the floor between them. She stared at it for a while.

'Will you be ok? I need to get this list back to the office. We can talk later.'

Thalia brushed her cheeks.

'Yes, go. I'm fine.'

She watched her sister walking up the path and decided there was only one place she wanted to be now. Thalia made her way to her father's grave. She had made him a promise that she would tell him if there was news of their family and she intended to keep it.

Chapter Thirty-Eight
Terpie

Terpie was wide awake. She didn't feel like she had been asleep long and the sky was pitch black so she assumed it must be the middle of the night, but had no means of knowing the time. Beside her, Thalia exhausted by her grief slept on. She wondered how it was possible that Thalia could sleep through the disturbance which had rudely barged in on her slumber. Feeling terrified, Terpie contemplated waking her sister for comfort but thought better of it. Thalia was cranky without sleep. This wasn't the first time planes and bombs had been heard over the prison recently and over the last few nights there had been unusual activity in the sky. Tonight, the bombs and sirens seemed closer, louder and the crashing and wailing in the distance took her back to when this ordeal began, huddling under the table at home with her family. With this thought an intense bout of homesickness gripped her, and she desperately craved the comfort of her parents. Silently she sobbed cradling her face in the crook of her elbow to drown out her grief. One after the other, a carousel of thoughts revolved around demanding her attention. First, her pappa. Gone was his calming presence in her life and his ability to make everything alright. There would be no one to look after her anymore, and that thought was frightening. The loss of her sisters, so young and full of life. Her home. A crushing weight on her chest made breathing difficult as she remembered her home did not exist anymore. There was no way back. Finally Benny. It pained her greatly to imagine a world without him, but if he were alive, he would have tried everything he could to get word to her, wouldn't he? Three years without any leads or letters and hope of his survival was fading like dying embers. To prevent her mind spiralling down a rabbit hole she liked to imagine a scenario where Benny had written to the convent. She convinced herself that it could be entirely possible with all the upheaval that any letter must have been mislaid, but eventually one of the Nuns would have found it and forwarded it on to the prison where it has been sitting in the backlog, waiting to be delivered. She was fully aware it was a fragile notion, but it kept the darkness at bay. No matter how often she re-read his previous letters or caressed the precious necklace around her neck like the genie's lamp, there wasn't a power in the world which could magic him back into her life. Rolling onto her back she listened, until the gaps between the explosions widened, eventually petering out into silence allowing her to steady her breathing once more. In competition with the nocturnal sounds, her stomach rumbled loudly, and she found it impossible to get back to sleep. Over the last few days the meals had been a paltry offering of rice only since the camp garden vegetable supply had been exhausted and there were no more Red Cross ration boxes to rely on. Even the guards were reduced to the same rations because the food shortages had become so awful. Staring at the stars until her eyes grew heavy, eventually she drifted back to sleep. When she woke, what seemed like only an hour later, Thalia was already awake, sitting beside her propped against the wooden divider with paper resting on her knees looking more cheerful than she'd seen her for many weeks.

'Morning. I woke early and wrote this. What do you think?' she said, excitedly shoving a piece of paper towards her.

'Hang on. I'm not awake yet. Did you hear the bombs again last night?' Terpie croaked, stretching her stiff limbs and yawning. She patted the taut skin on her face hoping it was not obvious she'd been crying and could pass it off as just a rough night. Slowly she repositioned herself to a seated position and took the paper. Her head was banging, and her eyes were like slits. Her tongue traced across her dry lips and she found it hard to swallow. She needed some water.

'No. I slept through it all,' replied Thalia, eagerly awaiting her sister's opinion. 'Come on, read it then.'

Rubbing the sleep from her eyes, she began to read.

'Well? What do you think?' asked Thalia keenly.

Terpie let the letter rest in her lap. 'I'm not sure.'

'What do you mean, you're not sure? Not sure about the content or writing at all?' Thalia asked, leaning forward demanding an answer.

'So much has happened. I don't know if it will help or add more stress to their situation. We can't tell them in a letter that Pappa has died. It's too harsh, but to talk about him as if he is still here giving them false hope, well that seems wrong too. I don't see how we can make contact and not open a can of worms and a whole lot of questions for them.'

'But they would want to know we are safe and alive. I think they have a right to know,' said Thalia.

'We don't know what state Mamma is in and if she is ready for the news. Let's wait a little longer before we decide. A few more weeks is not going to hurt is it?' Terpie noticed the slight tremble in Thalia's bottom lip and the way she bit it to curb an unwanted emotional response. The last few weeks had hit her younger sister hard, Terpie recognised how vital this news was for her, a lifeline to hold on to when they had lost everything else. 'Look, I know why you want to make contact. It's a good letter. All I'm saying is let's sit on it a little longer until we are sure of what we want to say, that's all.'

'Alright. I can't help thinking of Mamma with only Ino as company worrying about what has happened to the rest of us.'

'I'm being cautious that's all. We need to tell them about Pappa face to face, and God knows when that will be. Give it a week, and let's come back to it then,' said Terpie, and Thalia nodded in reluctant agreement, and the girls spoke no more about it and went about their morning routine. The two sisters joined the queue for breakfast, and Terpie sensed a strange but positive atmosphere from the women at the front of the queue. Squeals of delight and cheers floated down the line. Someone near the front shouted, 'The war is over!'

'Did you hear that?' asked Thalia. 'Surely this is someone's idea of a sick joke?'

Another voice from further down the line called out, 'We're free.' Terpie's stomach began to bubble with excitement. Could this be true? It seemed a preposterous notion but a wonderful one if it were true. There had been rumours recently the Japs were losing and coincidentally the guards had been behaving oddly, but both Terpie and Thalia were mindful not to take much notice of such gossip to avoid disappointment. Terpie concealed a huge smile behind her clasped hands and waited patiently until they reached the front of the queue. Instead of their usual breakfast, they were each handed a fried rice cake emblazoned with a "V" shape stamped in the centre. Thalia stared at it and traced her fingertips along the lines.

'What do you think this means?' she asked.

A women dancing barefoot in circles called out, 'It's a secret message. It's a "V" for victory. The war is over!' she shouted, punching the air in celebration.

'Do you think the war could really over?' said Terpie in shock.

'I hope it's true. We'll be free!' Thalia said, staring at the rice cake like it was a magical object with special powers. So desperate for food, Terpie wasted no time in devouring the puzzling communique in two bites. A group of women had gathered, all chattering in excitement.

'Ladies, ladies, listen.' came the booming voice of Mrs Halton, one of the camp representatives stepping away from the crowd so she could be seen. 'We've not been told anything officially yet as you know, the cogs of government take time to get the word out, but we have received news from outside the gates that after an atom bomb attack on two Japanese cities on sixth and ninth of August, the Japs have surrendered. As of today, the war is over. Isn't it wonderful!' She clapped her hands gleefully.

'I'm not sure whether to believe it, you know,' Terpie whispered to her sister standing close by.

'Why ever not? They wouldn't lie to us surely. Not after everything we've been through.'

Stupefied, the two sisters looked around at all the women crying and hugging one another.

'It's a terrible thing. Distrust. This place has made me question everything. I couldn't bear it if this was all a lie and we end up being stuck here.'

'I know what you mean. The Japs have lied to us so much but this news isn't coming from them. This is from our people,' said Thalia reassuringly. 'I think we have to trust it.'

Without warning, Terpie launched herself into Thalia's arms and clung to her younger sister allowing the tears of relief to flow freely.

'I wish Pappa had been able to hang on a few more months to see this day.'

'I know. It's so cruel but he wouldn't want us to be sad today.'

'We'll be able to eat proper food,' Thalia laughed through her tears.

'And have nice clothes and shoes without holes in,' giggled Terpie.

'I thought having your own bed would have been at the top of your list.'

'Oh my goodness, yes! And no offence, but to have a room to myself. We won't know ourselves.'

The girls parted, wiping their soggy faces, and all around them, women hugged, cried, laughed and danced at the joyous news. Amongst the feelings of celebration, a hint of disbelief lurked like an ominous cloud casting a shadow over Terpie's enjoyment of the moment. The announcement seemed too outrageous to be accurate and she didn't feel able to lean into the revelation wholly and would only believe it once she was on the other side of the gates. The girls walked away from the hubbub of revellers and sat down outside their hut.

'I don't mean to be a killjoy, but where will we go? Our home is gone. What are we going to do?' asked Thalia, staring into the distance. 'We have no money. I'm scared.'

'I am too. We can't think too far ahead and must trust that things will work out somehow. Besides, we'll need to get to India to find the others. I've no idea how we will manage that.'

'Will you… umm… look for Benny?'

Terpie, a little taken aback by the question replied faintly. 'I will when the time is right. We need to find Mamma first. She's our priority.'

Thalia returned an odd look she wasn't sure how to decipher.

Over the next few days, the atmosphere buzzed however, there were no noticeable changes to their living conditions, the prison routines continued as usual. The guards still guarded, the prevalence of hunger remained and the walls still imprisoned them from the outside world. Having completed her chores for the day, Terpie relaxed on the grass chatting with Greta and Julia whilst Thalia collected the laundry from the washing lines outside. Clutching the dried clothes to her chest, Thalia intently examined the patch of sky above.

'Can you hear something? Sounds like planes again,' she called over to the girls stunting their conversation to listen. Terpie wondered how long it would be, if ever, before the sound of aircraft did not fill her with utter terror.

'I see them. Look! They're dropping something,' said Julia.

A plethora of white paper floated down like snowflakes into the camp and crazed women jumped up and down to catch them. Screams of joy and laughter rippled through the camp and women came running outside from all directions to see what the commotion was about. Terpie was eager to get her hands on one but Thalia was quicker, leaping high she grabbed the leaflet and squealed as she began to read it. Very quickly the ground became littered with paper being kicked around like fallen leaves on an autumn day.

'What does it say then? Come on.'

Thalia briefly flashed the bit of paper in her direction, enough for her to read the bold lettering addressed to All Allied Prisoners of War.

Unable to wait for her excitable sister, Terpie grabbed one from the floor and began reading for herself.

The leaflet confirmed the Japanese had surrendered unconditionally and the war was over. Gripping the hard evidence in her hands, Terpie finally let go of her doubts and reservations, allowing the intoxicating rush of euphoria to flow through her body. Unsteady on her feet, she wobbled from the intensity of emotion and had to sit down.

Thalia read the note out loud:

'It says, *we'll get supplies brought to you as soon as possible and arrangements to get you out will follow but owing to the distances involved, it may be some time before we can achieve this.*'

'So we're stuck here then,' said Julia, slightly dejected.

'There's more. *You will help yourselves if you act as follows. Stay in your camp until you get further orders from us. Start preparing nominal roll of personnel with full particulars and list your most urgent necessities.*'

'I need new knickers and would kill for a cup of coffee,' laughed Terpie.

'I'm not sure your caffeine craving is what they meant,' she continued reading. '*As you have been starved or underfed for long periods DO NOT eat large quantities of solid food, fruit or vegetables at first. It's dangerous for you to do so. Small quantities and frequent intervals are much safer.*' Thalia dropped the paper into her lap. 'Well, that's disappointing but it's over!' She shouted, waving the piece of paper above her head like a flag. 'Waiting a few weeks is nothing really. It will pass quickly and before we know it we'll be out of this hell hole and can start living again,' said Thalia.

The girls set about picking up all the fallen paper scattered around and Terpie kept one in her pocket to add to her diary as a testament to this auspicious day.

Chapter Thirty-Nine
Thalia

After receiving the wonderful news that the war was over, prisoners continued with their tedious routines, but spirits remained high in the knowledge that freedom was almost in touching distance. It helped that the guards were keeping a low profile too. Thalia continued her work in the kitchens as people still needed to be fed and Terpie was kept busy assisting the officials to collect personal information from the women to aid with their repatriation to find a way home. Every man, woman and child were impatient to leave the confines of the prison, to be reunited with husbands, wives, children, family and get back to living and a normal existence again. Although, when the gates did eventually open, that would not be the end of it, each survivor would carry their own personal suffering and their lives would be forever tainted by the war. In time, wounds would heal, memories would fade, but the intrinsic trauma would remain an unsightly blemish on their personal history. With only their most treasured possessions packed in threadbare cases, they were waiting. Waiting for rescue. Thalia took advantage of the freedom to roam and strolled back from her father's grave, meandering along the stone path humming to herself and picking off the seeds on long strands of grass as she passed. Attending his grave had become a comforting daily ritual as she had so much to tell him and was mindful that one of these days, her visit would be her last. Since their liberation had been announced the grip of terror began to ease leaving her insides disentangled from fear. She had no doubt their road ahead would be difficult, but they were survivors and her desire to honour her father's memory gave her strength to go on. Whatever her future had in store, she wanted to make him proud. At only twenty-two, she had plenty of time to carve a new life and put this episode behind her. Perhaps one with a family of her own. The sound of planes overhead distracted her and she looked upwards from beneath the brim of her sun hat.

Thalia screamed with delight and ran. Liberating forces glided into the camp, carried by billowing parachutes and Thalia thought they resembled winged angels coming to rescue them and she brushed the impromptu tears of happiness from her cheeks. Their presence brought a sense of calm and safety, and could only mean one thing. Their release would be coming soon. She found Meena and her sister reading under the shade of a tree.

'Hey, did you see them?' called Thalia breathlessly as she approached.

'See what?' said Terpie glancing up from the pages of her book.

'Not what! Who! The British soldiers are here. They're heading to the main block. Let's go and check it out.'

The three girls quickly became swept along with the jubilant crowd also interested to know what was happening. The atmosphere crackled with energy through the corridors and the girls followed with no knowledge of where they were going or why. Like sheep, they bustled along until they arrived in the central hub and headed up the stairs to the gallery for a better view.

'What are we waiting for?' asked Meena.

'I'm not sure but it's the only entertainment we're going to get so might as well watch,' Thalia said, as they watched a stream of soldiers marching through the main corridor of the block beneath them.

'They must be getting rid of the Japanese,' said Meena excitedly. 'Good riddance!'

The girls watched eagerly as the prison swarmed with British soldiers taking command and within a short time the disgraced despots were removed from the camp. Thalia felt energised as she stood beside Terpie on the first-floor gallery as they witnessed the guard's shameful exit. Conceding to defeat, the familiar faces who had held them against their will filed out in steady procession and the building erupted with roars and cheers from the women as they passed. The ruckus was deafening with the sound of clanging against metal bars and stamping feet.

Thalia had never heard such a racket. Squalling women consumed by years of loathing spat and heckled the guards as they passed. A minor act of defiance for an insurgency long overdue. These cruel men had controlled and surveyed her every move and after today she would never see them again. Most of the guards walked with their heads bowed, but Sato she noticed lumbered past with his head high, his glaring frown fixed straight ahead. The show was over and the gates closed and friendly chatter resumed and the women dispersed, and with nowhere to be and nothing to do, Thalia and her sister opted to sit in the sunshine and enjoy the company of their friends. Later that afternoon, two women approached spreading the word that the camp representatives were holding a meeting at two o'clock in the dining room, and all must attend.

Thalia and Terpie gathered with the bemused women and fidgety children eagerly awaiting some positive news. Once everyone had arrived, Miss Foss, the camp superintendent, stood on a table and a sanguine hush descended as though a magic wand had been waved to silence them all. Miss Foss welcomed them with a warm smile. A sea of expectant faces tentatively smiled back as her mellifluous voice drifted over her audience. Her message was simple. Stay calm and be patient.

'I know you've all been through a terrible ordeal and want nothing more than to get out of here. The end is almost in sight, but we must be sensible. It would be irresponsible to allow people to leave until there is support in place on the outside.'

'How much longer do we have to wait?' shouted a disgruntled women from the front and other women chimed in to support her.

'The British government are sending aid and support so could take a couple of weeks, maybe more. I'll keep you updated as much as I can.'

Thalia sensed the frustration in the air as a groan of disappointment rippled through the room. Miss Foss waited for the crowd to settle.

'Look, I know this is hard. Please be patient. We're all in the same boat and have lives we're desperate to get back to. Remember the country is not the same as you left it and we must find places for you to stay and that takes time.'

Thalia wasn't bothered, she had nowhere to go and no one waiting for her on the outside. At this point her life was a blank canvass, her past had been whitewashed over. A few more weeks would not impact her life in any way. She still wasn't convinced her mother and Ino were alive. Thalia had become sceptical until she had seen evidence for herself. How accurate was the information they had received? Were her family really safe and well?

'All I can tell you for now is that within the next few days officials will be coming in to get the process underway. However, there is some more good news I want to share. Tomorrow, we have a very important visitor coming to the prison because she wants to meet you all. I won't say who it is and leave that as a surprise but if you could all meet in the parade square after breakfast and all will be revealed,' said Miss Foss with an air of mystery and placed her finger to her lips as shouts from the crowd questioned who was coming. The meeting concluded with confirmation that the barriers between the men and women would be removed so that families could at least mingle freely, resulting in cheers of celebration amongst the crowd.

The following day as instructed, the parade square was packed, and Thalia stretched on tiptoes, trying to get a glimpse of the surprise visitor making her way along the line with her staff carrying boxes behind her. There were whispers and rumours filtering down the line of who it could be. Being the tallest, Carol could see better than everyone else and informed the others.

'That's Lady Edwina Mountbatten, she's the Countess of Burma,' said Carol, nodding towards the vision of beauty heading their way.

'She's so elegant. I feel such a mess,' whispered Terpie, patting down her greasy hair.

'She's handing out things to people. I wonder what she's giving them,' said Thalia eagerly.

'We'll soon find out, she's on her way over,' said Carol.

When the royal visitor and her entourage reached them, the girls respectfully curtsied and in return were handed a pot of Pond's cold cream. The countess, dressed in a tailored khaki uniform, her dark wavy hair held back with a fabric band greeted them with a sincere smile and asked how they were faring and praised the girls for their bravery. Terpie found her voice and didn't hold back, making it known how awful the ordeal had been. Thalia simply thanked her and fondled the pot in her hands like she had just been handed a jar of pure gold.

Lady Mountbatten glided along the line and as soon as she had passed, like an eager child on Christmas day, Thalia twisted the lid open and scooped a large dollop and rubbed the silky-smooth cream into her desperately dry cheeks. Once the excitement of the royal visit was over, the women milled around with not much to do.

'Hey Meena, have you decided where you'll go when we get out of here?'

'I haven't made up my mind. I've nothing to keep me in Singapore but it's my home. I might go to see my uncle in Thailand. I don't think he knows about my parents, so I need tell him in person really. What about you two? Are you going to stay?'

'For the time being. We have no money and no home, so I've no idea where we'll end up. It's all a bit scary. Soon we'll have to say goodbye,' Thalia said, as if realising for the first time that they would not be together anymore. She looked down at the ground to mask the sadness in her eyes.

'I'm glad it is all over, but sad to lose a good friend,' Meena said and leaned in to embrace her with a hug.

'You won't lose me Meena. Your friendship helped me stay sane in here. We can stay in touch, can't we? Maybe you could pass me your uncle's address and we can write?' said Thalia into her friend's mane of thick black hair. Amongst all the good news and happiness there was also tinge of sorrow for the goodbyes which were inevitable. Meena pulled away and smiled.

'I'll give you the address. You've been my only true friend in here. Our friendship will last beyond these walls. I'll make sure of that,' said Meena.

With the Japanese gone, things began to change quickly and the following day a triage centre was established where officials in crisp uniforms sat behind desks with piles of various forms neatly stacked before them. The women were invited to queue up to seek assistance for their release. As news spread around the camp, the winding queue of women and children waiting in line extended down the corridors and looped out into the yard. It occurred to Thalia as she waited, observing mothers trying to keep their little ones entertained, that the younger children and the ones born in confinement, like Jacob, knew no different, this prison had been their only experience. Strangely she felt a pang of envy. These children would be entering a better and brighter existence but for her, the world she was returning to was greatly diminished. No one seemed to mind the long wait, and everyone seemed relaxed. Thalia observed the faces around her. Gone were the frowns and grimaces of woe and hardship. The weight of their incarceration and ill treatment was lifting and smiles and laughter flowed freely. They were survivors now. Thalia's insides bristled with anxiety of the unknown which was out of her hands. After two hours, they arrived at the front of the queue and Thalia took silent bets on which desk would become free first. She pinned her hopes on a good-looking officer with a twinkle in his eye and suffered slight disappointment when a woman with curly hair and thick rimmed tortoiseshell glasses called "next" and gestured them forward. The two sisters tentatively approached the desk before the Red Cross official whose face softened into a smile as they stepped forward. After checking their names off her list, the bespectacled woman tapped her pen lightly on the table, waiting for an answer to her question. She asked if they wished to use their free ticket to travel to England. The girls looked at each other in confusion. They had no reason to go to England, had no family or connections there. They were British citizens, born and raised in Singapore and this was the only life they had known. To go to England filled Thalia with terror. Their pappa had protected and guided them all their lives and making decisions had always been a family affair, so the stark reality of facing a new future without that stable hand to guide them was overwhelming. Thalia's mouth felt dry and for once she could not speak. She was relieved when Terpie took control.

'We have no connections in England. Will the ticket take us anywhere else? Our mother and sister are refugees in India. We got separated when they evacuated, and we need to get to them,' Terpie asked.

'Let me see what I can do. What are their names?' the woman asked, and when the reply came, promptly sifted through some papers from the top of the mountainous pile on her desk and scanned her index finger down a long list. The sisters waited in silence until the official found what she was looking for.

'Ah. Here they are. Your mother and sister are in a refugee camp in Nainital. We can arrange for you to be shipped there but it will take some time to arrange I'm afraid. It could be months. Do you have anywhere to stay locally until then?'

'No. Our house was bombed, and we've no other family. We've got nowhere to go,' said Thalia, her voice quivering. Just saying that out loud filled Thalia with despair and she bit down hard on her lip, almost drawing blood to vanquish the rising emotion bubbling to the surface like lava. It was like her life belonged to someone else. The official, sensitive to the nature of their plight jumped in.

'It's no problem girls, don't worry. We have accommodation set up around the city which can house you until such times as we can get you to where you need to be. Here are some forms you need to fill in so we can get you both sorted with identity cards and new passports which may take a little longer.'

Thalia and Terpie silently took the forms and pen which she handed to them. 'If you can complete these forms and pop them in that box over there. When the date for your release comes there will be transport provided to take you into the city and if you go through that door there,' she said, pointing to door behind her. 'You'll be given a bag of new clothes to get you started. You're safe now. Things will work out, I promise you.' The woman smiled warmly. 'I've added you to the list for housing and I'll see to it that you get issued a travel ticket to India.'

'Do you know when we'll be allowed to leave?' Terpie asked.

'Hopefully it won't be too long, a few weeks maybe. We must make sure there is a support network in place to help you all. Your poor souls have been through enough already, we don't want a situation where you're out on the streets. Now the war in Europe has ended, there are ships on their way with supplies and can collect refugees to be taken back to England.'

'Do you know anything about the soldiers in the camps? Where they will be sent? How can I trace someone?' Terpie asked with slight desperation.

'I'm sorry dear. No. I know nothing about the military side. Besides, there are prisoner camps all over the east so tracking anyone down will be like looking for a needle in a haystack.' The official observed Terpie's crestfallen face and added quickly, 'I'm sure once the dust settles, you'll be able to trace a loved one. Good luck with everything,' she said before the sisters turned to leave the hall to collect their new bag of clothes.

Chapter Forty
Thalia

The prisoners endured a month long wait before their final day of release came. Finally, on 8 September 1945, the four thousand or so survivors were granted their freedom to start rebuilding their lives, whilst coming to terms with what happened, the reality of losing loved ones and their homes. After walking through the gates with a few belongings, Thalia had never felt so adrift and lonely. By a cruel twist of fate, Terpie had become seriously ill with Beri Beri, caused by a deficiency of vitamin B, and was immediately admitted to hospital on the day of their release. Gradually, her body had lost muscle function and she could barely walk. Two months had now passed and Terpie was over the worst and would be discharged within the next few days.

During the uncomfortable period without her sister, Thalia tried to embrace the solitude. Being alone was scary and for a while she became petrified of losing Terpie too. Initially, she wore her vulnerability like a cloak, and became fearful of strangers, avoiding new situations whenever possible. She had to adjust to the wider world again after living a diminished existence under the strictest rules. As the weeks passed she relaxed into new routines, catching glimmers of the woman she was before all of this and her confidence returned. With Terpie in hospital, she had no alternative but to fend for herself, something she could never have imagined a few years ago.

Thalia had taken it upon herself to negotiate with the Red Cross and secured them both a crossing to India and in just under a month's time, they would be leaving the island to find their family. She had arranged new passports with the authorities and written to the camp in Nainital to prepare them for their arrival. Thalia no longer saw herself as the baby of the family. The cosseted life she once led as the youngest daughter of a wealthy merchant was now a thing of the past.

Heeding the warnings from the authorities, she kept to a restricted diet, and introduced new foods slowly, even though all she wanted to do was gorge on all the favourite things she had been denied. She must be doing something right because the condition of her skin improved, and her new clothes fitted better. As Thalia wandered through the streets, freedom to roam still felt like a luxury, instinctively she kept looking over her shoulder expecting to see guards around every corner. One of the many horrors which would take time to forget.

Gradually, the signs of Japanese rule were fading with the lowering of red ensign flags and tearing down of Kempeitai posters allowing the city and its occupants to breathe again. Life on the outside was still not easy and it would take years to remove the stain of the Japanese occupation. The city continued to grapple with food shortages where familiar shops and businesses simply did not exist anymore. Landmark buildings which once stood as stalwart silent sentries over the city tore a void in the landscape by their absence and Thalia drifted like a stranger in a foreign land. She walked amongst the sullied shops and houses with her arms tightly folded across her body, every location sparked a memory of a time with her family, her friends and even Charlie. Her loss weighed heavy in the centre of her chest, and in a state of melancholy she desperately wanted to find stability and a place her heart could rest easy.

Several times within the last few months, she had intended to make this journey, to visit her father's shop. The desire to satisfy a craving of closeness to his memory had finally forced her to face her fears, but the hope of nostalgic reverie dissipated quickly when she lay her tristful eyes on the wounded shop front before her. Gutted by enemy bombs, not much remained of the three-storey building which once housed her pappa's thriving business. The sooty stone façade had since been boarded up to hold back the rubble off the streets. With a sharp intake of breath, her hand covered her heart as if to contain the swelling ball of emotion and prevent it from expanding out if her chest. All his years of his dedication destroyed, and his presence eradicated from history. The sight would have horrified him and in a strange way, she was relieved he had not survived to witness its demise.

With glistening eyes, she turned her back on the blackened shop front and vowed never to return. The dependable Singapore sunshine tickled her skin with its warmth as she crossed the street. Her destination a large apartment block where she and Terpie had been housed temporarily until their papers were in order to allow them to travel. For now, Thalia carried her new identity card safely tucked in her purse beside the carving of the small bird crafted by her father's hand which she carried at all times. It had become a precious talisman.

Without access to money, Thalia got herself a job as a waitress in a local café and other than buying food, she was able to save her earnings and put them towards their travel fund. Their only other source of income would come from selling Emily's jewellery, but neither of the girls could bear to part with it and vowed it would be something they would do as a last resort. At some point, the girls needed to seek advice on how to claim their father's land and investments but it all felt too raw so it could wait. Arriving at the apartment, she quickly changed into fresh clothes and headed out to work. It felt good to be amongst people again, exposed to a variety of different faces, and listening to their stories as she served them tea. There was a shared cathartic release in being able to talk about their experiences to heal the trauma they had all been through. Although some remained silent, preferring to hold their nightmare close, and others just wanted to forget it happened and move on.

In no particular rush, Thalia strolled along the river in a daydream, a smile crept across her lips and a rosy flush reached her cheeks wondering whether she might see John today. Almost a week had gone by since she had seen him last. John was a regular customer at the cafe and she warmed to him instantly with his sparkling blue eyes and rugged jaw, looking smart in his Sergeants uniform. He always ordered a strong black coffee and a slice of the cake of the day. Initially she had been fascinated by his strong accent and would blush like a tomato when she couldn't understand a word he said and asked him to slow down. John made a joke out of it, and she giggled at his attempts at a British accent to make her feel better.

Over the weeks, their conversations broadened beyond small talk, and she learned he came from Motherwell in Scotland serving in the Royal Electrical and Mechanical Engineers having been sent to Singapore to assist with the rebuilding of the city and she found herself looking forward to his visits.

As the weeks went by, they became friends and eventually, John asked her out to dinner. Thalia did not respond immediately saying she would think about it. If she had been faced with the question three years ago, she wouldn't have hesitated, but trusting people came hard and her confidence to make judgements and decisions was shaken. With Terpie in hospital and with no one to ask for their opinion, she mulled the idea over and after two days concluded that she liked him, and deserved some fun. Initially, being in male company after years of separation made Thalia feel clumsy and awkward, but John was kind, patient and understanding. They sat in a secluded corner where flickering candlelight illuminated their faces and he listened intently whilst she told him her story, and about her beloved family and father who were her world. In return, he had spoken mostly about his military career and seemed reserved when it came to family, sharing minimal information. Thalia knew not everyone had the close family relationships she had been used to and respected his privacy.

Thalia's shift at the café was almost over. After wiping down the table, she balanced empty plates on her forearm to return to the kitchen when she saw John striding towards her clutching a small bunch of picked flowers to his chest. Dressed casually in a linen shirt and shorts, with his hair slicked back he looked relaxed out of uniform. Seeing him sparked a fluttering in her belly which scared her a little. She smiled coyly from beneath her fringe.

'I wondered if I might see you today,' Thalia said, putting down the stack of plates to receive the flowers. 'Thank you; these are gorgeous.'

'Well, I've been busy and wanted to take you somewhere this afternoon, if you're free?'

'I finish in a minute. So, where are you taking me? Sounds very mysterious.'

'Just wait and see. It's a surprise.'

'Give me five minutes to take these in.' She nodded at the plates. 'I'll get my things and we'll go.'

Thalia dashed into the darkness of the café and emerged a few minutes later minus her apron with her handbag over her shoulder. The couple walked and talked with ease, and it took Thalia a little while to realise that John was leading her back to Sime Road camp which was now fully accessible without gates or boundaries. Strangely, Thalia felt nothing being back here.

'This is a bit odd, John, it's the last place I would imagine for a surprise,' said Thalia, trying to keep the disappointment from her voice.

'That's because you don't know what it is. Come on,' said John, taking her hand and leading her onward. 'Trust me. I think you'll like it.'

Thalia relaxed as they wound their way through the roads once so familiar, and was flooded with memories of friends she had made and whilst they had the best intentions of keeping in touch, she wondered if their paths would ever cross again or would they just become characters in a shared a story. Soon it became clear where they were headed. The couple eventually arrived at the burial grounds and Thalia saw it instantly. John had tended to her father's grave. Rather than a non-descript, plain mound of dry earth, now her father had a proper resting place. The scruffy grass borders were replaced with neat stone edging and the centre was filled with pure white stones which sparkled in the bright sunlight and a wooden cross towered elegantly at the head of his grave. John had placed a stone slab with her pappa's name etched for all to see. The beauty of it took her breath away and she was stunned John had done this for her and for a man he had never met. Thalia was taken aback by his act of kindness and a swell of emotion knocked her off her feet and she fell into his arms and held him tight.

'Thank you, John, it's wonderful. I can't believe you did this!'

'Your pappa sounded like a special man. He deserved a better resting place. You like it?'

'Like it? I love it! I can't wait to show Terpie. No one's ever done anything like this for me. I'm so grateful,' said Thalia, standing on tiptoes to kiss him on the cheek.

John stepped back. 'I'll be over here. I'll leave you to it for a moment.'

John strolled around looking at the names of the other graves to give Thalia some privacy.

Thalia let her bag fall to the ground and knelt before the grave, whispering to her pappa to tell him not to worry.

'I'm ok Pappa. I've met someone who I think you would like. He's kind and thoughtful and he makes me happy. I'll come to see you again before we leave for India. Part of me doesn't want to go, especially now I've met John. I know, I know. That's selfish and of course I want to see Mamma and Ino,' she glanced over her shoulder to check John could not hear her. 'I never thought I'd feel so connected to someone again after Charlie. I think I might be falling for him Pappa and now I've got to leave.'

An echo of her father's voice drifted into her consciousness telling her that if it were meant to be, he would wait, and she smiled fondly. That was the kind of positive advice he would have given her. Thalia inhaled the sweet scent of the flowers before laying them against the cross and ran her fingers over the cool white stones. It dawned on her that John must think a lot of her to have gone to all this trouble. A fizz of excitement rippled through her body at this thought. This was the closest her pappa would come to meeting her new acquaintance and hoped he approved of her choice. Thalia said farewell to her pappa, blew kiss and turned to find John waiting patiently a few rows away until she was ready to leave.

On their way out of the camp, Thalia pointed out the forlorn hut where they had lived, the kitchen block and the area where the fence had been where her exchanges with Peter and Mickey took place. It was only here that her voice cracked with emotion because her valiant efforts to save her father were too little too late, but she managed to supress the feeling by quickly changing the subject. For John to see her tears would have been too embarrassing to endure. Having John by her side seemed to give her strength and together the couple walked hand in hand following the swooping paths out on to the main road. The next day, Thalia wasn't working and was waiting in the reception area of the hospital for Terpie to be discharged. She didn't have long to wait as her sister's pale form drifted towards her down the corridor with a small bag of belongings clutched tightly in her hand.

'You look so much better.'

'I feel great, I just want to get on with living and don't want to see another hospital bed a long as I live,' said Terpie.

'Are you sure you are up to this visit today? John can take us another time,' Thalia asked.

'No, we've left it too long already. Honestly, I'm fine. It's good of John to take us and I want to get it over with to be honest,' said Terpie as she looped her arm through her sisters for support as they shuffled slowly out to John waiting patiently in his car.

The girls had previously discussed making a visit to their house and both agreed they needed some closure and wanted to see it one last time. The house was the only link they had to their shared memories of their parents and siblings.

Terpie slid into the backseat and greeted John whom she had never met but heard everything about him on her sister's visits. The car wound its way through the city streets with the windows down and the warm air blowing in their faces. Thalia turned in the front seat to explain to Terpie what John had done to the grave and promised to take her there to see it. John drove in silence whilst the sisters caught up on missed gossip. As they approached the familiar driveway, Thalia had a knot in her stomach and felt nervous but couldn't explain why. For a split second, her mind provided her with a glimpse of how the house used to look from her memory before she was greeted with the stark reality. The shell of the house was still standing, and a stab of sorrow punctured her heart seeing it again after all these years. The debris had been cleared away but the remainder of the once green stanchions that used to support the roof now charred black stubbornly stood tall out of the ashes. In their absence, nature had thrived taking over and consuming the ruins with rambling climbers and leafy vines. Thalia had no idea whether Shi Min and Lim were still living here. She had no response to her post card she sent many months ago. John turned off the engine and the girls remained quiet, staring at the carcass of their home.

'It feels so strange to be back here,' Terpie finally said.

'I know, but I had to see it.'

The girls exited the car and approached the house apprehensively, leaving John to wait in the car.

'I wonder what happened to them?' asked Terpie looking over at the small abandoned wooden house. Smashed windows and missing wooden panels confirming Shi Min and Lim had not lived there for some time.

'I wonder if they left after the fire?'

Together the sisters climbed the stone stairs and stood on the spot where the beautiful carved veranda had once been. Where many nights the family had sat together, listening to music and hearing the stories of the day. Thalia felt choked by the rush of memories flooding in of happy times and she dug her fingernails into the palms of her hands to bring her back to the present moment. She made her way slowly towards to what used to be the entrance to the family room, the hub of the house now empty, dusty and charred black. Stepping over the wild tendrils, the girls glided around the remains and the timbers creaked underfoot as they trod carefully surveying the emptiness in silent contemplation. There was not much to see, only echoes of the past. Even though Thalia thought she had come to terms with losing her family, but being back here where the felt their presence more keenly opened the door to her grief. Reminding her of what she had lost and the pain bowled into heart almost knocking over. They would never be whole again. Each of the girls drifted through the ruins deep in their own private memories from when this was once a vibrant family home.

'It doesn't matter but I wonder what happened to all our belongings,' Terpie asked, scouting the empty rooms. Before Thalia had a chance to respond, John's voice drifted up to them from the driveway.

'Umm. Girls. There's someone here for you.'

Thalia looked at Terpie with a frown. 'Who could be here for us? No one knows we're here?'

When she reached the top of the stairs, Thalia's legs buckled beneath her when she saw a frail old lady standing beside John on the driveway.

'Oh my god, it can't be,' she gasped, sprinting down the stone steps with Terpie close behind. She embraced her Amah who she thought she would never see again and her tears flowed freely.

'I can't believe this. How did you know we were here?' she asked.

'I didn't child. I've been coming here every week for the last three years hoping that one day you would return,' said Shi Min.

The girls linked arms either side of Shi Min and led her to the stone steps to sit down.

'Did you get my post card I sent? Is Lim with you? Where are you living now?' Thalia had so many questions.

'No, I've not been living here since I lost him not long after the surrender,' said Shi Min, her pale blue eyes glistening with tears.

'What happened?' asked Terpie gently, taking her hand.

'The Japs. He went out shopping one day and never came back. Singapore was not a safe place for us, and thousands of Chinese people were murdered, got rid of,' she said slowly, wiping her tears on the back of her frail hands. 'It wasn't safe for me to stay so I moved to live with my cousin on the edge of the island. He's been good to me and brings me back here every Sunday. I knew there was a slim chance of ever seeing you again but I had to try, and today you came back to me.' Shi Min lovingly kissed each girl's heads and glanced towards her previous home. 'All my memories are here, you know. Of Lim, your parents and you children. Being here brings me closer to you all.'

'Oh Shi Min, I'm so sorry,' said Thalia, wrapping her arms around her beloved Amah.

'I can't tell you how happy it makes me to see you both looking so well. Tell me, what about the others? Do you have news?'

Terpie and Thalia exchanged a brief look.

Thalia spoke first, 'It's a long story. Are you sure you want to hear it?'

'Of course, I do! I've been thinking about this family every day for the last three years, wondering what happened to you all. I may look frail, but I can take the truth. I need to know. Are you the only survivors?'

Thalia and Terpie sat with Shi Min, holding her hands tightly, and over the next few hours, they filled her in on what they knew of their mother and the fate of their sisters. They described their time in the convent, their life in Changi, and their pappa. Shi Min asked about Benny too and Terpie told her as much as she knew.

Shi Min remained quiet and sighed heavily.

'It's so very sad. It should never have been allowed to happen. So many good people lost their lives.' She gripped the girls' hands tightly and her face hardened. 'Now, you listen to me. You girls are strong, and you've been brave. What's happened was a tragedy, but you must make a good life for yourselves now. It's what your parents would have wanted. Here, these belong to you,' said Shi Min, reaching into her pocket and pulling out a familiar bunch of keys and a metal whistle. 'I found them in the ruins and cleaned them up; your pappa would want you to have them. He loved that shop. I have some photographs that I managed to rescue back at home that you must have.'

Thalia took the keys in her hand and stroked the cool metal. A small paper label read "High Street" in her father's handwriting. Holding them brought her comfort; these keys had been handled by her pappa every day and she felt closer to him just by having them. She clutched them tightly to her chest.

'Thank you for these. It means so much to have them. I can't believe you've been coming here every week,' Thalia croaked.

'I had a feeling you would return one day and hoped I would get lucky,' said Shi Min, her eyes glistening. 'So, what will you do now? Are you going to India to find your mother and Ino?' Shi Min quizzed, looking from one to the other.

Thalia and Terpie exchanged a smile.

'Yes, yes, we are.'